The
BUTTERFLY
ROOM

Also from Lucinda Riley

The Seven Sisters Series
The Seven Sisters
The Storm Sister
The Shadow Sister
The Pearl Sister
The Moon Sister
The Sun Sister

Other Books
The Butterfly Room
The Love Letter
The Olive Tree
The Angel Tree
The Italian Girl
The Midnight Rose
The Light Behind the Window
The Girl on the Cliff
The Hothouse Flower

The BUTTERFLY ROOM

By Lucinda Riley

BLUE BOX PRESS

The Butterfly Room
By Lucinda Riley

Copyright 2019 Lucinda Riley
ISBN: 978-1-952457-07-4

Published by Blue Box Press, an imprint of Evil Eye Concepts,
Incorporated

Red Admiral
(Vanessa atalanta)

Posy

Admiral House
Southwold, Suffolk
June 1943

"Remember, my darling, you are a fairy, floating silently across the grass on wings of gossamer, ready to trap your prey in your silken net. Look!" he whispered into my ear. "There he is, just on the edge of the leaf. Now then, fly!"

As he'd taught me, I closed my eyes for a few seconds and stood on tiptoe, imagining my small feet leaving the ground. Then I felt the flat of Daddy's palm give me a gentle push forwards. Opening my eyes, I focused on the pair of hyacinth-blue wings and flew the two short steps I needed to swoop my net around the fragile frond of buddleia bush on which the Large Blue was currently perched.

The waft of air as the net landed on target alerted the Blue, who opened its wings in preparation for flight. But it was too late, because I, Posy, Princess of the Fairies, had captured him. He wouldn't be harmed, of course, merely taken off to be studied by Lawrence, King of the Magical People—who was also my father—before being released outside after enjoying a large bowl of the best nectar.

"What a clever girl my Posy is!" Daddy said as I made my way back through the foliage towards him and proudly handed over the net. He was crouching down on his haunches, so our eyes—which everyone told us were so similar—met in shared pride and delight.

I watched his head bend to study the butterfly, which remained stock-still, its tiny legs gripped to its white netting prison. Daddy's hair was a dark mahogany color, and the oil he put on it to flatten it down made it shine in the sun like the top of the long dining table after Daisy had polished it. It also smelt wonderful—of him, and comfort, because he was 'home' and I loved him more than anything else in my worlds, both human and fairy. I loved Maman too, of course, but even though she was at home most of the time, I didn't feel I *knew* her as well as I knew Daddy. She spent a lot of time in her room with something called migraines, and when she was out of it, she always seemed too busy to spend any time with me.

"He's an absolute corker, darling girl!" Daddy said, lifting his eyes to mine. "A true rarity on these shores, and no doubt of noble lineage," he added.

"Might he be a butterfly prince?" I asked.

"He might well be," Daddy agreed. "We shall have to treat him with the utmost respect, as his royal status demands."

"Lawrence, Posy...lunch!" called a voice from beyond the foliage. Daddy stood up so he was taller than the buddleia bush and able to wave across the lawns up to the terrace of Admiral House.

"Coming, my love," he called, quite loudly as we were some distance away. I watched his eyes crinkle into a smile at the sight of his wife: my mother, and unknowing Queen of the Magical People. This was a game only Daddy and I shared.

Hand in hand we walked across the lawns, smelling the hint of newly mown grass that I associated with happy days in the garden: Maman and Daddy's friends, champagne in one hand, croquet mallet in the other, the thwack of a ball hurtling across the cricket pitch Daddy mowed for such occasions...

These happy days had happened less since the war had begun, which made the memories of when they did seem even more precious. The war had also given Daddy a limp, so we had to walk quite slowly, which was fine with me because it meant it was longer that he was all mine. He was much better now than he had been when he had first come home from hospital. He had been in a wheelchair like an old person, and his eyes had looked gray too. But with Maman and Daisy nursing him, and me doing my best to read him storybooks, he had got better quickly. These days he didn't even need a stick to walk, unless he was going further than the grounds.

"Now Posy, run inside and wash your hands and face. Tell your mother I'm taking our new guest to settle him in," Daddy directed me with the net as we reached the steps that led up to the terrace.

"Yes Daddy," I said as he turned to walk across the lawn and eventually disappeared through a high box hedge. He was heading for the Folly, which, with its turret made of yellow sandy brick, made the most perfect fairytale castle for fairy folk and their butterfly friends to live in. And Daddy certainly spent a lot of time in there. Alone. I was only allowed to peep into the small, round room that lay behind the front door of the Folly—which was very dark and smelt of moldy socks—when Maman asked me to call Daddy in for lunch.

The downstairs room was where he kept his 'outside equipment,' as he called it: tennis rackets jostled with cricket stumps and mud-splattered wellington boots. I had never been invited up the stairs that went round and round until they reached the top (I knew this because I'd secretly climbed them when Daddy had been called by Maman to take a telephone call up at the house). It had been very disappointing to find he had already locked the big oak door that greeted me at the top of them. Even though I turned the knob as firmly as my small hands would allow me, it wouldn't budge. I knew that, unlike the room below it, there were a lot of windows in the room, because you could see them from the outside. The Folly reminded me a bit of the lighthouse in Southwold, except that it had been given a golden crown to wear on its head instead of a very bright light.

As I walked up the terrace steps, I sighed happily as I looked up at the beautiful pale red-brick walls of the main house with its rows of long sash windows, framed by lime-green tendrils of wisteria. I noticed the old wrought-iron table, now more green than its original black, was being set up on the terrace for lunch. There were only three placemats and water glasses, which meant that it was just us for lunch, which was very unusual. I thought how nice it would be to have both Maman and Daddy to myself. Stepping inside the house through the wide doors to the drawing room, I skirted between the silk damask sofas that sat around the enormous marble-encased fireplace—so big that last year, Father Christmas had managed to get a shiny red bicycle all the way down it—and skipped along the maze of corridors that led to the downstairs WC. Shutting the door behind me, I used both hands to turn on the big silver tap, then washed them thoroughly. I stood on tiptoe to look at my reflection in the mirror and check for smudges on my face. Maman was very fussy about appearances—Daddy said it was her French heritage—and woe betide either of us if we didn't arrive at the table spotless.

But even she could not control the wisps of wiry brown curls that continually escaped my tightly woven plaits, appearing at the nape of my neck and wriggling out of the slides that did their best to scrape the wisps back from my forehead. When he'd tucked me in one night, I'd asked Daddy if I could borrow some of his hair oil as I thought that might help, but he had only chuckled and twirled one of my ringlets around his finger.

"You will do no such thing. I love your curls, my darling girl, and if I were in charge, they would fly free about your shoulders every day."

As I walked back down the corridor, I longed again to have Maman's sleek, poker-straight mane of blonde hair. It was the color of the white chocolates she served with coffee after dinner. My hair was more like a *café au lait*, or at least that was what Maman called it; I called it mouse-brown.

"There you are, Posy," Maman said as I stepped out onto the terrace. "Where is your sunhat?"

"Oh, I must have left it in the garden when Daddy and I were catching butterflies."

"How many times have I told you that your face will get burnt and soon you will wrinkle up like an old prune," she admonished me as I sat down. "You will look sixty when you are forty."

"Yes, Maman," I agreed, thinking that forty was so old anyway, that by then I wouldn't really care.

"How's my other favorite girl this fine day?"

Daddy appeared on the terrace and swung my mother round into his arms, the jug of water she held slopping onto the gray stone paving.

"Careful, Lawrence!" Maman chastised him with a frown before extricating herself from his grasp and placing the jug on the table.

"Isn't this a glorious day to be alive?" He smiled as he sat down opposite me. "And the weather seems set fair for the weekend and our party too."

"We're having a party?" I asked as Maman sat down next to him.

"Yes we are, darling girl. Your Pater has been deemed fit enough to return to duties, so Maman and I have decided to have a last blast while we can."

My heart definitely missed a beat as Daisy, our maid of all things since the other servants had gone off to do war work, served the luncheon meat and radishes. I hated radishes, but it was all that was left over from the kitchen garden this week, as most things growing there had to go off to the war too.

"How long are you going for, Daddy?" I asked in a small, strained voice, because a big hard lump had appeared in my throat. It felt just like a radish had already got stuck there and I knew it meant I might very soon cry.

"Oh, shouldn't be too long now. Everyone knows the Hun are doomed, but I have to help with the final push, you see. Can't let my chums down, can I?"

"No, Daddy," I managed in a quavery voice. "You won't get hurt again, will you?"

"He won't, *chérie*. Your Papa is indestructible, aren't you, Lawrence?"

I watched as my mother gave him a small tight smile and I thought she must be as worried as I was because of it.

"I am, my love," he replied, putting his hand on hers and squeezing it tightly. "I surely am."

"Daddy?" I asked at breakfast the next day, dipping my toast soldiers carefully into my egg. "It's so hot today, can we go to the beach? We haven't been in such a long time."

I saw Daddy give Maman a look, but she was reading her letters over her cup of *café au lait* and didn't seem to notice. Maman always got lots of letters from France, all written on very thin paper, even thinner than a butterfly wing, which suited Maman, because everything about her was so delicate and slender.

"Daddy? The beach," I prompted.

"My darling, I'm afraid the beach isn't suitable for playing at the moment. It's covered in barbed wire and mines. Do you remember when I explained to you about what happened in Southwold last month?"

"Yes, Daddy." I looked down at my egg and shuddered, remembering how Daisy had carried me to the Anderson shelter (which I'd thought was called that because it was our surname—it had confused me a great deal when Mabel had said her family had an Anderson shelter too, as her surname was Price). It had sounded as if the sky was alive with thunder and lightning, but rather than God sending it, Daddy said it was Hitler. Inside the shelter, we had all huddled close, and Daddy had said we should pretend to be a hedgehog family, and I should curl up like a little hoglet. Maman had got quite cross about him calling me a hoglet, but that's what I'd pretended to be, burrowed under the earth, with the humans warring above us. Eventually, the terrible sounds had stopped. Daddy had said we could all go back to bed, but I was sad to have to go to my human bed alone, rather than staying all together in our burrow.

The next morning, I had found Daisy crying in the kitchen, but she wouldn't say what was the matter. The milk cart didn't come that day, and then Maman had said I wouldn't be going to school because it wasn't there any more.

"But how can it not be there, Maman?"

"A bomb fell on it, *chérie*," she'd said, blowing out cigarette smoke.

Maman was smoking now too, and I sometimes worried that she would set her letters on fire because she held them so close to her face when she was reading.

"But what about our beach hut?" I asked Daddy. I loved our little hut—it was painted a butter yellow, and stood at the very end of the row so if you looked the right way, you could pretend that you were the only people on the beach for miles, but if you turned the other way, you weren't too far from the nice ice cream man by the pier. Daddy and I always made the most elaborate sandcastles, with turrets and moats, big enough for all the little crabs to live in if they decided to come close enough. Maman never wanted to come to the beach; she said it was 'too sandy,' which I thought was rather like saying the ocean was too wet.

Every time we went, there would be an old man with a broad-brimmed hat walking slowly along the beach, poking the sand with a long stick, but not like the one that Daddy used to walk with. The man would have a large sack in his hand and every now and then he would stop and begin to dig.

"What is he doing, Daddy?" I'd asked.

"He's a beachcomber, darling. He walks along the shore, looking in the sand for things that might have been washed up from the ships out at sea or carried here from distant shores."

"Oh, I see," I'd said, although the man didn't have a comb of any kind, and certainly not like the one that Daisy dragged through my hair every morning. "Do you think he'll find buried treasure?"

"I'm sure if he spends enough time digging, he's bound to find something one day."

I had watched with growing excitement as the man had pulled something out of the hole and brushed the sand off it, only to see that it was an old enamel teapot.

"How disappointing," I'd sighed.

"Remember, my darling, one man's rubbish might be another man's gold. But perhaps we are all beachcombers in a way," Daddy had said, squinting in the sun. "We keep seeking, hoping to find that elusive buried treasure that will enrich our lives, and when we pull up a teapot rather than a gleaming jewel, we must continue to search."

"Are you still searching for treasure, Daddy?"

"No, my Princess of the Fairies, I've found it." He'd smiled down at me and kissed me on the top of my head.

After a lot of nagging, Daddy eventually gave in and decided to take me to a river to swim, so Daisy helped me put my swimsuit on and pushed a hat onto my curly hair, and I climbed into Daddy's car. Maman had said she was too busy preparing for the party tomorrow, but that suited me fine, because then the King of Fairies and I could welcome all the creatures of the river to our court.

"Are there otters?" I asked as he drove in the opposite direction of the sea and through the rolling green fields of the countryside.

"You have to be very quiet to see otters," he said. "Could you manage that, Posy?"

"Of course!"

We drove for a long time before I saw the blue snake of the river hiding behind the reeds. He parked the car, and together we hiked to the riverbank, Daddy carrying all of our scientific equipment: a camera, butterfly nets, glass jars, lemonade and corned beef sandwiches.

Dragonflies skimmed the surface of the water, disappearing quickly as I went splashing in. The water was deliciously cool, but my head and face felt prickly and hot beneath my hat, so I threw it onto the riverbank where Daddy had now changed into his bathers too.

"Any otters that were once here have surely scarpered at all this noise," Daddy said as he strode into the water. It barely reached his knees, he was so tall. "Now, look at all this bladderwort, shall we take some home for our collection?"

Together we reached into the water and pulled out one of the yellow flowers to reveal its bulbous roots. Lots of little insects had been living in it, so we filled a jar with water and then put our specimen inside it for safekeeping.

"Do you remember the Latin name, my darling?"

"Utri-cu-la-ria!" I replied proudly, getting out of the water and sitting down beside him on the grassy bank.

"Clever girl. I want you to promise you will keep adding to our growing collection. If you see an interesting plant, press it like I showed you. After all, I'll need help with my book while I'm away, Posy." He handed me a sandwich from the picnic basket and I accepted it, trying to look very serious and scientific. I wanted Daddy to know he could trust me with his work. He'd been something called a botanist before the war and had been writing his book for almost as long as I'd been alive. He would often lock himself in his Folly to do some 'thinking and writing.' Sometimes he'd bring the book back to the house and show me some of the drawings he'd made.

And they were wonderful. He explained how it was all about the habitat we lived in and there were beautiful illustrations of the butterflies and insects and plants. He'd told me once that if just one thing changes, it can throw everything out of balance.

"Look at these midges, for example." Daddy had pointed to an annoying cloud of them one hot summer night. "They're crucial for the ecosystem."

"But they bite us," I had said, slapping one away.

"It's in their nature, yes," he'd chuckled. "Without them, though, lots of species of birds wouldn't have a steady food source and their populations would plummet. And if the bird populations are affected, it has repercussions on the rest of the food chain. Without birds, other insects like grasshoppers would suddenly have fewer predators, and they would keep multiplying and eating all the plants away. And without the plants..."

"It would take away food from all the herb-vores."

"Herbivores, yes. So you see, everything hangs in a delicate balance. And one small beat of a butterfly's wings can make all the difference in the world."

I thought about this now as I chewed on my sandwich.

"I've got you something special," Daddy said, reaching into his rucksack. He pulled out a shiny tin and handed it to me.

I opened it up to see dozens of perfectly sharpened pencils in all the colors of the rainbow.

"Whilst I'm away, you must continue with your drawings so that when I come back you can show me how much you've improved."

I nodded, too happy with my present to speak.

"When I was at Cambridge, we were taught to really look at the world," he continued. "So many people walk about blind to the beauty and magic around them. But not you, Posy, you already see things better than most. When we draw nature we begin to understand it—we can see all the various parts and how they are joined together. By drawing what you see and studying it, *you* can help other people understand the miracle of nature too."

When we arrived home, Daisy scolded me for getting my hair wet and bundled me into the bath, which I thought didn't make sense as she was making my hair wet all over again. Once Daisy had put me to bed and shut the door behind her, I slipped out again and got out my new colored pencils, stroking the soft yet sharp tips of them. I thought that if I practised hard enough, by the time Daddy came back from the war, I could show him that I was good enough to go to Cambridge too—even if I was a girl.

The next morning, I watched from my bedroom window as cars began streaming along our drive. Each one was full to bursting with bodies; I'd heard Maman explain that all her friends had pooled their petrol coupons to make the journey from London. Actually, she called them '*émigrés*,' which, because she had spoken French to me since I was a baby, I knew meant 'emigrants.' In the dictionary it said this was a person who moved from their original country to another. Maman said that it felt as though the whole of Paris had moved to England to escape the war. I knew this wasn't true of course, but there always seemed to be more of her French friends than Daddy's English ones at the parties. I didn't mind at all, because they were so colorful, the men with their bright scarves and jewel-colored smoking jackets, and the ladies with their satin dresses and slashes of red lip paint. Best of all, they always brought me presents, so it was like Christmas.

Daddy called them 'Maman's bohemians,' which the dictionary said meant creative people like artists and musicians and painters. Maman had once been a singer in a famous Paris nightclub, and I loved listening to her voice, which was deep and silky-smooth like melted chocolate. She didn't know I was listening of course, because I was meant to be asleep, but when there was a house party that was impossible anyway, so I'd creep down the stairs and listen to the music and the chatter. It was as if Maman came to life on these nights, as if she was pretending to be an inanimate doll in between the parties. I loved hearing her laugh, because when we were by ourselves, she didn't do that very often.

Daddy's flying friends were nice too, although they all seemed to dress alike in navy and brown so it was hard to tell them apart. My godfather Ralph, who was Daddy's best friend, was my favorite; I thought he was very handsome, with his dark hair and big brown eyes. There was a picture in one of my storybooks of the prince who kisses Snow White and wakes her up. Ralph looked just like that. He also played the piano beautifully—before the war he had been a concert pianist (before the war, simply every grown-up I knew had been something else, except for Daisy, our maid). Uncle Ralph had some illness that meant he couldn't fight or fly planes in the war. He had what the grown-ups called a 'desk job,' although I couldn't imagine what one did with desks except sit behind them, which is probably what he did. When Daddy was away flying his Spitfires, Uncle Ralph would come to visit Maman and me, which really cheered us both up. He would come to Sunday lunch and then play the piano for me and Maman afterwards. I had realized recently that

Daddy had been away at the war for four of my seven years on this planet, which must have been miserable for Maman, with only me and Daisy for company.

I sat on my window seat and craned my neck through the window to watch Maman greet her guests on the sweeping steps that led up to the front door below me. She looked so beautiful today, in a midnight blue dress that matched her lovely eyes and, as Daddy joined her, slipping an arm around her waist, I felt very happy indeed. Daisy arrived to put me into the new dress she had made for me out of a pair of old green curtains. As she brushed my hair, then tied just a little of it back with a green ribbon, I decided I wouldn't think about Daddy going away again tomorrow, when a silence like before a thunderstorm would settle back on Admiral House and us, its residents.

"Ready to go down, Posy?" Daisy asked me. I could see she was red-faced and sweating and looked very tired, probably because it was very hot indeed and she had to make food for all these people with no help. I gave her my sweetest smile.

"Yes, Daisy, I am."

My real name wasn't actually Posy; I was named after my mother, Adriana. But as it would be far too complicated to have two of us answering to it, it had been decided to use my second name, Rose, after my English grandmother. Daisy had told me that Daddy had started calling me 'Rosy Posy' when I was a baby, and somewhere along the way, the second half of the name had stuck. Which was fine by me, because I thought it suited me far better than either of my real names.

Some of Daddy's older relatives still called me 'Rose,' and I would answer of course, because I had been taught that I always answered adults politely, but at the party, everyone knew me as Posy. I was hugged and kissed and little net parcels of sweeties tied up with a ribbon were pressed on me. Maman's French friends favored sugared almonds, which in truth I didn't like very much, but I knew how hard it was to find chocolate because of the war.

As I sat at the long trestle table which had been placed on the terrace to seat us all, and felt the sun beat down on top of my sunhat (which only made me hotter), and listened to the chatter around me, I wished every day at Admiral House could be like this. Maman and Daddy sitting together in the center, like a king and queen holding court, his arm draped around her white shoulder. They both looked so terribly happy, it made me want to cry.

"Are you all right, Posy darling?" Uncle Ralph, who was sitting next to me, asked. "Damned hot out here," he added, whisking a spotless white handkerchief out of his jacket pocket and mopping his brow.

"Yes, Uncle Ralph. I was just thinking how happy Maman and Daddy look today. And how sad it is that he has to go back to the war."

"Yes."

I watched as Ralph studied my parents and thought he suddenly looked sad too.

"Well now, with a fair wind, it will be over soon," he said eventually. "And we can all start to get on with our lives."

After lunch, I was allowed to play some croquet, which I did surprisingly well at, probably because most of the adults had drunk quite a lot of wine and wobbled the ball all over the place. I'd heard Daddy saying earlier that he was emptying the last of the wine cellar for the occasion, and it looked like most of it had been emptied into the guests already. I didn't really understand why adults wanted to get drunk; to my mind they just became louder and sillier, but maybe when I was an adult, I would. As I walked across the lawn towards the tennis court, I saw a man with his arms draped around two women lying under a tree. All three of them were fast asleep. Someone was a playing a saxophone alone up on the terrace and I thought what a good job it was that we didn't have close neighbors.

I knew I was lucky to live at Admiral House; when I had started at the local school and been invited round to tea by Mabel, a friend I had made, I had been amazed to find that her family lived in a house where the front door led straight into the sitting room. There was a tiny kitchen at the back, and an *outside* lavatory! She had four brothers and sisters who all shared the same tiny bedroom upstairs. It was the first time I had realized that I came from a rich family, that everyone did not live in a big house with a park for a garden and it was quite a shock. When Daisy collected me to walk me home I asked her why this was.

"It's the roll of the dice, Posy," Daisy had said in her soft Suffolk accent. "Some people get the luck and others don't."

Daisy was very fond of her sayings; half the time I didn't understand what she meant, but I was very glad that the 'dice' seemed to have rolled me into the lucky pile and I decided that I needed to pray harder for everyone that didn't get in.

I wasn't sure that my teacher, Miss Dansart, liked me very much. Even though she encouraged all of us to put up our hands if we knew the answer to the questions, I always seemed to be the first to do it. She would roll her eyes a little and her lips would make a funny shape as she said, "Yes, Posy," in a tired voice. I'd once heard her talking to another teacher in the playground as I was turning one end of a long skipping rope nearby.

"Only child...brought up in the company of adults...precocious..."

I had looked up 'precocious' in the dictionary when I got home. And after that, I'd stopped putting up my hand, even if the answer burned in my throat as I held it inside.

At six o'clock, everyone woke up and drifted off to change for dinner. I went into the kitchen, where Daisy indicated my supper.

"Bread and jam for you tonight, Miss Posy. I've got two salmon that Mr. Ralph brought to deal with and I can't make head nor tail of them."

Daisy chuckled at her own joke, and I felt suddenly sorry for her because she had to work so hard all the time.

"Would you like some help?"

"I have Marjory's two young 'uns coming in from the village to set the table and serve tonight, so I'll be all right. Thanks for asking," she said as she threw me a smile. "You're a good girl, you are."

When I'd finished my tea, I slipped away from the kitchen before Daisy could tell me to go upstairs and get ready for bed. It was such a beautiful evening, I wanted to go back outside and enjoy it. As I stepped onto the terrace, I saw the sun was hovering just above the oak trees, sending slants of butter-colored light onto the grass. The birds were still singing as though it was only noon and it was still warm enough to be comfortable without a cardigan. I sat down on the steps, smoothing my cotton dress over my knees and studying a Red Admiral that had settled on a plant in the sloping flower bed that led down to the garden. I'd always thought that our house was named after the butterflies that hovered so prettily in the bushes. I'd been terribly upset to find out from Maman that it had been named after my great-great-great (I think it was three 'greats,' or maybe four) grandfather, who had been an admiral in the navy, which wasn't nearly so romantic.

Even though Daddy had said Red Admirals were 'common' round here (which was what Maman called some of the children in my class at school), I thought they were the most beautiful butterflies of all, with their vibrant red and black wings and the white spots on the end of them, which reminded me of the pattern on the Spitfires Daddy flew. But that thought made me sad because it *also* reminded me that he was going away again to fly them tomorrow.

"Hello darling girl, what are you doing out here all alone?"

The sound of his voice made me jump, because I'd just been thinking about him. I looked up and saw him walking towards me across the terrace, smoking a cigarette, which he threw to the ground and stamped on with his foot to put it out. He knew I hated the smell.

"Don't tell Daisy you've seen me, will you, Daddy? Or she'll send me straight to bed," I said hurriedly as he sat down on the step next to me.

"Promise. Besides, no one should be in bed on a heaven-sent evening like this. I believe June is the best month that England has to offer; everything in nature has recovered from its long winter sleep, stretched and yawned and unfurled its leaves and flowers for us humans to enjoy. By August, its energy has burnt out in the heat, and it's all ready to go to sleep again."

"Just like us, Daddy. I'm happy to get into bed in the winter," I said.

"Exactly, darling. Never forget that we are inextricably entwined with nature."

"The Bible says that God made everything on earth," I said

importantly, having learnt this from my scripture lessons.

"Indeed, although I find it hard to believe he managed it in just seven days," he chuckled.

"It's magic, Daddy, isn't it? Like Father Christmas being able to deliver presents to all the children in the world in one night."

"Yes it is, Posy, of course it is. The world is a magical place and we must all count ourselves lucky to live in it. Never forget that, will you?"

"No, Daddy. Daddy?"

"Yes, Posy?"

"What time are you leaving tomorrow?"

"I must catch the train after lunch."

I studied my black patent shoes hard. "I'm worried you might get hurt again."

"No fear, darling. As your Maman says, I am indestructible," he smiled.

"When will you come back home?"

"The minute I get leave, which shouldn't be too long. Look after your mother while I'm gone, won't you? I know she gets miserable here by herself."

"I always try to, Daddy. She only gets sad because she misses you and loves you, doesn't she?"

"Yes, and golly, Posy, I love her. The thought of her—and you—is all that's got me through when I'm flying. We hadn't been married for long when this blasted war began, you see."

"After you'd heard her singing in the club in Paris and fallen in love with her that minute, then whisked her off to England to be your bride before she could change her mind," I said dreamily. My parents' own love story was far better than any of the fairy tales in my storybooks.

"Yes. It's love that makes the magic happen in life, Posy. Even on the drabbest day in the depths of winter, love can make the world light up and look as beautiful as it does now."

Daddy gave a deep sigh, then took my hand in his large one. "Promise me that when you find love, you will grab hold of it and never let it go."

"I promise, Daddy," I said, looking at him earnestly.

"Good girl. Now, I must be off to change for dinner."

He dropped a kiss on top of my curls, stood up, and walked back into the house.

Of course I didn't know at the time, but it was the last proper conversation I would ever have with my father.

Daddy left the next afternoon, and all the guests too. That evening, it was very hot and the air felt thick and heavy when you breathed, as if all the oxygen had been sucked out of it. The house fell silent—Daisy had gone on her weekly trip to take tea with her friend Edith, so there wasn't even the sound of her grumbling or singing (out of the two, I preferred the grumbling) over the washing-up. Of which there was a lot, still stacked on trays in the scullery waiting to be cleaned. I had offered to help with the glasses, but Daisy said I'd be more trouble than I was worth, which I thought was quite unfair.

Maman had taken to her bed the minute the last car had disappeared beyond the chestnut trees. She had one of her migraines, apparently, which Daisy said was a posh word for a hangover, whatever that was. I sat in my room, curled up on the window seat positioned over the portico at the front of Admiral House. This meant that, if someone was expected, I was the first one to see them arrive. Daddy called me his 'little look-out,' and since Frederick, the butler, had gone off to fight, I was usually the one who opened the front door.

From here, I had a perfect view of the drive, carved between lines of very old chestnut and oak trees. Daddy had told me that some of them had been planted nearly three hundred years ago when the first admiral had built himself the house. (I found this thought fascinating because it meant that trees lived on the earth almost five times longer than people, if the *Encyclopaedia Britannica* in the library was right and the average human life expectancy was sixty-one for men and sixty-seven for women.) If I squinted hard, on a clear day I could see a thin line of grayish-blue above the treetops and below the sky. It was the North Sea, which lay just five miles away from Admiral House. It was frightening to think that one day soon, Daddy could be flying across it in his little plane.

"Come home safely, come home soon," I whispered to the dark gray clouds that were pressing down on the sun as it set, about to squash it like a juicy orange (I hadn't tasted one of those for a *very* long time). The air was still and there was no breeze wafting through my open window. I heard the rumble of thunder in the distance and hoped Daisy wasn't right and God wasn't angry with us. I could never work out whether He was Daisy's cross God or the vicar's kind one. Maybe He was like a parent and could be both.

As the first drops of rain began to fall, soon turning into a torrent as streaks of God's anger flashed across the sky, I hoped Daddy had arrived safely at his base, otherwise he would get very wet indeed, or worse, struck by lightning. I closed the window because the sill was getting wet and then realized my tummy was rumbling nearly as loudly as the thunder. So I went downstairs to find the bread and jam Daisy had left me for supper.

As I walked down the wide oak stairs in the gloomy dusk, I thought how silent the house was compared to yesterday, like a nest of buzzing, talkative bees had arrived, then left just as suddenly. Another clap of thunder roared above me, breaking the silence, and I decided it was a good job I wasn't a scaredy-cat about dark and thunderstorms and being alone.

"Ooh, Posy, your house is creepy," Mabel had said when I had invited her home for tea. "Look at all them pictures of dead people in their old-fashioned costumes! They give me the willies, they do," she'd pronounced with a shiver, pointing up at the paintings of Anderson ancestors that lined the stairs. "I'd be too scared to leave me room to go to the lavvy at night in case of ghosts."

"They're my relatives from long ago, and I'm sure they would be very friendly if they did come back to say hello," I'd said, upset that she didn't love Admiral House immediately like I did.

Now, as I walked across the hall and along the echoey corridor that led to the kitchen, I didn't feel frightened at all, even though it was very dark now and Maman, who was probably still asleep upstairs in her bedroom, would never hear me if I screamed.

I knew I was safe here, that nothing bad could ever happen inside the house's sturdy walls.

I reached to turn on the light in the kitchen, but it didn't seem to be working, so instead I lit one of the candles that sat on a shelf. I was good at lighting candles, because the electricity at Admiral House, especially since the war, could not be relied upon. I loved their soft, flickering glow that just lit the area you were in and seemed to make even the ugliest person look pretty. Taking the bread Daisy had cut for me earlier—I might be allowed to light candles but I was forbidden to touch sharp knives—I slathered on the butter and jam thickly. Then, with a piece already in my mouth, I took the plate and the candle and went back upstairs to my bedroom to watch the storm.

I sat on my window seat chewing the bread and jam and thinking how Daisy worried about me when she left for her evening off. Especially when Daddy was away.

"It's not right for a little girl to be alone in such a big house," she'd mutter. I'd explain that I wasn't alone because Maman was here too and besides, I wasn't 'little' as I was seven, which was quite big.

"Hmph!" she'd reply as she took off her apron and hung it on the hook on the back of the kitchen door. "Never mind what she says, you go and wake your mum if you need her."

"I will," I always said, but of course I never did, not even when I'd been sick on the floor once and my tummy had hurt really badly. I knew Maman would get cross if I woke her up because she needed her sleep. In any case, I didn't mind being alone, because since Daddy had gone to the war, I was used to it. Besides, there was the whole collection of the *Encyclopaedia Britannica* from the library to read. I had finished the first two volumes, but I had another twenty-two to go, which I reckoned would take me until I was a grown-up.

Tonight, without electricity, it was too dark to read and the candle was now only a stub, so I watched the skies instead, trying not to think about Daddy going away or tears might start falling from my eyes as fast as the raindrops that were beating on the window.

As I looked out, a sudden flash of red caught my eye in the top corner of the pane.

"Oh! It's a butterfly! A Red Admiral!"

I stood up on the window seat and saw that the poor thing was doing its best to shelter from the storm by nestling underneath the window frame. I had to rescue it, so I very carefully opened the latch on the top pane and reached my hand outside. Even though it wasn't moving, it took me a while to clasp it between my forefinger and thumb because I didn't want to damage its fragile wings, which were firmly closed and very wet and slippery.

"Got you," I whispered as I carefully drew my hand—which was now soaking wet—back through the window and shut it firmly with my dry hand.

"Now then, little one," I whispered as I studied it sitting in the palm of my hand. "I wonder how I dry your wings?"

I thought about how they might dry if they were outside in nature because they must get wet all the time.

"A warm breeze," I said, and began to gently blow my own breath onto them. At first, the butterfly didn't move, but finally, as I thought I might faint from using so much breath, I watched as the wings fluttered and opened. I had never had a butterfly sitting still on the palm of my hand, so I bent my head and studied the lovely color and intricate pattern on the top of them.

"You are a real beauty," I told it. "Now, you can't go back outside tonight or you will drown, so why don't I leave you here on the windowsill so you can see your friends outside and I will set you free tomorrow morning?"

Very gently, I picked up the butterfly with the tips of my fingers and placed it on the windowsill. I watched it for a while, wondering if butterflies slept with their wings open or closed. But by now, my own eyes were closing, so I drew the curtains across the window in order that the tiny creature wouldn't be tempted to fly into the room and attach itself to the ceiling high above me. I would never be able to reach to get it down again if it did and it might die of hunger or fear in the meantime.

Taking the candle, I walked across the room and climbed into bed, feeling satisfied that I'd managed to save a life and that maybe it was a good omen and Daddy would not get hurt again this time.

"Goodnight, butterfly. Sleep well until the morning," I whispered as I blew the candle out and fell asleep.

When I woke, up I saw shards of light crossing the ceiling from the gaps in the curtains. They were golden today, which meant the sun was already out. Remembering my butterfly, I climbed out of bed and drew back the curtains carefully.

"Oh!"

I caught my breath as I saw my butterfly, wings closed and lying on one side with its tiny feet in the air. Because the underside of its wings were mostly dark brown, it looked more like a large, and very dead moth. Tears sprang to my eyes as I touched it just to check, but it didn't stir, so I knew its soul was already up in heaven. Maybe I had killed it by not setting it free last night. Daddy always said you had to release them very quickly and even though it hadn't been in a glass jar, it had been inside. Or maybe it had died of pneumonia or bronchitis because it had got so wet.

I stood there looking at it, and I just *knew* it was a very bad omen indeed.

Autumn 1944

I liked the moment when summer began to fade into the long dead winter. The mist began to hang across the tops of the trees like huge spiders' webs and the air smelt woody and rich with fermentation (I'd learnt that word recently when I went to visit the local brewery on a school trip and watched the hops being turned into beer). Maman said she found the English weather depressing, that she wanted to live somewhere where it was sunny and warm all year round. Personally, I thought that would be very boring. Watching the cycle of nature, the invisible magic hands that turned the emerald-green leaves on the beech trees to a shiny bronze color, was exciting. Or maybe I just lived a very dull life.

And it *had* been dull since Daddy left. No more parties or people coming to visit, except for Uncle Ralph, who turned up quite a lot with flowers and French cigarettes for Maman and occasionally chocolate for me. The monotony had at least been broken with the annual August trip down to Cornwall to visit Granny. Usually, Maman would come with me, and Daddy would join us for a few days if he could get leave, but this year, Maman announced I was old enough to go by myself.

"It is you she wishes to see, Posy, not me. She hates me, she always has done."

I was sure this wasn't true, as no one could hate Maman, with her beauty and her lovely singing voice, but the consequence was I went alone, with a bad-tempered Daisy accompanying me on the long journey there and back.

Granny lived just outside a small village called Blisland, which nestled on the western edge of Bodmin Moor. Although her house was quite big and quite grand, its gray walls and heavy dark furniture always seemed a bit gloomy to me after the light-filled rooms of Admiral House. Outdoors was fun to explore, at least. When Daddy came, we would walk onto the moor to pick samples of the heather and the pretty wildflowers that grew between the gorse.

Sadly, on this visit, Daddy wasn't there and it rained every day, which meant that outdoors was out of bounds. During the long, wet afternoons, Granny taught me to play Patience and we ate a lot of cake, but I was very glad when it was time to leave. When we arrived home, Daisy and I had climbed out of the pony and trap which Benson, our part-time gardener (who was probably one hundred years old) sometimes drove to collect people from the railway station. Leaving Benson and Daisy to bring in the suitcases, I ran into the house in search of Maman. I could hear 'Blue Moon' playing from the gramophone in the drawing room and had found Maman and Uncle Ralph dancing together.

"Posy!" she'd said, leaving Uncle Ralph's arms and coming over to hug me. "We didn't hear you arrive."

"It was probably the loud music in here, Maman," I'd answered, thinking how pretty and happy she looked, with her flushed cheeks and her lovely long hair, which had fallen out of its clip and was making a pale golden trail down her back.

"We were celebrating, Posy," said Uncle Ralph. "There's more good news from France, you see. It looks as though Jerry will soon surrender and the war will be finally over."

"Oh, good," I replied. "That means Daddy will be home soon."

"Yes."

There was a pause before Maman had told me to run along up to my room to wash and change after my long journey. As I did so, I'd truly hoped Uncle Ralph was right and Daddy *would* be home soon. Since the radio had begun to tell us in the news bulletins about the triumph of D-Day, I had been hoping to see him constantly. It was over three months ago now and he still hadn't come back, even though Maman had been to visit him when he had short leave, because it was easier. When I queried why he wasn't home yet when we'd almost won the war, she had shrugged.

"He is very busy, Posy, and will be home when he is home."

"But how do you know he is well? Has he written to you?"

"*Oui, chérie*, he has. Be patient. Wars take a long time to end."

The food shortages were even worse and we were down to our last two chickens, who hadn't had their necks broken because they were the best egg producers. Even they seemed down in the mouth, though I went to talk to them every day, as Benson said happy chickens produced more eggs. My chatter wasn't working, because neither Ethel nor Ruby had produced an egg for the past five days.

"Where are you, Daddy?" I asked the skies, thinking how wonderful it would be if I suddenly saw a Spitfire appear from between the clouds and there was Daddy, zooming downwards to land on the wide lawns.

November came, and each afternoon after school, I spent my time hunting in the sodden, frost-soaked undergrowth for kindling for the fire Maman and I lit in the morning room in the evening, because it was much smaller to heat than the great big drawing room.

"Posy, I have been thinking about Christmas," Maman said to me one night.

"Maybe Daddy will be home by then and we can spend it together."

"No, he will not be home and I have been invited to London to celebrate with my friends. Of course, it will be far too boring for you being with so many adults, so I have written to your grandmother and she is willing to take you for Christmas."

"But I..."

"Posy, please understand that we cannot stay here. The house is freezing, there is no coal for the fires..."

"But we have logs and—"

"We have no food on our plates, Posy! Your grandmother has lost her help recently and is willing to take Daisy too whilst she finds a local replacement."

I bit my lip, very close to tears. "But what if Daddy comes back to find us gone?"

"I will write to him and tell him."

"He may not get the letter, and besides, I would rather stay here and starve than spend Christmas at Granny's! I love her, but she is old and the house isn't my home and..."

"Enough! I have made up my mind. Remember, Posy, we must all do what we can to survive the last months of this brutal war. At least you will be warm and safe, with food inside you. This is much more than many others across the world who are starving or even dead."

I had never seen Maman so angry, so even though a torrent of tears was poised behind my eyes and making them ache, I swallowed hard and nodded.

"Yes, Maman."

After that, at least Maman seemed to cheer up, even if Daisy and I were walking about the house like pale spectres doomed for the rest of our existence.

"If I had any choice, I wouldn't be going," Daisy grumbled as she helped me pack my suitcase. "But the mistress tells me she has no money to pay me here, so what can I do? I can't live on buttons, can I?"

"I'm sure things will be better when the war is over and Daddy comes back home," I told her, comforting myself at the same time.

"Well, they can't get any worse than they've been. Things have come to a pretty pass here and that's for sure," Daisy replied darkly. "I've half a mind that she's getting us both out of the way so that she can..."

"She can what?" I asked her.

"Never you mind, young lady, but the sooner your dad is home, the better."

As the house was being shut up for the next month, Daisy went to work on cleaning every single inch of it.

"But why are you cleaning it if no one's going to be here?" I asked her.

"Enough of your questions, Miss Posy, and help me with these instead," she said, picking up a pile of white sheets und flapping them open like big white sails. Together we spread them over all the beds and the furniture in the twenty-six rooms of the house, until it looked like a large family of ghosts had moved in.

Once the school holidays began, I took out my colored pencils and my pad of clean white paper sheets and drew what I could find from the garden. It was quite hard because everything was dead. One chilly December day, I took my magnifying glass into the garden. It hadn't snowed yet, but there was a shiny white frost on all the holly bushes, and I took off my mittens so I could hold the lens to see the stems properly. Daddy had taught me exactly where to look to find the pupae of the Holly Blue butterfly.

As I did so, I saw the door of the Folly open and Daisy came out, her face flushed and her arms full of cleaning supplies.

"Miss Posy, what are you doing out here without your mittens on?" she scolded me. "Put them back on, you'll get frostbite and your fingers will drop off." With that, she stalked off to the house, and I looked at the door of the Folly, which hadn't quite swung shut behind her. Before I could think better of it, I slipped inside, and the door creaked shut behind me.

It was very dark, but my eyes soon got used to it, and I could make out the shapes of the cricket stumps and croquet hoops that Daddy kept in here as well as the locked gun cupboard that he had told me never to open. I glanced up at the stairs that led to Daddy's room and stood there in an agony of indecision. If Daisy had left the downstairs door unlocked, maybe the one to Daddy's private room was still open too. I wanted to see the inside of it so, so badly...

Eventually, curiosity won, and I tripped up the stairs that turned round and round quickly before Daisy returned. When I reached the top, I put my hand to the knob of the big oak door and twisted it. Daisy clearly hadn't locked it, because it opened, and one step later, there I was in Daddy's secret office.

It smelt of polish, and light illuminated the circular walls that surrounded the windows Daisy had just cleaned. On the wall directly in front of me hung what must be an entire extended family of Red Admiral butterflies. They were lined up in rows of four behind glass enclosed by a gilt frame.

As I took a step closer, I was confused, because I wondered how the butterflies could stay so still, and what they had found to eat inside their glass prison.

Then I saw the heads of the pins that stuck them to the backing. I glanced at the other walls and saw that they too were covered with the butterflies we'd caught over the years.

With a groan of horror, I turned and pelted down the steps and out into the garden. Seeing Daisy approaching from the house, I turned and ran around the back of the Folly and into the woodland that surrounded it. When I was far enough away, I sank down onto the roots of a big oak tree, gulping in breath.

"They're dead! They're dead! They're dead! How could he have lied to me?" I shouted in between sobs.

I stayed in the woods a very long time, until I heard Daisy calling for me. I only wished I could ask Daddy why he'd killed them when they were so beautiful, and then hung them up like trophies so he could look up and see their deadness on the walls.

Well, I couldn't ask because he wasn't here, but I had to trust and believe there was a very good reason for the murders in our butterfly kingdom.

As I stood and began to walk slowly back to the house, I couldn't think of a single one. All I knew was that I never wanted to set foot in the Folly again.

Butterfly Bush
(Buddleja davidii)

Chapter 1

Admiral House
September 2006

Posy was in the kitchen garden picking some carrots when she heard her mobile ringing from the depths of her Barbour. Pulling it out of her pocket, she answered it.

"Hello, Mum. I didn't wake you, did I?"

"Goodness no, and besides, even if you had, it's lovely to hear from you. How are you, Nick?"

"I'm good, Mum."

"And how is Perth?" Posy enquired, standing up and wandering through the garden and into the kitchen.

"Just starting to hot up as England begins to cool down. How are things with you?"

"I'm fine. Nothing much changes around here, as you know."

"Listen, I'm calling to let you know that I'm coming back to England later this month."

"Oh Nick! How wonderful. After all these years."

"Ten, actually," her son confirmed. "It's about time I came home, don't you think?"

"I do indeed. I'm over the moon, darling. You know how much I miss you."

"And I you, Mum."

"How long will you be staying? Could it be as long as to be the guest of honor at my seventieth birthday party next June?" Posy smiled.

"We'll have to see how things go, but even if I decide to come back here, I'll make sure I'm there at your party, of course I will."

"So shall I come and pick you up from the airport?"

"No, don't worry about that. I'm going to stay in London for a few days with my friends Paul and Jane as I have some business I want to sort out, but I'll ring you when I'm clearer on my plans and drive up to Admiral House to see you."

"I can hardly wait, darling."

"Nor me, Mum. It's been too long. I'd better go, but I'll be in touch soon."

"Righty-ho. Oh Nick...I can't quite believe you're coming home."

He heard the catch in her voice. "Nor me. Lots of love, and I'll call you as soon as I have things organized. Bye for now."

"Bye, darling."

Posy sank into the ancient leather chair next to the stove, feeling weak with emotion.

Of her two sons, it was Nick of whom she had the most vivid memories as an infant. Perhaps because he'd been born so soon after his father's tragic death, Posy had always felt that Nick was utterly hers.

His premature arrival—hastened almost certainly by the appalling shock of losing Jonny, her husband of thirteen years, so tragically—meant Posy, with three-year-old Sam on top of the newborn Nick, had found little time to wallow.

There had been much to sort out, a lot of hard decisions to make at a time when she was at her lowest ebb. All the plans she and Jonny had made for the future had to be shelved. With two small children to bring up alone—children who would need their mother's love and attention more than ever—Posy had realized it would be an impossible task to try and run Admiral House as the business they had planned.

If there was ever a particularly bad moment to lose one's husband, Posy thought, that had been it. After twelve years of being stationed around the globe, Jonny had decided to leave the army and fulfil his wife's longed-for dream: to return to Admiral House and give their young family—and the two of them—a proper home.

Posy put the kettle on to boil, thinking back to how hot it had been that August thirty-four years ago, when Jonny had driven them through the golden Suffolk countryside towards the house. She had been newly pregnant with Nick; anxiety mixed with morning sickness had caused them to pull over twice. When they'd finally driven through the old wrought-iron gates, Posy had held her breath.

As Admiral House had come into view, a flood of memories had washed over her. It looked just as she remembered it, perhaps a little older and wearier, but then again, so was she. Jonny had opened the door of the car for her and helped her out, and Sam had run up beside her and gripped her hand tightly as they had walked up the steps to the huge front door.

"Do you want to open it?" she had asked him, placing the heavy key into the palm of his small hand.

He had nodded and she had lifted him up so he could slot the key into the lock.

Together, they'd pushed open the heavy door, and the sun had shone a path into the dark and shuttered house. Going on memory, Posy had found the light switch. The hall was suddenly flooded with electric light, and they had all looked upwards at the magnificent chandelier hanging twenty feet above them.

White sheets were draped over the furniture, and dust had lain thickly on the floor, whirling up into the air as Sam had run up the magnificent cantilevered staircase. Tears had come to Posy's eyes, and she had shut them tightly as she had been assailed by the sights and smells of her childhood, Maman, Daisy, Daddy...when she had opened them, she had seen Sam waving from the top of the stairs and she had joined him up there to see the rest of the house.

Jonny had loved it too, though with obvious reservations about its upkeep.

"It's enormous, darling," he'd said as they'd sat in the kitchen in which Posy so vividly remembered Daisy rolling pastry on the old oak table. "And obviously in need of some updating."

"Well, it hasn't been lived in for more than a quarter of a century," she'd answered.

Once they'd settled in, the two of them had talked about how Admiral House could provide a much-needed income to supplement Jonny's army pension. They'd agreed that they could set about renovating the house and one day, open it as a bed and breakfast to paying guests.

Ironically, Jonny's death, after all his years in the military, had come only months later at the metal teeth of a combine harvester, which had hit him head-on as he negotiated a narrow bend only two miles away from Admiral House.

Jonny had left her his pension and a couple of life insurance policies. She'd also inherited her grandmother's estate when she'd died a couple of years before, and had put the money she'd received from the sale of the Manor House in Cornwall into investments. She'd also received a small bequest from her mother, who had died of pneumonia (a fact that Posy still found odd, given she'd spent many years in Italy) at the age of fifty-five.

She'd considered selling Admiral House, but as the estate agent she'd brought in to value it had told her, few people wanted a house of that size any longer. Even if she found a buyer, the price she'd get for it would be well below what it was worth.

Besides, she adored the house—had only just returned to it after all those years—and with Jonny gone, Posy needed the familiar and comforting walls of her childhood home around her.

So she'd worked out that as long as she remained frugal with their living costs, and braced herself to dip into her savings and investments to subsidize her income, the three of them could just about get by.

Throughout the lonely, dark days of those first months without Jonny, Nick's sunny, undemanding nature had provided endless solace, and as she'd watched her baby boy grow into a happy, contented child toddling around the kitchen garden, he'd given her hope for the future.

Of course, it had been easier for Nick; what he'd never known he couldn't miss. Whereas Sam had been old enough to acknowledge the chill wind of death as it blew across his life.

"When's Daddy coming back?"

Posy remembered him asking the same question every night for weeks on end after his father's death, her heart breaking as she saw the confusion in his big blue eyes, so similar to his father's. Posy would steel herself to tell him that Daddy wasn't coming back ever again. That he'd gone up to heaven to watch over them from there and finally, Sam had stopped asking.

Posy stood listening to the sizzle of the water beginning to boil. She stirred the coffee granules into the milk at the bottom of the cup, then topped it up with hot water.

Cradling her cup, she walked towards the window and stared out at the ancient horse chestnut that had stoically given generations of children a bumper crop of conkers. She could see the green, prickly husks already formed, heralding the end of the summer and the beginning of autumn.

The thought of conkers reminded her of the start of the school year—a moment she'd dreaded when her boys were younger, as it marked the buying of new school uniforms, the label-sewing and the trunks she'd heave up from the cellar. Then the dreadful silence when they'd left.

Posy had thought long and hard about sending her beloved boys away to boarding school. Even if generations of both Jonny's and her own family had been sent away, it had been the late seventies and times had changed. Yet she knew her own experience had not only given her an education, but independence and discipline. Jonny would have wanted his sons to go—he had often talked about sending them to his alma mater. So Posy had dug into her investments—comforting herself with the thought that her grandmother would approve too—and sent them away to school in Norfolk; not so far that she could never see them play rugby or appear in a school play, but far enough so she couldn't be tempted to fetch them on the occasions when one or the other of them was homesick.

Sam had been the most frequent caller—he'd struggled to settle and always seemed to be falling out with one of his friends. When Nick had followed his brother three years later, she'd rarely heard from him.

In the early days of her widowhood when both the boys were small, she had longed for time to herself, but when both her sons had left for school and she'd finally had it, the cool breeze of loneliness had blown through the damp walls and lodged in her heart.

For the first time in her life, Posy remembered waking up in the morning and struggling to find a reason to climb out of bed. She'd realized it was because the core of her life had been torn away from her and everything around the edges of it was merely padding. Sending her boys away was like going through bereavement all over again.

The feeling had humbled her—up to that point in her life she had never understood depression and had seen it as a sign of weakness, but in that dreadful month after Nick had first left for school, she had felt guilty for ever thinking one could simply snap out of it. She'd realized she needed a project to take her mind off how much she missed her boys.

She'd been in her father's study one autumnal morning and stumbled across an old set of plans for the garden in the drawer of his desk. From the look of them, he'd obviously been planning to turn the parkland gardens into something spectacular. Having been protected from light, the ink was still vivid on the parchment paper, the lines and proportions of the park rendered in her father's meticulous hand. She could see that beside the Folly, he had marked a space for a butterfly garden, listing nectar-rich perennials that she knew would be a riot of color in full bloom. A wisteria walk led to an orchard full of all of her favorite fruits: pears, apples, plums, and even figs.

Beside the kitchen garden, he had marked out a large greenhouse and a smaller walled garden, with a note that had read 'willow walkway for Posy to play.' Whimsical garden pathways were sketched in to connect the disparate parts, and Posy had chuckled at his plan for a pond near to the croquet lawn ('to cool off hot tempers'). There was also a rose garden marked 'for Adriana.'

So she'd gone out that afternoon with string and willow sticks and had started marking out some of the borders he'd planned, which would be filled with grape hyacinths, alliums and crocuses, all of which didn't need much attention and were perfect for attracting bees when they woke from their winter sojourn.

A few days later, with her hands deep in the soft earth, Posy remembered smiling for the first time in weeks. The smell of compost, the feel of the gentle sun on her head, and the planting of bulbs that would provide welcome color next spring had reminded her of her time at Kew.

That day had been the start of what had become a twenty-five-year passion. She'd laid out the vast area into sections, and each spring and autumn, she'd worked on a new part of it, adding her own designs to those of her father, including her personal *pièce de résistance*—an ambitious parterre below the terrace, comprising intricate curves of low box hedges enclosing beds of fragrant lavender and roses. It was an absolute devil to maintain, but the view it afforded from the formal reception rooms and bedrooms was sublime.

In short, the garden had become her master, her friend and her lover, leaving her little time for anything else.

"Mum, it's amazing," Nick would say when he arrived home in the summer holidays and she'd show him the new work in progress.

"Yeah, but what's for supper?" Sam would ask as he kicked a ball across the terrace. Posy remembered he'd broken the greenhouse windows three times as a boy.

As she gathered the ingredients together to whip up a cake to take over to her grandchildren later, Posy felt the familiar twinge of guilt prompted by any thoughts of her eldest son.

Although she loved Sam dearly, she'd always found him far more difficult than Nick. Perhaps it was simply that she and her youngest son shared so much in common. His love for 'old things,' as Sam had called them, watching his younger brother painstakingly restore an old chest rotting away from woodworm. Where Sam was all action—his attention span short and his temper quick to ignite—Nick was far calmer. He had an eye for beauty that Posy liked to think he'd inherited from her.

The terrible truth was, she thought as she stirred the eggs into the cake mixture, one could love one's children, but that didn't mean to say one would like them equally.

The thing that upset her most was that her two sons were not close. Posy remembered Nick toddling around the garden after his big brother when they were small. It had been obvious he worshipped the ground Sam walked on, but as the years had fled by, she'd noticed that Nick had actively begun to avoid him during the school holidays, preferring to spend time with her in the kitchen, or restoring his bits of furniture in the barn.

They were polar opposites, of course—Sam so outwardly confident and Nick introspective. Like a silken thread that had been spun through the decades from their childhood, their adult lives were connected, but had continued to take them in different directions too.

Since leaving school, Sam had flunked university and moved to London. He'd tried his hand at computers, cheffing and estate agency. All of these endeavors seemed to have melted away like snow after a few months. He'd returned to Southwold ten years ago, married, and after further failed start-ups, was at present trying to set up his own property business.

Posy always encouraged him as best she could when he came to her with a new money-making scheme. But recently, she'd made a pact with herself that there would be no more lending, however hard Sam pleaded with her. Besides, with most of her investment income eaten up by her beloved garden, she had little left to give. A year ago, she had sold one of her precious Staffordshire figurines to finance Sam's 'watertight' business plan to make films to help market local businesses. The funds from the figurine's sale had been lost forever when the company folded after only nine months.

The difficulty she had in saying no to Sam was compounded by the fact that he had managed to find himself an angel of a wife. Amy was a complete sweetheart who had even managed to smile when recently, for the umpteenth time, Sam announced they had to move from their rented house to another, smaller one, due to lack of cash.

Amy had borne Sam two healthy children—Jake, who was six, and Sara, four—*and* managed to hold down a job as a receptionist at a local hotel to provide an albeit small but much-needed regular flow of cash into the household, as well as stoically supporting her husband, which made Amy a saint in Posy's book.

As for Nick, Posy's heart filled with happiness that her son was finally returning to the UK. After he'd left school, he'd ignored the offers of a couple of excellent universities and instead announced he wanted to go into the antiques trade. After working part-time at a local auctioneer's, he'd managed to get himself an apprenticeship with an antique dealer in Lavenham, commuting daily from Admiral House.

When he was just twenty-one, Nick had opened his own shop in Southwold and had soon begun to garner a reputation for stocking interesting and unusual antiques. Posy could not have been happier that her son had chosen to live his life locally. Two years later, he'd rented the premises next door to double the space for his flourishing business. If he was away buying, Posy would leave her beloved garden and spend a day in the shop serving the customers.

A few months later, Nick had announced he had taken on a full-time assistant to run the shop when he was attending auctions. Evie Newman was not traditionally beautiful, her small frame and elfin features giving her the air of a child rather than a woman, but her huge brown eyes were haunting in their loveliness. The first time Nick had introduced Posy to Evie, she had watched her son watching every move Evie made, and had known without a doubt that Nick had fallen in love.

Not that Nick was able to do anything about his feelings. Evie had a long-standing boyfriend to whom she was seemingly devoted. Posy had met him once and been surprised that Evie could find the weasel-faced, pseudo-intellectual Brian attractive. A divorced sociology lecturer at the local community college and older than Evie by a good fifteen years, Brian had strong opinions and liked to air them as often as possible. Posy had disliked him on the spot.

As Nick spent more time away on buying trips, Posy had helped Evie learn the ropes at the shop. Despite the difference in age between the two women, they'd become firm friends. Evie had lost both her parents very young, and lived with her grandmother in a rambling Victorian house in Southwold. Having never had a daughter of her own, Posy reveled in the fondness she felt for her.

Sometimes Evie would travel with Nick and Posy would be left holding the fort at the shop. She loved to see Evie's sparkling eyes when she returned from a buying trip, her expressive hands conjuring up an elegant chiffonier they had got for next to nothing in a sale from a magnificent chateau in the South of France.

Despite her promise to herself not to rely on Nick's presence in her life, after years of coexisting happily at Admiral House, the shock she'd felt when, out of the blue, he'd told her he was selling up and moving to Australia had been devastating. This was compounded by Evie announcing soon afterwards that Brian had got a good job at a college in Leicester. He had asked her to marry him, apparently, and she had agreed. They were to leave Southwold imminently.

Posy had tried to discover exactly why her son felt he had to extinguish the successful business he'd worked so hard to build and move to the other side of the world, but Nick was not forthcoming. She'd suspected it was something to do with Evie, and given she was moving away too, something didn't quite fit.

The business sold almost immediately and Nick had left soon after for Perth, shipping stock over with him to give him a start in his new Antipodean venture. Posy had given no clue as to how lost she would feel without him.

The fact that Evie had not come to say goodbye before she'd left Southwold had cut Posy to the quick, but she'd accepted that she was an older woman in a young person's life. Just because she had strong feelings for Evie did not mean they were or should be reciprocated.

As winter had drawn in, again Posy had felt the familiar frost of loneliness. Due to the time of year, her precious garden was sleeping and there was little she could do until the spring. Without the comfort of that to bury herself in, Posy knew she had to find something urgently to fill the void. So she'd taken herself off into Southwold and managed to find herself a part-time job. Three mornings a week she worked at an art gallery. Even though modern paintings were not really her kind of thing, the job brought in some pin money and kept her busy. She had never admitted to the owner how old she really was and ten years later, Posy was still working there.

"Almost seventy," murmured Posy as she put the cake mixture into the oven to bake and set the timer to take with her. As she left the kitchen and headed for the main stairs, Posy thought what a Herculean task being a mother was. However old her two sons had become, she had never stopped worrying about them. If anything, she worried more; at least when they were small she had known exactly where and how they were. They'd been under her control and of course, as they had grown into adults and fled the nest, that was no longer the case.

Her legs ached slightly as she climbed the stairs, reminding her of all the things she tried not to think about. Even though she was of an age where she could legitimately start to complain about her health, she knew how lucky she was to be so fit.

"But," she said to an ancestor whose image hung on the landing, "just how long will it last?"

Entering the bedroom, Posy walked towards the windows and

drew back the heavy curtains. There had never been the money to replace them and the original pattern on the fabric had bleached beyond recognition.

From here, she had the best view of the garden she'd created. Even in early autumn as nature was preparing itself for sleep, the oblique rays of the afternoon sun caressed the leaves of trees that were slowly ripening to gold, and the last of the roses hung heavy with scent. Fat orange pumpkins sat in the kitchen garden, and the trees in the orchard were laden with blush-red apples. And the parterre, immediately below her window, looked simply stunning.

Posy turned away from the beauty outside and faced the enormous bedroom, where generations of Andersons had slept. Her eyes skimmed over the once exquisite chinoiserie wallpaper that was now peeling surreptitiously in the corners and spotted with damp, the threadbare rug that was past recovering from so many spills, and the fading mahogany furniture.

"And this is just one room; there are another twenty-five that need a complete overhaul, let alone the actual fabric of the building," she muttered to herself.

As she undressed, Posy knew that over the years she had done the bare minimum to the house, partly because of money, but mostly because, like a favorite child, she had thrown all her attention at the garden. And, like any neglected progeny, the house had continued crumbling away unnoticed.

"I'm living here on borrowed time," she sighed, and admitted to herself that this beautiful old house was beginning to feel like a yoke round her neck. Even though she *was* fit and able for a woman who had seen sixty-nine years, just how much longer would she be? Besides, she knew that the house itself was edging to the point of no return if it didn't receive serious renovation soon.

The thought of throwing in the towel and moving to somewhere more manageable appalled her, but Posy knew she had to be practical about the situation. She hadn't mentioned the idea of selling Admiral House to either Sam or Nick, but perhaps, now Nick was returning, she should.

Undressing, Posy saw her reflected image staring back from the cheval mirror. The gray in her hair, the wrinkles around her eyes, and the flesh that was no longer as taut as it used to be depressed her, and she averted her gaze. It was easier not to look, because inside, she was still a young woman full of youthful vigor, the same Posy who had danced and laughed and loved.

"Golly, I miss sex!" she announced to the chest of drawers as she searched for her underwear. Thirty-four years was an awfully long time not to feel the touch of a man, his skin against hers, caressing her body as he rose and fell inside her...

After Jonny had died, there had been men who had crossed her path occasionally and shown an interest, especially in the early days. Maybe it had been that her attention was on the boys, and later the garden, but after a couple of 'dates,' as her sons would call them, Posy had never found the enthusiasm to pursue a relationship.

"And now it is too late," she said to her reflection as she sat down at her dressing table and dabbed the cheap cold cream—the only beauty routine she regularly pursued—onto her face.

"Don't be greedy, Posy. To find two loves in your life is more than most people are ever granted."

As she rose, Posy put both dark and fanciful thoughts out of her head and concentrated on the far more positive thought of her son returning home from Australia. Downstairs, she took the cake out of the oven, emptied it from its tin and left it to cool. Then she walked through the kitchen door into the rear courtyard. She unlocked her battered Volvo and drove along the drive, turning right onto the road that would lead her on the ten-minute journey into Southwold.

She headed towards the sea front, and despite the chilly September wind, rolled down her window to breathe in the briny sea air, mingled with the perpetual scent of fried doughnuts and fish and chips from the shop by the pier, which reached out into the North Sea, a steel gray under a hazy blue sky. Smart white terraced houses lined the road, the shop-fronts beneath them filled with beach bric-a-brac, and seagulls patrolled the pavement for stray pieces of food.

The fabric of the town had hardly changed since she'd been a child, but unfortunately, its old-fashioned seaside quaintness had inspired hordes of affluent middle-class families to invest in holiday homes here. This had driven up property prices to obscene levels, and, although good for the economy of the small town, had undoubtedly altered the dynamics of the once tight-knit community. The second-homers flocked into Southwold in the summer, making parking a nightmare, then left at the end of August like a pack of vultures who had finished feasting on a carcass.

Now, in September, the town felt dead and deserted, as if all its energy had been sucked out by the hordes and taken away with them. As Posy parked in the high street, she saw an 'end of season sale' poster in the boutique, and the bookshop no longer had its trestle tables offering second-hand novels stationed outside.

She walked briskly along the street, nodding good morning to those who passed and acknowledged her. The sense of belonging gave her pleasure at least. Stopping at the newsagents, Posy collected her daily copy of the *Telegraph*.

Coming out of the shop with her nose buried in the headlines, she bumped straight into a young girl.

"Pardon me," she apologized, lowering her gaze to meet that of the brown-eyed child in front of her.

"That's okay," the girl shrugged.

"My goodness," Posy finally responded, "do forgive me for staring, but you look awfully like someone I used to know."

"Oh." The child shifted uncomfortably from foot to foot. Posy moved aside so she could pass by her and step inside the shop. "Goodbye, then."

"Goodbye." Posy turned and walked up the high street towards the gallery. As she did so, a familiar figure came running down the street towards her.

"Evie? It is you, isn't it?"

The young woman stopped dead in her tracks, her pale face reddening from embarrassment.

"Yes. Hello, Posy," she said quietly.

"How are you, dear girl? And what on earth are you doing back in Southwold? Visiting old friends?"

"No." Evie studied her feet. "We moved back here a couple of weeks ago. I...we live here now."

"Really?"

"Yes."

"Oh, I see."

Posy watched Evie as she continued to avoid making eye contact. She was far thinner than she used to be, and her lovely long dark hair had been chopped into a short crop.

"I think I may have seen your daughter just now outside the newsagent. I thought she looked very like you. Back for good, the three of you?"

"The two of us, yes," answered Evie. "Now if you'll excuse me, Posy, I'm in a terrible hurry."

"Of course, and," Posy added, "these days I work in Mason's Gallery, three doors down from The Swan. Any time you fancy a spot of lunch, you know I'd love to see you. And your daughter, whose name is...?"

"Clemmie, she's called Clemmie."

"Short for Clementine, I presume, like Winston Churchill's wife."

"Yes."

"What a lovely name. Well, goodbye, Evie, and welcome back."

"Thank you. Bye."

Evie headed towards the newsagents in search of her daughter, and Posy walked the last few yards down the road to the gallery. Feeling more than a little hurt at Evie's obvious discomfort in her presence, and wondering what on earth she had done to garner such a negative reaction, Posy took the keys to the gallery out of her bag.

As she unlocked the front door, entered and fumbled for the light switch, she thought about what Evie had implied: that Brian, her partner of all those years ago, was no longer in her life. Inquisitive to know more, Posy thought it unlikely she ever would. From Evie's reaction, it was more likely that she would probably cross the street to avoid her the next time they met.

However, the one thing she had learnt in her almost seventy years on this earth was that human beings were a queer lot and constantly surprised her. *Evie has her reasons*, Posy mused as she went to the office at the back of the gallery and switched on the kettle for her ritual second cup of coffee.

She only wished she knew what they were.

Chapter 2

"Please, Jake, go and find your shoes, now!"

"But Mummy, I haven't finished my Coco Pops and..."

"I don't care! We're going to be late. Now shoo!"

As Jake left the kitchen, Amy Montague wiped four-year-old Sara's cereal-smeared mouth with a cloth and knelt down to put on her shoes. The fronts were scuffed and her daughter's feet barely fitted inside them. Sara's nose was running, her hair was still tangled from a night's sleep and the pair of trousers passed down from Jake ended midway up her shins.

"You look like a gypsy child," Amy sighed, grabbing a brush from the detritus on the sideboard and attempting to pull it through Sara's mass of blonde curls.

"Ouch, Mummy!" screamed Sara justifiably.

"Sorry, darling, but Miss Ewing will wonder what kind of mummy I am if I send you to school looking like this."

"I'm going to school?" Sara's face fell. "But I hate it, Mummy."

"Oh sweetheart, your teacher says you're settling in really well, and Josie will pick you up and take you to her house with Jake afterwards. Mummy will pick you both up from there when she's finished work," Amy added.

"But I don't like school and I don't like Josie. I want to stay with you, Mummy." The little girl's face crumpled and she began to cry.

"Sara, darling, you *do* like school and you like Josie. And Mummy will get some chocolate cake for tea, okay?"

"Okay." Sara nodded, somewhat pacified.

"Jake?! We're leaving now!" Amy shouted, pulling Sara into the hall. She put on her daughter's anorak and her own coat, then fumbled for the keys in her bag.

Jake came crashing down the stairs, his shoes in his hands.

"Put them on, Jake."

"But I want you to do it, Mummy. Is Daddy still asleep?"

"Yes." Amy knelt and tugged Jake's shoes onto his feet. "Right, let's go."

"But I want to say bye-bye to him," whined Jake as Amy took Sara's hand and opened the door.

"Well, you can't."

"Why not?"

"He's tired. Now let's get a move on!"

Having dropped the children at their school, Amy drove to the garage to leave her car for the repairs it needed, having recently failed its inspection. Walking briskly home, she realized she only had an hour before she left for work; an hour in which to tidy the kitchen, do the washing and make a shopping list. How she was going to manage without a car, she really didn't know, but a difficult life was going to be rendered almost impossible. Besides that, she had no idea how they would pay for the repairs, but they'd have to find the money somehow; it was as simple as that.

Amy turned into the front path of the miserable little house which had become their home six weeks ago. Situated on a road on the outskirts of the town and with only the marshes between it and the sea, it was essentially an overgrown beach hut and utterly charming when the sun shone. It was only really intended for summer use and Amy knew its thin clapboard walls and huge windows would provide scant protection against the elements in the coming winter. There was no proper heating except a temperamental woodburner in the sitting room that, when she'd tried it last night, had smoked more than it gave out warmth. The house had only two dank bedrooms upstairs that were so cramped that most of their possessions stood in boxes in the shed in the back garden.

Even though she knew Sam's pride had taken a terrible knock when lack of money had forced them out of their last house, and she didn't want to upset him any further by telling him how much she loathed their current home, Amy was finding it hard to maintain her usual positive attitude. She knew her husband tried so hard for all of them, but he seemed to have endless bad luck, with one business venture after another folding. How could she tell him that Sara needed some new shoes, how small Jake's winter coat was for him, or just how exhausted she was trying to run the house and provide food on the meager amount she received from her job as a receptionist at a local hotel?

Sam was in the kitchen wearing his boxer shorts and yawning as he switched on the kettle.

"Hello, sweetheart. Sorry I was so late last night. Ken and I had a lot of things to thrash out."

"Did the meeting go well?" Amy looked up at him nervously, noticing his blue eyes were bloodshot and inhaling the smell of stale alcohol from his breath. She was glad she'd been asleep when he'd come in.

"Extremely." Sam looked down at her. "I think I'm going to be able to restore the fortunes of the house of Montague very soon indeed."

Usually, such comments were enough to lift Amy's spirits, but this morning, Sam's words had a hollow ring to them.

"Doing what, exactly?"

He pulled away and held her in front of him by the tops of her arms. "My darling, you are looking at the official managing director of Montague Property Development Limited."

"Really?"

"Yes. Want a cup of tea?"

"No, thanks. So how much will you get paid a week?" Amy asked hopefully.

"Oh, not very much, I don't think, but of course, all my expenses will be covered."

"But surely, if you're the managing director, you have to pay yourself a salary?"

Sam dropped a tea bag into a mug. "Amy, this is all about speculating to accumulate. I can't really ask for a wage until I've proved myself and got a project under way. Once that happens, I'll get fifty percent of the profits. And that will add up to a heap of cash."

Amy's heart sank. "But Sam, we need money *now*, not in a few months' time. I understand that this might make you rich in the future, but surely you realize that we just can't survive on what I bring home from the hotel?"

Sam poured boiling water into his mug and slammed the kettle onto the work surface with unnecessary force. "So what do you suggest I do? Go and work in a dead-end job in a shop or a factory to bring in an extra few pounds?"

This was exactly what Amy wished he would do. She took a deep breath. "Why do you have to view regular work so negatively, Sam? You've had a good education, lots of experience doing different things and I'm sure there's no reason why you couldn't get a perfectly well-paid office job—"

"Which will get this family nowhere in the long term, Amy. I have to look to the future, to finding a way to provide the lifestyle we want and deserve. We both know I won't do that working for someone else in a crappy office job."

"Sam, at present, all I care about is keeping the wolf from the door on a day-to-day basis. Personally, I think part of the problem is that we've looked to the future too often and speculated." Amy swiped her blonde hair away from her face in agitation. "It's not like it was when we first met. We have to realize we have responsibilities, children to house and support, and we just can't do that on thin air."

He stared at her as he sipped his tea. "So, what you're trying to tell me is that you've lost your faith in my ability to pull off the big one?"

"No..." Amy saw the look in his eyes and knew it spelt danger. "Of course I believe in you and your business ability, but wouldn't it be possible to do this project in your spare time and combine it with something that would give us some extra cash now?"

"Christ, Amy! You obviously have no idea how business works. If I'm going to get this property company off the ground, it's going to take up every minute of every day." Sam's face was now red with anger. He grabbed her arm tightly as she walked across the kitchen to the sink. "I am going to do this, darling, because unless I do, you and I and the kids are going to be stuck in this crappy little house for the rest of our lives. So rather than criticizing me for doing my best to dig us out of this hole, I'd appreciate it if you would support me as I try to turn things around!"

"I..." she said as the grip tightened on her arm, "Okay."

"Good." Sam let go of her, then picked up his mug of tea and walked to the kitchen door. "I'm going to get dressed, then I'm going out."

Amy sat down, nursing her sore arm and staying very still until she heard Sam climb the stairs, then, five minutes later, retrace his footsteps back down them. The whole house shook as the front door was slammed behind him.

Swallowing with relief and trying to hold back the tears that were threatening to erupt, Amy stood up and numbly made her way upstairs to the box room Sam and she shared, so they could fit two beds for the kids in the bigger bedroom.

Amy sat on the unmade bed and stared at the damp wall in front of her.

What had happened to the two of them in the past few years? Where had it all gone wrong?

She'd met Sam in the bar of The Swan in Southwold—she in her final year of art college and up from London for the wedding of a friend, he popping in for a quick drink on a Saturday night. His friend had been late and she'd needed a breather from the claustrophobic atmosphere of the nuptials. They had begun to chat, one thing had led to another, and he'd called her in London, asking her up for a weekend at his family home just outside Southwold.

Amy remembered seeing Admiral House for the first time. It was so perfectly formed, almost doll's-house-like in its prettiness, that she'd itched to paint it. Sam's mother, Posy, had been so welcoming, her stay so relaxed that she had returned to her small flat in London and dreamed of going back to the space and peace of Suffolk.

Sam had just started his computer business and had wined and dined her with energy and imagination. She'd found his enthusiasm for life captivating, his family delightful, and his bed warm and inviting.

When he'd asked her to marry him and move to Suffolk just after she'd finished her last term at art college, it had not been a hard decision to make. They'd rented a tiny terraced house in one of the quaint Southwold streets and settled down to married life. Amy began to take her easel along the sea front, painting the vistas and selling them to a local gallery for the tourists. But that work was only seasonal and when Sam's computer business had gone under, she'd had to take the first job she'd been offered as a receptionist at The Feathers, a comfortable if old-fashioned hotel in the center of town.

The past ten years had been a series of ups and downs, according to where Sam was with his businesses. When things were good, Sam would shower her with flowers and presents and take her out for dinner, and Amy would remember the fun-loving person she'd married. When things were bad, life was very different...

And, if Amy was honest with herself, things had been bad for quite a long time. When his film business had folded, Sam had sunk into a morass of despair and had hardly left the house.

She had tried so hard not to make it any worse for him. Even though he was at home during the day, she rarely asked him to pick up the children from school or do the shopping whilst she worked. She knew Sam's pride depended on him still thinking of himself as a businessman and she'd learnt from experience to leave him alone when he was in a downer.

"But what about me?"

The words came out of Amy's mouth before she could stop them. She was almost thirty and what had she achieved in her life so far? She had a husband who seemed to be permanently unemployed, they were broke and reduced to living in a rented hovel. Yes, she had two lovely children and a job, but it was hardly the glittering career as an artist that she'd dreamt of before she'd married Sam.

And as for his temper...she knew the aggression he showed her, especially after he'd had a few drinks, was getting worse. She only wished she had someone to talk to about it, but who would she tell?

Feeling horribly self-indulgent, Amy quickly put on her dark blue work suit and added some makeup to put some color into her pale cheeks. She was just tired, that was all, and Sam did try to do his best. She left the house, deciding to buy something special for supper. It only made things worse when they fell out on top of all their other problems and, despite her gut feeling that this new venture was doomed to failure like the rest, Amy knew that she had no choice but to trust him.

As it was Friday, and the start of the Southwold Literary Festival, the Feathers Hotel was chaotic. The other receptionist had called in sick, which meant Amy had taken no lunch break and had been unable to do the weekend shopping. She'd dealt with one double booking, a blocked toilet and a watch that had gone missing, presumed stolen, until it had mysteriously turned up half an hour later. Glancing at her own watch, Amy saw she only had ten minutes before she had to collect the children from Josie, the babysitter, and there was still no sign of Karen, the evening receptionist.

Mr. Todd, the manager, was nowhere to be found and when she tried to call Sam on his mobile to see if he could pick the children up, there was no reply. She fumbled in her bag to find her address book, then realized she had left it on the kitchen table at home. On the verge of tears, Amy called directory enquiries, only to discover Josie's number was unlisted.

"Is it completely impossible to get any kind of assistance round here?!"

The reception desk shook under the force of the fist being slammed onto it.

"I've called down three times now for somebody to try and get hot water running through my bloody taps!"

"I'm very sorry, sir, I have called maintenance and they promised to see to it as soon as they could." Amy knew her voice was wobbly because of the lump at the back of her throat.

"I've been waiting two hours, for Chrissakes! It's just not good enough and unless you sort it out within the next ten minutes, I'm checking out."

"Yes, sir, I'll get on to maintenance again now."

Her hand shook as she reached for the receiver, tears now gathering in her eyes no matter how hard she swallowed. Before she could lift it, she saw Karen arrive through the front entrance.

"Sorry I'm late, Amy. There's an overturned lorry on the way into town." Karen made her way round the reception desk and took off her coat. "You okay?"

Amy could only shrug and wipe a hand across her eyes.

"Go on, I'll deal with this. Now, Mr. Girault"—Karen smiled brightly across the desk—"how can I help you?"

Amy fled into the back office, found an old tissue in her

handbag, and blew her nose hard. She shrugged herself into her jacket and, head down, walked fast towards the front entrance. As she stepped out gratefully into the cool night air, a large hand was placed on her shoulder.

"I say, I'm terribly sorry. I didn't mean to upset you. I realize it's not your fault."

Amy turned round and saw the man she'd just encountered in reception looking down at her from his considerable height. In her earlier angst, she hadn't really taken in his appearance, but now she registered the broad shoulders, wavy auburn hair, and the deep-set green eyes which were currently full of concern.

"No please, don't apologize. It wasn't you, really. Now if you'll excuse me, I'm horribly late to pick up my kids."

"Of course," he nodded, "and I really am sorry."

"Thanks." Amy turned and hurried up off the road.

Arriving home with two disgruntled, exhausted children plus supermarket carrier bags, the sight of her mother-in-law standing by her front gate was almost enough to reduce Amy to tears again.

"Hello, Posy." She forced a smile as she unlocked the front door.

"Darling girl, you look beat. Here, let me help you." Posy tucked the tin she was holding under one arm and took some of the shopping bags with her free hand. Inside, she settled Sara and Jake at the kitchen table and told Amy to put on the kettle whilst she made toast and Marmite and warmed some tinned pasta for the children's tea.

"My goodness, it's freezing in here." Posy shivered.

"There's no heating, I'm afraid," Amy replied. "It's only meant to be used as a summer house."

Posy glanced round at the tiny, dreary kitchen, the one light bulb that hung uncovered from the center of the room showing up every smear of grime on the walls.

"Not exactly a palace, is it?"

"No," replied Amy, "but hopefully it'll only be for a little while, until we get back on our feet financially."

"You know, I have told Sam you can all come and stay with me at Admiral House for as long as you like. It seems ridiculous that I have it to myself whilst you are all cooped up here."

"You know Sam's pride will never let him do that."

"Well, my dear," said Posy, opening the tin and lifting out a perfect chocolate cake, "sometimes pride comes before a fall, and I almost can't bear to think of you living here." She cut the cake into slices. "There, Granny's best cake, for after you've finished your toast and pasta. Would you like some, Amy?"

"No thanks." Amy reckoned she might choke on it.

Posy eyed her daughter-in-law. Although she was still beautiful, Amy's skirt was hanging off her hips and her blue eyes were huge in her pale face. Her usually immaculate long blonde hair was fighting to escape from its ponytail and looked as if it needed a damned good wash.

"You're far too thin, dear girl. Are you eating enough?"

"Yes, Posy, I'm fine really." Amy wiped Sara's face. "If you'll excuse me, I need to bathe the children and put them to bed."

"Of course. Can I help?"

Amy thought of Posy's reaction to the squalid little downstairs bathroom, then shrugged. What did it matter? "If you'd like to."

Posy made no comment as the two of them bathed the children. After they were dry and in their nightclothes, she said she'd light the woodburner in the sitting room whilst Amy read them a story before bed.

With the children finally asleep, Amy came downstairs and sank down gratefully into a dog-eared armchair. Posy arrived from the kitchen, a glass of wine in each hand.

"Hope you don't mind that I opened the bottle, but you look as though you need it."

The wine had been a treat for her and Sam later, but Amy accepted the glass gratefully.

"Where is Sam, by the way?" Posy asked as she settled herself onto the old leather sofa.

Amy shrugged. "I don't know, but there's something brewing work-wise, so maybe he's at a meeting."

"At half past seven on a Friday night?" Posy raised an eyebrow. "I somehow doubt it."

"Anyway, I'm sure he'll be home soon."

"Does he help you much with the children?"

"Not during the week, but he's very good at weekends," said

Amy loyally.

"Amy, my dear, Sam is my son, and although I love him dearly, I also know him very well. Give him an inch and he'll take a mile."

"He does his best, really, Posy."

"Like tonight, you mean? If Sam isn't working at the moment, then surely he must help you with the domestic situation? He should have at least been around to pick up the children at five o'clock for you, or do the shopping. You look completely done in."

"I just need a good night's sleep, that's all. I'm fine, really." The last thing Amy felt capable of tolerating was a lecture on the failings of her errant husband, even if they were true. "So how are things with you?"

"I have received marvellous news!" Posy clapped her hands together. "Nick telephoned me a few days ago to say he's coming home!"

"After all this time," Amy mused, smiling. "You must be thrilled."

"I am indeed. And ironically, I saw Evie Newman in town that same day. She's back in Southwold too, with her little girl in tow."

"Isn't Evie the one who used to help run Nick's antiques shop?"

"Yes." Posy sipped her wine. "I can't remember; did you ever meet her?"

"Yes, but by the time Sam and I got married and I was living here permanently, she'd left Southwold."

"It is rather a coincidence that Nick and Evie are returning within a few weeks of each other," mused Posy.

"Yes. Do you know how long Nick is staying?"

"No, and to be frank, I'm too scared to ask. I'll take as much of him as I can get, and it will be wonderful to have him and his expertise at Admiral House. I was thinking only this week that the time has come to value its contents."

"Really? Are you thinking of selling them?"

"Perhaps. Certainly if I decide to sell the house too."

"Oh Posy, surely you're not serious?!" Amy was horrified. "That house has been in your family for generations. I...it's beautiful! You can't."

"I know, my dear, but those generations had the capital—and the staff, I might add—to maintain it," Posy sighed. "Anyway, enough about me. How's work?"

"Hectic, as it always is the week of the literary festival. The hotel is fully booked."

"Rather nice to have lots of interesting authors on one's doorstep. I'm going to hear Sebastian Girault speak about his book tomorrow. He sounds such an interesting man."

"Sebastian Girault?" Amy repeated numbly.

"Yes. His novel was shortlisted for the Booker Prize this year, but it sold heaps more than the actual winner. You must have heard of him, Amy."

These days, she felt reading the headlines on the front of the daily tabloid without disturbances was an achievement, let alone a book from cover to cover. "No, I mean, I hadn't heard of him until today. I met him this afternoon, actually. He's staying at the hotel."

"Did you indeed? Lucky old you. Rather attractive, isn't he? So tall and rugged," smiled Posy.

"I really didn't notice, to be honest. At the time he was screaming to me about the lack of hot water in his room."

"Oh dear, what a shame. I'd rather hoped he'd be as nice as he sounds on the radio. Mind you, he has had a difficult life. His wife died in childbirth a few years ago, taking the baby with her. Still, that's no reason to behave rudely to others. That's the trouble with all these celebrities, isn't it? They have the arrogance of fame and it changes them." Posy looked at Amy, then clapped her hands together. "I tell you what, why don't you come with me tomorrow? We could go for a spot of lunch at The Swan and on to the reading. It would do you good to get out."

"I can't, Posy. I've no one to look after the children."

"Surely Sam can manage for a few hours? It is Saturday, after all."

"I..." Before Amy could answer, she heard the front door open and Sam came in.

"Darling." Posy stood up and kissed her son on both cheeks. "Where've you been?"

"Out at a meeting."

"In the pub, was it?" asked Posy, smelling his breath.

"Don't start, Mum, please."

"I won't, but your poor wife has had the most appalling day and

I was just saying how much she needs a break. So I'm taking her out for lunch tomorrow and then we're going on to an event at the literary festival. You'll be fine with the children for the afternoon, won't you, Sam? I'll be off now, leave you two to eat your supper in peace. So I'll be here to pick you up tomorrow at twelve-thirty, Amy. Bye, both."

"Bye, Posy," said Amy, her face red from embarrassment.

The front door closed and Amy eyed her husband with trepidation, trying to gauge his mood. "I'm so sorry, Sam. You know when your mother has a bee in her bonnet, she won't let it rest. I'll phone her tomorrow morning and say I can't make it."

"No, Mum's right, you do need a break. I'll be fine with the kids tomorrow afternoon. And listen, I'm sorry I lost my rag this morning."

"And I'm sorry I doubted you," Amy said, relief flooding through her at his apology.

"That's okay. I can understand why, but you just have to trust me."

"I do, Sam, really."

"Good. Now, what's for supper and where's the rest of that wine?"

Chapter 3

"I don't want to go, Mummy, please!"

"Clemmie, Orwell Park is a wonderful school and it's a fantastic opportunity for you."

"But I don't care about that. I want to stay here with you, not go away. Please, Mummy, don't make me."

"Come here." Evie Newman took her daughter into her arms and gave her a hug. "Do you think I want you to go away?"

"Dunno," Clemmie sniffed.

"Well, of course I don't, but I have to think of your future. You're very clever and Mummy has to try and give you the best opportunities she can."

"But I liked my old school in Leicester. Why can't we go back there?"

"Because we live here now, darling. And even if we *were* still living in Leicester, I'd still be wanting you to go to Orwell Park."

"I just want us to go home. I want things back to the way they used to be," sobbed Clemmie into Evie's shoulder. "You need me to look after you, Mummy, you know you do."

"No I don't, Clemmie," Evie said fiercely. "I'm perfectly capable of looking after myself."

"But if I go away to school, you'll be all alone in this big house. What if..."

"Clemmie, darling, I promise you I'm going to be absolutely fine." Evie stroked her daughter's hair. "I feel very selfish that I've had you all to myself in the past few years. It's time you had a life of your own and stopped worrying about me."

"I'll never do that, Mummy. I like it the way it's been, just you and me."

"I know, and so do I, but remember, you'll be home every weekend and the holidays are far longer than at your old school. We'll have plenty of time to be together, I promise."

Clemmie pulled away roughly from Evie's embrace and stood up. "You just want to get rid of me. Well, I'm not going and you can't make me!" She ran from the room and slammed the door behind her.

"Bugger, bugger, bugger!" Evie thumped the sofa hard. Sending her beloved daughter away was tearing her apart, and there was no doubt that secretly she was as dependent on her daughter as Clemmie was on her mother. With just the two of them living together in their small terraced house in Leicester, and everything that had happened whilst they were there, Clemmie had had to grow up far too quickly and shoulder responsibilities that an adult would have found stressful.

Evie knew that, however much the initial parting hurt, it was imperative that Clemmie went away to school. It was time she began to live and laugh like a normal nine-year-old and develop her own world, outside of her mother's.

The doorbell rang downstairs. Feeling utterly drained, Evie heaved herself up from the floor, walked heavily down the three sets of stairs, and finally opened the front door.

"Hi, Evie. I know I'm early, but town is heaving."

Marie Simmonds, Evie's oldest friend, stood on the doorstep, smiling at her. They'd been nicknamed "Little and Large" at school: Evie so petite and thin, and Marie always a head taller than the rest of her classmates and decidedly plump. Just now, Evie thought, she'd swap places with her in a heartbeat.

"Come in. I'm afraid everything is still a dreadful mess." Evie led Marie through the hall and into the kitchen.

"God, Evie, you are lucky having this house. Give it to me and I'll sell it for you tomorrow, even if it is decorated circa nineteen fifty." Marie was the manager of a local estate agent, having worked her way up from her original position as receptionist.

"It's not been touched since my grandparents decorated it," Evie shrugged. "And no thanks. I want to live here, for the present, anyway."

"Well, the way things are going round here, with all the London lot desperate to secure a place and pay whatever it costs for the cachet of being in Southwold, I think you could count yourself as having millionairess status."

"That's nice to know, but if I don't intend to sell it, then there's not much point in thinking about it, is there? Coffee?"

"Yes please. Why don't I have a nice relative who's going to pop their clogs and leave their pile in Southwold to me?" lamented Marie, running a hand through her mane of healthy black curls.

"Because you have a lovely mother and father still alive," Evie said pragmatically, "which is something I haven't had since I was ten."

"Sorry, I didn't mean to sound callous or mercenary. I just occasionally feel rather bitter watching all this money change hands in the office whilst me and my family, who have lived in the town for generations, are forced to move outside it because we can't afford the prices."

"Slice of toast?" asked Evie, putting a coffee cup on the table in front of Marie.

"No, thanks. I'm on another diet. Honestly, Evie, I could really get to hate you: a huge house, plus a figure that hasn't changed since you were a schoolgirl, even after having a baby and eating whatever you want." Marie watched enviously as Evie plastered her toast with butter and jam.

"You wouldn't want my body, Marie, I promise," said Evie, sitting down at the table. "And I could envy you your happy marriage and the fact your kids still have both their parents together," she shrugged.

"How is Clemmie?"

"Miserable, difficult and over-emotional. She hates Southwold and wants to go back to live in Leicester. She's upstairs in a huff about going away to school. Honestly, I really don't know what I'm going to do. At the moment, she's refusing to go. I feel like a complete bitch. I just can't bear her to think that I don't want her at home with me, but for all sorts of reasons, it's important she goes."

"Is it?" questioned Marie. "She's very young, Evie. Couldn't she go to the local school for a few more years and then go on to boarding school a little later? Southwold Primary is rather good, actually. It's changed a lot since we were there. Obviously, it has none of the trappings of a posh private prep school, but my two are very happy there."

"No. For her sake, I want her to go now."

"I must admit, I wouldn't fancy sending mine away at nine," shrugged Marie. "I'd miss them like mad. And if she does go, you're going to feel the breeze. You'll be here all by yourself."

"Oh, I've got lots to occupy me. I'll be fine."

Marie sipped her coffee. "So how are you feeling about being back here?"

"Good," Evie answered shortly.

"Ever see Brian?"

"God, no. You know he left when Clemmie was a tiny baby and I haven't heard from him since."

"So he doesn't keep in touch with his daughter?"

"No."

"That's very sad—for Clemmie, I mean."

"I can assure you that we're both far better off without him. I look back and wonder what on earth I saw in him."

"He always did patronize you," agreed Marie.

"He treated me like a child. Nothing I ever did came up to scratch. I used to admire him so much, thought he was so much cleverer than I was, had seen so much more of life than me and initially I liked being looked after." Evie stood up and tipped the dregs of her coffee into the sink. "Now I can see that Brian was just a replacement for the father I lost when I was so young."

"Life hasn't been easy for you, has it?"

"Maybe not, but one could say that I've hardly helped myself to an easy ride. I've made some pretty awful mistakes."

"Everyone does when they're young, Evie. It's part of growing up. Don't punish yourself too much. Now, isn't it time we were on our way?"

"Yes. I'll go upstairs and see if I can extract Clemmie from her bedroom. She's already said she doesn't want to stay at your house whilst we go to the reading."

"She'll be fine once she gets there," said Marie. "Tell her Uncle Geoff is cooking pizza for lunch and that Lucy can't wait to see her."

Evie nodded. "I'll do my best."

Having dropped a morose Clemmie at Marie's house in the neighboring village of Reydon and issued instructions for Marie's husband, Geoff, to jolly her along as much as possible, the two women headed back into Southwold.

"My goodness, town's busy," Evie commented as they passed the brewery and headed for St. Edmund's Theatre, where the reading was taking place.

"And this time next week, once the literary festival's over, and with most of the children back at school now, it'll be as dead as a dodo," commented Marie. "Look, there's a queue already. Come on, let's get a move on."

Evie and Marie found good seats in the center of the small auditorium.

"Have you read the book?" asked Evie.

"No, but I've seen the author photographs and Sebastian Girault is definitely worth coming to see, if not to listen to," giggled Marie.

"He really is a wonderful writer...oh God! No! Look, it's Posy."

"Posy?"

"Posy Montague, see? Coming down the steps, just there," Evie indicated with her hand.

"Ah, I see her. She's with her daughter-in-law, Amy. Did you two ever meet?" Marie whispered.

"Briefly, a long time ago. She's very pretty, isn't she?"

"Yes. I know her, actually, because her son Jake is in the same class as my Josh. She's really sweet and long-suffering, as you can imagine, being married to Sam Montague and his knack for financial disaster." Marie rolled her eyes. "They're living in this dreadful house on Ferry Road, and there's Mummy Montague sitting in her enormous pile a few miles away."

"Ladies and gentlemen!" A hush fell over the audience as a woman appeared on stage to make the introductions. "On behalf of the Southwold Literary Festival, we're glad to see you all here today. I'm sure it's going to be an interesting afternoon as we listen to a reading of *The Shadow Fields* by the prize-winning author and journalist Sebastian Girault."

The audience applauded and Sebastian Girault strode onto the stage.

"Wow," Marie whispered as the author ran a hand through his thick auburn hair before beginning his opening speech, "he's gorgeous. No wonder the audience is mostly women. How old do you reckon he is? Early forties?"

"I have no idea," Evie said as the lights dimmed in the hall.

Amy closed her eyes as the lights dimmed in the hall. She felt completely exhausted. Sam had only arrived home at the eleventh hour to babysit the children, which had meant she and Posy had had to skip the planned lunch at The Swan and head straight for the theater. Not being able to find a parking space, they'd had to leave the car on the other side of town and run to make the start of the reading.

Amy wasn't interested in listening to Sebastian Girault talk about a book she'd probably never have time to read, but at least it was an hour in which she could sit down in the dark without being hassled by guests, children or her husband. Yet, as he began to speak, even Amy began to listen. There was something soothing about his mellow voice, a constancy that lulled and calmed her as he read excerpts from a tale of such intrinsic sadness that it made Amy feel guilty for ever complaining about her own existence.

The applause at the end of the reading was rapturous. Sebastian then took questions from the floor. Posy asked him how he'd managed to get the facts on the First World War so accurate, but Amy kept quiet, not wishing to have contact in any form with him again.

The audience was told that Mr. Girault would be in the foyer signing copies of his books.

"Come on, I want to get a signed copy just so I can gaze into those eyes," said Marie as she and Evie followed the audience out of the auditorium. "Then I can imagine him reading me his book in a rose-strewn bath, unlike my office-bound husband."

"But Geoff doesn't have the difficult artistic temperament to go with the brooding good looks and the talent," muttered Evie. "Brian was always surrounding himself with so-called intellectuals. I know his type and I don't find it attractive. I'll wait here while you get a copy."

Evie placed herself on a bench in the corner of the foyer and watched Marie join the queue to get her signed copy. When she saw Posy coming out with Amy, she put her head down and hoped she wouldn't be noticed. It didn't work. Posy made a beeline for her.

"Evie, how are you?" asked Posy, giving her a warm smile.

"Fine," she nodded, feeling her cheeks redden.

"Let me introduce you to Amy Montague, Sam's wife."

"Hello, Amy." Evie managed a polite smile.

"Hi. I think we met a long time ago," said Amy. "Are you back in Southwold for good?"

"For the foreseeable future, yes."

"Where are you living?" asked Posy.

"At my granny's house. She left it to me in her will."

"Oh yes, I did hear she died some months ago. I am sorry." Posy's steady gaze held Evie's. "What say you we all go to tea at The Swan? I'm dying to hear all your news, Evie, and you and Amy can get properly acquainted."

"Oh, I'm afraid I'm with someone and—"

"We'd love to come to tea," Marie interjected, appearing behind Posy. "I don't think we've ever met formally, Mrs. Montague, but I know where you live and I love your house. Hi, Amy," she added.

"This is Marie Simmonds. She's an old friend of mine and an estate agent," added Evie, embarrassed by Marie's easy attitude towards Posy, which made her own seem even more stilted.

"Hello, Marie. Right then, let's be off before all the comfy seats are taken," suggested Posy.

The four women headed for the exit.

"Excuse me? It is you, isn't it?"

Amy turned at the light touch on her shoulder and saw Sebastian Girault standing behind her.

"Pardon?"

"You're the receptionist from the hotel that I upset with my bullying tactics yesterday," he enlarged.

Amy knew that the eyes of the other three women were upon her. She felt herself blushing heavily. "Yes."

"Here." Sebastian stretched out his hand and offered Amy a copy of his book. "Probably the last thing you want, but it's by way of a peace offering. I really must apologize again."

"It's okay, honestly. I said last night it wasn't your fault."

"So you forgive me?"

Despite herself, Amy had to smile at his earnestness. "Of course. Thanks for the book. Goodbye."

"Goodbye."

Amy turned and followed the others out of the theater. Posy and Marie were agog to discover what that had all been about, so Amy had to explain.

"How nice to meet an old-fashioned gentleman," said Posy as they entered the cosy lounge of The Swan. Evie excused herself to head for the ladies', and the rest of the party settled themselves at a table.

"Hardly. He was an absolute pig to me yesterday," replied Amy.

"Well, at least you saved yourself the cost of his book for your trouble. I had to shell out fifteen ninety-nine for mine," sniffed Marie.

"Shall we order tea and scones all round?" asked Posy. "Gosh, this is such fun. All the girls together. I can't tell you how much I wish I'd had a daughter. Poor old Amy gets stuck with me rather a lot, don't you, my dear?"

"I don't mind, Posy, you know that," Amy replied.

Evie returned from the loo and squeezed herself next to Marie on the sofa, even though there was room next to Posy.

"We can't stay long, Marie. Clemmie might get worried." Evie clasped and unclasped her hands uncomfortably.

"She'll be fine," said Marie, enjoying herself far too much to take any notice of Evie's subtle hints.

"Your husband's so good with your children," sighed Amy, then, remembering Posy was there, added, "I mean, Sam's just so busy at the moment."

"So, Evie, are you enjoying being back here after all this time?" Posy asked pleasantly.

"Yes, thank you, Posy."

The tea and scones were set on the table, and to Evie's relief, Posy turned her attention to Marie and began questioning her on the state of the local property market.

"Why don't you let me come round and have a look at the house?" Marie said eagerly. "I could give you a valuation, so at least you know what it's worth."

"You're not really thinking of selling Admiral House, are you, Posy?" Evie caught the tail end of the conversation and couldn't stop herself from asking.

Posy saw a glint of the old Evie for the first time. "It has to be a possibility. As I have just said to Marie, the place needs lots of money spending on it and it's far too big for just me."

"But what about your sons?" Evie asked. "Surely one of them would want to—"

"Live there when I shuffle off my mortal coil? I doubt it. It would be an albatross around anyone's neck and therefore not a healthy gift to bequeath."

As Amy poured the tea, Posy watched Evie and wondered what on earth had happened to turn the lovely young woman full of vitality and intelligence into a pale and dreadfully thin version of her former self. Evie looked as though she had the weight of the world on her shoulders, and her brown eyes were filled with sadness.

"When does Clemmie leave for boarding school?" Marie asked Evie.

"Next week."

"Gosh, I went away to school and loved it," put in Posy. "Is she looking forward to it?"

"No, not at all," Evie replied.

"I can understand that, but once she gets there, I'm sure she will settle down quickly."

"I hope so."

Posy saw Evie was concentrating on her teacup, not able to meet her eye.

"Well, if you would like me to have a word, reassure her, as one who went away to school herself, I'd be more than happy to."

"Thank you, but I'm sure she'll be fine."

Posy searched around for something to throw into the now uncomfortable silence. "By the way, Evie, Nick is coming back from Australia shortly for a visit."

"Is he? That's nice. Now," she said, then stood up, "we really must go, Marie."

She took some money out of her purse, put it down on the table, and waited whilst a disgruntled Marie put on her coat.

"Bye, all," Marie said, managing to hand her card to Posy as Evie almost manhandled her to the door. "Give me a call."

"I will, once I've thought about it, my dear. Goodbye, Evie," Posy called to her disappearing back.

"We ought to be getting home too, Posy," said Amy. "It's past tea-time and I know Sam won't have fed the kids."

"Of course." Posy shook her head sadly. "You know, I wish I knew what I've done to upset Evie. We used to be great friends and she was such fun. All the stuffing seems to have been completely knocked out of her. She looks dreadful."

Amy shrugged. "Ten years is a long time. And she's obviously having some problems, what with her daughter going away to boarding school."

As Posy and Amy walked back to the car, Posy could not help remembering the expression on Evie's face when she'd mentioned Nick returning from Australia. There was something up, and Posy was damned if she wasn't going to try and find out what it was.

Chapter 4

"Answer the door, Clemmie, please! I'm just getting out of the shower," Evie called to her daughter from upstairs.

"Okay, okay, Mum, I'm going." Clemmie rolled off her bed, ran down the stairs, and unlocked the front door.

"Hello, Clemmie. I'm Posy Montague, an old friend of your mother's. Do you remember seeing me at the newsagents a few days ago?"

"Yes," nodded Clemmie. "Do you want Mum?"

"As a matter of fact, it's you I came to see. Ever been crabbing?"

"No," said Clemmie, looking apprehensive.

"Then it's high time you did. I've got bacon bait, lines and buckets in the car. If your mum says it's all right, we're going to row across the river to Walberswick. Do go and find her and ask if you can come."

"But...I don't—"

"Hello, Posy."

Evie had appeared in a bathrobe behind Clemmie, her face like thunder.

"Ah, Evie, good to see you again. Would you mind if I took Clemmie crabbing? It's such a beautiful day and I can have her back in time for tea."

"Well, it's very nice of you to offer, Posy, but we have a lot to do before Clemmie goes to school and—"

"Then I'm sure you'll get it done in double-quick time with a few hours to yourself. So, what do you say, Clemmie?"

Clemmie looked at Posy, realizing this lady was not going to take no for an answer. She shrugged. "Okay. If Mum doesn't mind."

"It's fine," Evie acquiesced, knowing she'd been outmaneuvered.

"Good-oh, bring a warm jacket in case it gets chilly later on."

Clemmie nodded and went upstairs to get ready.

"Dear Evie, forgive me for being an interfering old busybody, but I thought I could jolly Clemmie along about going away to school, tell her how much fun there is to be had."

"I'm at my wit's end, to be honest. She is point-blank refusing to go."

"Well, I'll do my best to cheer her up about the whole thing."

"Thank you, Posy." At last Evie managed a hint of a smile. "It's very kind of you."

"Not at all, a day's crabbing is always my pleasure. Right, young lady," she said as Clemmie came back down the stairs, "let's be off."

"Bye, Mum."

"Bye, darling. Have a fun time."

Evie waved them both off in the car and shut the door. Shivering in her bathrobe, she braced herself to climb the stairs and get dressed. She felt utterly exhausted—last night, the sun had been rising before she'd finally slept.

Slipping on her jeans and a sweater—she was always cold these days—Evie contemplated that, even though coming back here had to be the right thing for Clemmie, she had been a fool to hope she could return to Southwold and still somehow escape the past. If only she could tell someone, share the burden...Posy had been a surrogate mother to her ten years ago. The two of them had become close and Evie had adored her. It would be so comforting to sink onto her capable shoulder and let her troubles pour out.

Yet ironically, Evie thought as she lay down on the bed, feeling too weak to tackle the walk back downstairs, Posy was the last person she could confide in just now.

"Wow! A real wooden rowing boat," remarked Clemmie excitedly as they walked onto the narrow wooden pier and joined the small queue to cross the glistening water of the River Blyth, which separated Southwold from neighboring Walberswick.

"Surely you've been in a boat before?" said Posy as they watched the vessel coming back across the estuary, pulled by the oarsman.

"No. We weren't very near the water in Leicester, you know."

"I don't suppose you were," Posy agreed. "Never been there myself. Is it a decent sort of place?"

"I liked it," said Clemmie. "I didn't want to move because I had lots of friends there, but Mummy said we had to."

"Right, are you ready to go aboard?" asked Posy as the boat pulled in and the returning passengers climbed out.

"Yes."

The oarsman, whom Posy noticed was smartly dressed in a linen shirt, with a panama hat pulled jauntily over his brow to ward off the sun's glare, held out his hand to Clemmie and helped steady her as she stepped into the boat. Posy followed, throwing the two buckets full of bait in first.

"There we go, madam." The rich, modulated voice sounded familiar, and very different from Bob, the ex-fisherman who'd helmed the boat across the hundred yards of water for the past twenty years.

"Thank you." Posy sat down on one of the narrow benches as the rest of the passengers came aboard. "You can swim, Clemmie, can't you?"

"Yes, I had lessons at school."

"Good, because this boat has been known to sink under the weight of too many tourists," Posy teased as the oarsman behind them cast off and began to row across to Walberswick. "So Clemmie, I hear you're going away to school in a few days' time."

"Yes, but I don't want to go."

"I went away to school," Posy commented as she closed her eyes and lifted her head to catch the sun's rays. "I had a wonderful time there. I made lots of friends, had endless midnight feasts in the dorm and besides all that, got a very good education to boot."

Clemmie's lips pursed. "I'm sure you did, Posy, but I don't want to go, whatever you say."

"Look, we're here," said Posy briskly as the oarsman stood up and grabbed hold of a rope on the jetty to pull them in. He jumped out of the boat, then fastened it to the mooring. Being at the back of the boat, Posy and Clemmie were the last to step off. Posy watched as the oarsman swung Clemmie effortlessly onto dry land, his muscled forearms tanned and strong.

"Right," he said, turning to Posy and sweeping off his hat to mop his brow. "Goodness, it's warm today for the time of year." He smiled at her as she clambered over the narrow benches towards him. He reached out his hand to her, and she looked up into his eyes for the first time.

As she did so, Posy experienced the strangest sensation of time standing still. She could have stared at him for a second or a century; everything around her—the noise of the gulls above, the chattering of the other passengers as they walked away from the jetty—seemed to be somewhere far in the distance. She knew there was only one other moment in her life when she'd experienced a similar feeling, and that had been the first time she'd looked into the same pair of eyes over fifty years ago.

Posy came to and saw he was reaching out a hand to help her onto the jetty. She didn't know whether she might faint or in fact, vomit all over the rowing boat. Even though every instinct in her was telling her to flee from him and his proffered arm, she knew she was completely trapped, unless she threw herself into the water and swam back to the safety of Southwold, which was not a realistic option.

"I can manage, thank you," she said, ducking her head down and away from him, hands scrabbling for the jetty to haul herself up. But her legs betrayed her and as she wobbled precariously between boat and jetty, his arm moved to help her. At his touch, a bolt of electricity shot through her, making her heart slam against her chest as he put his other arm round her to virtually lift her onto the wooden platform.

"Are you quite all right, madam?" he asked her, as she stood above him, panting.

"Yes, yes, I'm fine," she managed as she watched his brown eyes study her and the dawn of recognition appear. She turned away quickly. "Come on, Clemmie," she said, forcing her jelly-filled legs to walk away.

"I...my God! Posy, is that you?" she heard him call from behind her. She did not look back.

"Are you okay, Posy?" Clemmie asked as Posy hurried her along the quayside.

"Yes, of course I am. It's just jolly hot today. Let's sit down on that bench and have a drink of water."

From her vantage point along the quay, Posy could see him

helping people onto his boat for the return journey. Only when it cast off and she saw him rowing back towards Southwold did her heart rate begin to slow down.

Maybe we could take a taxi back, she mused. *What on earth is he doing here...?*

Then she remembered it had been one of the things that had drawn them together originally, when they'd first met...

"So where do you hail from, Posy?"

"Suffolk originally, but I was brought up in Cornwall."

"Suffolk?" he'd said. "Well, that's something we have in common..."

"Are you feeling better, Posy?" Clemmie asked her, looking nervous.

"Much, thank you, the water has restored me. Now, let's go and find ourselves a good position and gather a bumper crop of crabs!"

She led Clemmie as far along the quay as possible, then they settled themselves on the edge of it. Posy showed Clemmie how to attach the bacon to the hook at the end of the line and throw it into the water.

"Now throw the line down, but don't wriggle it too much, because the crab has to jump on. Keep it close to the wall. There tend to be more rocks under which the crabs can hide."

Eventually, after a few false alarms, Clemmie triumphantly hauled out a small but lively crab. Posy extracted it from the line and threw it in the bucket.

"Well done, you! Now you've caught your first, lots more will follow, I promise."

Sure enough, Clemmie managed another six crabs before Posy declared herself hungry and thirsty.

"Right," Posy said, her heart giving a lurch as she saw the rowing boat approaching the jetty, "the perfect moment for a drink and a little light lunch at the local." They tipped the crabs back into the water.

Having found a table in the pub garden of The Anchor, Posy ordered herself a much-needed glass of white wine and Clemmie a Coke, plus two fresh prawn baguettes. As she stood at the bar, she remembered noticing how attractive he was when she'd first arrived at the boat. And when he'd taken his hat off to reveal what she'd always termed his "poet's head" of thick and now very white hair, swept back from his forehead and allowed to grow well below his ears...

Stop it, Posy! she told herself. *Remember what he did to you, how he broke your heart...*

Sadly, at least for now, she thought as she carried the drinks outside to the table where Clemmie waited, her rational brain wasn't listening, due to the extreme physical reaction of her body to his touch.

Do behave, Posy! You're almost seventy years old! Besides, he's probably married with a heap of children and grandchildren and...

"Thank you, Posy," Clemmie said as she put the glasses down on the picnic bench.

"The baguettes will follow, but I brought you a packet of crisps to stave off any hunger pangs. Cheers!" Posy chinked her glass against Clemmie's.

"Cheers," Clemmie repeated.

"So, dear girl, you're obviously not very keen on going to this new school of yours."

"No." Clemmie shook her head defiantly. "If Mummy makes me go, then I'll run away and come home. I've saved up my pocket money just in case and I know how to get on a train."

"I'm sure you do, and I understand just how you feel. I was horrified when it was suggested to me."

"Well, I don't understand why I have to go," Clemmie complained.

"Because your mother wants you to have the best start in life that you can. And sometimes grown-ups have to take decisions for their children that their children don't agree with or understand. Do you really think your mother wants to send you away?"

Clemmie sipped her Coke slowly through her straw as she thought about it. "Perhaps. I know I've been difficult since we moved to Southwold."

Posy chuckled. "My dear Clemmie, your behavior has nothing to do with her wanting you to go to away to school. When my boys left to go to board, I wept buckets for days afterwards. I missed them terribly."

"Did you?" Clemmie looked surprised.

"Oh yes," nodded Posy. "And I know your mother will feel the same, but like her, I did it because I knew it was the best for them, even if they didn't think so at the time."

"But, Posy, you don't understand, really you don't," replied Clemmie urgently. "Mummy needs me. And besides..." Her voice trailed off.

"Yes?"

"I'm scared!" Clemmie bit her lip. "What if I hate it? What if all the other girls are horrid?"

"Then you can leave," shrugged Posy. "It's pretty silly not doing something just because you think you might not like it. Besides, the school isn't far away. You'll be home for weekends, half term and holidays of course. You'll get the best of both worlds."

"What if Mummy forgets about me while I'm gone?"

"Oh my dear, your mother adores you. It's written all over her face. She's doing this for you, not for her."

Clemmie sighed. "Well, if you say it like that...and I suppose it might be fun to share a dorm."

"Well, how about you try it for a term or so? Take it in bite-sized chunks and see how you go? Then, if you really don't like it, I know your mother will allow you to leave."

"Will you make her promise, Posy?"

"We can ask her when I take you back home. Now." Posy looked up as the waitress placed two baguettes filled with prawns and crispy lettuce dressed in a rich piquant sauce, onto the trestle table. "Shall we tuck in?"

After another half hour of regaling Clemmie with jolly stories of school antics—some real, most imagined—a reluctant Posy and a far calmer Clemmie headed back for the boat. Thankfully, it was full and the oarsman had no time to say anything to her as he loaded the passengers on board. When they reached Southwold, Posy steeled herself as she waited to get off the boat. As he took her arm and helped her onto the jetty, he bent down towards her.

"It is you, Posy, isn't it?" he whispered.

"Yes." She gave a slight nod, knowing it would be childish to remain silent.

"Do you live locally? Because I'd really like to..."

By this time, she was safely on dry land. Without looking back at him, Posy walked away.

Chapter 5

Nick Montague viewed the early morning mist through the taxi window. Even though it was barely seven o'clock, cars were bumper to bumper on the M4 heading for London.

He shivered, experiencing the chill of an English autumn for the first time in ten years. In Perth, the spring was just beginning and temperatures were up in the early twenties.

As they drove into central London, Nick felt the tense momentum of the capital, so at odds with the laid-back atmosphere of Perth. It excited and unsettled him in equal measure and he knew it would take him time to get used to it. He was glad he'd decided to come here first, rather than heading straight to Southwold. He hadn't told his mother his exact date of arrival back in England, wanting some time to himself without her expecting his presence. He had decisions he wanted to make before he saw her.

In the past few months, he'd found himself homesick for England for the first time since he'd arrived in Perth. Maybe it was because originally, the challenge of establishing himself in a new country and forging a business had consumed him. He had eventually succeeded, and now owned a flourishing antiques emporium on the Left Bank and rented a beautiful apartment overlooking the water in Peppermint Grove.

Perhaps it had all been a little *too* easy, he acknowledged. Having hit Perth at a time when it was growing fast and gathering a clique of wealthy young entrepreneurs, and due to the lack of competition in the quality antiques business, he'd made far more money than he might have done in England.

He'd tried to enjoy his success but had known for some time he had to find himself a new challenge. He'd toyed with the idea of opening shops in Sydney and Melbourne, but the distances between the cities made it difficult, especially as far as shipping furniture was concerned. Besides, he'd now earned himself the money and experience to move into the big league, and if he didn't do it now, Nick knew he never would. Put simply, that meant coming home.

He'd decided to spend some time in London studying the antiques market, going to some top-notch sales and looking at a couple of shop sites in West London he'd researched on the internet. He also wanted to see how he felt about being back in England. If it didn't feel right here, maybe he'd head off to New York.

"Here we are, mate; Six, Gordon Place."

"Thanks," said Nick, paying the driver. The cab drove off, and Nick lugged his suitcase to the front door of the wisteria-covered town house. Even though they were only a couple of minutes' walk from the bustle of Kensington High Street, Nick was aware of the tranquility of this elegant residential neighbourhood. It was good to see houses that had stood for a couple of hundred years, rather than the endless new urban sprawl that covered Perth.

He walked up to the front door and rang the bell.

"Nick, g'day!" Paul Lyons-Harvey clasped him in a bear hug and slapped him on the back. "Look at you! You haven't changed one iota. Still have your own hair, unlike some of us." Paul stroked the bald patch on the crown of his head, then picked up Nick's case and took it inside.

"Nick!" He was hugged again, this time by Jane, Paul's wife, a tall, willowy blonde whose perfect symmetrical features had once graced the cover of *Vogue*.

"Doesn't he look in good shape?" said Paul, leading Nick down the narrow hall into the kitchen.

"He certainly does. Must be all that surfing that's helped keep the pounds off. I keep trying to put Paul on a diet, but it only lasts a day or so before he's back on the puds again," Jane remarked, kissing her diminutive and undeniably portly husband on his bald patch fondly.

"What I don't have in height, I've decided to make up for in girth," chuckled Paul.

"Too much of the good life, is it?" enquired Nick, sitting down at the kitchen table and swinging his legs underneath it.

"I must say things have gone rather well in the past few years. They had to, to keep the old lady in furs and jewels."

"You bet," agreed Jane, switching on the kettle. "I hardly married you for your stunning good looks, did I, darling? Coffee, Nick?"

"Yes, please," answered Nick, admiring Jane's long, jeans-clad legs and thinking yet again how his oldest friend and his wife might be physically mismatched, yet had one of the strongest marriages he knew. They were the perfect foil for each other: Paul the aristocratic art dealer, and Jane so elegant and down to earth, with a calmness that provided the balance to her more excitable husband. They adored each other.

"How tired are you?" Jane asked Nick, putting a coffee in front of him.

"Pretty," he admitted. "I might go and grab a few hours' nap, if neither of you mind."

"Of course not, but I'm afraid we do have a supper party here tonight. We arranged it before we knew you were coming to stay," Jane apologized. "We'd love you to join us, if you're up to it, but if not, don't worry."

"I'd come if I were you. Serious totty on the guest list," Paul chimed in. "A lovely girl from the good old days of Jane's time on the runway. I presume you still haven't got yourself hitched then?"

"No. The eternal bachelor, that's me," shrugged Nick.

"Well, with that tan, I give you twenty-four hours before women are throwing themselves against our front door," said Jane. "Anyway, I must be off. I've got a shoot at noon and I still haven't found a pair of shoes for the model to wear."

Having given up modeling some years ago, Jane was now a freelance fashion stylist, and, from what Paul had said in his emails, in great demand.

"You get some rest and see if you can garner the energy for tonight. We could do with another man." Jane massaged Nick's shoulders briefly before kissing her husband on the lips and disappearing from the kitchen.

"You are a lucky sod, Paul." Nick grinned. "Jane really is gorgeous. You both look as happy as you did ten years ago."

"Yes, I am lucky," Paul agreed, "but no marriage is without its problems, old boy. And we have our share like anyone else."

"Really? You wouldn't know it."

"No, but you may or may not have noticed the lack of the patter of tiny feet. We've been trying for almost six years, with no success."

"Paul, I didn't know. I'm sorry."

"Ah well, can't have everything, can one? I think it's worse for Janey, being a woman and all that. We've tried the lot, had all the tests and been through two rounds of IVF. And let me tell you, if there's an antidote to sex, that has to be it. There's something rather off-putting about having to perform to order, on a certain date, at a certain time."

"I can imagine."

"Anyway, we've decided not to go through it again. It was putting a huge strain on the marriage. Janey seems reasonably happy with her career and I'm certainly flying relatively high at present."

"Any finds?" Nick was as eager to change the subject as Paul obviously was.

"Only a Canaletto that I came across on my travels," he said lightly. "Got a good price for that, as you can imagine. It means I've sorted out our pension and anything else we earn is for fun. So how goes it with you?"

"Good. Well, financially, anyway, though I'm still searching for my Canaletto." Nick grinned.

"Well, I've sourced a couple of shop sites I think would be perfect for you if you do decide to open in London. As I'm sure you know, the antique market has been through a bit of a downer, what with the fetish for stainless steel and all things modernist. However, with a recession looming and everyone nervous about the markets, people are returning to buying what they hope will hold its value. Everyone knows so much more these days, what with the advent of all the television programs on the subject. People will pay a lot for top quality stuff, but it's harder to shift the rubbish."

"That's good news, because I'm going for the top end of the market, like I'd begun to in Southwold before I left," said Nick, stifling a yawn. "Sorry, it's been a long journey, Paul. I'm beat. I didn't sleep much on the plane."

"Of course. You go up and get some rest and I suppose I'd better show my face in Cork Street." He slapped Nick on the back again. "It's good to have you back and you know you can stay here as long as you want."

"Thanks." Nick stood up. "I really appreciate you having me here. And I love the house." He indicated his surroundings. "It's so...English. I've missed the architecture."

"It is indeed. You're on the top floor. Sleep tight."

Nick dragged his case up the three flights of stairs and opened the door to an attic bedroom. Like everything else in the house, the room was furnished eclectically, but cosily, and the big brass double bed with its lace counterpane looked enticing. Without removing his clothes, Nick fell onto it and went straight to sleep.

He woke when dusk was falling outside, kicking himself for not setting an alarm. He turned the light on and saw it was almost six in the evening, which meant the chances of him sleeping tonight were viturally nil. He opened a door, found it was a cupboard and tried another, which led into a small but well-fitted shower room. He pulled his wash-bag and some clean clothes out of his case, then went to shower and shave.

He wandered downstairs twenty minutes later and found Jane in the kitchen, chopping peppers and mushrooms in her robe.

"Hello, sleepyhead. Feeling better?"

"Yes, although I apologize if I want to stay up and chat until four in the morning tonight."

"That suits me, you know what a night-owl I am."

Nick took a slice of pepper from the chopping board and bit into it. "So you're enjoying your new job?"

"Yes, I am actually, far more than I thought I would. I did it initially as a favor for a photographer friend of mine. To be honest, I was just filling in time whilst...well, Paul and I waited for the babies to come along. Now that's no longer a possibility, it looks like I've got myself a career."

"Paul did mention earlier that you'd had a few problems," Nick responded carefully.

"Did he?" she sighed. "The odd thing is I'd never given having babies a second thought. In fact, I spent my late teens and twenties making sure I *didn't* have them. Rather ironic, really. I just never thought..." Jane stopped chopping and stared into space. "Well, I suppose one just assumes it's every woman's natural right. The trouble is, it's only when you realize that you can't have something that you begin to want it very badly."

"I'm so sorry, Jane."

"Thanks." Jane flicked a lock of blonde hair out of her eyes and began chopping again. "The worst thing is, I keep thinking how I punished my body when I was younger. I existed, like the rest of us models, on black coffee and cigarettes."

"The doctors haven't said it was you, have they?"

"No. We're one of a percentage of couples for whom there is no known cause. Anyway, the worst is over now. We've accepted we're going to be empty-nesters and I've just about got past the stage of sobbing every time I see a pram with a newborn in it."

"Oh, Janey." Nick moved towards her and gave her a hug.

"Anyway." Jane swiftly wiped her eyes. "What about you, Nick? There must have been someone special in the past ten years."

"Not really, no. There've been women, of course, but..." he shrugged, "none of them worked out. Once bitten and all that. I'm happy as I am."

The front door opened and Paul came hurrying along the hallway to the kitchen. "Good evening, darling!" He swung his wife into his arms and kissed her on the lips. "I have just acquired the most darling little cameo. We're investigating but we think it might be Lady Emma Hamilton, Lord Nelson's bit of totty on the side. Nick, my friend. How has your day been?"

"Sleepy," he replied. "Now, before I get in your way, I'm going to nip across to the pub. I have an absolute craving for my first proper pint of bitter on English soil and it must be satisfied."

"Be back here for eight, Nick," Jane called as he left the kitchen.

"Will do," he called back.

As he walked across the road to the pub, ordered a pint of foaming beer, and propped himself up on a barstool, he smiled in pleasure as he took his first sip. Savoring the beer and the unique atmosphere of the very British pub, he then thought that the last thing he wanted to do was to spend his first evening in England making polite conversation over supper with a group of total strangers.

Half an hour later, having treated himself to a second pint, Nick left the pub and strolled up Kensington Church Street, glancing though the windows of the many high-end antique shops along it. He paused and looked around him. Could he live here? Leave sunny, relaxed Perth with its amazing beaches for life in one of the most frenetic cities on earth?

"Not to mention the weather," he muttered as it began to drizzle. He gazed at a magnificent King George chest of drawers spotlighted in the window of the antique shop in front of him.

At this moment, Nick thought he could.

"Nick, we were getting worried. We thought you might have been abducted, you've been out of the big city so long. Come through and meet everyone." Jane, who looked elegant in leather trousers and a silk shirt, propelled him through to the sitting room. "A glass of champagne?"

"Why not?" Nick accepted the glass and nodded politely as Jane introduced him to the rest of the guests. Nick sat down on the sofa next to an attractive brunette, married, if he remembered rightly, to the aging Ronnie Wood-lookalike talking to Paul.

As she began to ask him vacuous questions about kangaroos and koalas, Nick sensed it was going to be a very long night. And the worst thing was, there really was no escape.

The doorbell rang and Jane left the room to answer it. She came back with a woman whose unusual beauty made even the world-weary Nick sit up and appreciate it. Tall, with skin like alabaster and a head of glorious Titian hair, he couldn't help but stare as Jane brought her over and introduced her. She looked as though she had stepped out of a fifteenth-century Florentine painting, wearing a long green velvet dress with a Chinese collar and tiny seed pearl buttons trailing all the way down to her ankles.

"Nick, meet Tammy Shaw, one of my oldest friends," she said as she handed Tammy a glass of champagne.

Tammy didn't answer. She was looking at him quizzically with her large, green eyes. Nick stood up and offered his hand. "Good to meet you, Tammy."

"Nick has arrived today from Australia," Jane said as Nick made space on the sofa and Tammy sat down next to him.

"So how do you know Jane and Paul?" he asked her.

"I met Janey years ago on my first shoot. She helped me through and we've been friends ever since."

"So you're a model too?"

"Was, yes," she nodded, taking a sip of her champagne and casting a glance around the room.

Nick felt the antipathy from her and understood. A woman who looked like her must have an endless queue of men chatting her up.

"To be honest"—Nick lowered his voice—"a supper party is not quite what I had in mind on my first night back, so forgive me if my conversation lacks a little substance."

"Personally I hate them." Finally, Tammy offered him a small smile. "Especially when you're invited as the token single woman. But Janey's my closest friend, so I make an exception for her. Do you live in London, Nick?"

"No, I'm staying here with Jane and Paul."

"Where did you meet them?"

"I met Paul at prep school when I was nine. I saved him from a bunch of bullies who were sticking his head down the toilet. We've been friends ever since." Nick's gaze moved to Paul with a smile. "He hasn't changed a jot since then, though I love to imagine that while he's been so successful, his toilet-flushing contemporaries have amounted to nothing."

"Boys can be so cruel, can't they? If I have kids, I'd never send them away. All the men I've met who went to boarding school seem to be messed up."

"Not all of us, I hope." Nick gave a grim smile. "And boarding schools have come out of the dark ages these days."

"Maybe," Tammy shrugged.

"So what do you do with yourself?" he asked politely.

"I sell vintage clothes on a stall in Portobello Road market."

Nick looked at her. "Really?" he said, his opinion of her making a seismic shift.

"Yup. I've hoarded them in a storage unit for years, because I love them. Now everyone else wants them too."

"How weird, because I'm an antiques dealer. Does that mean we both look to the past rather than to the future?"

"I've never thought about it like that," Tammy said as she scratched her nose, "but maybe you have a point. I've always felt like I was born in the wrong century. What kind of antiques do you sell?"

"Eclectic ones, i.e., no brown furniture. I find unusual things I think are beautiful and hope other people do too. I'm going to a sale tomorrow, as a matter of fact. There's a stunning Murano glass chandelier I've got my eye on."

"That makes me feel better, because I only buy clothes I love and want to wear too."

"And do they sell?"

"Yes they do, actually. But to be honest, I'm getting too old to be standing out in the rain on a freezing Sunday in January, not to mention that it doesn't do the clothes any good either. So I'm looking for premises."

"Right," Nick chuckled. "So am I."

"Okay guys, supper is served in the dining room." Jane stood at the door waving an oven glove.

Nick was relieved he was seated next to Tammy. Despite himself, she fascinated him.

"So how did you become a model?"

"By chance," she shrugged as she helped herself to the tapas laid out on the table. "I was doing my degree in philosophy at Kings in London," she continued between mouthfuls, "when I was spotted by a modeling agency in Topshop at Oxford Circus. I never expected it to last, to be honest, saw it as a bit of extra cash to subsidize my student grant. But it did and so here I am, a has-been."

"Hardly," Nick responded, glad to see that she seemed to have a healthy appetite. "Did you enjoy it?"

"Bits of it, yes. I mean, working with some of the top designers at the best ateliers in the world was a thrill, but it's such a cutthroat world I was glad to get out of it, get back to reality."

"You seem pretty real to me."

"Thanks. Not all models are brainless, cocaine-sniffing addicts, you know."

"Do you worry you're seen like that?" Nick asked her bluntly.

"Yup, I do," she admitted, a faint blush rising above the collar of her dress.

"Is what you're wearing one of yours?"

"Yes. I bought it when I was eighteen from an Oxfam shop. I've lived and died in it ever since."

"The problem is," mused Nick, 'that pursuing your passion doesn't always make you rich. I have a house full of lovely things back in Perth that I just couldn't bear to part with."

"I know exactly what you mean," Tammy agreed. "My wardrobe is bulging with clothes I just can't bring myself to sell. Nietzsche said that possessions are usually diminished by possession, and I try to remember that every time I pull something out to put on the stall," she smiled. "Anyway, tell me all about your business," she added as Jane served succulent pieces of fillet steak, new potatoes and fresh green beans.

Nick did so briefly, outlining his career from his days at the auction house in Southwold up to his possible move back to London.

"Do you have a life over in Australia?" Tammy asked him.

"If you're asking if I have a wife and family, then no, I don't. Do you?"

"I already told you I was single earlier," she reminded him. "It's just me in my tiny Chelsea mews house. I spent all my savings on it. Of course I should have bought a three-bedroom house..."

"But you fell in love with it," Nick chuckled.

"Exactly."

After dinner, Paul ushered the guests back into the sitting room where a fire was burning in the grate to ward off the chill. Jane appeared with a tray loaded with coffee and brandy. Nick saw it was past eleven o'clock and was amazed the time had gone so fast.

"So why haven't you ever married, Nick?" Tammy asked bluntly.

"Wow, that's quite a question," he said as Jane poured them both coffee. "I suppose I'm just crap at relationships."

"Or you've never met the right person," said Jane with a wink.

"Maybe. So now I can ask you the same question, Tammy."

"And I would give the same answer," she replied.

"There you go then," said Paul, who had followed behind Jane with the brandy. "Obviously made for each other."

Tammy looked at her watch. "So sorry to be rude, but it's late, and I have a lot of sewing waiting for me when I get back." She stood up. "It's been very nice to talk to you tonight, Nick, and I hope you find a suitable site for your business. If there are any going cheap, let me know, will you?" she said with a smile.

"Of course. Do you have a number I can reach you on?"

"Uh...yes, Janey has it. Bye, Paul," she said, kissing him on both cheeks. "Thanks for a great evening. I'll go and find your wife. Bye, Nick."

Tammy left the room and Paul sat down next to him.

"Did I say the wrong thing as usual?"

"You know you did, but don't worry about it."

"I will, actually, because it looked like the two of you really hit it off."

"She seemed great, and very bright too."

"Brains and beauty...the perfect combo. Tammy's very special. And independent," he added. "But you've always liked a challenge, haven't you?"

"Once upon a time, yes. But for now I'm sticking to business. It's far more straightforward."

An hour later, all the guests had left. Nick helped Paul and Jane clear up and they retired to bed while Nick sat alone in front of the fire nursing a second brandy. Despite himself, a picture of Tammy kept arriving in his head, and he admitted that he felt...excited. He tried to remember the last time a woman had had that effect on him. And realized that it hadn't been since *her*...

And look where that had left him; closing his successful business in the UK and running to the other side of the world to find sanctuary. Yet the fact that Tammy *had* stirred something inside him was good news, wasn't it? It meant that just maybe, he was finally cured.

And why shouldn't he see her again? The past ten years had been as lonely as hell. He'd been living a half-life and unless he wanted to be alone for the rest of his days, he had to be open to loving again. On the other hand, why would a woman such as her be interested in a man like him? Surely she could have anyone she chose?

Nick sighed deeply. He'd think it over tomorrow and then if he still felt the same, he'd give her a call.

Jane was in the kitchen when Nick arrived downstairs the following day.

"Good afternoon." She looked up at him from her laptop. "Sleep well?"

"Eventually," he shrugged. "I really don't do jet-lag well."

"How about an omelette? I was just about to make myself something for lunch anyway."

"I'll make it. Cheese and ham suit you?"

"Totally. Thanks, Nick. The coffee's over there. Help yourself. I just need to finish this mood board for the shoot and send it off to the magazine."

Nick puttered around the kitchen drinking strong coffee and collecting ingredients for the omelette. He looked out onto the small garden at the back of the house and saw the gorgeous colors of the leaves of the copper beech tree gleaming in the bright September sun. And was immediately reminded of Tammy's incredible hair.

"Done," said Jane, shutting her laptop.

"So's the omelette," Nick replied, using a spatula to place it on two plates.

"What a treat," Jane said as Nick put a bowl of green salad in the center of the table. "Maybe you could teach my husband to crack an egg at some point."

"He's always had you there to cook for him, whereas I've been on my own."

"True. And this is delicious. So you enjoyed last night?"

"Yes, though to be honest, I didn't get to speak to the other guests."

"No, so I noticed." Jane eyed him as she forked some salad from the bowl. "Tammy is usually standoffish with men, for obvious reasons. She really warmed to you."

"Thanks. She is remarkably beautiful. She must get hit on all the time."

"She certainly did as a young model. As you know, it's an unsavory world, with a lot of predatory men circling. She became an ice queen to protect herself, but underneath, she's an utter sweetie and very vulnerable."

"Did she, um, have many boyfriends?"

"A few, yes. There was a childhood boyfriend hanging around

for most of her career, but he went west three years ago or so. As far as I know, she hasn't seen anyone seriously since."

"Right."

"So will you give her a call?"

"I...maybe. If you'll pass on her number."

"I will, on the understanding that you don't break her heart."

"Why would I do that?" Nick frowned.

"You told me only last night you were a confirmed bachelor. I don't want Tammy to be just another notch on your bedpost, Nick. Tammy's worth far more than that. She wears her heart on her sleeve and is surprisingly naïve when it comes to men."

"I hear you, Jane, and I promise, I'm not up for a fling. I have far too much to do just now. And actually, I would like to see her again. There was definitely something there."

"I know. The whole table noticed it." Jane smiled. "I have to run to a meeting but I'll text you her number."

"Thanks."

After Nick had cleared up lunch, he heard a ping on his mobile and pulled it from his jeans pocket.

Hi, here's Tammy's no. C u tonite. J x

Nick added it to his address book, then wandered upstairs to his bedroom. He hadn't told Jane of course, but last night, when he'd eventually fallen asleep, he'd dreamt of Tammy. Pacing the room, he thought he should give it a couple of days before he called her or he might look too "predatory," as Jane had put it.

Could he wait two days...?

No. He wanted to see her now, to look into those incredible green eyes, touch that amazing hair...he missed her.

Christ, Nick, what has she done to you?

Whatever it was, a few minutes later, Nick pulled out his mobile and dialed the number Jane had given him.

Chapter 6

The bell which indicated a customer had entered the gallery tinkled in the back office. Posy left the computer and walked through to the showroom.

"May I help you?" she said automatically as she did so, to make sure the person wouldn't think the shop was empty and make off with a painting.

"Yes, you may. Hello, Posy."

She stopped short, her heart rate speeding up. She saw him standing in the center of the showroom, staring at her.

"I..." Posy put a hand to her throat to cover the blush that must surely be spreading up to her face. "How did you find me?"

"Well now," he said, taking a couple of steps towards her, "I wouldn't say that I had to employ a private detective. The first person I asked knew exactly where you worked. You're rather well known in Southwold, as I'm sure you realize."

"Hardly," Posy defended herself.

"Well, no matter, here you are."

"Yes. So what do you want?"

"I just...well, I suppose I just wanted to say hello properly after our rather strange meeting on the boat."

"I see." She averted her eyes from him, wanting to look anywhere else. He'd been incredibly good-looking in his early twenties, but now, just a couple of years older than her, he was without doubt the most handsome male she'd laid eyes on in decades.

And she didn't want her brain to be hijacked by another reaction of her body.

"How long has it been, Posy? Not far shy of fifty years?"

"Around that, I suppose, yes."

"Yes," he replied, and they both stood in silence for a while. "You still look exactly the same, you know."

"Of course I don't, Freddie! I'm an old woman."

"And I'm an old man," he said with a shrug.

There was another uncomfortable silence which Posy refused to end.

"Look, I was wondering whether you would let me take you out for lunch one day? I'd like to explain."

"Explain what?"

"Why I...well, why I left you."

"Really, there's no need. It's ancient history," Posy said firmly.

"And I'm sure you'd forgotten all about me until I popped up out of the blue on the boat, but at least let me take you out to lunch so we can catch up on all the intervening years. Please say yes, Posy. I've only been back in Suffolk a couple of months—I retired last year, you see—and I don't know many people here yet."

"All right, yes," Posy agreed before she could stop herself. Mostly because she wanted him out of here as soon as possible—she knew she hardly looked her best, having raced straight to the gallery from sweeping up leaves in the garden.

"Thank you. Any preference for where?"

"You choose."

"The Swan, then. It's all I know that's good. Can you make Thursday? It's my day off from the boat."

"Yes, I can."

"Does one o'clock suit?"

"Yes, that would be perfect."

"Right-oh. I'll see you on Thursday at one. Goodbye, Posy."

Freddie left, and Posy retreated back into the office to sit down and recover her composure.

"What are you doing, you stupid old woman?! He broke your heart last time, remember?"

Yet, despite the seriousness of Freddie Lennox walking like a ghost back into her life, Posy chuckled.

"Golly, that was even more awkward than when he arrived by mistake in your bedroom and you were naked!"

Posy felt ashamed of the effort she made to prepare for her lunch with Freddie. He was, after all, someone she had not seen for almost fifty years, but most importantly, he was not a distant memory, as he'd presumed. Their relationship and the abrupt ending of it had left an indelible stain on her heart. And in many ways, had shaped the path of her life.

Still, as she looked through her wardrobe and realized she hadn't bought a new piece of clothing for years, she knew that the lunch date was providing her with the proverbial kick up the backside she needed.

"You've let yourself go, Posy," she said sternly to herself. "You need a makeover, as those television shows call it."

So the following day, she took herself off into Southwold. She had a trim and some gentle highlights which painted over the gray that had sprouted onto her scalp in the past ten years. After that, she went into the boutique, which was having its end of season sale.

Having tried on most of the things in her size—still a twelve, she was proud to note—everything seemed too frumpy or too young.

"Mrs. Montague, how about you try these? They've just come in, so I'm afraid they're not in the sale."

The assistant was holding out a pair of black jeans.

"Surely they're for teenagers?"

"You have a fantastic pair of legs, Mrs. Montague, so why not show them off? I also thought this might go nicely with them."

Posy took the cornflower-blue cotton shirt and the jeans into the changing room. Five minutes later, she stood in front of the mirror, surprised at her reflection. The jeans did indeed show off her long legs—still firm from all her hours in the garden—and the shirt not only suited her complexion but was loose enough to cover that worryingly saggy skin around her midriff.

"A new bra too," she told herself as she undressed and saw the shapeless gray one covering her breasts.

Posy eventually emerged with two shopping bags. She'd bought two pairs of jeans, three new shirts, a bra and a pair of shiny black boots that stopped just below her knees.

"I hope I haven't fallen foul of the mutton dressed as lamb rule," she muttered to herself as she headed for her car. Then she thought of Freddie in his chinos, blazer and jaunty trilby, and decided she hadn't.

"My goodness, Posy, you look a treat," said Freddie as he stood up to welcome her to the table the next day.

"Thank you," she said as she sat down in the chair he'd pulled out opposite him. "You don't look so bad yourself."

"I took the liberty of ordering us a bottle of chardonnay. I remember you drinking white wine back in the day. When we weren't on the gin, that is," he smiled.

"Yes, a glass would go down rather nicely."

Freddie poured some wine into her glass, then lifted his own. "To your health."

"And to yours." Posy took a sip.

"It is rather strange, isn't it, that after all these years, fate should conspire for us to meet again?" he said.

"Well, we both come from Suffolk originally, if you remember, Freddie."

"Of course I do. How long have you been back?"

"Well over thirty years now. I brought up my family here."

"Where?"

"At my childhood home, just outside Southwold."

"Right." Freddie took a sip of his wine. Posy watched him pause before he continued, "And was it a good home for your family? No bad memories?"

"Not at all, why should there have been? I loved it there as a young child."

"Quite," said Freddie.

"Is something wrong?" Posy asked him, studying the all-too-familiar eyes. He'd always looked like he did now if there was a problem.

"Not at all, dear girl, not at all. I'm very glad you moved back there and were happy."

"*Am* happy, actually. I still live there."

"Do you indeed? Well, well."

"You seem surprised. Why?"

"I...don't know really. I suppose I always imagined you flying off intrepidly around the world, searching out rare flora and fauna. Now"—Freddie handed her a menu—"shall we order?"

Whilst Freddie read his menu, Posy studied him covertly over the top of hers, wondering what it was about her return to live at Admiral House that seemed to have rattled him.

"I'm having the catch of the day. You?" he asked.

"I'll have the same, thank you."

Freddie called over a waitress and once he had placed their order, Posy took another sip of her wine. "So tell me about you, Freddie. What have you been up to over the years?"

"My life has been pretty standard, to be honest. You might remember I'd already realized that a life dreaming of fame wasn't for me, so I went to Bar School and became a barrister. I married a solicitor in my thirties and we had a good life together. Sadly, she died two years ago, just after we bought a cottage here in Southwold. We were going to retire to it together, spend our sunset years pottering about on boats and traveling."

"I'm sorry, Freddie. You were married a long time. It must have been a horrible shock to suddenly be alone."

"It was, especially as Elspeth and I had never had children. She didn't want them, you see, was far too interested in plowing her way up to the glass ceiling with intent to shatter it. In retrospect, I don't think I could ever see Elspeth 'pottering.' She was driven and ambitious, so it was probably for the best that she died whilst she was still at the top of her game. I've always liked strong women, as you know."

Posy ignored the remark. "So where is your house?"

"At the end of a narrow lane right in the center of the town. Even if I would have enjoyed a sea view and a larger garden, one has to be pragmatic as one gets older and be within easy reach of the facilities. It's an old hophouse with an adjacent cottage where the original owners lived. I've almost finished renovating both, and intend to let the hophouse out eventually," he said as their fish arrived. "This looks excellent, I must say."

As they ate, Posy couldn't help but glance surreptitiously at

Freddie and wonder at their reunion. He hadn't changed a jot, the law student with the artistic soul whom she had once loved...the thought they were sitting here together after all this time made her feel quite emotional.

"So, Posy, what about you?" Freddie smiled at her across the table as the waitress cleared their plates. "You've already said you have a husband and children."

"Golly no! Well, at least, not a husband. Jonny died over thirty years ago. I've been a widow ever since."

"I am sorry to hear that. I presume your children were very young at the time? It must have been hard for you."

"It was, but one gets through. I actually have some wonderful memories of the time when my boys were small. It was the three of us together against the world. They kept me sane and focused."

"I'm surprised you never married again, Posy. A woman like you..."

"No one ever took my fancy."

"Although you must have had suitors?"

"I had a few over the years, yes. Now, are you up for pudding or shall we go straight to coffee?"

Over coffee, Posy continued to fill Freddie in on the story of her life.

"It was the garden that saved me, to be truthful. Watching it grow and flourish must be similar to the rush you felt when you won a case in court."

"I think it's a little more worthwhile than that, my dear. You have created something from nothing."

"Well, perhaps you'd like to come over to Admiral House and I'll give you a tour."

Freddie didn't reply. Instead he waved the waitress over and asked for the bill. "I'm getting this, by the way. It's been a real treat to catch up, Posy, but I'm afraid I must bring lunch to a close. I have an electrician due at three to fit the spots in the ceiling of the hophouse. You must come round and see it sometime."

She watched him put some notes on the table under the bill, then stand up. "Forgive me for rushing off. I'd lost track of the time. Goodbye, Posy."

"Goodbye."

As he left, she let out a big sigh before polishing off the rest of the wine in her glass. She felt totally confused, *shaken* by his abrupt departure. After all, it had been him who had sought her out, instigated the lunch, and she wondered what it was she had said or done to have him leave so hurriedly.

"Or perhaps he simply did lose track of time," Posy muttered as she stood up and prepared to leave. Whichever, she couldn't help feeling rather foolish as she walked along the high street in the bright September sun. She'd spent a lot of time in the past couple of days wondering whether, if he asked her out again, she could ever forgive him for dumping her so unceremoniously all those years ago. For her, at least, the physical attraction was there in spades and she had certainly enjoyed his company today.

"Oh, Posy, will you ever grow up and stop dreaming?"

As she drove home—carefully, due to the two glasses of wine—Posy remembered that the reason Freddie had suggested lunch originally was to tell her why he had left her. Yet he hadn't said a word.

"Men," she said as she changed out of her new shirt and jeans and donned her old and far more Posy-like cotton trousers and a moth-eaten sweater. Then she headed out into the garden.

Chapter 7

"Thanks so much for picking up the children," Amy said gratefully as Marie Simmonds let her in through her front door. "What with my babysitter having this awful cold virus, I was really stuck."

"No probs. Have you got time for a cup of tea?" suggested Marie. "All the kids have had supper and they're in the sitting room watching TV."

Amy looked at her watch. "Okay, if you're sure it's no bother."

"Of course not. Come in."

Amy followed Marie along the narrow hall to the small, immaculate kitchen. Despite the fact that the house was on a new estate with fifty others that looked exactly alike, and therefore not Amy's style at all, the warmth and orderliness of it compared to her own current accommodation made her feel envious.

"You know, any time you're stuck, Amy, I'd be happy to collect the kids for you and mind them for an hour or so. I only work until three so I can pick them up at half past. And Josh and Jake get on really well," Marie added.

"It really is kind of you to offer," said Amy, "but now I've got the car back from the garage, things should be a little easier."

"Milk and sugar?"

"Both, please," answered Amy.

"Another skinny-ribs, just like Evie," sighed Marie, making a black coffee for herself.

"Has Evie's daughter gone to her boarding school?" asked Amy.

"Yes. She's been there for a couple of weeks now and, after all the fuss, she loves it. Apparently it was your mother-in-law, Posy, who helped change Clemmie's mind. She really is an...interesting lady."

"Yes, she is," Amy agreed. "Posy's incredibly strong. Any time I'm feeling a bit low, I think of her and tell myself to pull myself together. So how is Evie feeling about losing her daughter to boarding school?"

"She's obviously missing Clemmie a lot. She must get so lonely, rattling around in that big house by herself."

"Posy has always been fond of Evie," commented Amy.

"Yes," Marie agreed, 'the two of them spent a lot of time together when they worked at Nick's shop."

"It's odd, though, because Evie seemed so uneasy with Posy when we saw her at the literary festival. Posy wonders what she's done to upset her."

"I honestly don't know." Marie shrugged. "Evie is a very private person—she always has been. Anyway, do you think Posy will sell Admiral House?"

"I can hardly believe she's considering it; it's been in her family for at least a couple of hundred years, but unfortunately, I don't think there's much money to help restore it."

"Maybe she'll leave it all to her sons in her will, then you'd part own it," suggested Marie. "And I think it might be a little bit more comfortable for you, Sam and the kids than your current home."

"Posy has offered lots of times to have us all to stay, but Sam always said no." Pride made Amy bristle. "Anyway, I do hope it won't be for much longer. Sam's got a big property project on the go."

"Yes, I've heard about that," nodded Marie.

"Really?" Amy looked at her in surprise. "How come?"

"It's no big mystery. I'm an estate agent and Sam has been into the office a few times looking for possible purchases. The kind of places he's looking for must mean he's got a few bob to spend. He must have a very rich backer."

Marie's general inquisitiveness was starting to irritate Amy. "I'm afraid I've no idea. I don't really get involved with Sam's business dealings." She drained her teacup and looked at her watch. "I really think we must be on our way."

"Of course." Marie eyed Amy as she stood up. "By the way, I saw a friend of yours the other day."

"Did you? Who?"

"Sebastian Girault. He was in the office inquiring about winter lets. Apparently he's got a book to write and he wants to rent something in Southwold where he can hole up for the next few months and get some peace and quiet."

"I'd hardly say he was a friend of mine, Marie, in fact, quite the opposite."

"You know what I mean." Marie gave a conspiratorial wink. "He seemed very interested in you that day of his reading. And he is sooo attractive."

"Is he?" Amy walked into the sitting room. "Right, kids, we're off home."

Driving the three miles back to the house, Amy felt unsettled by her conversation with Marie. Since she had met her with Posy and Evie a couple of Saturdays back, Marie had begun to chat to Amy in the playground, obviously eager to be friendly. She had undoubtedly come to Amy's rescue this morning at school, offering to take Jake and Sara home to her house until Amy could collect them, but something about the intimacy with which she spoke to Amy—as though she had known her for years—made Amy feel uncomfortable. Marie was obviously a gossip, eager for any tidbits thrown at her and even though she probably meant no harm, Amy, who regarded discretion as one of the great virtues, found it awkward.

"It's probably halfway round Southwold that I'm having an affair with Sebastian Girault," Amy muttered to herself as she pulled into the curb in front of the house.

Sam was out as usual, so Amy bathed the children, read them a story and put them to bed. She found her purse and took out twenty pounds to put in the emergency stash she kept in a tin at the bottom of the wardrobe where Sam wouldn't find it. Then she settled in front of the woodburner with Sebastian Girault's book and waited for Sam to come home. She only hoped he wouldn't be too drunk. As she began to read, despite her feelings about the author himself,

Amy could not help being enchanted and moved by his novel. Surely anyone who could write with such pathos and understanding of human emotions could not be all bad?

Amy gazed into the flames. What Marie had said earlier was plainly ridiculous. Why on earth would someone as glamorous as Sebastian Girault be the least bit interested in a very ordinary part-time receptionist and mother of two?

As she heard footsteps on the path up to the front door, she slammed the book shut. And just as it always did when Sam came back from the pub, Amy's heart rate rose. The front door opened and Sam appeared in the sitting room.

"Hi, sweetheart." Sam bent to kiss her and she smelt the familiar stench of beer on his breath. "See your car's back, thank God."

"You can say that again," breathed Amy. "The bad news is that it cost over three hundred pounds."

"Christ. What did you pay with?"

"Luckily, my salary's just arrived in the bank, so I paid by card. And it cleared some of the overdraft, but we're going to have to live on soup and baked potatoes for the rest of the month."

Amy waited nervously for his reaction, but Sam sank onto the sofa and sighed. "God, darling, I'm sorry, but with a bit of luck, all this will be behind us very soon."

"That's good," said Amy, relieved that Sam seemed positive and upbeat. "Are you hungry?"

"I got a pie and chips on my way home."

"Right. I'm so sorry, Sam, but I'm afraid you really are going to have to cut that kind of thing out for the next few weeks, otherwise we won't make it through financially."

"Are you saying that a man can't treat himself to a bag of chips after a hard day's work?"

"I'm saying we have a huge overdraft and we have to make our priority the kids until everything is sorted out. Sara's desperate for some new shoes, Jake needs an anorak and—"

"Stop trying to make me feel guilty!"

"I promise you I'm not. I'm just telling you the facts as they are. There's no money for anything this month, there really isn't."

"You know"—Sam shook his head and his eyes darkened—"you really are becoming the kind of wife men dread coming home to." He stood up and walked towards her.

"I'm sorry, I really am. I...I'm just going to go out. I need a breath of fresh air." She stood up, swiftly grabbed her coat and walked towards the front door and was out of it before he could stop her.

"That's right," he mocked her. "Walk out on an argument as usual, rather than having it out here and now. Miss Hard Done To, Miss Perfect Mother and Wife, Miss..."

Amy heard no more as she walked hurriedly away towards the town, tears stinging her eyes. She'd learnt that this was the best way of dealing with him when he was drunk. With any luck, if she left it long enough, he'd have passed out on the sofa before she got back. And the fresh sea air would help clear her mind. It was a pleasant night and Amy walked briskly along the sea front until she found a bench. She sat down and looked out into the blackness, hearing the waves breaking on the sand below her.

The vastness of the ocean always made her feel insignificant, which in turn helped to put her problems into perspective. She sat breathing deeply with the break of the waves, trying to calm down. Across that ocean, there were millions of humans whose lives were destroyed by war, poverty and famine. There were children dying every day as a result of terrible diseases, or homeless, orphaned, crippled...

Amy counted her blessings. Even if life—and Sam—were difficult, she had two healthy children, a roof over her head and food on the table.

"Remember, you're just one of billions of ants crawling across the face of the earth, trying to survive," she said to the air.

"Very poetic. And very accurate."

A voice from behind her made her jump up from the bench and turn round, her arms instinctively going across her chest. She stared at the tall figure in a long coat, a felt hat pulled down over his face to protect him from the wind. Amy knew exactly who he was.

"Sorry to startle you. I believe we have met before."

"Yes. What are you doing here?"

"I could ask you the self-same question. As for me, I was just taking an evening stroll before cooping myself up in my hotel bedroom for the next eight hours."

"I saw you're not staying at our hotel anymore."

"No. I prefer somewhere with more reliable hot water so I don't have to reduce the receptionist to tears."

"Oh." Amy turned round and sat back down on the bench.

"I presume you're here because you want to be left alone?"

"Yes," she answered shortly.

"Well, before I go on my way, I must make sure that my harsh words to you a couple of weeks ago have no bearing on your present state of mind."

"Of course not. Really, can we just forget it?"

"Yes. Just one more question; have you had a chance to read my book?"

"Some of it."

"And?"

"I love it," answered Amy truthfully.

"I'm glad."

"You're an author. Of course you're glad someone likes your work."

"Yes, but I'm particularly glad *you* like it, that's all. Well, I'll be off then. Leave you to your ocean."

"Thanks." Amy turned round, feeling suddenly guilty for her rudeness. "Look, I'm sorry if I've been offhand. I'm just feeling a bit down, that's all."

"Don't apologize. Believe me, I've been there, and still revisit occasionally. All I can say, from bitter experience, is that life usually gets better, as long as you try to be positive."

"I've been trying to be positive for years, but it really doesn't seem to help."

"Then maybe you have to look a little deeper, find out the real cause of your unhappiness and do something about that."

"You sound like a self-help book."

"Yes, I do. Done the course, got the therapy T-shirt, me. Sorry."

"Excuse me for saying so, but personally I think all that kind of stuff is self-indulgent crap. Try having two kids, a full-time job and no money. You just have to get on with it."

"So you're part of the 'pull yourself together' brigade, are you?"

"Absolutely," Amy nodded vehemently.

"Which is why you're sitting alone on a bench in the dark falling apart."

"I'm not falling apart. I just needed...some air."

"Of course. Anyway, I've already taken up too much of your space. I'll see you around."

"Yes, see you around."

Out of the corner of her eye, Amy watched Sebastian Girault stride off down the road. Objectively, she could understand why women such as Marie thought he was so attractive. He was a very striking man.

Walking home, she *did* feel calmer. This was her lot, her life and she just had to make the best of it. Yet she couldn't help but hear Sebastian's words about discovering the root of her misery and acting on it.

She paused in front of her house for a few minutes, dreading going back inside. With a heavy heart, Amy reluctantly acknowledged what that root might be.

Chapter 8

"Can I call you Monday with a final decision?" asked Nick. "I just have to make sure the finances are in place and give myself forty-eight hours to mull it over. But I'm ninety-nine per cent sure I'll take it."

"Good. I'll look forward to hearing from you Monday, Mr. Montague."

The two men shook hands and Nick stepped out of the front door. He turned round to face the shop and imagined the currently dreary frontage repainted in a deep emerald green, with his own name above the windows in gold.

He felt confident that it was the right showroom in which to place his antiques: lots of window space to attract passersby as well as the spacious ground floor, a large basement with enough room for a workshop and storage.

He crossed the busy Fulham Road and felt satisfied the location was perfect. Right in the heart of a stretch of pavement littered with high-quality antique, interior and bespoke design showrooms. Admittedly, he would have to pay more for the lease than he had originally budgeted for and it was a high-risk operation; ten years abroad had left him with no track record here and he would have to start from scratch.

Yet it was none of the above which daunted him, had made him want to think twice before a gentleman's handshake sealed the deal. The decision was much more fundamental: was he absolutely sure he wanted to live his life in the UK?

Nick's mobile rang. "Hi, Tam...Yes, I think I've found it. Where are you? Okay, what about the Bluebird halfway up Kings Road? My treat. I'll see you in ten minutes. Bye."

Seeing the road was gridlocked with traffic, Nick decided to skip a taxi and walk the half mile or so to the restaurant. Even though he could feel the chill of autumn beginning to creep into the air, the sun was shining and the sky was an azure blue. As he walked, Nick pondered how amazing life was. After feeling as if he'd been treading water emotionally for the past ten years and avoiding all thoughts of returning home because it was just too painful, two weeks back in England and here he was, experiencing what could only be described as happiness.

Surely he must still be jet-lagged, confused, on some kind of an initial high? There must be some explanation for the way he felt, as though the darkness had suddenly lifted and he was being propelled back towards the human race at a rate of knots.

And if it wasn't any of those things—and Nick had to admit it was doubtful it was—that meant there was only one explanation for his current euphoria: Tammy.

Since their first meeting at Jane and Paul's supper party, they'd seen each other constantly. With both of them on the hunt for premises for their businesses, they'd met up for coffee, a sandwich or an early evening drink to share their experiences. They'd bemoaned endlessly the price of finding somewhere suitable, then forgotten about business and talked to each other about their lives, their philosophies and their hopes and fears for the future.

Nick could not remember ever feeling so comfortable with another person, especially a woman. Tammy was grown-up, together and bright. Best of all, Nick hadn't had a hint of the usual neuroses that seemed to plague most single women he knew. She seemed happy in her own skin, calm and confident, and if she possessed any bunny-boiling tendencies, she was yet to reveal them.

So far, things had developed no further than friendship. In fact, as he paced along the street, Nick admitted that he had no idea whether Tammy liked him as a friend, or perhaps felt more. A woman like her could have anyone.

As he walked, Nick knew that Tammy had completely confused

the picture. He felt it was now impossible to make a rational decision about his future. If he stayed here in London, would it be because of her?

He could hardly tell Tammy of his quandary. She'd think him more than a little mad that he might base his future on whether she might be in it. The last thing he wanted to do was frighten her off by being pushy, but perhaps it would be possible to somehow glean if she did have any feelings for him over lunch. And take it from there.

He walked into the restaurant fifteen minutes later and saw Tammy sitting on a sofa in the bar, her long legs clad in jeans, with a green cashmere sweater that matched the color of her eyes. He'd never seen her look more beautiful.

"Hi, Tam." He leant down and kissed her warmly on both cheeks.

"Hi, Nick," she smiled up at him.

"Shall we go through? I'm starving."

"Sure." Tammy stood up and they both followed a waiter to a table. "This place is a bit of a notch up from our usual lunchtime meeting points. You must have good news."

"Hopefully, yes. How about a glass of champagne?" Nick asked as they sat down.

"Lovely. It is Friday, after all."

"Absolutely," he nodded. "Any excuse."

"Nick?"

"Yes?"

"Why are you staring at me like that?"

"Sorry...I was just thinking...about something."

"What?"

Nick mentally slapped himself out of his romantic daydream which, as he'd looked at her, had involved a small velvet-covered box and her delicate white finger. He told himself firmly he really was losing it and picked up the menu. "Nothing important. Posh fish and chips for me. How about you?"

"The same, I think."

Nick ordered two glasses of champagne and the fish and chips. "I do like a woman who likes her food."

"Well, you wouldn't have liked me a few years ago. I was obsessed with my body. I hardly ate at all," said Tammy. "Let's face it, my entire career depended on my figure. Then I gave up modeling, decided to eat exactly what I wanted and what do you know? I've hardly put on an ounce since. Which just goes to prove it's mostly to do with your metabolism and very little else. So tell me about the premises on the Fulham Road."

They sipped champagne and Nick told her.

"So I have the weekend to make up my mind," he finished.

"Surely there's no decision to be taken? It sounds perfect, absolutely perfect."

"It is, but life isn't quite as simple as that," sighed Nick. "It's a big move, to close up in Australia and start again here."

"But I thought it was what you wanted?" said Tammy.

"I think it is, and I'm ninety-nine but not a hundred percent sure."

Tammy's face fell. "Oh Nick, I hope you're not going to go back. I'd really miss you."

"Would you?"

"Of course!"

"Tammy, I..."

Typically, the momentum was broken by the arrival of the waiter with two plates of fish and chips. Nick ordered another couple of glasses of champagne. He needed as much Dutch courage as he could get.

Tammy stared at him across the table. "Is there something you want to say? You've been tense since you walked in here."

"I have, haven't I?" Nick took a large gulp of his drink. "Look, I'm rubbish at this kind of stuff, but I'll try and explain as best I can."

"Go for it," Tammy encouraged him.

"The thing is, Tam, the last couple of weeks have been fantastic. I've really enjoyed your company and stuff, but, well..."

"What?" Tammy's eyes were anxious. "Are you trying to tell me you don't want to see me again?"

"God no! Completely the opposite. We've become such good friends so quickly and I really do seem to have become very fond of you...more than fond, actually, and I was wondering...Well, the truth is, I was wondering whether this is as far as you want to take it."

"You mean whether I'd prefer to remain 'just good friends'?" she clarified.

"Yes."

"As opposed to what?"

"Instead of, you know, taking it further."

"Nick, are you saying you might quite like to ask me out? I mean, officially, like teenagers do?"

She was playing with him now, but he didn't care. "Yes, I would, very much."

"So"—Tammy forked up a chip—"ask me then."

"Okay," nodded Nick, his heart pounding, "would you like to go out with me?"

"No, not really." She shook her head firmly.

"Oh."

Tammy offered her hand to him across the table.

"I said that's what we'd do if we were teenagers, but we're not. And we've been 'out' on lots of dates already. In fact, we're in the middle of one right now. So how about we behave like the consenting adults we are, and after we've eaten these delicious chips, cut the crap and go back to my house?"

He looked at her, relief flooding through him. "I can't think of anything I'd like more."

The late afternoon sun streamed through Tammy's uncurtained bedroom window. It looked out on a pretty roof terrace that she'd filled with pots full of flowers and a trellis that sported a clematis in high summer. The flowers were past their best now, but she still loved looking out at her little patch of nature in the center of the city. The tiny house was her haven and she'd populated it with treasures from her travels around the world.

Small dust motes danced in the air and Tammy watched them through half-closed eyes as Nick caressed her back softly with his hands and his mouth. She felt totally peaceful, sated after two hours of blissful lovemaking.

Usually she dreaded the first time with a new lover. Even though there was the surge of excitement that could only be felt at the touch of a new, unknown body, there was also the tension of not knowing whether she would please him, or he her.

But with Nick, it had been wonderful.

He had a beautiful body, tanned from the Perth sun, strong and slim, with just the right amount of male brawn where it should be. And he'd touched her so gently, without any hint of clumsiness or hesitation, and whispered so many loving endearments that she'd been able to respond fully to her body's urges in safety and without any embarrassment.

"You are totally and utterly gorgeous," Nick murmured into her neck. "And I completely adore you."

She rolled over to face him, then stroked his cheek. He took her fingers to his lips and kissed them.

"So can I say that we are officially going out?" he asked softly.

"Just because I sleep with you doesn't mean you are my boyfriend," she giggled.

"Blimey, how things have changed. Used to be it was the other way round," he teased.

"I'd love to 'go out' with you," nodded Tammy. "Apart from the fact that, just for now, I'd far rather prefer to stay in."

"Absolutely, as much staying in as possible, please." He twisted a lock of her Titian hair around his fingers. "By the way, I'm going to call my mum this weekend and let her know I'm back. She lives in Suffolk and I'll probably go up to see her next week. Would you like to come with me?" he added, unable to stop himself.

"I'd love to meet your mother at some point, but perhaps you should go and see her alone first? You'll have a lot to talk about and I'm sure she'll want you all to herself, at least for a few hours."

"You're right." Nick felt the color rising in his cheeks at his impromptu suggestion.

"Do you have any brothers or sisters?"

"Yes, I do." Nick's face darkened. "An older brother called Sam. For various reasons he's not my favorite person, I'm afraid. He's a total waster and I have no time for him whatsoever."

"They say you can choose your friends, but not your family," said Tammy.

"Absolutely. Anyway, let's not talk about Sam. So where shall we go on our first official date tonight? That's if you're not doing anything else?"

"The local takeaway, I'm afraid. I've got some repairs to do on a couple of dresses before the weekend on my stall. God, I can't wait until I find some premises and I can employ a seamstress who can help me. I've got stacks of beads waiting to be re-sewn on." Tammy pointed to the plastic boxes that were cluttering up the area she used as her dressing room. "Goodness, it's nearly six. Sorry, darling, but I've really got to get up and get on."

"Okay. Would you prefer me to go?"

"No, not at all, as long as you don't mind chatting to me while I work and fetching a curry," Tammy smiled.

"Of course not."

"Can you go and get it now? I'm starving."

"You're food-obsessed, woman," grinned Nick as he watched her climb out of bed.

On the way to get the curry, Nick had a sudden feeling of euphoria. For better or worse, this afternoon his mind had been made up. He would stay and take his chances on a new life in London. And on Tammy.

Large Blue
(Phengaris arion)

Posy

Admiral House
December 1944

I was a little upset that Maman didn't look *more* upset as we climbed up onto the pony and trap on a frosty December morning. Even though it was not even seven o'clock in the morning, Maman was wearing one of her pretty dresses and had red lipstick on.

"You look nice today," I said as she appeared at the front door and walked down the steps towards us.

"Well, it is nearly Christmas, *chérie*, and we must all make an effort," she shrugged as she reached up so she could kiss my cheek. "Now, be a good girl for your grandmother, won't you?"

"Yes. Merry Christmas, Maman," I said as Benson snicked the pony's flank in preparation to leave. "See you in the New Year," I added as the pony began to clop along the drive.

But Maman had already turned away and was walking up the steps and into the house.

Christmas wasn't actually as miserable as I had imagined it would be. For starters, on the day before Christmas Eve, it began to snow. Living near the sea, I'd only been treated to three or four snowy days in my entire life, the white covering disappearing within hours as it began to rain. Here, on the edge of Bodmin Moor, the snow came down like great dumps of icing sugar and didn't seem inclined to go away. It sat on the windowsills outside as the light from the fires and the Advent candle flickered inside. Bill the young man who did all sorts of odd jobs for Granny and brought in logs for the fire, presented me with an old sled he himself had once used in the winter. I followed him through the snow that reached up to my knees, and followed his pointed finger to a slope. Small, bright bundles were careening down it on all manner of sliding equipment, from tin trays to old wooden pallets.

He took me across to the bottom of the slope and introduced me to a tiny figure whose face was so camouflaged in a pink knitted hat and scarf I could only see a pair of bright blue eyes.

"This be my god-daughter, Katie," Bob said, his Cornish accent as thick as the cream from the cows that dotted the landscape. "She'll take care of ye."

And she did. Even though she only came up to my shoulder, it turned out Katie was the same age as me and obviously a power to be reckoned with in this remote community. We trudged up the slope, Katie shouting and waving at her pals as we did so.

"That be Boycee, the butcher's son, and that be Rosie, the postmaster's daughter," she informed me as we reached the summit of the snow-covered tor. "My da's the milkman."

"My daddy...da is a pilot," I said as Katie showed me how to lie face down on my sledge and use my hands to paddle in the snow to give myself a start downwards.

"Off you go!" Katie shouted as she gave the sledge an enormous push and I went sailing at speed down the steep slope, screaming like a baby and loving every second of it.

I went up and down the tor countless times that day, and of all my childhood memories, it always stood out as the best fun I'd ever had, apart from catching butterflies with Daddy of course, but I couldn't think about that any more without wanting to cry. The other children were very welcoming, and after I'd enjoyed the hot Ovaltine brought by one of the mothers and doled out into tin cups to warm us all up, I went home feeling happy that I'd made a lot of new friends. It was a feeling that warmed my insides as much as the Ovaltine.

Christmas Eve came, and Bill and I traipsed through the snow to a small pine wood on the edge of the village. I chose a small tree, which, even though it could never compete with the enormous one that always stood in the hall at Admiral House, looked so pretty with

Granny's old and rather tarnished silver decorations and the candles that stood on the branches flickering in the firelight.

The village residents passed through Granny's house all day to enjoy a fresh mince pie. Daisy had been overwhelmed to see six jars of spiced mincemeat sitting on the top shelf of the pantry. Granny had chuckled and asked how anyone could be surprised at this when mince pies were only eaten for a couple of days a year; she explained to Daisy that the batch her old cook had made before the war began had been large enough to feed half the Western Front and it kept forever. Then Granny, Daisy and I sat down to enjoy a scrumptious dinner of toad in the hole. There weren't many sausages, but the crispy golden batter and thick gravy more than made up for it. It seemed to me that this little village on the edge of the moor had eaten better during the war than dukes and duchesses in London.

"That's because we've all pulled together," Granny had explained. "I've had my vegetable garden and chickens, and I swap my carrots and eggs for milk and meat. We're a self-sufficient lot down here. We've always had to be, living where we do. Just look outside." She pointed to the snowflakes whirling beyond the windowpanes. "The road will be impassable by tomorrow, but there will still be fresh milk on the doorstep come morning, you'll see. Jack's never failed to get through yet."

And indeed, as Christmas Day dawned, Daisy brought in the still-warm milk left in a small tin canister on the doorstep. This was a moorland community where people looked after each other, isolated as it was from the rest of the world. Bodmin was the nearest town, and that was ten miles away. As I looked at the snow piled outside in great heaps where the heavens had deposited it, I thought it could easily be a thousand miles. I felt cocooned from reality in a soft, safe, snowy nest. And even though I missed Maman and Papa and Admiral House dreadfully, it was a feeling I liked.

We opened our presents to each other after church and I was delighted with the book of botanical drawings by Margaret Mee, who was once an explorer for Kew Gardens, that Daddy had sent me in the Christmas box addressed to Granny, which had arrived a few days earlier.

Christmas 1944
For my darling Posy—have a merry time with Granny and

counting the days until I see you again. All my love, Daddy xxx

Well, I thought, at least he knows where I am, which was just as comforting as the lovely present, which would keep me occupied for many a long, snowy day. Daisy had knitted me a woollen hat with flaps that came down over my ears and tied under my chin.

"Perfect for sledding!" I said as I hugged her and she turned pink from pleasure.

Granny had given me a set of leather-bound books by ladies called Anne, Emily and Charlotte Brontë.

"They are probably a little grown-up for you now, Posy my dear, but I loved those stories when I was a gel," she'd smiled.

Daisy had been invited to join us for Christmas lunch, which I found most surprising. Never, ever could I imagine Daisy sitting up to table at Admiral House, but Granny had insisted, saying how wrong it would be for Daisy to eat alone in the kitchen on the most holy day of the year. I liked Granny for that a lot, the way she didn't mind where in the "lottery" someone came from or what they did for a living. In fact, I was growing to like Granny more and more.

I also noticed that, after a couple of whiskies, Granny became much more talkative. As we sat in front of the fire on Christmas night, me in my nightgown sipping hot cocoa before bed, she told me the story of how she and Grandfather had met. It had been during something that Granny called "the Season," when Granny had "come out" (I was not sure where from), which seemed to have to do with an awful lot of parties and dances and something called a "deb's delight." Grandfather had been one, apparently.

"I saw him at the very first ball...well, how could one miss him?! He was six foot four and just down from Oxford. With those big brown eyes, which both you and your father have inherited, he could have had any young lady during the Season, even though he wasn't titled like many of them. His mother had been an 'Hon.'..." (I wasn't sure what this meant, but it was obviously something good.) "so, by the end of the Season, we were affianced. Of course, the marriage meant that I had to leave my beloved home here in dear old Cornwall and move to Suffolk, but that was what young ladies did in those days. They followed their husbands."

Granny took another sip of whisky and her eyes took on a dreamy expression. "Oh, my dear, we were so happy for those first two years before the Great War came. I found myself pregnant with your father and everything was so perfect. And then…" Granny gave a deep sigh. "Georgie enlisted the moment war was declared and was shipped off to the trenches in France. He didn't even survive long enough to see his son born."

"Oh Granny, how awful," I said as she dabbed her eyes with a lace handkerchief.

"Yes, it really was at the time, yet so many of us women were losing their men, and with some in the village left virtually destitute because of it, I felt that it was my duty to help them. And that, plus your darling father being born, was what got me through. Lawrence was such a good baby and a sweet toddler—perhaps too gentle for a boy if one was being completely honest, but of course, I indulged his passion for nature, because I shared a love of the outdoors too. He adored his butterflies even then and had quite a collection of other insects too. That was why I gave him the top of the Folly; I simply couldn't bear him sleeping in the same room with jars of insects and spiders," Granny shuddered. "One never knew when they might escape. He's a clever chap, your father, albeit his head is ruled by his heart. And even though he is a gentle soul, once he has a bee in his bonnet, there is no stopping him."

"What is a bee in a bonnet, Granny?"

"It means that when he knows what he wants, he goes after it. All his schoolmasters thought he was quite bright enough to study law at Oxford like his father, but Lawrence wasn't having any of it. Botany was the path he wished to tread and he did so at Cambridge. Then of course, he was determined to have your mother, even though…" Granny stopped short suddenly and took a breath. "She was French," she added. Rather limply, I thought.

"Is there something wrong with being French?" I asked her.

"No, no, not at all," Granny replied hurriedly. "They simply had to learn each other's languages, that's all. Now, look at the time! It's past nine o'clock, far too late for little girls to be up and about. Off with you to bed, young lady."

I was glad the snow stayed put after Christmas, because it meant I was kept very busy. I was out with the village children every day, sledding or having snowball fights and snowmen-building competitions. I really liked the fact that we lived close enough to the village for Katie to call for me, or I for her, because at Admiral House, which was miles from any other building, only Mabel had ever come to call. And even though Granny lived in the grandest house in the village, the other children didn't treat me differently, just teased me about my accent, which I thought was quite ironic, considering it took a lot of concentration to understand a thing that any of *them* said to me.

On New Year's Eve, the entire village went to church to attend a special service of remembrance for all the local men lost to the war. There was quite a lot of sniffing and weeping, and I prayed hard for Daddy to return safely (even though Granny said the war was all over "bar the shouting," whatever that meant, and she was hoping to hear from him any day soon). After church, there was quite a lot of drinking in the hall next door. Katie surreptitiously offered me some punch that she had sneaked from one of the big bowls while no one was looking. I tried it and was almost sick because it tasted and smelt like petrol mixed with bruised apples and gone-off blackberries. Then someone produced a fiddle and someone else a flute and soon the whole village, including me, Granny and Daisy (who danced with Bill) were hopping and skipping and twirling around the room. It really was great fun, even if I hadn't a clue what I was doing.

In bed that night, even though I was exhausted from all the dancing and the walk home through the snow afterwards, I managed to send my love up to both Maman and Daddy.

"Happy New Year. Sleep with the angels," I murmured, before falling contentedly into a deep sleep.

Two days later, when the snow had finally begun to turn to slushy fondant during the day, but was freezing treacherously at night, Granny got a telegram. We were having breakfast together at the time, deciding what Daisy would cook for supper that night when the front doorbell rang. Daisy brought in the telegram and I watched Granny's face turn as white as the previous night's ashes still lying in the fire.

"Excuse me, my dear," she said as she rose from the table and left the room. She didn't come back, and after I had been up to my room to wash my face and hands after breakfast, I came down to be told by Daisy that Granny was on the telephone in the study and not to be disturbed.

"Is everything all right, Daisy?" I asked tentatively, knowing full well "everything" was not.

"Yes, now, look who has come to call for you!" she replied as we both saw Katie cycling up to the front door. As Daisy opened it, I saw relief on her face. "Morning, Katie, that's a smart bicycle."

"I got it from Father Christmas, but I ain't bin able to ride it because of the snow. Will you come for a spin with me, Posy? I'll let you have a ride on her. Mam says you're to come for lunch with us too."

I could see how proud Katie was of her bicycle, but also how it was not at all new; there was rust on the wheel covers and a worn basket that sat at a precarious angle at the front. I thought of my beautiful shiny red bicycle sitting in the stables at Admiral House, which then made me think of Papa, and the terrible color Granny had turned when she had read the telegram. I turned to Daisy.

"Are you sure everything is all right?"

"Yes, Miss Posy, now off you go with your friend and I'll see you later."

All that day, even though it was fun to ride a bicycle again and I liked sitting round the big table with Katie's three siblings eating the meat and potato pastry they called a "pasty" here, there was a knot of dread in my tummy that wouldn't go away.

When I returned home it was already growing dark. I saw the lights were burning in the sitting room, but the fire—which was usually glowing merrily at this time of day—was not.

"Hello, Miss Posy," Daisy greeted me at the door. Her expression was as dark as the dusk outside. "You have a visitor to see you."

"Who?"

"Your mother is here," she said as she helped me out of my coat and untied the strings of the knitted hat she had made me for Christmas. I saw her hands were shaking slightly as she did so.

"Maman? Here?!"

"Yes, Miss Posy. Now, you go and wash your face and hands

and brush your hair, then come back down and I'll take you into the sitting room."

As I walked up the stairs to my bedroom, my legs felt as if they were puddles of melting ice beneath me. And while I was standing in front of the mirror re-plaiting my hair, I heard the sound of raised voices coming from the sitting room beneath me. Then my mother crying.

And I knew, just *knew*, what I was going to be told.

"Posy, my dear, come in."

My grandmother ushered me through the door and put a gentle hand on my shoulder to steer me over to the wing-backed chair in which my mother was sitting beside the unlit fireplace.

"I will leave you alone for a while," Granny said as I looked down at Maman and she looked up at me through tear-soaked eyes. I wanted to ask Granny to stay—her solid presence held a sense of comfort that I just knew Maman would not be able to give me, but she walked across the sitting room and closed the door behind her.

"Posy, I..." Maman said as her voice cracked and she began to cry again.

"It's Daddy, isn't it?" I managed to whisper, already knowing that it was and therefore hoping at the same time that it *wasn't*.

"Yes," she replied.

And with that one word, the world I had known shattered into a trillion tiny pieces.

Bombing raid...Daddy's plane hit...flames...no survivors...hero...

The words went round and round in my brain until I wanted to pull them out through my ears so I didn't have to hear them any more. Or understand what they meant. Maman tried to hug me, but I didn't want to be hugged by anyone other than the one person who could never hug me again. So I ran upstairs and once in my room, all I could do was hug myself. Every sinew of my body ached with anguish and horror. Why *him*, and why *now*, I asked, when everyone had said the war was almost over? Why had God—if there really was one—been so cruel as to take Daddy away right at the end, when he had survived for so long? I hadn't even heard about any raids on the radio recently, just about the Germans retreating through France and that they couldn't hold out much longer.

I didn't know the words to describe how I felt—maybe there

just weren't any—so instead I keened like an injured animal until I felt a gentle hand being laid on my shoulder.

"Posy, my dearest girl, I am so very, very sorry. For you, for me, for Lawrence, and of course," Granny added after a pause, "your mother."

I opened my mouth to answer, because even now, in this terrible moment, I had been brought up to be polite and reply to any grown-up that spoke to me, but nothing came out. Granny gathered me up in her arms and I cried more tears against the comfort of her bosom. How my body was producing so much liquid I didn't know, because I hadn't had a drink of water since lunchtime.

"There, there," she soothed me and eventually, I must have dozed off. Perhaps I imagined it, but I was almost sure I heard the soft sound of sobbing which, as I was half-asleep, could only be coming from Granny.

"My dearest, dearest boy...how you must have suffered. And after all you had been through...I understand, my darling, I understand..."

I must have fallen asleep completely then, because the next thing I knew, I was waking to see the dreary gray light of a new day. My brain took only a few seconds to remember the terrible thing that had happened, and the tears started all over again.

Daisy arrived in my bedroom with a tray not long after and placed it on the bed. Like Granny, she took me in her arms.

"Poor little mite," she crooned, releasing me. "See? I brought you a fresh boiled egg and some toast soldiers to dip in. That'll make you feel better, won't it now?"

I wanted to reply that nothing, *ever*, could make me feel better again, but I opened my mouth automatically as Daisy fed me the egg and soldiers like I was a toddler.

"Is Maman awake?" I asked her.

"Yes and getting ready to leave."

"Are we going back to Admiral House today? I need to pack!" I pulled back the covers and jumped out of bed.

"Get dressed first, Miss Posy. Your mum wants to see you downstairs."

I did so and found Maman sitting by the fire in the drawing room. Her lovely skin was as white as the melting snow outside and I saw her hand shaking as she lit a cigarette.

"*Bonjour*, Posy. How did you sleep?"

"Better than I thought I would," I said truthfully as I stood in front of her.

"Sit down, *chérie*, I want to talk to you."

I did so, comforting myself that whatever she had to tell me could not ever be as bad as yesterday's news.

"Posy, I..."

I watched her fingers twine and untwine around each other as I waited for her to speak.

"...I am so very, very sorry for what has happened."

"It isn't your fault Daddy's dead, Maman."

"No, but...you did not deserve this. And now..."

She paused again, as if she didn't have the words either. Her voice sounded husky, barely there. As her eyes turned to me, I couldn't quite read the emotion in them, but whatever it was, Maman looked utterly miserable.

"Posy, Granny and I have been talking about what is best for you. And we think, especially for now, that you should stay here."

"Oh. How long for?"

"I really don't know. I have...many things to sort out."

"What about Daddy's..." I gulped and screwed up my courage to say the word, "funeral?"

"I..." Maman looked away from me into the fire and gulped too. "Granny and I have decided it is best for us to have a memorial service in a few weeks' time. They have...they have to return his...*him* from France, you see."

"Yes," I whispered, blinking hard. I realized then that I *had* to be strong for Maman. Be the "big brave girl" that Daddy had called me when I'd sliced my finger on a thorn in the garden or fallen off the swing he had made me. She was hurting terribly too. "For how long? School starts next week."

"Granny says you have made lots of friends in the village, so we thought that, for now, you could go to school here."

"I could, yes, but for how long?" I couldn't help repeating.

"Oh, Posy," Maman sighed. "I cannot answer that. I have so many things to sort out, you see. Decisions to be made. And while I am doing all that, I will not be able to give you the attention you need. Here, you will have Granny and Daisy all to yourself."

"Daisy is staying too?"

"I have asked her and she has agreed. I hear you are not the only one to have made new friends in the village." For the first time, Maman gave me a weak smile and a little flush came into her cheeks, warming the color of her skin, which reminded me of the grayish pastry Daisy made with lard. "So Posy? Do you think this is the best plan?"

I rubbed my nose as I thought about it. And what Daddy would say I should say.

"I will miss you and Admiral House terribly, Maman, but if it makes it better for you, then yes, I will stay here."

I noticed a glimmer of relief cross her face and knew I had given her the right answer. Perhaps she'd thought I would shout and scream and beg to go home with her. Part of me desperately wanted to do that: to go "home," and have things as they were before. But then I realized that nothing would ever be the same again, so what did it matter?

"Come here, *chérie*." Maman opened her arms to me and I went into them. I closed my eyes and smelt the familiar musky scent of her perfume.

"I promise that this is best for you, for now," she whispered. "I will write to you of course and come back for you as soon as I have settled things."

"Promise?"

"Promise." She pulled out of our hug and her hands dropped to her sides. She looked up at me from her chair, then reached up to gently touch my cheek. "You are so very like your Papa, *chérie*: brave and determined, with a heart that loves deeply. Don't let that destroy you, will you?"

"No, Maman, why should it? It's a good thing to love, isn't it?"

"*Oui*, of course it is." She nodded, then stood up, and I saw the despair in her eyes. "Now I must get ready to leave. I have to go to London to visit your father's solicitor. There are many things to organize. I will come and say goodbye when I have packed."

"Yes, Maman."

I watched her leave the room, then, with my legs giving way beneath me, I sank into the chair she'd been sitting on and silently wept into its arm.

August 1949

"So Posy, your mother and I have been talking on the telephone, for I have come up with a suggestion."

"Oh. Is she opening up Admiral House and wants me to go back?"

"No, dear girl, as we have discussed, it's far too large for just you and her. Maybe one day, if you marry, you can return and fill it with the big happy family it so deserves. As your father is...gone, it belongs to you, after all."

"Well, I wish I could go and live there tomorrow, with you of course, dear Granny."

"Well, when you come of age and inherit the house and your trust officially, you can make that decision. For now, it's sensible that it remains closed. As you will no doubt find out one day, the running costs are astronomical. Now then, I was telling you about my idea. I think it is best for you if we consider the idea of you going away to boarding school."

"What?! Leave you and all my friends here?! Never!"

"Please calm yourself, Posy, and hear me out. I understand that you have no wish to leave us, but it's becoming obvious that you need a far more sophisticated education than the village school can offer you. Miss Brennan herself came to see me and said the same thing. She is having to set you a completely different level of work to the rest of the class and admitted you were close to outstripping her own level of knowledge. She too thinks you should be in a school that can give you the breadth of education your academic gifts deserve."

"But..." I could feel myself pouting and couldn't help it, "I'm happy at school, and here, Granny. I don't want to go away, I really don't."

"I do understand, but really, if your father were alive, I'm sure he would say the same."

"Would he?" Still, five years on, I found it desperately painful to talk about him.

"Yes, and in a few years' time, you may well be thinking of a career, like so many women are these days."

"I haven't really thought about it," I admitted.

"No, well, why should you? That's what myself—and your mother, of course—are here for: to look to your future. And goodness, Posy, if I had been born in a time when women could have an education, and perhaps even go to university, I'd have jumped at the chance. Do you know that, before I met your grandfather, I was a suffragette? A fully paid-up member of the WSPU and a great supporter of Mrs. Pankhurst? I chained myself to the railings, fighting for women's right to the vote."

"Goodness, Granny! Did you really?"

"I most certainly did! But then of course, I fell in love, became engaged and all that caper had to stop. But at least I feel I made a contribution, and now times are changing, thanks in no small part to what Mrs. Pankhurst and my other brave comrades did back then."

I looked at Granny with fresh eyes, suddenly realizing that she had been young once too.

"So, Posy, the school I'm proposing for you is in Devon, not so very far away from here. It has an excellent reputation, especially in the sciences, and manages to get a number of its intake into university. I've spoken to the headmistress and she is very keen to meet you. I think we should go and take a look next week."

"And if I don't like it?"

"Let's wait and see if you do. I don't like negativity before the fact, as you know. And by the way, you have a letter from your mother upstairs in your room."

"Oh. Is she still in Italy?"

"Yes. She is."

"But I thought she was only going for a holiday and that was a year ago now? Pretty long holiday, if you ask me," I muttered.

"Enough of your cheek, young lady. Go upstairs and wash, please. Supper will be ready in ten minutes."

I went up to my bedroom, no longer temporary as it had been when I'd arrived here, but instead filled with all the paraphernalia of my past five years of living in it. It—and I—had adapted; we'd had to after I'd eventually realized, after two long years of waiting every day for Maman to send for me, that she wasn't going to. Any time soon, at least. After Daddy's death, she had gone back to Paris—the war had ended and many of her friends were returning there, so she had told me in one of the occasional postcards she had written to me. Whereas I, on the other hand, wrote to her every week of those first two years, on a Sunday afternoon before tea. And I always asked the same two questions: when was she coming to get me, and when was Daddy's memorial service to be held? The answer was always the same: *"Soon, chérie, soon. Please try to understand I cannot yet return to Admiral House. Every room is filled with memories of your Papa..."*

So, eventually, I had accepted that for now, my life was here, in this tiny community, physically and mentally cut off from the rest of the world. Even Granny's precious radio—which she used to listen to religiously every day for news of the war—had apparently broken just after Papa had died. It had miraculously managed to rouse itself for an hour when Victory in Europe had been announced, and I had hugged Granny and Daisy and all of us had done a little jig around the sitting room. I still remembered asking why we were celebrating, when the person we loved most would never be returning to us, like some of the other fathers and sons in the village subsequently had.

"We must find it in our hearts to be glad for them, Posy, even though our own beloved is no longer with us," Granny had said.

Perhaps I was a bad person, but when the village had gathered together to celebrate VE day in the church hall, I hadn't been able to feel anything in my heart except a big, numb lump of nothing.

Little had changed after VE Day, although Granny started traveling regularly to London, citing the fact that there was "paperwork" to attend to. The paperwork must have been very tiresome indeed, because Granny always came home looking dreadfully gray and exhausted. I vividly remembered her returning from the last visit she had made. Rather than arriving back and coming to find me immediately with some small treat she had brought back from London, she'd disappeared straight to her room and had not emerged for three days. When I'd asked to see her, Daisy had told me she had caught a bad chill and did not wish me to catch it.

I'd decided then and there that if I ever had children, even if I was dying of something dreadfully infectious like cholera, I would still let them in to see me. Grown-ups that you loved, barricaded behind closed doors, were so awfully unsettling for a child's constitution. And I had experienced my fair share of it over the years.

Eventually, Granny had emerged, and I only just managed to stifle a gasp at the amount of weight she had lost. It was as if *she* had been suffering from cholera. Her skin looked waxy and her eyes had somehow sunken deeper into their sockets. She looked very old and not at all jolly, as she used to.

"Darling Posy," she'd said, forcing a smile that didn't reach her eyes as we'd shared a cup of tea by the fire in the sitting room. "I do apologize for my absences in the past few months. You will be pleased to know they are at an end. Everything is done with and there is no need for me to return to London now—if ever. I simply *loathe* that godless city, don't you?" she'd shuddered.

"I've never been, Granny, so I couldn't say."

"No, although I am sure you will visit one day, so I mustn't spoil it for you, but it does not hold good memories for me..."

Her poor, sunken eyes had drifted away from me, then snapped back, with what I felt was false brightness.

"Anyway, what is done is done. And now it is time to look to our future. I have a surprise coming for you, Posy."

"Do you? How nice," I'd said, not sure quite how to respond to this new, different Granny. "Thank you."

"I won't spoil it by telling you what it is, but I thought you should have something of your father's to remember him by. Something...practical. Now then, would you throw another log on the fire? This chill has crept into my bones."

I'd done so, and after a chat about what I had been up to since she'd been away—which was nothing much, although I could have told her that Daisy had been entertaining Bill in the kitchen more often than I thought was necessary—Granny had said she was exhausted and needed to go up for a rest.

"Come here and give your Granny a hug first."

And I had, and even though she looked so frail, her arms had gripped me tightly, as if she would never let me go.

"Well now," she'd said as she stood up. "Onwards and upwards, Posy. That's the way forward."

Three days later, a small van had arrived outside the front door. I'd wandered into the hall and seen a brawny man heaving big boxes into the study. Granny had appeared beside me as I looked up at her askance. She'd laid a hand on my shoulder.

"They're all for you, darling girl. Go and see, and then you can arrange them to your liking on the bookshelves. I've cleared enough space to make room for them."

I went into the study and tore the thick tape off the top of one of the boxes. And there inside, covered in their familiar soft brown leather, were my beloved *Encyclopaedia Britannica*s.

"They will keep you occupied on a dark Cornish night," Granny had said as I'd lifted one out and placed it on my knee. "I bought them all for your father, every Christmas and birthday. I know he would want you to have them."

"Thank you, Granny, thank you so much," I'd said, as my hands caressed the leather and my eyes glittered with tears. "It's the best thing I could possibly have to remember him by."

Over the next year, I'd watched Granny slowly begin to revert to how she used to be. Even though I often saw sadness in her eyes, I was glad that she was returning to herself as she bustled about the house and, as winter subsided, applied her energy to the large expanse of garden behind the house, which was fast awakening from its months of hibernation. When I wasn't at school or up on the Moor with my friends, I'd taken to helping her. As we worked, she taught me about the various species we were planting or tending. In the old lichen-covered greenhouse, she showed me how to germinate and nurture seeds. She'd even presented me with my very own set of gardening tools, contained in a sturdy willow basket.

"Whenever I feel sad," she'd told me as she'd handed them over, "I dig into the rich earth and think of the miracles it produces. It never fails to lift my spirits. I hope that you too may feel the same."

And to my surprise I *had*, and I'd found myself spending more and more of my spare time either getting my hands dirty or poring over Granny's gardening books and magazines. Daisy took me under her wing in the kitchen and I spent many happy hours baking and rolling pastry. I had also continued with my botanical drawings, as Daddy had asked me to.

One afternoon at the end of March, Granny had invited the vicar to tea to organize the annual Easter egg hunt (which was always held in our garden, because it was the largest in the village). I couldn't help feeling a surge of pride as the day of the egg hunt dawned and all those who took part commented on how well cared for and pretty the garden looked.

It was around about that time that I'd started getting postcards from Maman in Paris. Apparently, she was singing again. There wasn't a lot of room to say much more on a postcard, but she'd sounded happy. Which I'd tried to be glad about, but given the *inner* Posy was as hollow as an empty coconut shell (despite the *outer* Posy pretending she was just the same as she always had been), I'd found it almost impossible. Granny was always talking about "generosity of spirit," and as my own couldn't be generous to my own mother, I'd decided I must be a very horrible person. The truth was, I wanted her to be as miserable as I was. To find it impossible to be "happy" when the person we had both loved most in the world had gone forever.

In the end, I'd confided my feelings to Katie, who, despite never having ventured further than Bodmin (and that was only once, to a great-aunt's funeral) and being completely clueless during lessons, possessed a great deal of common sense.

"Aye, well, maybe your Ma is pretendin' to be happy just like you are, Posy. You thought of that?" she'd asked me.

And with that one sentence, everything had become a little easier. Maman and I were both playing a game of 'pretend'; Maman was throwing herself into her singing just as I was throwing myself into my lessons and my very own patch of garden, which Granny had recently given me to nurture and plant whatever I wished. We were both doing our best to forget while we still so painfully remembered. I also thought of Granny, and how she was striving to get back to normal. I only knew she was still hurting about Daddy's death because of the sadness I saw sometimes in her eyes. I couldn't *see* Maman's eyes, and after all, if Granny had written me a postcard from a foreign country, I'm sure she would have written something jolly too.

The postcards had become more infrequent in the last two years, and then, a year ago, I'd had one from Rome with a picture of the Coliseum on the front of it, telling me she was taking a "*petite vacance.*"

"More like a *grande vacance,*" I complained again to my reflection in the mirror as I twisted my impossibly unruly hair into a plait. I'd tried not to mind that she hadn't visited me once since she'd left just after the news of Daddy's death, but I couldn't help minding sometimes. She was my mother, after all, and it had been five long years.

"At least you have Granny," I added to my reflection. "*She* is your mother now."

And as I went downstairs to join her for supper and talk about this boarding school she'd mentioned, I realized it was true.

"Right, that's everything," Daisy declared as she closed the lid to the shiny leather trunk Granny had had sent from London, along with the bottle-green school uniform, which I personally thought was hideous. But then I supposed it was probably meant to be hideous. It also didn't help that it had been ordered without me trying it on, so every item drowned me.

"Room for growth, Posy," Granny had said as I'd stood in front of the mirror in a blazer whose arms covered my fingertips and had enough room across the shoulders for Katie to climb in with me too. "Both your mother and father were tall, and doubtless you will shoot up like a young sapling in the next few months. In the meantime, Daisy will tack the sleeves and the skirt, so you can let them down easily when you need to."

Daisy bustled around me, pinning the blazer sleeves and the hem of the kilt, which currently brushed the top of the black leather lace-up brogues, which felt—and looked—like I was wearing boats on my feet. It was quite hard for her to "bustle" actually, as she had an enormous bump in her stomach and was due to give birth any day. I was desperate to see the baby before I left for school, but it became more unlikely as each day passed.

Out of the three of us, Daisy was the one who had found true contentment on the Cornish moors. She and Bill—Granny's odd-job man—had married two years ago and the entire village had attended the wedding, as they did for any celebration, or, for that matter, wake. Daisy now lived with Bill in the cosy gardener's cottage which stood in the grounds of the main house. The pale, whey-faced girl I'd known at Admiral House had blossomed into a pretty young woman. *It is obviously true love that makes one beautiful*, I thought, and as I looked at myself decked out in bottle-green in the mirror, I wished I would find some myself.

Over our last supper together later that day, eaten outside in the balmy late August evening, I asked Granny if she was going to be all right on her own.

"I mean, with Daisy about to have her baby, and me gone, how will you manage?"

"Goodness, Posy, please don't write me off just yet. I'm only in my fifties, you know. And I will still have Bill and Daisy—having a baby does not mean that one becomes incapacitated. Besides, it will be wonderful to have a little one about the place. New life always lightens the spirits."

As long as that baby doesn't replace me in your affections, I thought, but didn't say.

The next morning, as I climbed into the ancient Ford motor car for Bill to drive me to Plymouth station, I had to hold back my tears as I kissed Granny goodbye. At least she didn't sob all over me as Daisy had done, although her eyes certainly looked brighter than usual.

"Take care of yourself, darling girl. Write to me regularly and let me know what you've been up to."

"I will."

"Work hard, and do your father—and me—proud."

"I promise I'll do my best, Granny. Goodbye."

As Bill drove me along the drive, I looked behind me. And knew that, whatever the pain I had suffered since arriving here five years ago, the small community I'd lived in had protected me. And I would miss it dreadfully.

Boarding school was...*fine*. I mean, if one ignored the frosts that formed on the inside of the dormitory windows as winter drew in, the utterly inedible food and the "PE" that they made us take in the gym three times a week. "Perfectly execrable," I called it, because it was. A lot of gawky teenage girls trying to hop over a pommel horse had to be one of the most inelegant sights possible. On the other hand, I took to hockey—which I had never played before, much to the horror of Miss Chuter, the burly games mistress—like the proverbial duck to water. I had a "low center of gravity," apparently, which I felt was just a euphemism for having two feet planted firmly on the ground, but it suited the game and I soon became our team's top scorer. I also excelled at the cross-country runs, having spent most of the past five years outdoors on the Cornish moors.

This propensity for games at least helped the fact that the other girls thought me far too keen on lessons—which I was—and nicknamed me "Swotty." Just as they didn't understand my enthusiasm for academia, I couldn't see why they weren't lapping up the knowledge that was freely offered every day. After years of learning most of what I knew from the hallowed pages of the *Encyclopaedia Britannica* (Granny had of course been right about Miss Brennan struggling to keep up with me), to have a living, breathing human being bringing subjects to life was simply wonderful. Used as I was to being an only child, and the odd one out, even when I'd been "in" a group with Katie and my other Cornish friends, the fact that the girls at my new school mostly viewed me with suspicion did not hurt me the way it might have done. It helped that there was another girl in my year who was also thought of as strange, due to her passion for ballet dancing. And that created a bond between us.

Like was said to be drawn to like, yet, beyond our supposed mutual strangeness, Estelle Symons could not have been less akin to me if she'd tried. Where I was already tall compared to my classmates, solidly built and, as I saw it, rather plain, Estelle had a tiny, delicate frame, and even when she walked, she reminded me of a wisp of gossamer floating on a breeze. To add to that, she had a thick mane of shiny blonde hair and big, china-blue eyes. Whilst I spent any free time I had in the library, Estelle was in the gymnasium, practising her leg-lifts and twirling in front of the mirror. She told me she came from a "bohemian" family; her mother was an actress, her father a well-known novelist.

"They've sent me here because my mother is always travelling to some theater or other, and Pups—my father—always has his nose in a manuscript, so I was in the way." Estelle had shrugged pragmatically.

She had also confided in me that one day, she would become a famous ballerina like Margot Fonteyn, who I had never heard of, but of whom Estelle spoke in hushed tones. Due to her obsession with dancing, Estelle had little time for her schoolwork, so I did my best to finish her prep for her, making sure I added spelling and grammar mistakes so it looked like her own work. Alongside her ethereal physicality, Estelle had a dreamy, "otherworld" personality to match it. I sometimes thought that if they ever made a ballet about a beautiful, blonde-haired fairy, they would choose Estelle to dance her.

"You are so clever, Posy," she said with a sigh as I handed her back her mathematics workbook. "I wish I had brains like you."

"Personally, I think it must take a lot of brains to remember all those dancing steps and which way to move your arms."

"Oh, that's easy; my body just knows what to do, a bit like your brain knowing the answer to an equation. Every human has their own unique talent, you know. We are all blessed."

The more I got to know Estelle, I realized that her being a dunce at lessons was simply because she wasn't interested in them, since she was actually very bright when it came to the world—and far more philosophical than I was. To me, a spade really was a spade, whereas, to Estelle, it could be something far more imaginative. She made me think back to the days when Daddy would call me "Princess of the Fairies," with him as king, and I realized that I had lost that magic somewhere along the way.

As autumn and winter passed and we all returned for the summer term, the two of us would lie in a shady spot under an oak tree and share confidences.

"Do you think much about boys?" Estelle asked me one sunny June afternoon.

"No," I answered honestly.

"Surely you want to get married one day?"

"I've never thought about it, probably because I can't imagine any boy wanting me. I'm not beautiful and feminine like you, Estelle." I looked down at my pale freckly legs, stretched out in front of me, thinking they were both reminiscent of the tree trunk I was leaning against, and then at Estelle's perfect ones, tapering down to a pair of elegant thin ankles, that Maman had always said were a thing that men loved. (She had them, of course, unlike her daughter.)

"Oh, Posy, why do you say such things about yourself?! You have a fit, athletic body that doesn't have an ounce of fat on it, gorgeous hair the color of autumn leaves and a lovely pair of big, brown eyes," Estelle chided me. "And that's apart from that brain of yours, of course, which is a match for any man's."

"Maybe they won't like that either," I sighed. "It seems to me that men want women to have their babies and make their homes comfortable, but never express an opinion on anything much at all. I think I would make a very bad wife, because I would have to correct my husband if he was wrong. Besides," I confessed, "I want a career."

"So do I, darling Posy, but I can't see how that means I wouldn't be able to have a husband too."

"Well, I can't think of one woman I know who is married and has a job of her own. Even my own mother gave up singing when she married my father. And look at the schoolmistresses here: all single, the lot of them."

"Perhaps they bat for the other side," Estelle giggled.

"What do you mean by that?"

"Don't you know?"

"No, so stop talking in riddles."

"It means that perhaps they like each other."

"What?! A girl likes a girl?" I said, astounded at such a concept.

"Oh, Posy, you might be clever, but you can be so naïve. You must have noticed how Miss Chuter moons around over Miss Williams."

"No," I replied abruptly. "I don't believe that can be true. It's...well, it's simply against the laws of nature."

"Don't get botany mixed up with *human* nature. And just because the subject isn't in one of your fat encyclopedias doesn't mean it doesn't exist. It does," Estelle said resolutely. "And men liking men too. Even you must have heard about Oscar Wilde, put in prison for his relationship with a man."

"You see? It's illegal, because it isn't natural."

"Oh Posy, don't be such a square! In the theatrical world, such things are standard. And besides, surely it's not their fault? People should be allowed to be who they are, whatever society's rules, don't you think?"

And, thanks to Estelle, I *did* begin to think. Not just about photosynthesis and chemical compounds as I had done up to now, but about the way that the world had laid down rules of what it believed was acceptable and unacceptable behavior. And I began to question it.

I was growing up.

November 1954

"So Posy, we need to discuss your future plans."

Miss Sumpter, the headmistress, gave me a smile from the other side of her desk. However, I only saw it out of the corner of my eye, as every time I'd looked at her over the past five years, my eyes were immediately drawn to the wart that sat to the left of her chin and the long gray hairs that sprouted from it. For the umpteenth time, I wondered why she didn't use a pair of scissors to cut them off, because the rest of her face was actually quite pleasant to look at.

"Yes, Miss Sumpter," I replied automatically.

"You leave us next summer, and now is the time that you must start thinking of applying to university. I am presuming that this is what you want?"

"I...well, yes. Where would you advise?"

"Given your academic prowess, I feel you should aim for the top and give Cambridge a shot."

"Golly," I said, feeling a sudden lump come to my throat. "My father went there. Do you really think I'd have a chance? I understand the competition for places—especially for women—is intense."

"It is indeed, but you are an outstanding student. And we must add that your father attended to your letter of application. The old school tie never does any harm," she smiled.

"Even if it is to be worn by a woman?" I said wryly.

"Quite. As I am sure you already know, Girton and Newnham are the two established female colleges, but I wonder if you have heard about New Hall? It opened this September with only sixteen students, and the tutor of the college, Miss Rosemary Murray, is an old friend of mine. It would mean I could put in a good word, although your admission would solely depend on passing the three-hour written exam. Last year, four hundred young women applied for just sixteen places. Competition is stiff, Posy, but I honestly believe you stand a very good chance of gaining entry. I'm presuming you would wish to study a science?"

"Yes, I'd like to take botany," I replied firmly.

"Well, Cambridge is renowned for its Botany School. You could not do any better."

"I must of course discuss this with my grandmother before I go any further, but I'm sure she will be very supportive. Though of course, I might not get in, Miss Sumpter."

"One doesn't achieve anything if one doesn't try, and out of all the pupils I have had through my doors, you are amongst the most gifted. I have every faith in you, Posy. Now, off you go and enjoy Christmas."

Although the anticipation I felt at returning home to Cornwall—especially for Christmas—no longer prevented me sleeping for a week before due to the uncontrollable fizz of excitement in my tummy, it was still a special moment as Bill drove us through our tiny village. A mist had begun to descend, and the darkening sky indicated dusk was imminent, even though it was just past three o'clock. I smiled with pleasure as I saw the colored lights on the magnificent pine tree that sat in Granny's front garden. She had told me her own grandparents had planted it one Christmas in the hope it would take root. It had, and now the entire village gathered for the traditional switch-on of the lights on the day of the winter solstice.

"Darling Posy, welcome home!"

Granny stood on the doorstep, arms outstretched, but before I could reach them, a small boy pushed past her and hurtled towards me.

"Posy! It Christmas! He's coming!"

"I know, Ross. Isn't it exciting?!" I leant down and took the boy in my arms, kissing the top of his head, which was covered with straw-colored hair just like Daisy's, and carried him inside.

Daisy was hovering in the hall, waiting to greet me. Ross wriggled in my arms to get down, desperate to show me a painting of Father Christmas he'd made that hung on one of the kitchen cupboards.

"Miss Posy can see your picture later, Ross," Daisy chided her son affectionately. "She's had that long a journey, I'm sure she just wants to sit in front of the fire awhile and have a nice cup of tea and a scone."

"But..."

"No buts," Daisy steered him towards the kitchen. "Come and help me make the tea."

I followed Granny into the sitting room, where a cheerful fire was burning. The inside tree had been erected in its pot of soil, but had not yet been decorated.

"I thought I'd leave you the pleasure of doing that," Granny smiled. "I know how much you love it. Now, come and sit down and tell me all about your final Michaelmas term."

Over tea and scones, I told Granny all about the past three months. She had been so very proud when I'd been made Head Girl in September.

"I haven't liked all the responsibility that has come from it, though; having to dole out punishments to some of my friends has been the hardest bit. I caught Mathilda Mayhew smoking in the woods at the start of term. I let her off because she promised me she wouldn't do it again, but she did, and I had to say something. She was gated for three weeks and she now loathes me," I sighed.

"Yes, but has it stopped others who might have been tempted to do the same?"

"It has, yes, or at least, the girls are far more careful to make sure I don't catch them. But all that means is that they steer clear of me and don't let me in on their fun. It doesn't help that I now have a room to myself, either. I feel isolated, Granny, and school hasn't been half as much fun since."

"As you're learning, with responsibility comes all sorts of challenges and hard decisions, Posy. I am sure the experience will fit you out for the future. Now, tell me more about applying to Cambridge."

So I told Granny about the new ladies' college and how Miss Sumpter thought I had a good shot at winning one of the few places available. I watched her eyes fill with tears.

"Your father would be so terribly proud of you, Posy, as am I."

"Hold on, Granny, I haven't got in yet!"

"No, but just the fact she thinks you might is enough. You're growing into a very special human being, and I am so very proud of you."

It was sweet of Granny to say so, but as the Christmas season progressed and we attended the traditional village get-togethers, I realized that, even here at home, in the community where I'd done a lot of my growing up, my "specialness" had definitely affected my friendships here too. Katie, who was normally knocking on the door the moment she saw Bill's car pass the front of her family's cottage, didn't appear until Christmas Eve, at the drinks party Granny always threw for the village. At first glance, I hardly recognised her, for she'd had her gorgeous red hair cut off and permed into a "poodle cut," which (I thought cruelly) made her look rather like one. She wore a lot of makeup, the pancake foundation forming a tidemark around her jawline, which, with the naturally pale skin of her neck beneath it, made her look as though she was wearing a mask.

"You should come round one evening and I'll do your face up like mine," she offered as we stood outside in the cold whilst she dragged on a cigarette. "You got lovely eyes, Posy, and with some black liner, it would really make them stand out."

She told me how she'd just got a job as a trainee hairdresser in Bodmin. She was living with a relative there and had met a young man called Jago.

"His da owns the butcher's shop in Bodmin an' he'll take over the business one day. There's a lot of money in meat," she assured me. "So what've you been up to, Posy? Still studying at that school o' yours?"

I confirmed I was and that I was hoping to get into Cambridge University, which she'd never heard of.

"Judas, seems to me you'll still be at your lessons when you're an old maid! Don't you want to have some fun? Go out dancing with a lad sometimes?"

I tried to explain that I found lessons fun, but I knew she didn't understand. I saw her a couple more times after that before she had to return to Bodmin, but it was blatantly obvious we had nothing left in common. It made me terribly sad. And on top of that, maybe it was my imagination, but the little household I'd once felt very much at the center of seemed to have motored on without me. The new focus was on little Ross—who was, to be fair about it, enchanting— and even Granny seemed to spend more time with him than she did with me. Once Christmas had passed, I actually found myself counting the days until I was back at school.

Yet you couldn't wait to come home, Posy, I thought to myself as I went for a solitary walk across the moor one afternoon. *You don't belong here either...*

So, where do I belong? I asked myself as I trudged back home, feeling rather self-indulgently like the quasi-orphan I'd become since Maman had left me here almost ten years ago and never bothered to return.

The truth was, I just didn't know.

The day before I left to return to school, I received an airmail letter, postmarked Rome, in Italy. It was my mother's writing, so I took myself upstairs to my bedroom to read it.

My dearest Posy,

Forgive me for not writing sooner, but the past year has been such a whirlwind and I didn't want to say anything until I was absolutely certain of my plans. The truth is, chérie, that I have met an absolutely delightful man by the name of Alessandro. He is an Italian and a Count to boot!—and he has asked me to marry him. This will happen in early June—the most glorious time of the year here—and of course, I want you to attend as my very special maid of honor. I will send more details and a proper invitation for both you and your grandmother of course, but before that, there is the question of having a dress made for you.

I know you are still at school, but I was thinking that perhaps, sometime in your Easter break, you could fly out to have a fitting and also meet darling Alessandro. You will love him, I know. We will base ourselves in his palazzo in Florence— imagine a much warmer and older version of Admiral House (some of the frescoes date from the thirteenth century) with cypress trees in place of the chestnut trees. It is utter heaven and your Maman is currently the happiest woman on the planet.

Posy, I do know how you loved your Papa—as did I—but the past ten years have been so miserable and lonely as I have grieved his loss. So I hope you can find it in your heart to be happy for me. We must all move on and even though I will never forget your darling Papa, I feel I deserve a little joy before it is too late.

Please let me know when your Easter holidays are, then I can book you a seat on the aeroplane, which I promise, is an adventure in itself.

I cannot wait to see you in person and hear all your news. Granny tells me you are a star pupil at school.

A million kisses, chérie,

Maman

A few seconds was all it took to catapult me out of the house and have me running towards the moor, where I screamed my head off in a place no one could hear. Tears spurted out of my eyes as I yowled like I imagined the Beast of Bodmin Moor would do at the horror of what I'd just read.

"How *dare* she?! How *dare* she?!" I cried to the rough grass and the skies over and over again. Those three words encompassed all the wrongs she had done me: firstly, and worst of all, expecting me—Daddy's beloved daughter—to be "happy" that she had found such a new and wonderful love. Secondly, after not even bothering to visit her daughter for so many years when I—especially at the start—had been distraught and grieving so terribly, to just assume that she could simply order me to board a plane to have a fitting for a *dress*, when I would be in the midst of studying hard for my final school examinations and my Cambridge entrance test, was just so dreadfully selfish. And the June wedding itself—had she not even bothered to *think* that it was the actual time when my exams took place?!

And...on top of that, my eighteenth birthday was also in June. I had overheard Granny whispering to Daisy in the kitchen about some form of celebration and it had crossed my mind then that Maman might—just might—return to England for it, but it was obvious that she was so busy planning for her own celebration that her daughter's eighteenth birthday had never entered her head.

"Of course it hasn't, Posy! Golly, she's only spoken to you by telephone a handful of times since she left," I said out loud, pacing back and forth across the coarse moorland grass. "What kind of mother does that make her?!" I shouted to the gray clouds scudding across the sky.

I sat down abruptly, the emotion of the moment turning my legs to jelly as I, Posy—no longer the frightened little girl I had been, but Posy, the almost-woman—finally accepted the truth. Over the years, even if the thought had fluttered through my consciousness, I hadn't allowed it to enter my head, for fear of what it would mean: that my mother didn't love me. Or at least, she loved herself more than she loved me.

"She's a *terrible* mother," I told the moors, anguish in my words and my heart. I realized that even in the old days at Admiral House, she had left me mainly to the care of Daisy. Even though it was quite normal for a wealthy family to have staff to look after their children, I tried to remember a single occasion when Maman had come to collect me from school, or to my bedroom to kiss me goodnight, or read me a bedtime story. However hard I searched through the mists of time, not one of those occasions came to mind.

"She was never cruel to you, Posy," I told myself, wary of how easily I could slip over into self-indulgence, "or hurt you physically. And you were always fed and clothed," I added for good measure.

And I was, and when Daddy had been there to give me all his laughter and love, I'd had everything I'd needed; like the seedlings on my windowsills at home and school, with the right balance of sunlight, water and *nurture*, I had blossomed.

I then thought about Granny, and how wonderful she had been, stepping into the role of my mother, and immediately, I realized how lucky I was. Nobody's life was perfect and even if I had an absentee mother (who had probably been absent from the start) I had to count my blessings. Not everyone was born with the maternal instinct that made it easy to care for and love their child; I thought of animals in the wild who would abandon their young at a few hours old. Maman had certainly not done that.

"Posy, you have to accept her as she is," I told myself firmly, "because she will never change, and it will only cause you pain to think she might when she won't."

On the walk back home, I gave myself a good talking-to, knowing from what I'd read of psychology that it wasn't only the things that happened to one that mattered, it was often how you *dealt* with them.

"From now on, you must see Maman as an auntie, or maybe a godmother," I told myself and my psyche. "Then it won't hurt any longer."

However, there was still the problem of the Italian wedding.

"How can I possibly go, Granny?" I asked her the next morning over breakfast when I'd had time to calm down.

"I am sure if you write and explain that it is right in the middle of your final exams, she will understand that you can't attend. And I must tell her I cannot go either."

"Are you busy too?"

"I...yes," Granny replied after a slight pause. "June is always a busy month in the village, what with the fête to organize."

I understood then that Granny didn't want to go either—the fête wasn't until the end of the month and it hardly took more than a few days to hang some bunting around the garden and set up the cake stall. It made me feel better somehow, and also made me wonder whether, if I hadn't had a valid excuse, I would have gone anyway. I certainly had no interest in meeting Maman's new husband and raising a glass to their "love." How could I? And more importantly, how could *she* think I would? Maybe if we had been closer, spent time together in the past ten years and I'd seen her grieve in person for Daddy, it might have been different, but this bolt from the blue had only ignited anger inside me.

It took me ten drafts to compose a letter back to her. I asked Granny to read it before I sealed it and sent it off.

"It's very good, Posy. The best thing on these occasions is simply to state the facts calmly and that is what you have done."

So I sealed it, popped it into an airmail envelope and took it down to Laura, the village postmistress. Then I packed my trunk and set off back to school for the most important six months of my life.

Vervain
(Verbena officinalis)

Chapter 9

Admiral House
October 2006

Posy was in the middle of pruning the roses when she saw a Red Admiral alight on the purple flowers of the vervain, supping on the last of the nectar before the impending winter. Its wings were open to display its striking black, red and white pattern, and Posy watched it, fascinated, its presence taking her back to another, long-ago moment...She jumped when she heard her mobile ringing from her trouser pocket, and just managed to whip off her gardening glove to answer it before it stopped.

"Hello?"

"Mum, it's Nick."

"Nick! Darling boy, how are you?"

"I'm fine, Mum, you?"

"Yes, I'm very well indeed, Nick, thank you."

"Listen, are you doing anything on Wednesday? I thought I might drive up and take you out for lunch."

"But..." It took a few minutes for Posy's brain to compute this information. "Nick, are you saying you're in England?"

"Yes, London, to be precise. I've had some business I wanted to sort out before I came to see you. I've done that now."

Posy was torn between sheer happiness that Nick was back on British terra firma and maternal jealousy that he'd not let her know until now. "Well of course, I would absolutely love to see you."

"Fantastic. I'll be there by noon and we'll go to a restaurant of your choice. I've got a lot to tell you."

And I've got a lot to tell you, mused Posy silently. "That would be splendid."

"Okay, Mum, all news when I see you. Bye."

Posy leant back in the weak October sun, thinking with joy of Nick, home after all these years...

She was then aware of the sound of a car snaking up the long drive towards the front of the house.

"Dammit! Who on earth can that be?" she asked herself, eager to get the roses pruned before the winter frost set in. The Red Admiral, perhaps irritated by all the noise, had fluttered off.

She decided it was probably the nice chap who brought the parish magazine round once a month. She'd normally ask him in for a cup of tea, but today, she'd pretend she was out and he could simply push it though the letter box.

"Posy?"

She jumped. The voice was very close and she looked up to see Freddie striding towards her.

"Hello," she said, shielding her eyes from the sun and, despite herself, wishing she'd put some lipstick on earlier.

"Forgive me for barging in on you like this. I did knock a number of times—the front doorbell doesn't work, by the way—but I saw your car and took a guess you were in the garden."

"I'm...it's fine, and yes, I must get that damned bell fixed," she agreed.

"It's a beautiful house, Posy. I presume it's Queen Anne from the symmetrical perfection of it."

"It is, yes."

There was a short silence as Posy waited for Freddie to explain why he was here. She certainly wasn't going to ask.

"I...Posy, do you fancy a cup of tea?"

"No, but I could certainly do with a glass of water." She stood up and watched Freddie surveying the gardens around him.

"My God, Posy! This is quite incredible! Have you really made this all by yourself?"

"Apart from the laying of the pathways and the gardener who mows the lawns and does the trimming and weeding in the summer, I have, yes. Mind you, it's taken almost twenty-five years. I started when the boys went to boarding school."

"Do you ever open it to the public?"

"I used to, yes, during the annual village fête. I've also had a couple of photographers here taking pictures for their design magazines, which was gratifying, but to be honest, I was only thinking this morning that it needs far more attention than I have the energy to give it these days. I've created a monster that needs to be fed and watered constantly."

"Well, it's a glorious monster, Posy, however demanding," he said as they walked along the path back to the house, passing the copper beech, still resplendent in its glorious colors.

Freddie suddenly halted in his tracks, looked to his left, and pointed. "What is that building?"

"The Folly. My father used it as his den. He collected butterflies and I used to help catch them—I thought he just studied them and let them go. When I managed to sneak inside, I was horrified to see them hanging on the walls, all dead, with great pins stuck through their middles. I haven't been near the place since," she shuddered.

Freddie was silent for a while as his gaze rested on the building, then on Posy. He sighed heavily. "No. Well, I don't blame you."

"Now then," Posy could feel the atmosphere was heavy with ghosts from the past, and it was her fault. "Let's go inside and I'll make you a nice cup of tea."

She busied herself around the kitchen as Freddie sat silently at the old oak table. She was positive Health and Safety would probably insist on it being destroyed, due to the amount of bacteria that had collected in its wooden grooves over the years, but she had very happy memories of lunches and dinners eaten at it as a family.

"Are you quite all right, Freddie?" she asked him as she put a cup of tea in front of him. "You seem awfully subdued."

"Sorry, Posy, perhaps seeing you has taken me back to a different moment in my life. And made me realize how old I am," he added with a shrug.

"I'm sad my presence depresses you," she said as she sat down opposite him with a glass of water. "Slice of cake?"

"No thank you, I'm trying to watch my waistline. But really, Posy, I'm thrilled that we have been reacquainted after all these years."

"You don't look it," Posy said brusquely, deciding she just needed to be honest. "Won't you tell me what's up? We were having such a lovely lunch and then suddenly you upped and left."

"I...look, Posy, the truth is," Freddie sighed heavily, "there was a reason back then and a reason now why I can't...pursue the relationship I'd so very much like to have with you. And it has absolutely nothing to do with you. It's all...*me*. Putting it simply, I have...issues."

A hundred thoughts floated through Posy's head: *Is he a closet gay? Does he have a mental disorder like bipolar? Is there another woman lurking in the background...?*

"Why don't you tell me what it is? Then maybe I can decide whether or not it's important."

"I'm afraid I can't do that, Posy," Freddie replied gravely. "And now I feel very guilty for even coming here. I swore to myself I wouldn't, but...seeing you again, it rekindled the feelings I had for you all those years ago and, well, I just couldn't keep away."

"Talk about mixed messages, Freddie," Posy sighed. "I do wish you would just tell me what it is."

"Could you accept I can't, for now, anyway? Because if you can, then I do think there is no reason why we can't have a friendship, at least."

Posy realized that all she could do was agree. If she said that she couldn't, it would make her sound either churlish, or needy for more than he said he could give her.

"That's fine by me," she shrugged.

Finally, a smile crossed Freddie's face. "Then I am a happy man. May I take you out to dinner tomorrow night, if I promise not to rush off towards the end of it like some blushing virgin who thinks his virtue is about to be stolen?"

That made Posy chuckle and eased the tension somewhat. "Yes. Dinner would be lovely, thank you."

By the time Freddie had left, it was too dark to go back into the garden. She made herself beans on toast, then went into the morning room, which had served as the sitting-room for years as the drawing room was simply too large to heat. She knelt to light the first fire of the autumn, then sat in her favorite chair and watched the flames jump in the grate.

"Why is life so complicated?" she asked herself with a sigh. It seemed ridiculous that, with both of them around seventy years of age, there had to be "issues" that precluded a proper relationship between them. Still, she thought, it was nice to think of dinner tomorrow night, even if Freddie had made it obvious there would be no goodnight kiss on the menu afterwards.

"Perhaps he simply doesn't fancy me, and maybe he never did," she said to the flames. "Which was maybe what the problem was in the first place. Yes, I'll bet that's what it is, but he just can't bear to tell me."

What little confidence Posy had garnered from Freddie's recent attentions, plus the haircut and the jeans, floated away into the ether.

"Stop it, Posy!" she told herself firmly. Instead, she would focus on the fact that her darling Nick was due here in a couple of days' time after ten long years.

Chapter 10

Amy listened to the wind howling round the thin walls of the house. She could hear, in the dead of the night, the waves crashing onto the shore only a quarter of a mile away from her. The other residents of the houses on Ferry Road had long since left for warmer, more substantial shelter.

Next door, Sara coughed in her sleep. Amy shifted restlessly, knowing she must take her daughter to the doctor's tomorrow. The cough had been going on for too long now.

Sam was snoring next to her, oblivious to the anxious thoughts keeping his wife awake. He was coming in later and later these days, citing his heavy workload as the reason, and she made sure she was in bed feigning sleep before he arrived home.

There was no doubt their marriage was going through a crisis. And it wasn't as if she could blame their current circumstances, either. They'd been here before, struggling for money time and again when one of Sam's deals hadn't worked out. Perhaps not as dramatically as this, but still, their life together had never been a bed of roses.

Everything was bloody, bloody awful. The thought of spending a long winter in this ghastly house was almost unbearable. She'd once believed it didn't matter where they lived or how much money they had as long as they were together, but actually it *did*, because it made life so much harder. She was tired of putting on a brave face to the world, tired of defending herself from her husband's anger when he was drunk and, on top of that, exhausted from trying to do her job and be a good mother to her two children.

Although Sam was lying only a few inches away from her, the emotional chasm between them was vast. And since that night she had met Sebastian Girault on the sea front, Amy had begun to question whether it was just because life was so difficult at present, or, more disturbingly, whether her current feeling of depression was because she just didn't love Sam anymore. In fact, she admitted, he disgusted her when he was drunk, but what could she do?

The following morning, Amy got up as usual, leaving Sam asleep in bed. She drove Jake to school, then sat in the doctor's surgery with a poorly Sara on her knee.

"Sara has a temperature and a nasty cold and cough. A couple of days tucked up in a nice, warm bed should see her better. If she doesn't improve, bring her back and we can think about prescribing some antibiotics, but let's see how some old-fashioned nursing goes down first, shall we?" suggested the doctor.

Amy's heart sank. The news meant she'd have to cancel work for two days, which meant she'd lose two days' money. On the way home, she called in to the hotel and told them she'd be unable to work, then popped quickly next door to the supermarket to get supplies. Sara whined and cried in the front of the cart as Amy sped round the aisles, eager to get her home.

"Darling, I won't be long, I promise. Let's get you some Ribena and..."

As Amy turned fast into the next aisle, her trolley collided with a shopping basket sticking out from the arm of a man.

"Sorry, sorry." Amy's heart sank when she saw who it was.

Sebastian Girault raised an eyebrow at her. "We really must stop meeting like this. People will talk."

"Yes we must. Sorry and excuse me." Amy reached past him for a bottle of Ribena. Sebastian waved her arm away, took a bottle down and placed it in her trolley. Sara began to scream.

"Oh dear, she doesn't sound happy."

"She's not. She's sick. I need to get her home."

"Of course. Bye then."

"Bye."

Sebastian watched as Amy hurried along the aisle and

disappeared round the corner. Even in her dishevelled and obviously anxious state, she really was a beautiful woman. He wondered who she was and where she came from. In this small seaside town, so full of middle-aged and retired gentlefolk, Amy and her youth and beauty stood out like a beacon.

Sebastian was just about to move off when he saw a small pink mitten lying on the floor. Obviously, Amy's daughter had dropped it. He retrieved it and rushed down the aisle after her. He reached the checkout and saw Amy getting into her car outside. By the time he got to the exit, she'd driven off.

Sebastian looked down at the tiny glove. Not quite Cinderella's slipper, but it would have to do.

Amy was actually relieved to return to work a couple of days later. Being stuck in the house with only a sick, whiny four-year-old for company as the rain had poured down outside had just about been the icing on her cake. The only positive had been that she had taken the time to catch up with some housework and laundry and at least their hovel was tidy now, if not welcoming.

"How is Sara?" asked Wendy, the hotel housekeeper, as she passed by the reception desk.

"Much better. It's me that needs the Valium." Amy rolled her eyes.

"There's nothing worse than a poorly little one," Wendy clucked. "Still, she's on the mend now."

Amy's heart sank as Sebastian Girault entered and marched up to the reception desk.

"Yes, it's me again. Sorry, but I came to return something that was yours—or should I say, your daughter's." He placed the tiny mitten on the counter. "She dropped it in the supermarket."

"Oh, er, thanks," said Amy perfunctorily, not looking up to meet his eyes. Sebastian hovered at the desk and Amy realized he had something more to say. "What?"

"I'd like you to come for a drink with me at lunchtime."

"Why?"

"Why not? Because I want you to," he shrugged.

"Mr. Girault"—Amy lowered her voice to prevent being

overheard, her cheeks pink with embarrassment—"you don't even know my name."

"Yes I do. Mrs. Amy Montague," he read from the badge pinned to her blouse. "There you are, you see."

"Exactly. Mrs.," Amy almost hissed. "It may have escaped your notice, but I'm a married woman with two children. I can't just go waltzing off with some strange man for a drink."

"Admittedly, I am strange," Sebastian agreed, "but I haven't quite revealed my ulterior motive, which is that I have been speaking to your friend Marie and—"

"Excuse me, Mr. Girault, I must deal with this customer's bill." Amy indicated the man standing patiently behind Sebastian.

"Of course. I'll see you in the back bar of the Crown at one, then." He smiled at her and left the hotel.

When Amy had finished dealing with her customer, she immediately called Marie.

"Oh," Marie giggled down the line, "it's my fault. I suggested something to him when he was in our office yesterday. He's still looking for somewhere to rent for the winter."

"What did you suggest? That he came and stayed with us on Ferry Road?"

"Ha ha, no. You'll have to go and meet him and find out, won't you?"

"Marie, please, I don't like games, just tell me."

"Okay, okay, keep your hair on. Sebastian is desperate for a place to write this novel of his. So far everything's been too big, too small, too old, too new—you name it—but it's not been right. Anyway, yesterday when he walked in, I'd just had a call from your mother-in-law, Mrs. Montague, to say she is seriously thinking of selling and would I go round and value Admiral House. And I suddenly thought what a fantastic place it would be to write a book."

"So why didn't you suggest Sebastian got straight in touch with Posy rather than involving me?" asked Amy crossly.

"Because I barely know your mother-in-law and it would be unprofessional to start giving out her telephone number to a stranger. I thought it would be better if Sebastian spoke to you and then you could act as a go-between. That's all. I'm sorry if I've done the wrong thing, Amy, really."

"No, no, of course you haven't," Amy said hastily, feeling guilty for her suspicious mind when Marie had obviously acted in all innocence. "It's just that I seem to bump into him at every turn."

"Well, I doubt you'll come to much harm in the back bar of the Crown," said Marie sensibly.

"No, and I'm sorry. Thanks, Marie." Amy put the receiver down and wondered who she was becoming. Her usual sunny demeanour seemed to be deserting her. She was grumpy with everyone, especially the kids. After she met Sebastian, she'd go to the deli and take them home something special for supper.

Sebastian was already ensconced behind a copy of *The Times* in a corner of the bar when Amy arrived. Looking nervously around her, she was relieved to see that, apart from a couple of oldies drinking pints of Adnam's beer, the bar was deserted.

"Hello, Mr. Girault."

He looked up from behind his paper. "Sebastian, please. What can I get you to drink?"

"Nothing, I can't stay. I have some shopping to do." Amy felt breathless, her heart banging against her chest.

"Okay." Sebastian shrugged. "Will you at least sit down, then? I swear I will not ravish you where you stand, madam, that my intentions are honorable," he smiled, his green eyes full of amusement at her discomfort.

"Don't make fun of me," said Amy under her breath. "This is a very small town with a lot of big mouths. I do not want it to get back to my husband that I was seen having a drink with you."

"Well, you've already said you're not having a drink, so that solves half the problem," Sebastian replied rationally. "And I hardly think you'd choose the most popular bar in town in which to have a secret liaison, but anyway...I *am* having a drink. Excuse me."

Amy moved aside to let him pass. She watched him walk to the bar and realized how childish he must think her behavior was. She followed him.

"Sorry, Sebastian. I'll have an orange juice and lemonade, please."

"Coming right up."

Amy went and sat down.

"There we go, one orange juice and lemonade."

"Thank you. I'm sorry for behaving so defensively earlier and just now."

"That's okay. I do know what small towns are like. I used to live in one too. Cheers." Sebastian took a swig of his beer. "No doubt you called your friend Marie—"

"I wouldn't call her a friend exactly," cut in Amy. "I hardly know her."

"Okay, you called Marie to find out what she'd been saying to me."

"Yes I did," nodded Amy.

"And what do you think?"

"I have no idea how Posy would feel about having a tenant." Amy shrugged. "Or how you would feel about Admiral House. It's not exactly luxury accommodation, you know. There's no heating at all upstairs."

"That doesn't bother me. I went to public school so I'm used to freezing my balls off, if you'll pardon the expression. I have to say, having exhausted the rental possibilities, your mother-in-law's place sounds just the job. I need lots of room to pace."

"There's certainly pacing room at Admiral House, that's for sure. Heaps of it," acknowledged Amy. "Well, all I can do is ask Posy and see what she says. How long would it be for?"

"A couple of months to begin with. It's hard to tell how quickly I'll get on."

"You'd certainly be well fed. Posy is a wonderful cook."

"My goodness, I wasn't hoping for board as well, but that would be absolute heaven. I never manage much more than the odd slice of toast and a pot noodle when I'm writing."

"Oh, I'm sure Posy would love to feed you. I know she misses cooking for her family."

"So you are married to one of her sons?"

"Yes. Sam, the eldest."

"She lives alone in the house, does she?"

"Yes, but not for much longer. I think she's finally decided to sell it. Marie said something about going in to value it later this week."

"I'd better get in there soon, then. Will you ring your mother-in-law for me? Put in a good word? Tell her I'm clean, house-trained and willing to pay, but a little on the eccentric side when it comes to the hours I keep."

"I'll do my best." Amy nodded.

"So where do you live? In some equally gracious pile, I presume."

"Hardly," she snorted. "The Montagues are no longer the wealthy family they once were. All that remains of the glory days of the past is Admiral House. Sam has to make his own living."

"I see. And what does your husband do?"

Usually, the word "business entrepreneur" would slip easily from her tongue when people asked her what Sam did. Today, Amy could not bring herself to say it. She shrugged. "Oh, this and that. At the moment he's involved in some property company which, given Sam's track record, will probably go belly-up within the next six months."

"I see."

"Oh God, that sounds so awful, doesn't it?" Amy put her hand to her mouth in shame. "What I meant to say is that Sam's a nice man and I love him to bits, but he really hasn't had much luck in the career department."

"That must have been very difficult for you," acknowledged Sebastian, "especially with children. Didn't you say you had two?"

"Yes. And you're right, it's not all been plain sailing, but then whose life is?"

"No one's, I guess." Sebastian looked at his watch. "I'm afraid I have to go. I have an appointment at half past one. Thanks very much for coming, and if you do get a chance to speak to your mother-in-law in the next couple of days, I'd be very grateful. She could always contact me at The Swan if she'd like to meet me." Sebastian stood up. "Bye, Amy." He nodded at her and left the bar.

Amy sat nursing her St. Clements, suddenly feeling very low. The fact that Sebastian had arranged another appointment half an hour after meeting her made Amy feel even more stupid. He'd obviously had no dishonorable intentions at all.

And why should he? Amy drained her glass and stood up. She was, after all, hardly the kind of woman Sebastian would be used to—or interested in—in his high-flying, literary world.

And there was her, acting like some uptight teenage virgin whose innocence was about to be threatened. Amy shuddered. She was absolutely positive that, after her behavior today, it was the last she would see of Sebastian Girault. She was surprised to find that the thought upset her.

From his vantage point in a hidden corner of the hotel lounge, Sebastian watched Amy leave. Strolling back into the bar to the table she had just vacated, he ordered another pint and settled down to finish his newspaper.

Chapter 11

When Posy saw the car traveling along the drive towards the house, it was all she could do to stop herself running out to meet it then and there. She walked to the front door, opened it, and stood on the porch in an agony of anticipation as the car drew to a halt in front of her.

At last, her tall, handsome son drew his long legs out from behind the wheel and met his mother halfway across the gravel.

He flung his arms around her. "Hello, Mum."

"Nick, my dear, dear boy. It's so wonderful to see you!"

"And you, Mum, and you."

They stood hugging for some time, both trying to compose themselves before speaking further. Nick released Posy and looked at her.

"Mum, you look amazing! If anything, younger than when I left."

"Oh, go on with you, Nick, of course I don't, but thank you anyway."

He put an arm round her shoulder, and they headed towards the house. He stopped short in front of it and looked up. "My memory has served me well. It's exactly as I've remembered it for all these years."

"Good," said Posy as they walked into the hall, "but I'm afraid you'll be able to spot ten years' further wear and tear inside."

As they entered the kitchen with its familiar comforting smell,

Nick was assailed by memories of his childhood. It had always felt to him like a safe haven and he saw it hadn't changed. It still contained the same thick iron saucepans hanging on the wall, the eclectic mishmash of rare and valuable porcelain arranged in no particular order on the dresser, and the huge station clock above the stove that had hung there since he was a toddler.

"Mmmh, what is that smell?" said Nick. "It's not..."

"Yes, liver and bacon, your favorite," said Posy.

"But, Mum, I wanted to take you out, to treat you."

"You told me it was my choice and I wanted to cook for you at home. We can go out any old time. Oh Nick, I just can't tell you how wonderful it is to see you. You haven't changed one jot, either. Coffee, tea, or how about a beer?"

"A beer, please, and yes I have, Mum. I'm thirty-four already and beginning to sprout gray hairs and lines around my eyes," he sighed. "So how are you?" he asked as he took a swig of beer from the bottle she handed him.

"My joints are starting to stiffen up, especially in the morning, but I'm basically hale and hearty." Posy poured herself a glass of wine. "Here's to you and your safe arrival home after all this time." She raised her glass to him.

"I can't tell you how good it feels to be back, sitting in a house that's older than a few years and isn't a bungalow."

"I want to hear everything that happened in Perth. You must have liked it to stay there so long."

"I did and I didn't," said Nick. "It's so completely different to the UK, and Southwold in particular, which is what I needed."

"You know, I always wondered whether you were running away."

"Of course I was, but I'm back now."

"How long for?" Posy hardly dared ask.

"That's the million-dollar question," grinned Nick. "Now, how about some of that liver and bacon? I'm starving."

Posy's appetite had vanished with excitement, so she pushed her own lunch round her plate as she listened while Nick told her all about Perth and brought her up to date with his plan for a shop in London.

She drank a little too much wine, plucking up courage to tell Nick about the impending sale of Admiral House.

"So if you've been investigating shop leases in London, does that mean you might be thinking of staying permanently?" asked Posy.

"Well, the reason I didn't contact you the moment I got back to England was that I wanted to explore things before I saw you. Now I've found the right premises, I've decided I'm going to give it a go."

Posy's face lit up and she clasped her hands together in pleasure. "Darling Nick! I can't tell you how happy that news makes me."

"You'll probably be seeing no more of me than you have in the past ten years, I'll be working so hard," chuckled Nick.

Posy made to clear away the plates but Nick pushed her gently back down into her chair. "I'll do it, Mum."

"Thank you, darling. The rice pud's in the bottom of the stove, if you wouldn't mind retrieving it. So, what was it that made you come to this momentous decision now?" Posy asked as Nick served the rice pudding into two bowls and brought them to the table.

"Oh, all sorts of things," Nick replied as he sat down. "Perhaps the biggest one being that I've realized you can run away as far as you wish, but you can never escape from yourself."

Posy nodded, waiting for him to continue.

"And to be honest, I missed England, especially this." Nick indicated his rice pudding. "I suppose that it just wasn't home."

"But you're glad you went?"

"Absolutely," answered Nick, stirring his spoon around his bowl. "It was an awfully big adventure that had the advantage of making me a shed-load of money."

"You've always been rather good at doing that," agreed Posy. "Everything you touch turns to gold. Completely the opposite to poor old Sam."

Nick's face darkened. "He's still struggling?"

"Yes."

"Well, he does rather bring it on himself, doesn't he, Mum? I mean, one hare-brained scheme after the next. Is that sweet wife of his still hanging in there?"

"Oh yes, Amy's still with him and of course, you haven't met their two children, Jake and Sara. They are delightful."

"They haven't taken after their father, then," said Nick bluntly.

"My goodness, Nick, you talk of Sam with real venom," sighed Posy, sadness in her voice. "He might be rather a disaster when it comes to business, but he's not a bad person, you know."

"I appreciate he's your son, and my brother, but I'm afraid I can't quite agree on that point, Mum."

"By which you mean what?"

Her son sat opposite her, stoically silent.

"Nick, please tell me so that I can try to understand," Posy pleaded. "There's nothing more upsetting for a mother than to see her children at loggerheads."

Nick shook his head. "Look, Mum, it doesn't matter. Let's move on to happier subjects, one of them being the fact that, believe it or not, I've met somebody. Somebody special."

"Nick! You dark horse! Where is she? Who is she? I presume she's Australian?"

"Er, no, that's the odd thing. I actually met her the day I landed back in the UK. She's a friend of my old friends, Paul and Jane Lyons-Harvey. Her name's Tammy, she's extremely beautiful, and she runs a vintage clothes business."

"Goodness, Nick, that's fast."

"I know. Should I be worried?"

Posy thought back to the first moment she'd laid eyes on Freddie and shook her head.

"Definitely not. If the feeling's there, it's there, in my book anyway."

"Well, it's never happened to me so fast before, and it's scary, Mum. I really, *really* like her."

"Good. Then when can I meet her?"

"I was thinking I might bring her up here next week, if she can spare the time. She's busy setting up her business just like I am."

"Oh do, Nick. If you could make it a weekend, then even better. I could invite Sam and Amy...whatever you feel about your brother, you should meet your nephew and niece."

"Of course, Mum. We're all grown-ups after all. And I'd love to see Amy again, and meet the kids of course. So how about next weekend?"

"Perfect!" Posy clapped her hands together. "Do warn your lady friend to bring some warm pyjamas, won't you? The nights are drawing in."

"I will, Mum," he said, looking at the mischievous grin on her face. "Now, before I leave, I'd love to see what more you've done to the garden."

After they'd wandered round the garden and Posy was making tea in the kitchen, Nick walked through the hall towards the morning room. He paused to look up at the massive chandelier and saw how the light showed up the huge cracks stretching across the vast ceiling, the peeling paintwork and the crumbling cornicing. In the morning room, he reached for the heavy black light switch and then moved across to light the fire. The room was very cold, and the smell of damp was noticeable. The beautiful silk curtains he remembered hiding behind as a child were frayed and rotting.

Rather like a silent movie queen ravaged by the passage of time, the sight of this once elegant room reduced to its current state brought a lump to Nick's throat. He busied himself with lighting the fire as his mother entered with a tea tray and her famous Victoria sponge cake.

"There," he said as he crouched in front of the flames. "The first fire I've lit in ten years. Wow, that makes me very happy."

"Have you decided where you're going to live yet?" Posy asked him.

"No, Paul and Jane have said I can stay with them as long as I want. I'll get the business sorted out first and then move on to finding myself a place."

"Well, when you're up next weekend, I'd like you to take a look around the house. Most of the furniture is probably worth nothing, but there might be the odd piece that's worth something."

"Are you stuck for cash, Mum? You know I've told you over and over to ask if you are."

"No, Nick, I'm absolutely fine. The thing is...I really feel that I must think about selling Admiral House. I'll be seventy next year."

Nick stared at her, then at the flames in the fireplace. Eventually he said, "Right."

"Nick, tell me how you feel, please."

"To be honest, Mum, I'm not sure: a mixture of stuff, I suppose.

Sadness, obviously—this was my childhood home, and yours for that matter—but I understand why you're thinking about selling it."

"It's perhaps a little like caring for an old and infirm pet," Posy said sadly. "You love it and will be heartbroken when it's gone, but you know it's for the best. That's how I feel about Admiral House. It needs a new owner, someone who can nurse it back to its former glory. It's gently crumbling to bits and I must do something before it's past the point of no return."

"I understand, Mum."

Nick looked up and saw the large damp patch that had been there since he was a small child. He remembered thinking how it resembled a hippopotamus. Now other patches had joined it, creating a fresco across the ceiling.

"I have a local estate agent coming in to value it next week," Posy told him, "but of course I have to ask you whether you would consider taking it on."

"Firstly, Sam would never forgive me if I did. He's the eldest son and heir, after all. Besides, my life isn't here; plus I'm going to need every penny I have to sink into the business. Sorry, Mum."

"Of course, Nick. I had to ask, that's all."

"Where will you go once you've sold it?"

"I really haven't given it much thought. To a smaller place that doesn't need much upkeep. With at least some form of garden outside," she smiled. "I do hope whoever buys it doesn't demolish this one."

"I'm sure they won't. It's a wonderful feature. You just need some rich city type with a trophy wife and an army of staff to come along and take it on."

"Well, I can't imagine there are too many of those, but we will see."

"As you've always said to me, what will be will be. And now, I'd better be on my way."

Nick stood up, as did Posy, and they walked together to the front hall.

"Before you go, I must give you this." Posy picked up a letter from a side table by the front door and handed it to him. "It was hand-delivered to the gallery yesterday, so what luck that I was seeing you today to pass it on."

Nick took it and looked down at his name written in her familiar sloping black ink. He swallowed hard, trying not let his shock show. "Thanks, Mum," he said after a moment.

"It's been wonderful to see you," she said as she kissed him. "And I'm absolutely thrilled you're coming home for good."

"So am I, Mum." Nick smiled. "Bye now."

Nick made his way out to the car and turned the engine on. He drove along the drive, then pulled to a halt just outside the entrance. The letter was on the passenger seat, willing him to open it. His fingers shaking, he picked it up, opened it and read the words she'd written to him.

Then he sat staring into space, trying to decide what to do. He could tear this up now and head straight back to London and Tammy. Or he could drive into Southwold, hear what she had to say, then lay the ghost.

Nick turned right and drove towards Southwold. The town looked as pretty in the autumn dusk as it always had. He drove up the High Street, noting that his old shop had become an estate agent's, but nothing much else seemed to have changed. On a whim, he parked his car and took a walk along the sea front.

As he walked, he let the memories wash over him, knowing it was important not to bury them. Perhaps if he saw her, with a newfound focus and Tammy in his life, he could finally exorcise them for good.

He hung over the railings, watching the sea slip gently in and out of the shore, and remembered the sheer agony he'd felt last time he'd stood here. Yes, he had loved her. Perhaps he would never love like that again, and in retrospect, he prayed he wouldn't. He'd realized that kind of love was not a force for good—it was overwhelming, all-encompassing and destructive.

Nick walked back to his car, started the engine, and headed for her house.

Chapter 12

Tammy signed the papers with a flourish, then handed the pen back to the agent. "There we go, all done and dusted at long last."

"I believe these are now yours." The agent dangled a set of keys in front of her.

"Yes. Thank you." Tammy took the bunch and placed them safely in the zip pocket of her handbag. "Is there anything else?"

"No, everything is in order." The agent checked his watch and smoothed a strand of hair across his bald pate. "It's nearly lunchtime. How do you fancy joining me for a glass of champagne to toast your new venture's future?"

"Er, thanks for the offer, but I'm obviously eager to get straight to my new premises and start sorting things out."

"As you wish. Good luck, Miss Shaw."

"Thank you, Mr. Brennan."

Safely outside the office, Tammy hailed a taxi.

"Number four, Ellis Place, please. It's just off Sloane Street, at the Sloane Square end," she added proudly as she jumped in the back of the taxi.

As they sped along the King's Road, Tammy gazed through the window, hardly able to believe her luck. Only last week, she'd told Nick she despaired of ever finding suitable premises. Location, location, location, was what it was all about, but there seemed to be nothing available in her price range in the right areas.

Then Jane had called her from a photo shoot and said she'd just heard on the grapevine that a clothes boutique had just gone under and the liquidators were looking to sell off the fixtures, fittings and, of course, the rest of the lease. Jane gave her the number to call and Tammy did so immediately.

She'd decided it was perfect before she'd even stepped inside. Tucked away in a small side street just off Sloane Street, the tiny shopfront stood between an up-and-coming shoe designer—whom she had read about in *Vogue* recently—and a hatter. Inside, the shop was almost exactly as Tammy had imagined her own would be: small but tastefully decorated and with just enough room to display her clothes. There was an office and tiny kitchen at the back and a dry downstairs basement, which, as well as providing storage space, could seat a seamstress. The fact the shop was only a five-minute drive from her mews house was another big incentive.

Tammy had had her heart in her mouth when she'd asked the agent the price. It was definitely at the absolute top end of her budget, and criminal for the amount of space she'd be renting, but she was convinced it was the right thing to do.

They'd shaken on it then and there, and now, only a few days later, Tammy stepped out of the taxi, walked to the front door, her hands shaking a little, and turned the key in the lock.

She stood for a few minutes, hardly daring to believe she'd finally done it before letting out a shout of triumph. She took out her mobile and dialed Nick's number. Even though he was visiting his mother today and she expected his voicemail, she wanted him to be the first to know.

"Hi, darling, it's me. I just wanted to say I'm in! And it's wonderful and I'm so happy. We'll crack open the champagne when I see you later. Give me a ring and let me know what time you'll be back. I'll probably still be here at the boutique, so maybe you could come and collect me. Bye, darling."

She smiled fondly at her mobile as she put it in her bag. It was a long time since she'd been this happy. Nick made her laugh and she missed him when he wasn't with her, to the point where she had begun to wonder whether she might be falling in love with him. She hugged herself in the pleasure of the moment: a gorgeous boyfriend and the dream of her own boutique coming true. Her cup really was running over at present.

"Right, Tam, enough of all that euphoria. Every second in here is costing about a fiver, so get to work, my girl," she told herself.

The next three hours were taken up with ferrying her sewing machine and the plastic boxes of jewels and beads to the shop. Then she drove to her storage unit to fetch a selection of her vintage clothes. She spent far too much time hanging her clothes in various different orders and messing around with ideas for the window, rather than cracking on with the nitty-gritty of moving in, but surely she was allowed just a few hours of indulgence?

Tammy was boogieing to Robbie Williams on the radio, with one of her floatier dresses pulled on over her sweater and jeans, when there was a tap on the door.

"Hi," said Tammy, mid-boogie, as an attractive Indian girl entered the shop.

"Hi. I'm Joyti Rajeeve from the shoe shop next door. I just thought I'd come and say hello."

"I'm Tammy Shaw, and I'm a great fan of your shoes. They're really starting to attract some attention in the glossies, aren't they?"

"Yes, fingers crossed," said Joyti. "This is a very good place to be and it matters a lot that your neighbors are doing well, because the street gets a reputation and you get each other's passing trade."

"Absolutely," agreed Tammy. "Well, I hope I don't let the side down, like the last business in here."

"From the look of that dress, I'm sure you won't. It's gorgeous!" Joyti fingered the delicate beading on the chiffon.

"Yes, I got it for a song in an estate sale—though the owner hadn't taken care of it at all. I had to re-do all the beading by hand, but hopefully not for much longer. I need staff," Tammy added, "but my budget is very tight."

"Well, interestingly enough, I may know someone who might be prepared to help you and who comes with the highest qualifications."

"Really? Well, I probably couldn't afford her then."

"Oh, you probably could. She's my mum, actually."

"Oh, I see." Tammy didn't want to sound condescending, but she needed a professional.

"And she was, in her day, one of the most famous bespoke sari makers in the business," Joyti continued. "Her close-work is second to none. She gave it up to retire a year ago, but now, of course, she's bored rigid at home."

"Why doesn't she pop along to see me then?" Tammy offered.

"I'll ask her. It would work to my advantage to keep her occupied and get her out of my hair," Joyti giggled. "Anyway, I'll leave you to it, but if you fancy a drink after work any time, just give me a knock. Oh, and by the way, I have the perfect pair of shoes to go with that dress. Maybe we could do some cross-marketing. See you around," said Joyti as she left the shop.

Tammy's mobile rang at eight o'clock and she answered it, expecting to hear Nick.

"Hi, Tam, it's Jane. How's it going?"

"Fantastic! I've been dancing around the shop with excitement!"

"Good. Decided on a name for the shop yet?"

"Nope." It was the one thing Tammy was stuck on.

"Well, you'll have to decide that before you have your big opening."

"Yes, I will, won't I?"

"Want me to come over and we'll go to the Fifth Floor at Harvey Nicks and have a bottle of champagne to celebrate?"

"Oh Jane, it sounds wonderful, but I'm promised to Nick tonight."

"Of course. But tomorrow night, I insist you come with me to the opening of the new Gucci store."

"Yuck," groaned Tammy. "I hate all that stuff."

"I know, but you really should be putting yourself about as much as possible in the next few months, letting people know about your new venture."

"Yes, okay, you're absolutely right," agreed Tammy. "How about we pop in to the party for an hour or so, then go off somewhere for a nice gossip and some supper?"

"Sounds good to me," agreed Jane. "I'll pick you up tomorrow at seven from your new premises. Congratulations again, darling."

"Thanks. Bye, Janey."

At nine o'clock, now ready to go home, Tammy tried Nick's mobile. It was still on voicemail. She decided to head home for a bath and wait for him to call her there. Maybe there'd been so much to talk about with his mother, he hadn't noticed the time ticking on. Still, it was very unlike him not to call.

Having had her bath, Tammy paced her sitting room, unable to settle. At ten, she tried Nick's mobile again, and, still getting the voicemail, tried Jane and Paul's house. Their answering machine was on too.

Tammy slumped onto the sofa. She was starving, so she warmed herself a slice of pizza and opened the bottle of champagne.

"Cheers to me," she toasted herself half-heartedly, then took a healthy slug, but all the pleasure seemed to have drained from the day and now she felt both cross and frustrated. If Nick had phoned to say he couldn't make it, she could at least have gone out with Jane and celebrated. She didn't understand. Nick knew how much this day had meant to her.

"Bloody men, they're all the same," she growled on her third glass of champagne.

At midnight, chucking the empty champagne bottle into the bin, Tammy walked unsteadily to the bedroom, lay down on the bed and fell into an alcohol-induced sleep.

The next morning, hung over and irritable, she went to the boutique and began to organize her clothes. She had purchased some expensive black velvet hangers, and she hung the evening gowns on them, arranging them by era and style. Then she wrestled a structured deep red 1950s dress onto a mannequin, the skirt falling voluminously to the ground, and busied herself with sorting through the vintage accessories she'd collected, placing the costume earrings onto little velvet pads and the bracelets onto a porcelain jewelry tree.

And still, there was no word from Nick.

"Wow," said Jane when she arrived that evening. "Someone's been busy."

"I have, yes, but there's still so much to do. What do you think of the window? I've ordered lots of fake flowers and bushes to dress it. It's going to have a Midsummer Night's Dream kind of theme."

"I think it's a wonderful idea. And you look fantastic in that dress," Jane said admiringly. "A walking advert for your wares, darling."

"Thanks. The only thing I have to decide, as you mentioned yesterday, is the name."

"That's one for tonight over supper. Come on, we don't want to be late and miss all those smoked salmon canapés." Jane tucked her arm through Tammy's and they headed for the party.

Tammy made pleasant conversation with the A-listers invited to the opening of the new boutique. Even though she'd been off the celebrity circuit for a couple of years now, it was still the same faces; ironically, many looking younger than when she'd last seen them. The paparazzi recorded the affair for their newspaper diaries and the glossy magazines, and even though she found it facile, Tammy knew she had to recognize that this would be part of her life again if she wished to make it in the fashion business.

"At least I'll be the one pulling the strings," she muttered to herself as she watched the celebrity designer surrounded by It girls and minor royalty.

Jane came and found her after an hour, and they took a cab to a cosy Italian restaurant just off the King's Road.

"Is it champagne tonight?" asked Jane as they sat down at their table.

"Well, I had an entire bottle to myself last night. Nick didn't turn up," Tammy answered abruptly.

"Really?" Jane frowned. "I am surprised. He wasn't home with us either, so I presumed he was with you."

"Nope." Tammy shook her head. "He's gone AWOL. I haven't heard from him today either."

"That really is unlike Nick. He's usually Mr. Reliable. God, I do hope he's okay, that nothing's happened to him."

"Well," Tammy shrugged, "I can hardly call the police and put out a missing person alert for a thirty-four-year-old who's been away for one night, can I?"

"No, but if you don't hear from him, and he doesn't turn up at our place either, perhaps you should at least call his mother."

"I don't have her number. Now, how about that champagne?"

"Actually, I won't, but please have one yourself. I'm good with water."

"Really? Are you on a detox?"

"Yes, sort of. I...Well, the thing is, I..." Jane shook her head. "Oh shit, I wasn't going to say anything. I mean, I haven't even told Paul yet, but, well..."

"Oh my God! You're pregnant, aren't you?"

Jane's eyes shone and she nodded. "Yes, yes I am. I can hardly believe it. I'm still in complete shock."

"Oh Janey!" Tammy's eyes filled with tears and she reached across the table to take her hand. "That is just the most wonderful piece of news. I am so, so happy for both of you."

"Thank you." Jane's eyes were wet too and she reached in her handbag for a tissue and blew her nose. "But it's very early days yet. I'm only six weeks and there's every chance things could go wrong."

"Well, you're going to have to take every precaution to make sure they don't. Lots of rest, healthy diet, no booze...the works. So, how on earth did it happen?"

"In the same way as it always does," Jane chuckled. "You know all about us trying for years, spending a bloody fortune on IVF, not to mention nearly losing my mind and my marriage with the pressure of it all." She chewed on a bread stick. "You remember me saying that Paul and I had agreed to forget the whole idea, just accept we would be childless and that would be an end to it. The ironic thing is, I really feel we've finally achieved that."

"Maybe it's because you've relaxed so completely that your body has decided to get on with it by itself," said Tammy.

"Yes, that's what the doctor said."

"When will you tell Paul?"

"I don't know. I want to tell him, obviously, but you know what he's like; he's a big kid himself. He'll be so overexcited and go out and start finding antique cradles and suitable original prints for the nursery. I just couldn't bear it if something went wrong for us. He'd be devastated."

"God, Janey, if it was me, I doubt I could keep it to myself, but I understand why you are."

"Maybe I'll tell him in a couple of weeks' time. Every day I hold on to the baby is one day less to worry about, and once I get to twelve weeks, I can relax a little."

Tammy raised her champagne glass. "To you, Janey, for totally making my day. Cheers."

"And to you, and your soon to be famous, but currently nameless, business," added Jane.

They clinked glasses.

"Anyway, forget about my shop, when is this little one due to be born?"

"May." Jane paused and looked at Tammy. "'Born'...or rather, 'reborn'? How about that as a cool name for your boutique?"

"'Reborn'...'Reborn.'" Tammy rolled it round her tongue and imagined it above the window of the shop. "Oh my God, it's perfect! I love it! You are clever, Janey."

"Thank you."

"Now I can get a signwriter in and start on the invitations for the opening party."

"Which will be when?" Jane asked as their pasta arrived.

"As soon as possible, because every day I'm not open is another day without dosh. November maybe. A lot of the clothes still need work to restore them, but my new neighbor says her mum might be able to help me. God, I have so much work to do."

"Well, at least your name is going to drag the great and the good to the opening, even if it's only for the booze and a nose. I could try and pull a few strings and see if I could get you and the clothes a feature in a good mag."

"Janey, that would be fantastic!"

"I'll do my best." Jane watched her friend as she pushed her pasta around her plate. "Not hungry?"

Tammy shrugged. "No, not very."

"You're worried about Nick, aren't you?"

"Yes, it's just that everything has been going so well between us, I've begun to believe that it might just work out. I really feel something for him, and"—Tammy took a gulp of her champagne—"once again, I've been let down. Last night was so important to me, and Nick knew it was."

"Look, Tam, I've known Nick for a long time and he is not, and never will be, a bastard. Whatever has happened to him in the past twenty-four hours has got nothing to do with the way he feels about you, I'm sure of it. I've seen the way he looks at you. He absolutely adores you, Tammy, really."

"I don't know," she sighed. "I was just getting to the point where I'd begun to feel reasonably secure and now, well, it doesn't take much for me to be frightened off."

"I understand, but you just need to trust."

"Do you know if he had lots of women before he left for Australia or since?"

"I don't think so, although I do remember Paul telling me of someone he was very keen on just before he left for Perth. I think he said she worked for him at the shop he had in Southwold. He can't have been that keen, anyway, if he went to the other side of the world soon after."

"Unless he went because it didn't work out." Tammy shrugged. "Anyway, we'll just have to see what he has to say for himself when he eventually turns up, *if* he turns up."

Tammy arrived home around eleven, feeling calmer after her chat with Jane. It was pointless worrying until she knew the whole story, but the anxiety she felt was the very thing that unsettled her. It meant that Nick had got under her skin.

Knowing she wouldn't be able to sleep, Tammy took out some paper and began to fiddle with designs for the lettering of the name of her new shop.

Her mobile rang at midnight.

"Hello?"

"Tam, it's me, Nick. Did I wake you?"

Where the hell have you been, you shit?! was what she wanted to say. Instead, she said, "It's okay. I've been doing some work."

"Look, I'm so, so sorry about last night and not calling you. Something came up and...well, I just couldn't get away. Is it too late to come round now and crawl on bended knee for your forgiveness?"

She knew she shouldn't let him, but she was so relieved he was okay and desperate to see him. "If you want," she said as casually as she could, "but I'm very tired."

"I'll see you in fifteen minutes."

Tammy ran to the bedroom to brush her hair and clean her teeth, promising herself she would act with dignity and decorum and not show just how upset she really was.

Nick pulled his hire car into a petrol station, switched off the engine and sat in the darkness. He felt completely drained, mentally and emotionally.

Having experienced the total euphoria of arriving back in the UK, meeting Tammy and starting to set up his business, he'd been fooled into believing that the gods were smiling on him and the past was well and truly behind him. In the last twenty-four hours he'd been dragged back into it, kicking and screaming. He looked at his hands and saw they were still shaking with adrenaline.

All the way from Southwold, he'd ruminated on what he should tell Tammy. How could he expect her to understand? The ramifications of what he'd learnt were something even he was struggling to come to terms with, to believe. And though he and Tammy had become close, the relationship was still very new, and therefore fragile.

Nick ran a hand through his hair. He didn't want to lie, but if he told her, tried to explain, there was every chance the situation would frighten her off and he'd lose her. Besides, nothing was yet one hundred percent certain. Perhaps the most sensible thing was not to say anything for now, wait for confirmation and take it from there.

Tears came to his eyes, whether from exhaustion or frustration, Nick didn't know. All he did know was that nothing in his emotional life seemed to come without a price, and he could only hope he wouldn't end up paying the highest cost of all.

Tammy heard the buzzer and went to open the front door.

"Here." Nick piled three bunches of wilting flowers, obviously bought from a petrol station, into Tammy's arms. "Can I come in?"

"Of course." Tammy stepped aside to let him pass. She shut the door and followed him into the sitting room. She stood there silently, waiting for him to speak.

"I'm so sorry, Tam." Nick shrugged despondently. "What happened was...unavoidable."

"What on earth have you been doing? You look like you've been dragged through a hedge backwards."

"I feel like it," he agreed. "Would you mind if I took a quick shower? I'm sure I smell foul."

"Help yourself," Tammy said coolly and went back to her sewing whilst he used the bathroom.

He emerged in a towel ten minutes later, looking much more like his old self, walked over to her, and laid his hands gently on her shoulders.

"Darling..." he murmured as he kissed her neck, "tell me how cross you really are?"

"I feel let down, yes, but more than that, I've been worried to death. I saw Jane for supper tonight and she said you haven't been at theirs, either."

"No."

A silence settled on the room.

"Anyway," said Tammy, breaking it, "I'm not your keeper and I have no right to know your movements every step of every day."

"Of course you have a right to know where I am, Tam. We're having a relationship, for God's sake! What I did last night was unforgivable, but there was something I just had to sort out."

"To do with a woman?"

"Partly." Nick sighed and slumped into an armchair. "It's a very complex story and I really don't think I'm up to telling it tonight."

"Okay," she replied coldly.

"Look, Tam, the one and only thing you must know is that none of it affects the way I feel about you."

"Right. And I just have to take your word for that, do I?"

"Yes," he nodded sadly, "unfortunately you do. That's what it's all about, isn't it, trusting one another? And the good thing about last night is that, even though I may have let you down, I do know now that, however ridiculous, given the short time we've been together, I love you."

She looked up at him, wanting to feel euphoria that he'd just told her he loved her. But the expression in his eyes was one of such intrinsic sadness that she couldn't.

"Tam?"

"Yes?"

"Do you believe what I've just told you? That I love you?"

"I...no, not tonight. Anyone can say those words."

"Yes, they can. But will you at least give me the chance to prove to you that I do? Please?"

Tammy yawned. "We're both exhausted, Nick. Let's go to bed and get some sleep. We can talk more in the morning." She stood up, switched off the desk lamp and held out her hand to him to follow her.

"Can I hold you?" Nick asked as he climbed into bed next to her.

She nodded and snuggled into his arms, feeling frightened at just how good she felt there.

He stroked her hair gently. "I'm so sorry, Tam, I am so sorry. I never want to hurt you. I love you, I really do."

And I love you too.

"Hush now, enough," whispered Tammy.

Chapter 13

Posy looked up as the bell on the gallery door jangled.

"Hello, Freddie." She smiled as he entered the showroom. "How are you?"

"Very well, very well indeed." He walked over to the desk at which Posy was sitting. "I was wondering whether you fancied going to the flicks tomorrow night? They're showing that French film that's had rather good reviews."

"That sounds like an offer I can't refuse. You're on."

"Good-oh," he said. "Shall we meet at six outside the cinema?"

"That would be perfect."

"I'll see you tomorrow. Goodbye, Posy."

"Goodbye, Freddie."

He tipped his hat, then walked to the door and left the shop.

Posy sighed. Although she tried not to think about it, she was struggling with their so-called "friendship." They'd had a few pleasant dinners and lunches together since his appearance in her garden. There had certainly not been a shortage of conversation—Freddie had regaled her with fascinating stories from his days as a criminal barrister and she had filled him in on the details of her life since they'd last seen each other.

Yet it felt very much as though it was what was *unsaid* that mattered; why he had left her first time around and, fifty years on, could only offer her his company, rather than his heart.

It didn't help anything that, as Sam used to say, she "fancied the pants" off him. And despite telling herself endlessly that she just had to accept and enjoy what he *could* give her, it wasn't working. Seeing him was like some kind of beautiful torture and, Posy realized, she was always going to be doomed to disappointment. When they parted, there had never been any attempt by Freddie to make physical contact other than a neat peck on the cheek.

She left the gallery at lunchtime and made her way home. Marie was arriving at two o'clock to value the house. Posy tidied the kitchen and lit the fire in the morning room, knowing there was little more she could do to make the house look welcoming.

Just before one, the telephone rang and she picked up the receiver.

"Hello?"

"Is that Posy Montague?"

"Yes, speaking."

"It's Sebastian Girault here. I believe Amy, your daughter-in-law, has spoken to you about me."

"She did mention you might call, yes."

"Would you be at all interested in having a lodger? It would only be for a couple of months or so. I'd be out of your hair by Christmas."

"Well, you're welcome to come and see the house, Mr. Girault, but I'm afraid I don't think it will be suitable. It really is very basic."

"I know that. Amy has described it to me and it sounds perfect. Would you mind if I did come to take a look?"

"Not at all. As a matter of fact, I'm home this afternoon. If you wanted to pop in at four, that would be perfect. The house is easy to find; there's a tree-lined lane off the Halesworth Road on the way into Southwold, and "Admiral House" is written on the postbox."

"Don't worry, I have a GPS. Thanks, Mrs. Montague. I'll see you at four, then."

Posy put the phone down, knowing that once Sebastian saw the house, he'd think better of it, but having his company for half an hour or so after the house had been valued might lift the pall of gloom that Marie's visit would undoubtedly leave.

At two o'clock on the dot, Posy heard a knock on the front door.

"Hello, Marie. Do come in, and please call me Posy."

"Thank you." Marie stepped inside, armed with a clipboard. She looked up at the chandelier. "Wow. This is absolutely stunning. What a fantastic entrance hall."

"Thank you. Would you like a cup of tea or coffee before you start?" offered Posy. "I imagine it'll take you quite a while."

"No, thank you. I have my children to pick up at three so I'd best get going here."

"I thought I might show you round the gardens and the ground and first floors, then leave you to look at the attic floor yourself. My legs aren't what they once were, and the stairs are really quite steep."

"That would be fine, Posy."

The two women started off outside, then came back in and walked from room to room, Marie exclaiming over the many original features and scribbling on her clipboard.

After showing her round the six bedrooms on the first floor, Posy came downstairs to boil the kettle and warm some scones she'd made before work. At least Marie was not a sharp-suited wheeler-dealer, because she really didn't think she could have borne such a character poking round her precious home.

Marie eventually arrived in the kitchen and they drank tea and ate the fresh scones at the refectory table.

"These are yummy, Posy. I wish I could bake like this."

"Years of practice, that's all, my dear."

"But not as yummy as this house, and as for the garden, well, wow! I can't believe you made that all by yourself."

"It was a labor of love, and therefore a pleasure, Marie."

"And maybe that's what makes it special. Right, I suppose we should get down to business." Marie looked at her. "Posy, the house too is absolutely spectacular. The original features are just stunning. The fireplaces, cornicing, the shutters on the windows...the list is endless. The room sizes are amazing and the grounds are something else."

"But..." Posy pre-empted it before it came.

"Well." Marie rubbed her nose. "It goes without saying that the person who buys this house will have to make a huge long-term commitment in terms of both time and money. I'm sure you realize how much work the house needs to restore it. And therein lies the problem."

"Yes," agreed Posy.

"My honest feeling is that you'd be very lucky to find someone to take it on. The country-house market has cooled off recently, plus even though Southwold is a very popular spot for second homes, this is far too large to be one of those. It's quite unlikely that someone would want to commute to London from here, given the journey, and I can't see the retirement lot being interested because of the size and the amount of work."

"Marie, my dear, just spit it out. What are you trying to say?"

"I suppose I'm trying to say that, unless we can find a pop singer or a movie star with enough money to purchase their country estate and then spend the time and money required to renovate it, the field for buyers is extremely narrow."

"I can understand that, yes."

"Posy, I'm sure you're going to hate the idea, but I really feel your best shot would be to sell it to a developer who would probably turn it into some tasteful apartments. Although very few people want a house as big as this these days, they do want the setting and the grandeur."

"I had considered that is what you might suggest. It would break my heart, of course, and my ancestors will turn in their graves, but..." Posy shrugged. "I have to be realistic."

"Yes. The problem is, there's no doubt a developer would want to purchase it as cheaply as they could. There would be so much work for them to do and they'd have to think about the end profit. The only advantage is that we wouldn't have to put you through the ignominy of the house going on the open market. Our office knows a few developers who may well be interested. We can put them in touch with you, they can have a look and the deal can be handled quickly and discreetly."

"So how much do you think such a developer would pay for it?"

Marie shrugged. "It's very difficult to say, but I would put the figure around a million."

Posy had to chuckle. "Goodness, and there's poor departed Mrs. Winstone's three-bedroom cottage on the High Street selling for over half that."

"I know, it does seem ridiculous in comparison," agreed Marie, "but that cottage is right in the center of Southwold and perfect for a second home. Posy, I really wouldn't be at all hurt if you wished to get another estate agent into value it. In fact, I think you should."

"No, no, dear, I'm sure you're absolutely right. And, let's be honest, a million pounds is an awful lot of money. An amount I'll never spend in my lifetime, but lovely for my sons to inherit."

"Yes, it is. Now I must be off to collect the kids. Thank you very much for the tea and scones." Marie stood up. "I'm going to put all I've said in a letter to you. When you've had a chance to consider it and chatted to your sons, give me a call."

"I will." Posy walked with Marie to the door and shook her hand. "Thank you for making the experience reasonably painless. I'll be in touch when I've made a decision. Goodbye, dear."

Posy watched Marie drive off and went back to the kitchen for another cup of tea and some thinking.

Shortly after that, Sebastian Girault arrived on the doorstep.

"Good to meet you, Mrs. Montague." He shook her hand firmly.

"Do call me Posy." She looked up into his piercing green eyes and wished she was thirty years younger. "Please, come in." She closed the door behind him and led him to the kitchen, where she put the kettle on again. "Do sit down, Mr. Girault."

"Thank you. And it's Sebastian, please. What an absolutely amazing house this is."

"So Amy says you want somewhere to write in peace?"

"Yes, and space. That's very important."

"Well, I may not have a reliable heating system, or many modern conveniences, but I do have space," chuckled Posy. "I'll show you the bedrooms that might be suitable, then you can tell me they're freezing and dusty and we can come downstairs, forget the idea and have a nice cup of tea."

At the end of the corridor on the first floor was one of Posy's favorite bedrooms. Placed on the corner of the house, it had full-length windows that overlooked the gardens on two sides.

"Beautiful," Sebastian breathed as Posy led him into the next-door bathroom—a relic from the nineteen-thirties. The huge cast-iron bath sat in the middle of the room, the floor covered in original black, and very worn, linoleum.

"There. What do you think? I really won't be offended if you say no."

Sebastian walked back into the bedroom. "Do you think the fireplace is usable?"

"Probably. It would need its chimney swept."

"I would pay for that, of course, and..." Sebastian walked over to the window. "I could set my desk just here, so I can enjoy the view whilst I stare into space." He turned to her. "Posy, this is perfect. If you're happy to have me, I'd love to come and stay. I'd pay you well, of course. How about two hundred a week?"

"Two hundred pounds? That's far too much." Posy didn't earn nearly that in a week at the gallery.

"It's still less than I'd pay if I rented a cottage in town. And how about you throw in the odd meal too?" suggested Sebastian. "I've heard you're a fantastic cook."

"Not fantastic, just consistent," corrected Posy. "Of course I'll cook for you. I have to for myself, anyway. But are you sure you're going to be comfortable in here? I can provide you with a couple of heaters, although they tend to be quite expensive to run."

"I promise I will cover all costs of my stay. And by nature of my profession, I doubt I shall disturb you, although I do tend to keep strange hours when I'm writing."

"That's no problem, as I sleep at the other end of the house. There is one thing I should mention, mind you. I had an estate agent round this afternoon, as I'm thinking of selling the house. I'm sure nothing will happen before Christmas, but I'm not sure how long you're wanting to stay."

"My deadline is February, but as I mentioned, I hope to have written the first draft by the middle of December. I can work on the rewrites at my flat in London, so I should be out of your hair for Christmas. So do we have a deal?" Sebastian tentatively stretched out his hand.

Posy put her hand to his. "Yes, Mr. Girault, I think we do."

Sebastian and Posy returned downstairs, forgot the tea and instead had a glass of wine to celebrate the arrangement. He noticed the framed photo of Posy's father in his RAF uniform, which sat on the occasional table in the morning room.

"My new book is going to be set in the Second World War. Do you happen to know if your father ever flew Spitfires?"

"Oh yes, he did. He was involved in some of the biggest battles, including the Battle of Britain. Sadly, he died shortly before the war ended, on one of the last sorties."

"I'm so sorry, Posy."

"Thank you. I adored him, as any daughter does her father."

"Of course. Would it upset you if I interrogated you at some point about what you remember of the war here in Southwold?"

"Not at all, although I was very young at the time."

"That would be fantastic. Now, just so you know I'm serious, I want to pay you the first week's rent up front." Sebastian opened his wallet and took out some cash. "When can I move in?"

"As soon as you like, although I must warn you that the family is coming en masse for Sunday lunch, so it won't be as quiet as usual."

"No problem. I promise I'll make myself scarce."

"Nonsense. You're most welcome to join us," she said as she walked towards the front door and opened it. "My goodness, I shall have to give you a key," Posy chuckled.

"That would be useful, yes. Now, goodbye, and thank you for everything." He kissed her warmly on both cheeks.

"Not at all. It's going to be a delight having you here. Goodbye, Sebastian. Let me know when you want to move in."

Chapter 14

The following morning, Posy had just finished dressing when she heard the sound of a car coming up the drive. She was surprised to see Sam's ancient red Fiat pull to a halt in front of the house. She walked downstairs to find Sam standing in the hall, staring up at the chandelier.

"Hello, dear. What a nice surprise."

"Hi, Mum." Sam came over and kissed her. "How are you?"

"Oh, you know, chugging along, as always. Long time no see. To what do I owe this visit?" she asked him.

"Sorry, Mum, I know I've not been to see you for a while," said Sam, "but I've been really busy with this new company of mine. Anyway, I was just passing and I thought, I must pop in and say hello. Any chance of a coffee?"

"Yes, a quick one." Posy checked her watch. "I have some bits to do in town."

Sam followed her into the kitchen and paced around it whilst she put the kettle on to boil. "This really is a spectacular room," he said, parking himself at the kitchen table. "You could fit four modern kitchens into it, no problem."

"Yes, you probably could," agreed Posy.

"The windows really aren't in bad shape, considering they're so old," he added.

"No." Posy made her son a coffee and set it down next to him on the table. "How are Amy and the children? I haven't seen them for a while."

"They're fine, just fine," said Sam, who now had his eyes on the floor. "These are original York stone flags, aren't they?"

"Yes. Did Amy tell you I've invited you all to lunch on Sunday? You know Nick is back in England, don't you?"

"Yes. Lunch will be fine. Mum?"

"Yes, Sam?" Posy had been waiting for the question. Sam only visited her when there was something he wanted.

"A little bird told me you had the house valued yesterday, with a view to selling it."

"My goodness, news travels fast. Yes, I did. Are you upset by the thought?"

"Well, obviously it's my old home and I wish we could keep it in the family and all that..." Sam paused, obviously working out how to phrase his next remark. "And it just so happens that I might have found a way in which we could, sort of, do just that."

"Really? Have you secretly won the lottery, Sam, and come to tell me that all your financial problems are over?"

"In a way, yes."

"Pray, do continue," suggested Posy, steeling herself.

"Well, you know I've recently gone into partnership and am a director of a property development company?"

"Amy has mentioned something about it to me, yes," answered Posy slowly, the penny beginning to drop.

"I have a backer who is prepared to fund the projects that I source. I organize the project and see it through to its conclusion. We then split the profits from the sale of the property that's been developed."

"I see," said Posy, determined to act as though she was innocent as to where this conversation was leading.

"Now, Mum, the thing is that Marie, in her capacity as estate agent, has been charged with informing me if anything suitable for our needs might be coming onto the market. I just happened to speak to her yesterday afternoon and she told me she'd been here to value it."

"Right."

"Mum, Admiral House is just what my company is looking for. A fantastic house, full of character, that could be turned into four to six smashing apartments."

Posy looked at Sam silently for a while. Then she said, "Sam, did Marie tell you what she valued it at?"

"Yes, around a million."

"And you're telling me that your company has a million spare pounds to purchase Admiral House?"

"Absolutely," nodded Sam confidently.

"Plus the money to do the renovation and alteration work, which I'm sure would run into hundreds of thousands, if not the same amount again?"

"Yep, no probs at all."

"Well, well, we're obviously talking the big league here," mused Posy.

"We are. My partner is a very, very wealthy man. He doesn't want to mess around with two-bit projects."

"And how many other 'projects' have you got off the ground so far, Sam?"

"Well, this one would be the first. We've only been going for a few weeks."

"So what is it exactly you've come to ask me?"

"I want to know whether you'd be prepared to sell Admiral House to my development company. We'd pay the full market price, I wouldn't ask for any family favors or anything. It really would work to your advantage, Mum. There'd be no need to put it on the market, we could just conduct the deal discreetly between us. And there would of course, be an incentive for you."

"Really? What?" Posy asked.

"I discussed it with my partner and he agreed that if you were to sell it to us, we'd offer you one of the apartments at a discount. That way you could still live here! What do you think of that?"

"I've no idea what I think, Sam. I have to decide whether I want to sell the house in the first place."

"Of course, but if you do decide to sell, would you give me first refusal? A project such as this would put me and the company on the map, establish us in the major league. It would give other potential sellers the confidence to trust us. If not for me, do it for Amy and the kids. You've seen where we're living at present."

"I have and I was horrified," Posy agreed.

"They deserve better and I'm desperate to give it to them. So please, Mum, will you think about selling it to me?"

Posy looked at her son, his blue eyes—so like his father's—beseeching her to answer in the affirmative.

"I promise that when I have decided, I will consider your offer first."

"Thanks, Mum." Sam stood up, then walked towards Posy and gave her a hug. "I promise you could trust me to take care of the old place, and if it has to happen, isn't it better it's still in family hands, rather than some stranger who sees it only in terms of bricks, mortar and profit?"

"Of course." Posy wanted to laugh at Sam's unabashed emotional blackmail.

"I won't rush you, I promise. Take your time. I have to say, though, that the house really is starting to deteriorate rapidly."

"Well, it's stood here for three hundred years already so I doubt it will crumble round my ears in the space of a few weeks," Posy replied briskly. "Now you must excuse me. I have to leave in five minutes."

"Of course. Well, as soon as you've made up your mind, please let me know. It would be great to have the deal done and dusted so we could get going on the work in the spring. It's so much more cost-effective to build through the summer months."

"I thought you said you wouldn't rush me," chided Posy as she left the kitchen and headed to the front door.

"Sorry, Mum. I just know this would be the making of me. And Amy and the kids."

"Bye-bye, Sam." Posy sighed wearily and kissed her son on the cheek. "I'll see you on Sunday."

That night, as arranged, Posy met Freddie outside the Arts Centre. With everything crowding into her thoughts, Posy admitted afterwards that the finer points of the film had rather gone over her head.

"And mine, dear girl. God only knows what that scorpion was a metaphor for."

"Obviously it meant something for those with far more intellect than us." Posy smiled.

"Listen, how do you fancy a snifter back at mine? It's only a few minutes' walk from here."

"Why not?" Posy heard herself say, mentally kicking herself for agreeing so readily.

They walked along the High Street in companionable silence. Freddie turned along a narrow lane which eventually opened up into a small courtyard with a flint cottage and an old hophouse edging it. A Japanese maple sat in the courtyard and two small bay trees stood on either side of the freshly painted front door. Freddie unlocked it and led her inside.

"Freddie, this is delightful!" she said as she stepped into a heavily beamed sitting room with a huge inglenook fireplace taking center stage.

"Thank you." Freddie gave a mock bow as he took Posy's coat from her shoulders and hung it on a hook in the hall. "I must admit I am rather pleased with it. Come through and see my favorite room, the kitchen."

Posy followed him into an airy space, realizing the three walls in front of her were made entirely of glass. Freddie flicked a light switch and Posy gazed through the windows into the small but immaculate garden.

"This was no more than a two-up, two-down cottage when I came here, so I added what is in essence a conservatory. It's trebled the space, not to mention the light."

"I love it." Posy clapped her hands in delight. "And just look at all your modern appliances," she said, turning round and admiring the sleek stainless-steel fridge, oven and dishwasher housed under a thick marble worktop. "You put me to shame."

"I am so glad you like it," said Freddie. "Brandy?"

"Yes, please. This is exactly the kind of thing I'd love to buy. Small, manageable, but with character," she said, feeling cheered that maybe there *was* an alternative if she sold Admiral House.

"Are you thinking of moving, then?" asked Freddie lightly as he handed her a brandy and led her back into the sitting room.

"Yes." For some reason, Posy had so far not felt comfortable about mentioning the valuation and possible sale to Freddie.

"That's a big decision," he said as he sat down.

"Yes, it is."

"But perhaps the right one. Sometimes it's healthy to move on, put the past behind you," Freddie mused.

"Surely only if that past has been difficult? Admiral House is filled with happy memories for me," she replied defensively.

"Yes, of course. So you'd be selling for purely practical reasons?"

"I would, yes. As a matter of fact, I already have an offer of sorts. Sam, my eldest son, appeared this morning and announced that he wanted to buy it and convert the house into apartments," sighed Posy. "I have to say it's left me in rather a quandary."

"And why is that?"

"For starters, I only had it valued yesterday. It was more a furtive gesture to find out how much it was worth than a definite plan."

"And now you already have an offer?"

"Yes, and the problem is that I'm stymied. If I do decide to sell, how can I not accept an offer from my own son? But, to be blunt, his track record in business is utterly appalling and this new company of his is fledgling and untested. Admiral House, from what I gather, would be their first big project."

"Are you sure he would have the money for it?"

"Sam says so, yes, but do I believe him? Not completely, no."

"But he's not asking for any favors?"

"He's offered the asking price."

"Right. Is it likely he would try and double-cross his own mother?"

"I would like to think not, no, but then I'm his mum and will always think the best of him. Even though I'm aware he has his faults, I have to believe his heart is in the right place."

"Of course you do, but it's a very difficult position that Sam's put you in. Of course you feel duty-bound to sell it to him. My barrister past also tells me that any financial deal between close relatives can often end in tears."

"I know," nodded Posy.

"I think the only thing you can do is to be relatively hard-nosed about it. The house has been valued by an independent estate agent, so you know what it's worth. Why don't you give Sam and his company first refusal and a deadline by which they must exchange contracts and put down a hefty deposit? You're in no hurry, so if

Sam fails to close the deal, you won't have lost much more than a few weeks anyway. Then at least you've given him the chance."

"Yes, thank you, dear Freddie. You really are so sensible. I think you're absolutely right. I shall do just as you suggest."

"Glad to be of use, milady."

"By the way, I was going to ask you whether you'd like to join us for a family lunch at Admiral House on Sunday. My son Nick and his new girlfriend, plus Sam, Amy and their children are coming."

"I'll have to ask Joe to take over the boat for me, but yes, that sounds marvellous."

"Good." Posy stood up. "Now I really must go. Thank you for a delightful evening and your words of wisdom."

Posy made her way into the hall and Freddie helped her into her coat.

"Goodnight Posy, and thank you too." He reached in to kiss her and for a split second, she thought he was heading for her lips. Yet at the last minute, he diverted and a gentle peck was planted on her cheek.

"Goodnight, Freddie."

She gave him one last glance as she turned to walk down the lane. And wondered why he looked so terribly sad.

Chapter 15

"Nick! What on earth is this?" laughed Tammy as she stepped into the passenger seat of an ancient but immaculate tomato-red sports car.

"This, my dear Tammy, is a vintage Austin Healey."

"I like the color," Tammy said as she climbed in and smelt leather and polish. "It won't break down, will it?" she added as Nick tried to start the engine and failed.

"Maybe, but we'll just have to push."

"What is it with you and old things?" she asked him as the car finally started and they pulled away from the curb.

"Does that include you?" he smiled as he changed gears, then reached for her hand.

"Charmed, I'm sure."

"Not nervous about today, are you?" he asked as they sped east across a largely deserted London still waking to a leisurely Sunday morning.

"You mean meeting your mum—and your brother and his family—for the first time? A little, I suppose."

"I'm sure Mum will love you, and probably Sam too, for all the wrong reasons. He's always wanted anything I had, but I'm confident you'll like Amy. From what I can remember, she's a sweetie. I know you'll charm them all."

"I hope so," sighed Tammy, wondering why she felt it was so important she did.

Posy had just finished laying the kitchen table and was arranging multi-colored asters, which she grew in abundance because they provided late-season nectar for hibernating butterfly species, in a vase for a centerpiece. She'd woken up this morning in a state of high excitement—the anticipation of having her entire family together for lunch for the first time in years filled her with pleasure. Apart from her brief trip to the garden to pick the flowers, she'd been in the kitchen since seven, baking and preparing the beef she'd bought yesterday.

The telephone rang. "Hello?" she said, picking up the receiver.

"Posy, it's Freddie. I am most terribly sorry at the short notice, but I'm afraid I can't make it over for lunch today after all."

"I see."

Posy waited for Freddie to offer an explanation, then she realized the silence meant there was none forthcoming.

"That's a shame. I was looking forward to introducing you to my family."

"And I was looking forward to meeting them. It can't be helped, I'm afraid. I'll ring you during the week. Goodbye, Posy."

She put the phone down, feeling a little of the gloss slip from her day. He'd sounded so abrupt, so cold...

"You look deep in thought, Posy."

Sebastian's voice behind her made her jump. He'd moved in a couple of days ago and she was still getting used to someone else being present in the house.

"Do I?" She turned to him. "Sorry."

"Would you mind if I make myself a coffee?" Sebastian asked. "I promise to go and purchase my own kettle tomorrow, so I don't have to keep disturbing you down here."

"You're not disturbing me at all, really." Posy walked over to the table and began removing Freddie's place setting. Sebastian watched her.

"Someone canceled?"

"Yes," said Posy, filling up the empty space by shuffling the placemats along. "My friend Freddie."

"Excuse me for saying so, but it's rather short notice, isn't it?"

"Yes." Posy sighed, then, still holding the cutlery, sank into a chair. "You're a novelist, Sebastian, and a man. Maybe you can tell me what it means when somebody seems...very attentive and eager to be with you one moment, and yet the next, he's cold and distant and cancelling the date."

"Who knows?" Sebastian spooned some instant coffee into a mug. "As you know, men generally tend to be much more basic than women; for the most part, less emotionally complex. They call a spade a spade, whereas women are more likely to say it's a metal digging implement used in the garden."

The analogy made Posy smile.

"Therefore, I would deduce that your Freddie can't come today because he has a straightforward reason for not doing so."

"Then why doesn't he just tell me what it is?"

"God knows." Sebastian removed the kettle from the hob and poured boiling water into his mug. "In my experience, when men get together, it's all beer and sport with a few jokes thrown in for good measure. They can be extremely bad at communication, especially—if you'll forgive me saying so—men of a certain generation, who have been taught from the cradle to keep their thoughts and emotions to themselves. And British men have got to be the worst. They were born with a stiff upper lip."

"Well, you're obviously out of a different mold altogether. You express yourself quite beautifully."

"It must be the French in me," Sebastian said as he stirred his coffee.

"I'm half French, you know, on my mother's side," said Posy, taking out the huge joint of beef and basting it.

"Are you now?" Sebastian smiled. "That must be why I like you."

"Well, as I'm a woman *and* half French, I'm going to be very forward and ask whether you'd fill in for Freddie at lunch today?"

"Really? Are you sure you want me with all your family coming?"

"Absolutely, I told you before you moved in that you'd be welcome. Besides, they're far more likely to be civil if there's a stranger present."

"Are you expecting pistols at high tea?"

"I hope not, although I'm not sure Nick will be too pleased if

Sam mentions he intends to buy this house and turn it into apartments. Nothing's decided yet."

"I don't think I'm too pleased either, and I'm not even related to you," Sebastian admitted ruefully. "I've fallen completely in love with the place. Anyway, I'd be happy to join you for an hour or so, if you're sure."

"Completely sure," said Posy. "Besides, you are now my official date."

"Then I'll be down at one o'clock prompt. See you later."

At just past noon, Posy saw an old red sports car making its way up the drive and parking on the gravel. A pair of long, slim legs encased in chic suede trousers emerged from the passenger door, followed by an elegant torso and a tumbling mane of red-gold hair.

"My goodness, you're a beautiful woman," murmured Posy, feeling disappointed. She'd met few beautiful women in her life that she'd actually liked and she only hoped Tammy would be the exception.

Within ten minutes of meeting Tammy, Posy realized that this lovely, open young woman *was* going to prove the exception. Even though she was obviously nervous, which Posy found endearing, she seemed as bright as a button, friendly and completely unaffected by her looks. Most importantly of all, as she watched the way Tammy reached for her son's hand and her eyes followed him around the room, she obviously adored Nick.

"Can I give you a hand with anything, Posy?" Tammy asked as the three of them stood in the kitchen drinking a glass of wine.

"No, I..."

"Sam and Amy have just arrived, Mum." Nick was peering out of the kitchen window. "My goodness, just look at my nephew and niece! Excuse me whilst I go out and introduce myself as their uncle, will you?"

"Of course."

"Posy, this is such a beautiful house," said Tammy.

"Thank you, Tammy, I love it too. More wine?"

Tammy accepted a refill.

"You know, I don't think I've ever seen Nick look happier,"

commented Posy, topping up her own glass. "You must be good for him."

"I hope so," ventured Tammy. "I know he's good for me."

"It's so healthy that you're both successful in your own right. I think it makes for a much more balanced relationship."

"Well, I'm untried and untested at the moment, Posy. My boutique could end up being a massive flop."

"I doubt it will, dear, and even if it was, I'm sure you'd pick up the pieces and move on to something else. Ah, I can hear the patter of tiny feet." Posy turned towards the door.

Nick came into the kitchen, Sara in his arms, Jake by his side.

"Now, come and meet your Auntie Tammy." Nick brought them both over to Tammy, set Sara down and the two children smiled up at her shyly.

"Hello, you two." Tammy bent down towards them.

"Are you married to Uncle Nick?" asked Jake.

"No, I'm not."

"Then how come you're our auntie?" he queried.

"I love your hair," said Sara quietly to Tammy. "Is it real?"

Tammy nodded seriously. "Yes. Do you want to touch it to make sure?"

Sara reached out her small, chubby hand and caught a strand of burnished copper. "It's as long as my Barbie Princess hair. Hers isn't real though."

"Hi, Posy, how are you?"

Tammy looked across the kitchen as a very pretty blonde woman came through the door.

"Amy!" Posy kissed her warmly. "You look lovely. Now, come and meet Tammy. Tammy, this is Amy, my dearest daughter-in-law."

"That's because at present, I'm her only daughter-in-law," smiled Amy, and Tammy knew the two of them would get along just fine. "Hi, Nick, it's so good to see you again after all these years."

Tammy watched as Amy wrapped her arms around Nick and he hugged her tightly back.

"You look fantastic," said Amy, smiling up at him. "And by the way, I apologize in advance for anything my children do or say over lunch. Just don't let their sticky little fingers anywhere near those beautiful suede trousers you're wearing, Tammy."

"Hi, Mum."

Tammy saw a short but broad-shouldered man with blonde hair kiss Posy on the cheek. She felt Nick stiffen beside her as he walked over to join them.

"Nick, old chap, good to see you."

"Hello, Sam," Nick said stiffly. He extended his hand and his brother shook it heartily.

Tammy studied Sam and thought that, of the two brothers, Sam had aged the least gracefully. His hair was already thinning on his crown and he had a noticeable beer belly. Apart from a similar nose, he looked nothing like Nick at all, who took after his mother.

"So what brings you back to the old country? Business fallen on hard times back in Perth, has it?"

Tammy saw the muscles in Nick's jaw tighten.

"As a matter of fact, things have gone better than I could have ever expected," Nick replied coldly.

"Good. Well, seems you might have some competition from your big brother soon," remarked Sam. "But I'll tell you about that later."

"I can't wait to hear," said Nick, the sarcasm obvious in his voice.

Tammy caught Amy's eye and they exchanged a glance of mutual understanding.

"Right, who's for a glass of the champagne that Tammy and Nick have so kindly brought me?" Posy interrupted at just the right moment.

"I'll open it, shall I?" Nick suggested and moved across the kitchen to retrieve the bottle.

"So, sweetheart, where did Nick find you?" Sam turned to Tammy, his eyes sweeping up and down her body. Tammy knew instantly she was dealing with a man who used his charm to great effect, the kind of man Tammy had met time and again throughout her adult life...the type of man she could not stand.

"We have mutual friends."

"You're obviously not Aussie then, with your accent?"

"No, Sam, Tammy is a well-known model," interrupted Posy.

"Used to be," corrected Tammy. "I'm more of a businesswoman these days, actually."

"Well, I can tell you don't have kids, the way you look," said Sam. "Childbirth and sleepless nights age women, don't they, darling?" He cast a less than complimentary eye over his wife. "Right, I'll leave you ladies to it. Got to have a word with Mum." Sam winked at them as he walked away.

Tammy felt the familiar and awkward sensation of standing next to a woman whose husband had just made it obvious he found her attractive. She wasn't quite sure what to say until Amy broke the silence by sighing.

"Sam's right, you know. What I'd give for a lie-in, and some time to choose matching clothes before I go out, but that's the penalty of having children."

"I don't know how women do it. But it must be worth it, I mean, look at your two over there," Tammy smiled. "They're gorgeous."

Both Sara and Jake were with Nick, giggling at something their newfound uncle was saying.

"Perhaps, but I have started to wonder whether motherhood is nature's big joke. Of course I'd be shot dead in the playground if I ever admitted I found it less than stimulating spending the day with a four- and a six-year-old watching endless Tweenies videos, but sometimes I want to scream."

"At least you're honest enough to say it," said Tammy, liking Amy more and more. "From the outside, it seems to me that motherhood is ninety percent hard work, ten percent pleasure."

"Well, of course it's worth the pain in the long run; everyone says it's fantastic when they grow up and become your friends. The problem is, most adult children I know seem to find visiting their parents a chore. Oh dear," giggled Amy, "not exactly a walking advert for family life, am I? But I really wouldn't be without them."

"I get it, Amy; you're just saying that on the odd occasion, you'd like to have a little time for you."

"Exactly. Look, Tammy," Amy said, watching her children with Nick, "now there's a man who looks very comfortable with a couple of kids hanging off his knee. You could end up like me: a complaining, exhausted mum. Now I'd better go and rescue him."

"Champagne, everyone. Gather round." Posy was pouring out glasses on the table. "I just wanted to raise a glass to Nick and say welcome home."

"Thanks, Mum." Nick nodded.

"And a very warm welcome to Tammy, too," Posy added. "Right, lunch will be ready in ten minutes. Would you carve, Nick?"

Tammy saw Amy's husband narrow his eyes as he watched his mother fussing over his younger brother. A cloud of jealousy wafted from him like a strong scent.

Sebastian strolled into the kitchen just as everyone was beginning to sit down at the table.

"Perfect timing," said Posy, indicating the chair between herself and Tammy. "Everybody, this is my new lodger, Sebastian Girault."

"Hi." Sebastian smiled briefly at the assembled group and sat down. "Hope no one minds me crashing this special occasion."

"Not at all. Nick Montague." Nick reached across the table to shake his hand. "I read your book and loved it."

"Thank you."

"I'm Sam Montague, and this is my wife, Amy."

"Yes. Amy and I have already met at the hotel," Sebastian replied. "How are you?" he asked her.

"Fine, thanks."

Tammy noticed the color in Amy's cheeks rise as she lowered her eyes.

"So what are you doing at Admiral House, Sebastian?" Sam asked, tipping back the last of his champagne and reaching for more.

"Writing my next book. Your mother kindly offered me board and lodging."

"You're a dark horse, Mum," teased Nick.

"Yes, for a moment then, when Sebastian walked in, I thought you'd found yourself a toy-boy," said Sam.

"Chance would be a fine thing," smiled Posy. "Now has everyone got everything they need?"

Over the next hour, Posy sat at the head of the table and felt the warm glow of contentment as she watched her family together after ten years. Even Sam and Nick seemed to have put their sibling tension to one side and Nick was filling his brother in on his time in Australia. Tammy and Sebastian were chatting comfortably together, and the only person who seemed un-relaxed was Amy. It was probably because of the children—Posy remembered all too well how she'd taken her boys out for Sunday lunch and remained on tenterhooks lest they misbehave. She looked exhausted and Posy couldn't help comparing Amy's haggard, worried expression to that of Tammy's fresh, unlined brow.

"Now, Posy, I must return upstairs to work, or more truthfully, after all that excellent wine, for a nap before I do start to work," said Sebastian, standing up. "See you again, folks." He waved at the assembled company and left the kitchen.

Whilst Posy made coffee and Amy cleared the table, Nick moved round to sit by Tammy. He put an arm proprietarily round her shoulder.

"Hello, darling," he kissed her on the neck. "Long time no see. What did you think of Mum's lodger, then?"

"He was great," said Tammy. "Not at all arrogant, considering he's such a literary star."

"Mummy, I want a wee-wee," piped up Sara from the other end of the table.

"Okay, you come too, Jake, and then we'll go exploring for a bit and give everyone some peace." Amy took the hands of her children and left the kitchen.

"So I presume Mum's told you about her selling Admiral House to me?" drawled Sam, refilling his wine glass.

"What?! No. Why haven't you told me, Mum?"

Posy's heart sank as she placed the coffee tray on the table. "Nothing's definite yet, Nick, that's why."

"You're selling Admiral House? To Sam?" Nick was incredulous.

"To my company, yes, and what's wrong with that?" said Sam. "As I said to her, if she's got to sell it, then it's better to keep it in the family. And I've promised Mum a discount on one of the apartments, so she could stay here if she wants."

"Now, Sam, really, I've told you there's no guarantee—"

"Apartments?! What on earth is he talking about?" The color had drained from Nick's face.

"Mum's going to sell the house to my property development company and we're going to turn it into a few classy apartments. They're all the rage these days—you can get a real premium for them, especially in a big retirement area like this. No garden maintenance— we'd employ someone full-time to look after it—good security and the like."

"God, Mum." Nick shook his head, trying to control his anger. "I just can't believe you couldn't have discussed this with me first, given me an opportunity to express my opinion."

"Let's face it, bruv, you've been on the other side of the world for the past ten years. Life goes on," cut in Sam. "Mum's been struggling alone with this place for ages."

"Well, it's obvious you've got it all worked out between you and you don't need me interfering." Nick stood up, quivering with rage and indignation. "Come on, Tam, it's time we were going."

Tammy stood too, head lowered in embarrassment, wishing she could disappear through the floor.

"Nick, please don't go. Of course I was going to discuss it with you, ask your opinion. I..." Posy shrugged helplessly.

"Sounds as if you've already decided what you're doing." Nick walked round to Posy and gave her a cursory peck on the cheek. "Thanks for lunch, Mum."

"Yes, thank you so much," said Tammy, watching Posy's stricken expression as Nick marched towards the door. All she could do was follow. "I do hope we'll meet again soon. Bye."

The kitchen door slammed shut behind them and Posy put her head in her hands.

"Sorry, Mum," Sam shrugged airily. "I obviously presumed he knew. He'll get over it. As a matter of fact, I was going to suggest that maybe I should offer to show Nick the pl—"

"Enough, Sam! You've done sufficient damage for one day. I do *not* wish to discuss this any further. Do you understand?"

"Of course." He had the sense to look chagrined. "Now I'll help you with the clearing up, shall I?"

Amy wandered round the first-floor bedrooms, playing a half-hearted game of hide and seek with the children. She looked at her watch and hoped Sam would want to go home soon. She had a heap of ironing to do when she got back. How wonderful to be Tammy, she thought, just to be able to go home and read a book by the fire without being disturbed.

"Mummmeee! Come and find me!" a muffled voice said from

the other end of the corridor.

"I'm coming," she answered and followed the sound into a bedroom.

Sebastian was sitting at a desk in front of a laptop. The desk was placed in front of one of the full-length windows, with its gorgeous view over the parterre and gardens.

"God, sorry, I thought..."

"Don't worry." Sebastian turned to her. "I'm glad of the distraction, to be honest. That excellent red at lunch has killed off another few thousand brain cells and I'm struggling."

"How many pages have you written?"

"Not nearly enough. I'm about a third of the way through and discovering penning number two is much harder than number one."

"I would have thought it was easier, that you'd have gathered more experience from writing the first."

"True, but sometimes experience can be detrimental. When I wrote *The Shadow Fields*, I just threw it out onto the page, not having any idea whether it was good or bad and not really caring either way. It was a stream of consciousness, I suppose. But of course, with that having been such a success and well reviewed, I'm hoisted by my own petard, because everyone will be waiting for me to fail."

"That's a very negative approach, if you don't mind me saying so."

"I agree, but there's every chance I may be a one-book wonder," Sebastian sighed. "This one really feels as though I'm having to write it and I've no idea if it's good or utter rubbish."

"Mummee! Where are you?!"

"I'd better go." Amy raised an eyebrow.

Sebastian smiled at her. "I enjoyed lunch. You have a very good family."

"Tammy seems very nice. And so beautiful," said Amy admiringly.

"Yes, she's a lovely, warm lady, though not really my type."

"What is your type?" It was out of her mouth before she could stop herself.

"Oh, petite, slim blondes with big blue eyes." Sebastian eyed her. "Funnily enough, a bit like you."

A frisson of excitement jumped its way clumsily up Amy's spine as they held each other's gaze for a moment.

"Mummy!" Sara appeared at the door, pouting. "I waited and you didn't come."

"No, I..." Amy broke off eye contact. "Sorry, darling. We should be going anyway."

"Goodbye, Sara. Bye, Amy," Sebastian gave them a small wave, an amused glint in his eyes. "See you soon."

Amy found Jake underneath his grandmother's bed and the three of them walked down the stairs. What on earth had possessed her to say that to Sebastian? It had been tantamount to flirting and most unlike her. Perhaps it was the wine, or perhaps...perhaps it was the fact that, even though she hated to admit it to herself, she *did* find Sebastian attractive.

They walked into the kitchen and found Sam and Posy silently plowing through the washing-up.

"Where are Nick and Tammy?" she asked.

"They've gone back to London," answered Posy abruptly.

"You should have called me. I'd have liked to say goodbye."

"They just upped and left," said Sam. "Something I said upset Nick, I'm afraid."

"Sam told Nick I was considering selling Admiral House to him. Naturally, it was a shock. I'd have preferred to have told him gently myself, but there we go," explained Posy.

"Sorry, Mum."

Amy thought Sam didn't look very sorry at all.

"Well, it can't be helped. I shall have to call Nick and talk to him." Posy made an effort to smile. "Now, anyone for a cup of tea and a slice of Granny's chocolate cake?"

"I just can't believe it! How Mum could even contemplate selling Admiral House to Sam! It's just...madness!"

Tammy sat quietly in the passenger seat as Nick drove back to London at top speed, his knuckles white with anger on the steering wheel.

"Darling, I'm sure your mum was going to tell you. It's just one of those things."

"I saw her for lunch last week and yes, she did mention she was getting the house valued, but nothing at all about selling it to Sam. No, I bet the real reason is she knew exactly how I'd react."

Having listened to his outpouring for the past forty minutes, Tammy wasn't sure whether Nick was more upset about the sale of Admiral House—his beloved childhood home—or the fact his mother was selling it to Sam.

"Nick, it is terribly sad, but you have to understand your mother's point of view. That house is far too much for her, anyone can see that. It's not her fault she doesn't have the money for the upkeep and restoration, is it? And if Sam's company can buy it, then at least it sort of stays in the family, as he said."

"Tammy, you really have no idea what kind of person Sam is. When I say that he'd screw over his own mother to get what he wants, I'm not joking."

"And you think that's what he's doing?"

"I've no idea, because Mum has chosen not to involve me, remember? She's made it obvious she doesn't need my help or advice. Well, she's made her own bed and she can damn well lie in it!"

Chapter 16

Posy drove into Southwold the following morning feeling very low. Having looked forward so much to having her family around her, the way the lunch had ended had devastated her. She'd spent the night trying to think how best to resolve the situation and had reached for the telephone this morning on more than one occasion, then replaced the receiver. Nick was very much like her; she knew he needed time to cool down before he'd listen to anything she might have to say.

She opened up the gallery, made herself a cup of tea and watched the rain pour down outside the window. The worst thing was that she knew she must come to a final decision on the sale of Admiral House. All this shilly-shallying was unsettling for all of them, not to mention the upset it had already caused. All she had to do was to pick up the telephone and tell Sam he had first refusal. Then she could hand the entire thing over to her solicitor and set about finding herself a new home.

An hour later, the gallery door opened and Freddie appeared through it, shaking the rain from the shoulders of his raincoat.

"Good morning, Posy. It's foul out there, absolutely foul," he said as he walked towards her.

"Hello, Freddie."

Even Posy could hear the limpness of her greeting.

"Look, I know you must be livid with me, canceling lunch yesterday at such short notice."

"Really, don't worry about it, Freddie."

"Well, I have and I am." Freddie began to pace around the gallery. "Good God, this is frustrating!"

"What is?"

"Just..." He looked at her, despair in his eyes. "Nothing," he said, shaking his head.

"Forgive me, Freddie, but one way and another, I'm not in the mood for any more dramatics. Especially when I have absolutely no idea what they're about. So if you still refuse to tell me, I'd be very grateful if you'd leave."

Posy could feel that she was close to tears, which really wouldn't do at all. She turned away from him and made to walk back to the office.

"Posy, I'm so very sorry. I really didn't mean to upset you further," he said, following her.

"It's not you, really," she said, reaching for a tissue from the box on the desk and blowing her nose hard. "It's all to do with the sale of my damned house. It's caused a big upset between my sons."

"Posy, please don't cry, I can't bear it..."

Freddie put his arms around her and pulled her to him. Despite herself, Posy felt too low to resist. She *needed* a hug, and despite herself, in Freddie's arms she felt safe and protected. She heard him sigh heavily above her, then looked up at him as he leant down to kiss her gently on the forehead. The bell that indicated a customer was entering tinkled and they pulled apart immediately.

"Listen, how about I take you to The Swan for a bite to eat once you've finished here? Then you can tell me all about it. See you at one?"

"Yes, that would be lovely, thank you, Freddie."

Posy watched him leave and thought that, whatever the state of their relationship, she needed a friend. *And at the very least,* she thought as she walked towards the customer, *Freddie is that.*

After a restorative gin and tonic and an attentive Freddie listening to her tale of woe, Posy's spirits were somewhat revived.

"Dearie me," Freddie sympathized as they munched their way through excellent fish and chips. "This sounds far more complicated than the issue of the sale of the house. A bad case of sibling rivalry, as much as anything else."

"Of course it is," Posy agreed. "Sam has always felt second-rate to Nick's business success. He wanted to crow to him about his new company and buying Admiral House. Nick was terribly upset I hadn't told him of my plans, not to mention the fact that he genuinely loves the house. And there you have it. This is how a family falls apart," she sighed, "and I just can't bear for it to happen to mine."

"Well, you must talk to Nick, who, if you ask me, sounds as if he was being more than a little petulant."

"Perhaps," Posy said, "but even though Nick is usually the more easygoing of my sons, once he gets a bee in his bonnet he can be very blinkered and stubborn, especially when it comes to his brother."

"I'm sure he'll come round, Posy, and look, at the end of the day, I'm afraid that for once, you have to put yourself and your needs first. That house of yours seems to have caused you nothing but grief lately and I really think you should just get on and sell it."

Posy studied the vehemence on his face. "You really don't like Admiral House, do you?"

"What I like or dislike is completely irrelevant. What *is* relevant, and what matters to me, is seeing you happy. And if you want my humble opinion, it's time you moved on."

"Yes, you're right. Okay," Posy breathed as she drained her gin and tonic. "I'm going to do as you suggested and give Sam first refusal."

"Good. Letting go is always difficult—when I sold the house in Kent after my wife died, it was the hardest decision I've ever made. But there's no doubt it was the right one."

"I'll go and see Marie at the estate agency when we're finished here," Posy promised.

"That's the spirit," Freddie said, signaling for the bill. He looked at her for a long time before he thumped his fist on the table.

"Hang it all! Life is too short not to!"

"Not to what, Freddie?"

"To ask you if you would like to come to Amsterdam with me the weekend after next. I've been invited to the seventieth birthday party of one of my oldest friends, Jeremy—we were at Bar School together. I'd love you to come with me, Posy, I really would."

"Right. Well..."

"Look, I understand I'm guilty of giving you mixed messages, but I really think that a weekend away from Southwold would do us both a power of good—breathe in some fresh air unencumbered by the past."

"*Our* past, you mean?"

"Yes, that, and..." Freddie shook his head. "I think we deserve some fun, Posy, both of us. No strings attached of course, separate rooms and all that in the hotel."

"Of course."

"So?" Freddie eyed her.

"Why not? I haven't been abroad for years and as you say, life's too short. So yes, I accept your invitation," Posy smiled as they walked through the bar over towards the exit.

"Mum! Hello there."

Posy felt a blush rise to her cheeks as she saw Sam on a bar stool, drinking a pint of Adnams.

"Hello, Sam."

"And who is your friend?" he asked her, glancing at Freddie and giving his mother a sly smile.

"Freddie Lennox, pleased to meet you." Freddie held out his hand and gave Sam's a firm shake.

"And you. Made a decision on our little deal yet, Mum?"

Feeling this wasn't the moment to inform Sam of the choice she'd just made, Posy merely said, "I will let you know as soon as I have. Bye now." Then she walked swiftly through the bar to the lobby. "Right, Freddie, thank you for lunch and the advice. Now I intend to act on it. I'm off to see Marie before I change my mind."

Having walked to the estate agent's and told Marie that Sam had first refusal but that she was not to contact him until a solicitor was instructed, Posy hurried through the rain to her car. Starting the engine, she decided she didn't want to go home and sit and stew once more on the Nick/Sam situation. Remembering Amy had said yesterday that the children were on half-term and she was having to take a week off from the hotel to look after them, Posy parked in front of the bakery, dashed inside to buy a cake, then headed down Ferry Road to see her daughter-in-law and grandchildren.

"Hello, Amy, how are you?" Posy said as Amy opened the door. "I brought you a cake."

"I...thanks..." A paler than usual Amy put a hand to her unbrushed hair and Posy noticed her eyes were red. She looked as though she'd been crying. "I wasn't expecting any visitors," she said as she led the way through the cluttered hall and into the sitting room. The floor was covered in children's toys and the sofa in a large pile of unironed clothes. Jake and Sara were both sitting in front of a grainy television and barely acknowledged their grandmother's presence.

"Why don't we leave those two whilst they're engrossed and go and make some tea?" suggested Posy gently.

"Okay, but the kitchen's in a worse state than this."

"I've come to see you, I don't care about the housekeeping," Posy said as she followed Amy into the kitchen. "Are you all right, my dear? You don't look too good."

"Oh, I think I've got that bug that's been going around, that's all," said Amy, switching on the kettle and blowing her nose on some kitchen roll.

"Then you should be in bed."

"I wish." Amy leant over the stained worktop and Posy saw her shoulders were shaking.

"Amy, my dear." Posy went towards her, then pulled her into her arms and held her as she sobbed. "There, there, tell me what the matter is," she comforted.

"Oh Posy, I can't," Amy sobbed.

"Yes you can, and if it's about Sam, I really won't feel you're being disloyal. I know his faults better than anyone. I'm his mother."

"I..." Amy hiccupped as she tried to speak. "I just don't know how we're going to get through this month, I really don't. We're at the limit of our overdraft, we've got hundreds of pounds of bills to pay, including the telephone, gas and electricity, which is already overdue, and all Sam can do is spend what we do have drinking in the wretched pub! The kids are being a nightmare and I feel so ill and...I'm so sorry, Posy." Amy slumped onto a kitchen chair. "I'm at the end of my tether, I really am."

Posy tore off some more kitchen roll and handed it to Amy, who wiped her face and blew her nose again. "Of course you are, Amy dear. Everyone reaches their limit when their cup of endurance fills up so much that it overflows. That's what's happened to you. To be honest, I'm amazed you've held out this long."

"Are you?" Amy lifted her eyes to Posy's, who sat down next to her and took her hands.

"Yes. Everyone who knows you thinks you're incredibly loyal to Sam. You've had such a tough time, Amy, and you've never complained."

"Up until now."

"Well, it's high time that you did, for your sake if nobody else's. You're not a saint, just human like the rest of us."

"I've tried to be positive, I really have, but it's so difficult when you're stuck in a miserable hole like this with the rain pouring down, and feeling there's just no hope."

"You're absolutely right, this is a hole, but I promise you, there is hope," reassured Posy. "Now, let me make you some nice hot tea and we can talk about what you're going to do to at least start trying to solve the financial problems."

"I could get a sub on next month's wages, but the problem is, that'll leave us even shorter in a few weeks' time."

"I think you have to live from day to day at present," said Posy as she switched the kettle on. "Is Sam earning nothing at all?"

"No, not until he gets one of these projects off the ground. At the moment, it's all—as usual—speculative."

"Well, I do have a little good news, Amy. I've just been to see Marie and told her that Sam can have first refusal on Admiral House."

"Really? Well, that will cheer him up," Amy agreed. "Are you absolutely sure, Posy?"

"No, but at least Sam can now have a shot."

"I meant about selling."

"Of course not, but as a very good friend said to me earlier, one must move on. And at least if the project does go well, then you really could be looking to a brighter future," suggested Posy.

"I suppose so. Sam certainly seems more committed and excited about this project than I've seen him for a long time. But things have gone wrong so many times in the past, I almost don't dare to hope."

As Posy passed Amy her tea, the door opened and a little ragamuffin with tousled hair and a dirty face came in. Sara climbed onto her mother's knee and stuck a thumb into her mouth.

"Cuddle, Mummy," she said.

"Now, Amy, the other thing I think you should seriously consider is moving in with me until the situation improves. I really don't think this house is equipped to see a young family through a long winter. You'll end up catching your deaths. The draughts here are far worse than at mine," said Posy, shivering involuntarily.

"We can't. You know Sam would never consider it."

"Well, Sam has got to start thinking of his family and their welfare before his silly pride. Now, Sara, I'm going to make your Mummy a hot water bottle, then tuck her up in bed with a couple of aspirin."

"No, Posy, really, I'm fine."

"You're exhausted and besides, Sara and I are going to bake jam tarts for tea, aren't we?"

Sara jumped off her mother's knee and came to hug her grandmother. "Yes please!"

There was no sign of Amy by teatime, so Posy fed the children, then bathed them, thinking how much good it would do Amy to rest. She was just reading them a bedtime story when the key turned in the lock and Sam arrived home. Kissing both children goodnight, Posy crept past Amy's bedroom and down the stairs.

"Hi, Mum. What..."

Posy put a finger to her lips. "Hush. Amy's sleeping. She's not at all well. Come into the kitchen. We'll talk there."

"What's been going on?" asked Sam, looking confused.

"I arrived here this afternoon to find your wife hysterical."

"What about?"

"Perhaps the fact that there seems to be no money to pay any bills, that she's reduced to living in a house that isn't fit for dogs, that she works all hours God sends and takes care of the children, with, it seems, little if any support from you, might have contributed to her current state of mind."

"My God, she has been having a bitch about me, hasn't she?"

"Sam, I would say that it is not in your interest to anger me at present. Sit down, please."

Sam recognized that rare cold undertone from childhood in his mother's voice and did as he was told.

"Now listen to me, please. Your wife is on the edge of a nervous breakdown. If you *dare* to criticize her for letting her troubles pour out, you'll find no sympathy from me. Amy has supported you through thick and thin for years without complaint. I and others have often wondered why she's done it, but for whatever reason, you're a very lucky man."

"Please don't lecture me, Mum. I realize I'm married to a saint, everyone tells me, and that I must be grateful and—"

"Sam, you are at risk of losing Amy unless you get your act together and fast. And I really don't want to see that happen, for the children's sake, if not yours. Therefore, I'm prepared to help you."

"How?"

"I've written a check made out to you for five hundred pounds. From what Amy says, that should at least pay the utility bills and keep the wolf from the door for a while."

"I really don't think things are as bad as Amy made out, Mum..."

"I think they are. Here," Posy handed over the check. Sam took it and read it.

"Thanks, Mum, I'll pay you back when things get going, of course."

"Of course." Posy took a deep breath. "And the other thing you should know is that, for the sake of Amy and the children, I'm prepared to give your company first refusal on Admiral House."

Sam's face lit up. "Mum, that's fantastic! I don't know what to say."

"You can say whatever you wish, but it'll be to my solicitor, who will be dealing with it from here on in," Posy said briskly. "It will obviously take time to organize everything, so I won't want to move out before February, but there's no reason why the paperwork can't be completed as soon as possible. I'll contact my solicitor tomorrow and let him know of my decision. I think it's far better if this is conducted on a purely business basis. I'm giving you the opportunity, but if you mess it up, then it's down to you."

"Of course, Mum. I'm thrilled." Sam made to hug her, but Posy pulled away.

"I just pray that for your family's sake you make a success of the project. And now I really must be going."

"Are you sure you don't want to stay? I'll run out and get a bottle of champagne to celebrate."

Posy sighed. "I hardly think, in your current financial predicament, that champagne is within your range. Please give my love to Amy and tell her I'll see her soon. Goodbye, Sam."

"Bye, Mum."

As soon as the door closed, Sam let out a whoop of triumph.

Chapter 17

Nick threw his mobile down onto the passenger seat of his car. He stared into the distance, not really knowing what to think or feel.

So now he knew for sure. The question was, where did he go from here? Did he tell Tammy the truth, come straight out with it and try to explain an inexplicable situation? Or was it better to get through the next few weeks, do what he had to do whilst covering his tracks, and then when things were more settled, tell her?

Who knew how things would turn out? Perhaps it was kinder if he shouldered the burden alone for a while. The situation would obviously mean he'd have to play it very carefully and there was no doubt it would add a lot of extra pressure to his already pressurized life. But what could he do? Under the circumstances, he could hardly walk away, which, if he was honest, was what he desperately wanted to do at this moment.

Nick pondered how one's life could be running perfectly smoothly and happily, then in the space of a few short weeks, everything could change. If he was in the mood to be self-indulgent, then he could say that fate had dealt him a very rough hand, but he knew there were others who were currently suffering a far worse plight than he was.

Nick sighed deeply, then pulled himself together and climbed out of the car. As he put his key into the lock of Paul and Janey's house, he told himself he'd cope. At the end of the day, he had no other choice.

The doorbell rang and Evie shouted for Clemmie to answer it.

"Hi, Clemmie. How are you?"

"I'm good, thanks, Marie. Mum's upstairs."

"Right. I was going to ask you whether you wanted to come round to ours for lunch and a play with Lucy," Marie said as she followed Clemmie inside and up the stairs.

"I'd love to. It gets boring in the hols, especially because I don't know anyone around here."

"School's going well?"

"Yes. I love it," she said as she pushed open the door to her mother's bedroom. Evie was in bed, propped up on pillows.

"Hi, Marie. How are you?"

"Fine, thanks."

"I just asked Clemmie if she wanted to come for lunch at ours. She does."

"That would be great." Evie nodded.

"You okay?"

"I've got this bug that's going around, but I'm all right, thanks."

"Would you like a cup of tea, Marie? I'm just going to make one for Mum."

"I'd love one, thanks, Clemmie."

"Wow, Evie." Marie whistled as Clemmie left the room. "Your daughter's special. I'm still waiting for Lucy to make me anything in the kitchen department."

"Yes, she is, but she's had to be, one way and another."

"She says she's enjoying school anyway."

"Yes. I'm very relieved she's happy."

"So..." Marie perched on the end of Evie's bed. "Have you heard the news about Posy Montague?"

"No, I don't listen to town gossip."

"She's selling Admiral House."

"Really?"

"Yes. To her son, Sam."

"I see. And what will he do with it?"

"Turn it into luxury apartments. I'm brokering the deal," Marie added. "I do feel sorry for that poor wife of his, though. It's obvious that they've got no money, but..."

"Then how can Sam be buying Admiral House, if that's the case?"

"Sam told me he has a sleeping partner, a chap called Ken Noakes. From what I gather, he's seriously rich."

"Posy must be devastated, having to sell her lovely home," mused Evie.

"Well, I hope to be able to find her somewhere nice to live in the next few weeks. I've already sent her some details. You know, she seems awfully fond of you, Evie. Why don't you go and see her?"

"I might when I'm better."

"And I'll tell you who I saw driving out of town recently, in a vintage Austin Healey..."

"Who?"

"Nick Montague, Sam's baby brother."

"I know who he is, Marie. I used to work for him, remember?" Evie said coldly.

"Yes, of course you did, sorry. Anyway, he must have done quite well for himself, being able to afford a motor like that."

Clemmie brought up the tea and Evie decided seeing Marie was a bit like eating at McDonald's; you looked forward to it, but then felt sick halfway through.

"Thanks, Clemmie," said Marie. "Give me ten minutes and we'll be off."

"Okay." Clemmie wandered out of the room.

"Do you ever miss having a man around the place?"

"Nope," Evie said firmly. "I like my own company."

"You always were different from me. I need people and chat around me all the time," Marie admitted. "I'd go mad living by myself."

"Sometimes I get lonely, but very rarely."

Marie studied Evie for a while, then said, "Are you sure you're okay? You look awfully pale, and even thinner than usual."

"Do I? Well, I'm not," insisted Evie.

"And you seem...tense."

"I'm fine, really."

Marie sighed. "Okay, okay, I get the message. Whatever it is, you don't want to talk about it. I just worry about you, that's all. I have known you for most of your life and I know there's something wrong."

"Will you bloody well stop treating me like one of your kids, Marie! I'm a grown woman and I'm completely capable of looking after myself!"

"Sorry." She stood up. "I'll drop Clemmie back around five."

"Thanks. I don't mean to be snappy and...yes, you're right," she sighed. "I do have a...situation and it's giving me sleepless nights, but I'll be fine once I've sorted it out."

"Well, you know I'm here if you want to talk about it."

"Yes, thanks. And I'm really sorry I shouted."

"Don't worry. We all have our bad days. Now you have a rest and I'll see you later."

Just after Marie and Clemmie had left, the telephone rang. Evie heaved herself up to answer it.

"Hello?"

"It's me, I'm just checking in. How are you?" he asked.

"Okay."

"You don't sound it."

"I'm okay," she repeated.

"Having a bad day?"

"A bit, yes."

"I'm so sorry, Evie, I wish I could be there for you more often. So are we still on for the weekend?"

"Yes."

"God, I'm nervous."

"You'll be fine, really," she reassured him.

"I'll do my best."

"I know you will—please don't worry."

"I'll try not to. Anything you need, just call me on the mobile. Otherwise, I'll see you both at noon tomorrow."

"Yes, see you tomorrow." Evie put the phone down, sank back onto the pillows, and let out a long, deep sigh. How she would break the news to her daughter, she wasn't sure—the thought of hurting her was like sticking a knife into her own heart, but she had no choice.

She closed her eyes, feeling nauseous at the mess she had made of her life and how that would affect Clemmie.

Some things were out of her control, but now she had to do everything to sort out her daughter's future as best she could.

"Hello, Amy, what a nice surprise." Posy looked up from her desk in the gallery. "How are you?"

"Oh, much better, thanks," said Amy as she walked towards Posy and put a bunch of lilies down on the desk. "I brought these to say thank you so much for being so kind to me the other day and looking after the kids."

"That's what family is for, Amy," said Posy, picking up the flowers and smelling them. "What time did you eventually wake up?"

"The following morning," Amy admitted. "I slept right through, but it did me the world of good. I feel much more positive. And I also wanted to say thank you for the check. Sam told me you'd given it to him and it really is very kind of you. He's put it in the bank and paid off some of the bills."

"Well, as I shall technically be a millionairess in a few months' time, I thought it was the least I could do."

"As you can imagine, Sam's over the moon about Admiral House. In fact," said Amy, "he's a different person. I can't thank you enough for giving him the opportunity, Posy."

"Actually, while you're here, I have something for you." Posy reached down into her handbag and pulled out an envelope. "There."

"What is it?"

"An invitation to the launch of Tammy's boutique. She wrote to thank me for lunch and enclosed it for you. She said you and Sam were welcome to stay with her for the night at her house in London."

"That's really sweet of her, except I can't go," said Amy, opening the envelope and looking at the smart invitation.

"Of course you can. I'll have the children for you, then you and Sam could go together, make a night of it."

"That's very kind of you, Posy, but I've got work."

"I'm sure you could arrange to swap shifts with one of the other girls, Amy. It would do you the world of good to have a break."

"Maybe, but I don't have a dress to wear to some posh London party."

"Stop making excuses, young lady." Posy wagged her finger at

Amy. "Leave it to me. I'll come up with something, all right?"

"You sound like my fairy godmother, Posy."

"Well, I do feel you're entitled to a little fun occasionally, my dear. And talking of fun, guess where I'm going next weekend?"

"Where?"

"To Amsterdam!"

"Goodness! Who with?"

"A gentleman friend of mine. Do forgive me, Amy, but I just had to tell someone. Though I'd obviously prefer it if you said nothing to Sam. He might not approve."

"Well, I think it's wonderful. Are the two of you...?"

"Goodness, no, but I do so enjoy his company. At my age, one just has to seize the day and not worry too much about the future, and," Posy added with a smile, "that's just what I intend to do in Amsterdam."

Chapter 18

Tammy kissed a dusty Nick on the top of his head. "How are things going?" she asked as he stood up from examining the bottom of an enormous painted bookcase.

"Woodworm, it's got bloody woodworm! I can't believe he didn't notice it. Five grand and I'll be lucky to see two!"

"Hello to you too, darling." Tammy watched as Nick thumped the bookcase with his fist.

"Sorry. Hello, sweetheart."

"God, it's cold down here," Tammy remarked with a shiver. "The showroom upstairs is already starting to look good though."

"Thanks. I reckon I'll be able to open the doors in about a month. God, I'm pissed off about that bookcase," he sighed.

"Fancy some supper at the Italian round the corner?" Tammy asked.

"As a matter of fact, a bath and a take-away pizza in front of the TV hold more appeal tonight."

"Okay, I'm easy. Come back to mine." She watched as Nick switched off the lights in the basement and they walked upstairs together. Tammy flung herself onto a huge four-poster bed placed in the center of the showroom.

"Good sir, come ravish me, right here, right now! Why not put this in the window with us on it? That would get the customers in," she giggled as she looked up at him and saw her joke hadn't even mustered a grin. "Oh dear, you really do look totally stressed out."

"I am," Nick shrugged. "Sorry."

Over a Neapolitan pizza and a bottle of wine in Tammy's sitting room, Nick outlined his woes.

"What with the shop to organize and open and all that entails, not to mention the sale of the business in Perth, I've got no time to do the rounds and actually do the buying myself. If I'd been at the sale, rather than phoning the bid in, I would have seen the woodworm on the spot. My reputation here in London will rise or fall purely on the quality of my stock. Anyway." Nick ran a hand through his hair. "Ignore me, as you said, I'm stressed. Tell me about you."

"I'm very happy. I really have managed to find the most wonderful back-up."

"You mean your neighbour's mum, the Sari Queen of Brick Lane?"

"I do, yes. Meena might be nearly sixty, but my God, she has more energy than I do. Her beadwork and sewing are just superb and totally put mine in the shade, but it's more than that, Nick. She's just so capable. I went in today at nine and Meena was already there, having addressed a further fifty envelopes on my party guest list. If she has nothing to do, she'll find something."

"Can she come and work for me?" murmured Nick.

"Hah, no. She even brings me in little Tupperware pots of Indian food to feed me up. I've offered her a job as my second in command and if we get really busy, I'll just employ someone else to do the repairs. Meena says she has lots of friends who would help."

"Is your stock all ready?"

"Not yet, no, but at least with Meena on the case, I should have enough stock to open with. And guess what? Darling Janey has managed to organize a feature on me and the clothes in *Marie Claire*. I've also had a Sunday mag and a couple of dailies wanting to interview me too."

"That all sounds great, darling."

"Sorry, Nick, I don't want to sound happy when you're feeling low."

"Don't be silly." He pulled her towards him and stroked her hair. "I'll be fine once the business is up and running. The sign-writer's coming in at ten tomorrow, so at least I'll have my name over the window."

"That's good. By the way, Janey called. She's invited us for supper on Saturday night to celebrate their big news. Can you make it?"

"I'm afraid I've already said I can't. There's an auction at a country house in Staffordshire on Sunday, with viewing on the Saturday. I'll be away all weekend."

"That's a shame, but never mind. Why don't I come with you? I'm sure Janey and I can organize another night to celebrate."

"You could, but you'd be bored out of your mind. Talking of Jane, I really think it's time I sorted out my accommodation situation. I know I spend most nights here, but my stuff is still there and it's not fair on Jane and Paul. So I thought I should go house-hunting in the next few days."

"You could always move in here, you know."

"Could I?"

Tammy nodded. "Yes."

"That's a big step. After all, we've only known each other a few weeks."

Tammy felt suddenly irritated by Nick's lukewarm response to her offer. It was a big step for her too, but obviously one Nick was not ready for.

"Anyway," she shrugged, "it was only an idea."

"Thanks, and I really appreciate it, but I just think I might be hell to live with in the next couple of months. To be honest, I'd prefer to wait until things have settled down and I'm in a more positive state of mind about the future. Okay?"

"Okay."

"What's wrong, Tammy?"

Tammy looked up at Meena as she put a hot coffee on her desk in the tiny office at the back of the boutique. The older woman was immaculately dressed as always, her generous frame clothed in a bright pink suit with a multi-colored scarf thrown jauntily over her shoulder. Her shiny ebony hair was pinned neatly into a chignon and her makeup was expertly applied.

"Nothing, I'm fine," said Tammy as she sat opening the post.

"We've received another ten acceptances to the party. I'm getting concerned whether there'll be enough air for everyone to breathe in here."

"That is good news, isn't it?" Meena smiled broadly, revealing a set of faultless white teeth. "So tell me, why do you look so glum?"

"I don't."

"Pah!" Meena waved her beringed fingers in the air. "You have a call from *Marie Claire* to organize a photo shoot yesterday and you arrive this morning looking like the dog ate your favorite dinner. Tell me, what's up?"

"I'm sure I'm just being oversensitive, that's all. I suggested Nick move in with me last night and he said he wasn't ready to. So I've ended up feeling like I'm pushing the relationship faster than he wants."

"Men!" Meena sniffed. "He gets the offer of a warm bed with a beauty like you in it, and he turns it down because he is 'not ready.' You mark my words, he will live to regret his decision."

"Will he?" Tammy sighed. "I just don't know. My relationship with Nick sometimes feels like one step forward, two steps back. There are times when he's fantastic, and I feel very secure and happy and I really believe he loves me and it's going to work out. Then out of the blue, he'll do or say something that will really rock my faith. It doesn't help that he's spending so much time out of London hunting for stock either. I miss him, Meena. It makes me wonder whether I'm in far too deep."

"Oh, you are, there is no doubt about that," nodded Meena. "You love this man, that is obvious. Once you have it, you are stuck, like me and Sanjay. Just think, if I had not set eyes on a young man standing behind his stall at the Brick Lane market thirty years ago, I could perhaps have married a Maharajah, not a sari manufacturer."

Tammy giggled. "Do you still love him?"

"Yes, but more importantly, I like him and I respect him. He is a good person. And from what I have seen of your Nick, he is too. Seize the moment, Tammy. Enjoy the fact you are young, beautiful and in love, for in no time you will be like me, an old crone."

"Meena, if I look like you in my fifties, I will be thrilled," she said, studying her assistant's unlined caramel skin. "So I mustn't pull away from him, is that what you're saying?"

"No. Embrace it!" Meena held out her arms wide. "The pain will only make the pleasure heightened. It is what life is all about. And you are young enough to bounce back if it goes wrong."

Tammy nodded. "Yes, you're right. And if I end up an old maid with only my memories, at least I can say I've lived."

"Yes, Tammy. That is right."

The front doorbell and the telephone rang at the same time.

"Time to forget about love and become a businesswoman," said Meena. "I'll answer the call, you let the delivery man in."

Chapter 19

Amy was feeling more upbeat than she had for ages. In the past ten days, since Posy had arrived like the cavalry and given Sam the go-ahead on Admiral House, the atmosphere at home had lightened considerably. Sam had said last night that Ken Noakes, his partner, was so pleased Sam had managed to nab the project that he'd offered him a small weekly wage whilst he worked on the deal.

"It's still not a lot, and we won't see the real money until I get my cut when the project's finished, but I reckon we could maybe afford to move out of here in the spring."

"Oh Sam, that would make all the difference," Amy had said with relief as she'd served up their bangers and mash.

"I know how difficult it's been for you, sweetheart. Tell you what, when all this is over and we're sitting pretty with the money in the bank, I'm going to take you abroad on a really special holiday."

"That sounds like bliss," Amy had replied, glad to see her husband so positive, and not drinking as much as usual either, which made her life so much easier.

"By the way, I'm not going to be around tomorrow night," Sam had mentioned. "Ken is flying over from Spain and wants to meet me for dinner at a hotel in Norfolk. He's got another project going on there at the moment, so he's booked me a room for the night. I think he wants to celebrate the Admiral House deal."

"Okay," Amy had agreed, thinking Sam had so rarely been around in the evenings recently that a few more hours after midnight would make no odds. "You go and have a good time. You deserve it, darling."

This morning, Amy had kissed Sam goodbye before she'd left for work and thought how she was looking forward to a night to herself. Marie was collecting the kids from school, and when she got home, she was planning to put the children to bed, then curl up by the fire and finally finish Sebastian's book.

"Weather's looking grim for tonight," commented Karen, the other hotel receptionist, as she posted the daily weather report on the reception desk. "Gales and torrential rain are forecast."

"Oh God," said Amy. "I don't think it would take much for the roof to blow off our house."

"No, you're not exactly protected there, are you? Mind you, I'm sure it's survived a few gales in its time and it's still standing."

By the time Amy arrived at Marie's house, the weather had indeed deteriorated.

"Not a nice night," said Marie, letting a dripping Amy in through the door. "I've fed the kids and they're fine. Now, how about a glass of wine before you go home?"

"Just a small one, thanks. I don't want to get back too late. I hate it when winter starts to set in. It's nearly dark already and it's only twenty past five," said Amy, accepting the glass of wine Marie handed to her.

"I know. It'll soon be Christmas. Cheers." Marie raised her glass. "Here's to your property mogul husband. Is he pleased?"

"Very," nodded Amy.

"Good. I reckon he could make a fortune if he does the job properly."

"Let's hope so," agreed Amy. "But there's a long way to go yet."

Twenty minutes later, Amy piled her children into the car and they headed home. The rain was beating down so fast, she could hardly see out of the windscreen. She pulled up in front of the house, grabbed the shopping from the boot and ran with Jake and Sara up the path to the front door.

"Let's get inside, have a nice hot bath and warm up," she said as she unlocked the front door and reached for the light switch. Nothing happened. She tried it again and let out a groan of frustration. Obviously the storm had tripped the fuses. Putting Sara down and shutting the front door behind her, Amy stood in the pitch-black hallway and tried to remember where the fuse box was.

"Mummy, I'm scared," whined Sara as Amy fumbled her way into the sitting room, then located first the mantelpiece, then the matches.

"There we go." Amy lit a match and hurriedly scanned the room for a candle to give more permanent light. Her eyes alighted on a half-inch of wax sitting on a saucer on the window-ledge. "Right." She made her way back to Sara and Jake, their little faces full of fear. "You two follow me and we'll go and get some lights back on."

The three of them made their way carefully through the kitchen and into the small lobby beyond. Amy pulled open a box which she was thankful to see housed the fuses and scanned the trip-switches. To her confusion, none of them seemed to have switched themselves off, but she tried them all anyway, to no avail.

"Mummy, I don't like the dark. I see monsters," complained Jake. "When will the light come back on?"

"Mummy, I'm cold," added Sara.

"I know, but Mummy's just got to take a minute to think what to do. Perhaps the storm has turned off the electricity in lots of houses. It might come back on in a minute. Anyway, I'll phone the electricity people and find out, shall I?"

With her two little ones holding tight to the back of her coat, Amy dug in her handbag for her mobile. Searching up the number, she dialed the emergency hotline.

"Oh, hello, I was just enquiring whether there's been a power cut in Southwold? I live on Ferry Road and we've come in to find no electricity. No? Oh, well then, we need someone to come out and find out what the fault is. My full name and address...yes, of course."

Amy imparted the necessary information and waited as the operator put her on hold to make enquiries. Finally, the voice came back at the other end of the line.

"I'm very sorry, Mrs. Montague, but our computer is showing that your electricity supply has been terminated."

"What?! Why?"

"Because we have still not received payment for the last quarter. You were sent a letter over two weeks ago, informing you that if you did not pay the bill within the next fourteen days, we would be terminating the supply."

Amy's heart started to thump against her chest. "Yes, I received it, and I know for a fact that my husband paid it."

"I'm afraid no payment is showing up on our system, Mrs. Montague."

"But he did pay it, he told me he had. Perhaps it's got lost," said Amy desperately.

"Perhaps," said the operator, obviously having heard it all before.

Amy bit her lip. "So what do I do?"

"The fastest way is to make a cash payment at your nearest post office, then call us to let us know the money has been sent. We will reinstate your supply immediately upon receipt."

"But...but what about tonight? I've got two young children, it's dangerous for them here in the dark." Amy could feel the tears welling up and constricting her throat.

"I'm sorry, but there's nothing we can do until you've made that payment, Mrs. Montague."

"Well, I...thanks for nothing!" Amy ended the call and sank down into a chair.

"Mummy, what's happened?" asked Jake, his little face full of concern.

"Nothing, nothing at all, Jakey." Amy brushed the tears away harshly with her sleeve as she tried to think what was best to do. They couldn't stay here for the night. They had no more candles and it was far too cold for the children. She was sure Marie would put them up, but pride would not allow her to ask.

No, there was only one place they could go. She dialed Posy's number. The line was engaged, which at least meant Posy was at home. Rather than sit here another minute, Amy decided to pile the children into the car, drive straight to Admiral House and beg a bed for all of them for the night.

"Come on, kids, we're off on an adventure. We're going to Granny's to stay there for the night."

"We're going to sleep in that big house?" said Jake, who, having lived no more than ten minutes away from his grandmother, had never needed to stay over.

"Yes, won't that be fun?" Amy lifted Sara up into her arms and picked up the candle to light them to the front door.

"But what about our pyjamas?" Jake enquired.

"I'm sure we'll find something for you to wear at Granny's house," she soothed, wanting to get out of the house as soon as possible. "Right, Jakey, you run down the path to the car whilst Mummy locks the door."

Amy was soaking by the time she had managed to belt both children into their car seats.

"What about Daddy? Won't he come home and wonder where we are?" asked Jake as they set off.

At this precise moment Amy only wished some very painful accident would befall Sam so she'd never have to see him again. "Daddy's away for the night, darling. We'll be back home tomorrow by the time he arrives," she reassured her son.

The storm was in full force as Amy drove through the deserted streets of Southwold and out of the town towards Admiral House. As she turned off onto the lane that led to the entrance, she could feel the ferocity of the wind buffeting the little car.

"Nearly there now," she soothed as she pulled into the drive. "I'm sure Granny will have some kind of nice cake in her pantry for us."

She pulled up outside the house and turned off the engine, relieved to see lights on downstairs and in a couple of rooms upstairs.

"You two wait here whilst I go and speak to Granny."

Amy opened the driver's door and struggled to close it again against the wind. She ran to the front door and rang the bell. When there was no reply, she tried knocking loudly instead. The rain was dripping from the ends of her hair as she ran round to the kitchen door at the side of the house. That too was uncharacteristically locked. Running back to the front door, she hammered on it insistently.

"Posy? It's me, Amy!"

There was still silence from inside the house.

"Oh Christ, what on earth do I do now?" she asked herself desperately.

Banging her fists on the door again, Amy realized she'd just have to swallow her pride and throw herself and the children on the mercy of Marie. Turning away from the front door, she headed miserably back towards the car. Halfway there, she heard the sound of bolts being drawn back and turned to look. Sure enough, the front door was opening.

"Thank God, thank God," she breathed as she rushed back towards the door. "Posy, it's me, Amy. I..."

Amy stopped short as she saw not Posy, but Sebastian Girault, with only a towel wrapped round his midriff, standing on the doorstep.

"Amy, my God, you're drenched. Posy's not here."

Amy's heart sank. "Where is she?"

"She left to go to Amsterdam this morning."

"Shit! She told me last week but I'd forgotten." Amy gulped, knowing she was going to cry again at any minute.

"I think you'd better come in anyway, at least until you've dried off," he suggested. "You'll catch your death."

"I've got my children in the car. Oh God, I don't know what to do, I don't know what to do."

"Look, grab the kids and come inside, okay?"

Half an hour later, all three of them having climbed gratefully into the hot bath she'd run for them, the two children were wrapped in blankets on the sofa in the morning room. Amy sat cross-legged by the fire, wearing Posy's ancient velour dressing gown.

Sebastian appeared from the kitchen with hot chocolate for the children and handed her a large brandy. "Drink it. You look as though you need it."

"Thanks," said Amy gratefully.

"I've hung your wet clothes over the stove. They should be dry by the morning."

"I hope you don't mind us crashing on you like this," said Amy. "We just had nowhere else to go."

"Don't be silly. You're Posy's daughter-in-law," said Sebastian, who had now covered his modesty with a pair of sweatpants and a sweater. "She'd hang me out to dry if she thought I hadn't offered you full hospitality. Mind you, you're bloody lucky I heard you. I'd just got into the bath and was listening to Verdi on my headphones. If I hadn't left the soap by the basin and had to get out to retrieve it, I would never have known what a tragedy was unfolding on the doorstep. If you don't mind me asking, what exactly has happened?"

Amy put a finger to her lips and indicated the children. "Come on, you two, it's time for bed. I've decided you can share with Mummy tonight and I've already put hotties in to warm the sheets."

"Do you want a hand?" Sebastian asked as Amy wearily heaved a sleepy Sara up into her arms. "Like a piggy-back?" he suggested to Jake.

"Yes please." Jake nodded shyly.

"Come on then, old man, let's be having you."

Amy managed a smile as Sebastian went charging up the stairs at top speed, a squealing Jake hanging on to his neck.

They tucked the children under a cosy eiderdown in the double bed in one of the spare rooms.

"Story, Mummy, story!"

"Oh darling, Mummy's a bit tired tonight and it's very late and..."

"I'll do the story, Jake," cut in Sebastian, "but as I'm a professional storyteller, I might have to make some kind of charge for my services, like Mummy going downstairs and filling up my wine glass from the bottle in the fridge. Would that be fair do you think, Jake?"

"Oh yes, what's the story to be about?"

Amy kissed Sara, who was virtually asleep already, then hugged Jake, who was obviously eager to get rid of her.

"We...ell," Sebastian winked at Amy as she left the room. She walked slowly downstairs, touched by the natural way Sebastian obviously had with children. As she picked up his wine glass, refilled it and took it back upstairs, where a rapt Jake was hanging on every word Sebastian spoke, she couldn't help but compare him to Sam. She had to virtually beg Sam to read the kids a story, or in fact spend any time playing with them whatsoever. Amy had recently come to the conclusion that, even though he undoubtedly loved them, Sam didn't actually much like *being* with them. She could only hope the situation would change as they grew up and became more civilized.

Amy went back down to the morning room, settled herself by the fire, and picked up the remains of her brandy. She thought how much she loved this house, so bruised and battered, yet so full of character. It felt safe and secure, like the home she currently yearned for would be.

"What are you thinking?"

Amy jumped and turned to see Sebastian standing in the doorway. She'd been so deep in thought she hadn't heard him come in.

"I was thinking how much I adore this house and how grim it'll be to see it turned into apartments."

"Don't," groaned Sebastian. "I hate the thought too. And how Posy must feel doesn't bear thinking about."

"Well, imagine how I feel. It's my husband whose company will take the sledgehammer to it."

"So I've heard." Sebastian padded to the sofa and sat down. "Oh well, he'll make some money and that'll help you and the family, won't it?"

"Perhaps," Amy conceded. "But as it's his complete incompetence that's landed us on your doorstep tonight, I really can't say I hold out much hope."

"Am I allowed to ask?"

"Yes." Amy sighed wearily. "He didn't get round to paying the electricity bill and they've cut us off."

"I see. Was this an oversight or due to lack of funds?"

"Definitely an oversight. I know for a fact he had the money. Posy had very kindly given him a check. Of course, he may well have spent it on booze..." Amy shrugged. "Let's face it, whichever way you look at it, it doesn't bode well for the future."

"No, quite. Er, where is he exactly? Did you leave him at home in the dark?"

"He's off in some swanky hotel in Norfolk having dinner with his business partner. Sebastian, would you mind awfully if I made myself some toast? I've had nothing to eat since lunchtime and my head's swimming from the brandy."

"Help yourself. As a matter of fact, I might join you. After all this excitement, I feel quite peckish." He followed Amy into the kitchen.

"How about cheese on toast?" she asked.

"Wonderful. I'm glad you came."

"Please don't let me hold up your work. If you need to get on, just say," said Amy, placing cheese onto slices of bread.

"No, I wasn't considering doing any more work tonight and besides, I've had some rather good news today."

"Really?" said Amy, putting the bread and cheese into the oven. "What?"

"A Hollywood film company has just bought the rights to *The Shadow Fields*. Apparently, they're going to turn it into next year's blockbuster."

"Oh my God, Sebastian! That's amazing. Will it make you rich?"

"Possibly. Not that I'm exactly poor now," Sebastian stated without a hint of arrogance. "They'll probably wreck it, of course, but I hope there'll at least be some essence of the original."

"There you go." Amy put the meal down on the table. "Not exactly much of a celebration dinner, is it?" she said with a small laugh.

Sebastian looked at her as she sat down. "I happen to think it's just perfect."

"Well, congratulations anyway on the film deal."

"Can I offer you a glass of wine to toast my success?"

"Go on then." Sebastian poured them both some wine, then they tucked into the food.

"It is strange that you turned up here on the doorstep tonight. Obviously serendipity taking a hand," said Sebastian. "Posy said she's not been away anywhere for years..."

"And I've certainly never needed to ask her for a bed for the night before," added Amy.

"I wonder what your friend Marie would make of it, if she could see us both sitting here now eating cheese on toast in your mother-in-law's kitchen," mused Sebastian. "Posy in Amsterdam, your husband away..."

"Don't," shuddered Amy, "I know exactly what she'd think."

"Well, even the most cynical mind might contemplate the fact that fate has seemed rather eager to throw us together. And one must therefore ask, why?"

Amy had stopped eating and was looking at Sebastian. "And what would be your answer?"

"If I was in creative-writer mode, I'd say that from the first moment we laid eyes on each other, there was a connection between us."

"You shouted at me and made me cry," rejected Amy.

"Yes, and I was then, for some reason quite unknown to me, impelled to follow you out onto the street to apologize to you."

"Surely that was just good manners?" Despite herself, Amy couldn't help joining in with his flirtatious banter.

"Amy, my dear, sadly, you don't know me at all well. Apologies from me are as searched-for as the Golden Fleece. No," he shook his head, "it was definitely something else. And then I was compelled at my reading to force my book into your hands free of charge. Which, I might add, is also definitely not like me. Shall we move back into the morning room and take our wine with us?"

They moved next door, Amy settling herself once more in front of the fire and stoking it. "I have to say, I really didn't like you very much at all, you know. But then I read your book and thought that anyone who could write so movingly couldn't be completely bad."

"Thanks," Sebastian acknowledged. "I'll take that as a compliment. And I'll let you into a secret, shall I?"

"If you want."

"I think," he said, nursing his wine glass in both hands, "that I wanted to stay and write in Southwold because of you."

"What? We'd only met twice before you decided. If you're trying to give me compliments so you can have your wicked way with me, it won't work," she added, blushing.

"Did I mention anything as sordid as that?" Sebastian feigned horror. "Madam, I am a gentleman. I respect your honor."

"Good," nodded Amy with a conviction she didn't feel.

The air was suddenly charged with tension and both of them sat silently sipping their wine.

"Anyway, you remind me far too much of Posy in that dressing gown," Sebastian finally quipped. "So tell me, Amy, and I want the truth, do you feel nothing at all for me?"

She looked up at him and saw his eyes were no longer laughing, but deadly serious.

"I..." she shook her head, "I don't know. I mean, I like you, but you're a rich, successful, international novelist and I'm a downtrodden, broke mother from the sticks. How could I even begin to think of...anything?"

"And what if I said that I've thought about you non-stop since the first moment I met you, that every time I've bumped into you, the feeling has got stronger?" he murmured slowly. "That no matter what I do, or how often I tell myself you're unavailable and not interested, I just can't get you out of my mind?"

Amy couldn't answer. She stared at him, too shocked to speak.

"Amy, I know it's ridiculous and I understand it can probably never go any further, but unfortunately, I think I love you."

"You can't. You don't even know me." Her voice was no more than a hoarse whisper.

"Will you come here? I promise, I just want to hold you, nothing more."

Amy's heart was pounding. "I shouldn't, I really shouldn't..."

"Look, I promise that if fate hadn't sent you here to me tonight, I'd have probably suffered in silence. But it did. Will you come here?" Sebastian stood up and held out his arms to her.

"The children...I..."

"I only want to hold you."

She stood up and walked slowly towards him. His arms went around her and she laid her head against his chest, feeling his heart pounding as fast as her own. Strange erotic frissons were shooting around her stomach as she breathed in his scent and experienced the physicality of him for the first time.

"Do you, Amy?"

"Do I what?"

"Feel anything for me?"

She looked up at him and nodded sadly. "Of course I do, and I hate myself for it. I mean, I'm standing here, in your arms, a married woman, wanting to..."

Sebastian bent his head to hers and kissed her, hard and passionately.

Amy could do nothing but respond with equal ardor.

"Amy, Amy..." His mouth was on her neck, his hands caressing her hair. As they sank to the floor, he tore Posy's dressing gown from her shoulders and ran his fingers lightly over her breasts. Her nipples stiffened beneath his touch as she took her turn to pull off his clothes and felt his flesh against hers.

"You are so beautiful, so beautiful," he said as he finally yanked the robe away from her body. He kissed her again as his hand trailed down to her stomach, then along her inner thigh. Amy groaned in pleasure, knowing she was more ready than she'd ever been as he moved between her legs, pushing himself easily inside her, riding her until they were both panting and Amy cried out, unable to hold on any longer.

He sank onto her, continuing to kiss her face, her neck, her breasts.

"I love you, I love you, Amy," he whispered. "I'm sorry, but I do."

They lay there, as still now as they had been active before. Amy found her eyes filling with tears.

"What have I just done?" she asked.

"Made love with me," he answered.

"How could I?"

"Because you wanted to."

"But...the children, they could have—"

"Well, they didn't, sweetheart." Sebastian propped himself up on one elbow to study her and brushed a lock of hair out of her eye. "Please don't tell me you regret it," he said quietly.

Amy shook her head. "I don't know...I'm married, for God's sake! I've never been unfaithful to Sam. What kind of wife does this make me?"

"From what I've heard from Posy, the most loving, supportive and long-suffering one."

"Yes, but that doesn't excuse what I've just done: 'Oh, sorry, Sam, I've had a bit of a rough day so I made love with someone else.' Christ!" Amy stood up and went in search of Posy's dressing gown. She put it on, then sat on the sofa staring into the fire, her hands clasping and unclasping in agitation.

Sebastian stood up and came to sit beside her. "Amy, did I force you to do that just now?"

"God, no. That's the worst thing about it. I wanted to. I really wanted to."

Sebastian pulled her into him and held her tightly. "I just needed to know that."

They sat silently for a while, each lost in their own thoughts.

"So," he said eventually, "where do we go from here?"

"What do you mean?"

"Exactly what I say. Is tonight the end of a beautiful friendship or the start of a new love affair?"

"I can't think about tomorrow. I can only think about what's just happened," sighed Amy, hating herself for feeling so happy in his arms. "I'm far too confused."

"You're right. Stop worrying about tomorrow. We have all night, don't we?" He tipped her chin upwards. "And whatever happens beyond this, we must seize the moment," he added as he reached down to kiss her yet again.

Several hours later, Amy left Sebastian's arms and crept into the bed in which her children were sleeping. She felt the warmth of their little bodies next to her and bit her lip guiltily.

Her head spun as she tried to make sense of what had taken place. All she knew was that, right or wrong, she had never experienced anything like it before in her adult life. The passion and excitement she'd felt as they'd made love again and again had only seemed to grow as they'd explored each other and familiarized themselves with the intimate map of each other's bodies.

At some stage, Sebastian had led her upstairs to his bed and they'd lain in the darkness, listening to the roar of the storm and watching the clouds scud across the moonlit sky. Sebastian had talked to her as they lay entwined, told her a little of his life, his first wife and the loss of both her and their baby. And Amy had talked too, told Sebastian of her days at art college and her dreams of becoming an artist before she met Sam.

Finally, in severe danger of falling asleep, Amy had said she must go and slip into bed with the children.

He had tugged her arm to stop her leaving as she tried to climb out. "Don't go. I can't bear it."

"I have to."

"In a minute." He'd pulled her back next to him, kissed her and held her tight. "I just want to say, Amy, that if you should decide this can never happen again, I will remember this night for the rest of my life. Goodnight."

"Goodnight." She'd kissed him gently on the lips, then staggered on weak, wobbly legs to the children's room.

And now she lay, sleepless, her body aching, parts of her actually sore from the endless lovemaking.

And no matter how hard she tried to remind herself of the dreadful act of betrayal she'd just committed, all she could feel was utter joy...and the sense that she'd finally come home.

Chapter 20

Posy and Freddie touched down at Schiphol Airport at two o'clock in the afternoon. Posy felt exhausted. She'd had a sleepless night worrying about her decision to accompany Freddie to Amsterdam, and all that it might entail. She'd finally dropped off to sleep at five but had to be up at a quarter to seven to be ready for Freddie's arrival.

She'd packed and unpacked her suitcase, unable to decide what to take with her and what to wear to the party. Sebastian had sweetly carried it downstairs for her and she'd introduced him to Freddie.

"May I say that I very much enjoyed your book, Mr. Girault."

"Sebastian, please. Perhaps we could go out for a beer at some point? Posy says you're a child of the Second World War like her."

"I'd be glad to."

"Good. Take care of her now, won't you?"

"Of course." Freddie had smiled.

"Goodbye, Sebastian," she'd called as Freddie had carried her suitcase to the car and put it in the boot next to his own.

"All set?" Freddie had asked her.

"I think so, yes."

He'd held her by the shoulders and kissed her lightly on the cheek. "You look terrified, my dear Posy. This is meant to be fun, you know."

"There's just been so much to organize. I think I've got out of the habit of going away."

"Well then, we must nurse you gently back into it, mustn't we?"

She'd resolved then and there to stop being such a silly old woman and enjoy the weekend.

They had driven to Stansted Airport, chattering about all sorts of things, and finally Posy had started to relax. At the airport, she felt a frisson of excitement as they checked in.

"Do you realize that it's over twenty years since I was on an aeroplane, and that was only to Jersey for a holiday with the boys?" she'd said to Freddie as they'd walked through to departures.

"Well, just to warn you that they don't make you wear a flying mask and goggles any more," Freddie had quipped.

Posy had thoroughly enjoyed the smooth flight and was rather sad when they came in to land. Freddie, who was obviously a seasoned traveller, led her though passport control and into the baggage hall, where they retrieved both suitcases from the carousel.

They took a taxi and as they entered the city, Posy looked eagerly out of the window at the tall, gabled houses leaning precariously along the web of tree-lined canals that made up the core of central Amsterdam. Everyone seemed to be on bicycles, haring along the narrow cobbled streets, bells tinkling to alert pedestrians and cars alike to their presence.

The taxi stopped in front of an elegant seventeenth-century town house overlooking a canal. "What a beautiful city," she murmured as they climbed out.

"I came here to stay with Jeremy many years ago and fell in love with the place. I've always wanted to come back. The wonderful thing is that you can walk to virtually anywhere, the city is so compact. Or take a boat." Freddie indicated a barge going under the bridge on the canal. "Right, let's check in and then we can go and explore."

The reception area was tastefully furnished, understated and homey. Posy sat herself in a chair whilst Freddie checked them in.

"Right," he said, handing her a key, "how about we unpack and then go out for a stroll?"

They spent the next couple of hours wandering around the maze of canals, stopping at a small cafe for hot chocolate and to check the map to see where they were.

"You know what else you can buy in here, don't you?" Freddie raised an eyebrow.

"What?"

"Any kind of cannabis that might take your fancy." Freddie indicated the blackboard propped up against the bar, displaying the menu of different kinds of grass and hash. "Ever tried it?"

"No, I always refused it in the old days. Have you?"

"On the odd occasion." Freddie's eyes twinkled. "Fancy a quick joint with your hot chocolate?"

"Why not?"

"Really?"

"Really," nodded Posy. "My philosophy is that one must try everything once."

"Okay then." Freddie nodded and headed off to the bar to make a purchase. He came back with a roll-up and a box of matches. "I asked for the mildest stuff, by the way." He lit it and breathed in, then passed the joint to Posy, who took it and put it to her lips. She took a drag, but as the acrid smoke went straight to the back of her mouth, she choked helplessly.

"Yuck!" she shuddered, handing it back to Freddie.

"It's an acquired taste, but at least you tried it. Any more?"

"No, thanks." Wiping her streaming eyes, she laughed. "Goodness me, if only my sons could see me now, sitting in a cafe in Amsterdam with a man and smoking pot!"

"I'm sure they'd admire you for it. As I do," Freddie added, stubbing out the joint into the ashtray. "Shall we go?"

Posy took her time getting ready for dinner that evening, sitting in front of the mirror in her lovely room overlooking the canal and applying her mascara and lipstick a little more carefully than usual.

Freddie collected her from her room, dressed in a crisp blue shirt and a smart jacket.

"You look lovely, Posy," he said. "Ready to go?"

They went to a wonderful French bistro the hotel receptionist had recommended. Over a good bottle of Chablis and a delicious steak, they discussed where they would visit tomorrow before the party in the evening.

"I'd love to go to the Van Gogh museum if possible," said Posy as Freddie refilled her glass.

"And I'd like to see Anne Frank's house, which is only a stroll away from our hotel. Perhaps we had better make that our first port of call, as I'm told the queues are fairly horrific," said Freddie. "What about the seedier side of the city? I've heard the live shows in certain districts are...educational, to say the least!"

"I plucked up the courage to try some pot, but I think I draw the line at a live sex show," admitted Posy. "But don't let me stop you."

"Not my scene, either, I can assure you. Now, what shall we order for dessert?"

After supper, the two of them walked companionably back to the hotel. Even though it was late October and there was a chill in the air, it was a pleasant, crisp night.

Posy linked her arm through Freddie's. "I feel a little tipsy," she admitted. "I've drunk far more than I'm used to."

"It doesn't hurt once in a while, does it?"

"No." They had reached the front of the hotel. Posy turned to Freddie. "I just want to tell you how much I like it here and how glad I am that I came."

"Good," he said as they walked into the lobby. "A brandy before bed?"

"No, thank you, Freddie. I'm utterly exhausted and I want to be fresh for tomorrow."

"Of course," he said as Posy collected her key from reception. He leant down and kissed her gently on the cheek. "Sleep well, my dear."

He watched her as she walked easily up the stairs to her room. No one would guess that she was almost seventy—she had the physical stamina of a woman far younger. And the same zest for life she'd had as a twenty-one-year-old.

Freddy went into the cosy bar and ordered himself a brandy. He looked at other couples chatting together in the comfortable chairs and sighed heavily. That was what *he* wanted, and he wanted it with Posy. Due to circumstances he couldn't have dreamt possible, he'd been denied it once before, so when he'd seen her there in his boat, he'd felt a wave of euphoria that fate had perhaps thrown them a second chance.

Of course, he'd presumed prematurely that she would have *known*. It had been almost fifty years since he'd last seen her, after all. Surely someone would have told her...?

Freddie took a sip of his brandy. After that first lunch, when it had become clear that she still didn't, he'd simply had to get up and leave. He'd been too upset to stay.

"What to do?" Freddie muttered under his breath. He knew they couldn't carry on like this, that he'd have to walk away just like he'd done before. What he knew would have broken her then; the question was, would it break her now?

He finished his brandy and took his key from reception. He needed someone to talk to, he decided, someone who knew Posy relatively well, but could give him a rational overview.

Freddie thought he knew just the man.

Posy looked out of the window as the plane took off from Schiphol airport. It had been a wonderful three days and she'd enjoyed every second of it. The party had been huge fun, and Freddie's friend Jeremy and his lovely wife Hilde welcoming.

She glanced at Freddie sitting next to her, his eyes closed.

I love you, she thought to herself sadly. That had been the only negative during the weekend—as always, Freddie had been the perfect gentleman and she only wished he hadn't been. It felt—as it often had between them—that there was so much that was left unsaid.

Don't be greedy, Posy. Be thankful for what you have with Freddie, not what you don't, she told herself firmly.

Having collected their suitcases, Freddie drove towards Suffolk in silence, staring at the road in front of him.

"Are you all right?" she asked, noticing his grim expression.

"Sorry, Posy." Freddie roused himself and gave her a weak smile. "I'm fine. Maybe a little tired, that's all."

When they arrived at Admiral House, Freddie carried her suitcase inside. Sebastian was in the kitchen, making himself a cup of tea.

"Hello, you two wanderers. How was Amsterdam?"

"Wonderful," said Posy. "Do excuse me, but I must use the facilities."

As she left the kitchen, Sebastian offered Freddie a cup of tea.

"No thank you, I must be on my way. But actually, how about arranging a time for that drink? There was something I wanted to discuss with you..."

Swallowtail
(Papilio machaon)

Posy

Mansion House
Bodmin Moor, Cornwall
June 1955

"Now, on the auspicious occasion of her eighteenth birthday, I would like to say a few words about my granddaughter, Posy. I can honestly say I could not be prouder of her. And I know I speak for her father...and of course her mother, too."

I saw tears twinkling in Granny's eyes as she glanced at me next to her.

I'd found tears were the most infectious plague on the planet and soon enough there were some in my own eyes too.

"As well as winning a coveted place at Cambridge University and excelling in her final school exams, I also want to say that, despite the trials she has been through since she came to live with us here, Posy has never wallowed in self-indulgence. You will all know how she has always maintained a smile for anyone who greets her, been willing to help out in times of crisis, and provided a listening ear to those who needed it."

"'Ear, 'ear!" I heard Katie call out from the crowd gathered around me in the garden. People chuckled at her probably accidental play on words.

"So let us all wish her well as she embarks on adulthood and her next great challenge. To Posy!"

"To Posy!" everyone chorused as they lifted their glasses of fizz. I did too, unsure whether I was actually meant to toast myself, but wanting to take a sip anyway. It was awfully hot today.

After that, lots of the villagers came up to me to give me their own personal congratulations, and then we ate the fine spread Daisy had put on before the sandwiches went stale in the heat.

Later that night, when everyone had left, I opened the presents that had piled up on the table. Most of them were homemade and I now had enough initialled handkerchiefs to keep me going throughout my three years at Cambridge and probably into retirement. Yet I knew that each one had been sewn with love and my heart swelled at the kindness this village had shown me. It went some way to filling the empty void caused by the disappointment that Maman had not made an appearance at my party. Even though it had always been highly unlikely she would, the part of me that was still a little girl had thought that perhaps Granny had been keeping her arrival a secret, even though she had gently told me a month ago Maman could not attend.

"They are on an extended honeymoon. She said she was dreadfully disappointed not to be here, but she sent you this."

The envelope was still sitting on the present table, along with Granny's card, which was attached to a gift wrapped in shiny silver paper. Its size and shape resembled a slim volume and I'd already guessed it was a book.

"Will you open your mother's card now?" Granny reached for it and handed it to me.

Part of me wanted to tear it up or set fire to it to save me the pain of reading what I knew were simply hollow words, platitudes to a daughter she no longer even knew.

But I did open the envelope, gritting my teeth and wondering why, after all the talking-tos I'd given myself about how I had to accept her as she was, I felt on the verge of tears.

The card said "Happy 18th Birthday!" and had a picture of a champagne bottle and two glasses on the front. It was the kind that I'd had from many of the villagers.

Goodness, Posy! What were you expecting? A hand-painted watercolor?! I chided myself as I opened it. There was another envelope inside, which I placed on my lap while I read the inscription inside the card.

Darling Posy,
On the occasion of your 18th birthday,
All our love,
Maman and Alessandro
Xx

I bit my lip at the sight of *his* name, struggling not to let more wasted tears fall. I set the card on the table with the others and opened the envelope still on my lap. I pulled out a photograph and studied it. It was of Maman and a man who was smaller and fatter than she was. Maman was wearing a beautiful wedding dress with a long train and a sparkling tiara and looking down adoringly into her new husband's eyes. The two of them were standing on some steps with an enormous castle in the background. This, I presumed, was the palazzo, my mother's new home.

"Here," I passed the photograph to Granny while I pulled out the other item in the envelope, which was a check with a note folded round it.

Darling Posy, as we weren't sure what to get you, Alessandro thought that this might help with your university expenses. Do come and visit us soon— Alessandro can't wait to meet you. Much love, M and A x

I suppressed a shudder, then looked at the amount on the check and gave a little gasp. It was made out for five *hundred* pounds!

"What is it, Posy?"

I showed Granny the check and she nodded sagely. "That will come in handy in the next few years, won't it?"

"Yes, but Granny, it's a fortune! And we both know that Maman doesn't have that kind of money, which means it's actually from her husband, who doesn't know me and has never met me and..."

"Stop it, Posy! It's perfectly obvious from what your mother has said that she has married a very wealthy man. You—whether you like it or not—are technically his new stepdaughter, and if he wishes to give you such a gift, then simply accept it with grace."

"But surely it means that I'm somehow..." I searched for the word, "*beholden* to him?"

"It means you are family, Posy, and he is recognizing that fact. Goodness, you've had nothing at all for years from your mother, and however you feel about the situation, or where the money has really come from, do not look a gift horse in the mouth."

"I shan't touch it," I said stubbornly. "It feels like I'm being bought. Besides, I won a scholarship, Granny, so I don't even need it!"

"You know already that, as your trustee, I used some of your inheritance from your father to pay for your school fees and we've agreed to do the same to cover your living expenses at Cambridge, but it's not a fortune by any means. Why don't you let me put it away and you can call it your rainy-day money? You never need touch it if you don't need it, but it's there if you do."

"Okay, but I just don't feel right about it. And it means I will have to write a 'thank you' note," I said sulkily.

"Now then, we're sounding churlish. Enough of this on your birthday. Why don't you open my gift? Although I have to say, it's hardly impressive after that," Granny smiled.

I reached for the slim package and tore off the paper. At first I thought it was a leather-bound book as I'd suspected, but as I lifted it from its wrapping, I saw it was a box. I opened the clasp and saw a string of creamy pearls laid on the indigo-blue satin lining.

"Oh Granny! They are beautiful! Thank you."

"They were actually my mother's, so they really are quite old, but they are real pearls, Posy, not these cheap cultured ones that are all the rage these days. Here." She stood up. "Let me put them on for you."

I sat still as she fastened the dainty clasp around my neck. Then she walked round to look at me. "Lovely," she said with a smile. "Every young woman should have a string of pearls." She kissed me on the cheek. "Now you are ready to go out into the world."

I arrived in Cambridge with my two suitcases and my folder of botanical drawings at the beginning of October. It took Bill and me some time to negotiate the warren of cobbled streets at the epicenter of the city. We must have passed Trinity and King's College three times in our search for Silver Street. As we pulled up in front of the Hermitage, where the residents of New Hall were housed, I felt a twinge of disappointment run through me. The Hermitage was a fine, large house, but it certainly wasn't one of the gorgeous four-hundred-year-old boys' colleges with their ubiquitous dreaming spires.

I was greeted warmly at the door by Miss Murray, the tutor-in-charge at New Hall, whom Miss Sumpter, my old headmistress, had known from her own boarding school days.

"Miss Anderson, you have made it, all the way from Cornwall! Heavens, you must be exhausted. Now I shall show you up to your room—admittedly, it's small and right at the top of the house—the first tranche of girls last year bagged all the best rooms—but it has the most delightful view over the town."

Miss Murray had been correct—the room was indeed small. I surmised it had once belonged to a servant, being in the attic, but it had a dear little fireplace and sloping ceilings, plus a window which did indeed have a wonderful view over the rooftops and spires. The lavatory and bathroom were on the floor below, but Miss Murray assured me she had plans to convert the broom cupboard next door to me into a more accessible facility.

"Obviously, doubling our numbers because of this year's new intake has been a challenge and many of the girls are sharing the larger rooms downstairs. I had an inkling you would prefer your own space, however small. Now I will leave you to unpack and settle in, and then do come down at six to the dining room, where you can meet the rest of the girls."

The door closed behind me, and I stood where I was for a moment, breathing in the smell of dust and, maybe I was imagining it, old books. I wandered over to the window and stood looking at Cambridge laid out beneath me.

"I did it, Daddy," I murmured to myself. "I'm here!"

As I walked downstairs an hour later, my heart beat faster at the thought of meeting the other girls. I was exhausted, not only from the long drive but from the sleepless nights that had preceded it. I'd tortured myself with thoughts of how clever and worldly-wise and almost certainly prettier the other girls would be, and how I'd probably only got in because of Miss Sumpter's friendship with Miss Murray.

Taking a deep breath, I walked into the dining room and found it already packed with females.

"Hello there, which newbie are you?" asked a tall young woman who was wearing what looked like a man's suit. She was proffering a tray of sherry.

"Posy Anderson," I said, taking one of the small glasses. I needed it for Dutch courage.

"Ah, right. You're studying botany, aren't you?"

"Yes."

"Andrea Granville. I do English myself. There are only a handful of us women on the entire course and I'm sure there'll be even fewer in your department. You need to get used to dealing with a herd of silly little boys making fatuous jokes at your expense as fast as you can."

"Right-ho, I'll try my best," I replied, knocking back the sherry.

"The sad thing is, Posy, half of them are only here because their forefathers were," Andrea barked (she had a very loud voice). "Lord Hoighty-Toity's sons and grandsons aplenty, I'm afraid. Most of them will leave here with a third or a 2:2 at best, then go back to living off their trust funds and ordering their servants round the family pile."

"Oh Andrea, that's not true of all of them, you know. Don't let her scare you," said a girl with glorious black curly hair and enormous violet eyes. "I'm Celia Munro, by the way. I'm reading English too."

"Posy Anderson." I smiled back, liking her immediately.

"Well, Posy, I'm off to share the sherry around, but just watch out for toads in your desk and whoopee cushions on your chair. Oh, and you should know that we are all lesbians, according to the boys," Andrea added as her parting comment.

"Honestly," Celia shook her head. "We're meant to be helping you feel comfortable here, not scaring you witless. Take no notice, Andrea's a good sort, just awfully pro-women's rights. You'll find a lot of that here amongst the female contingent. I totally agree, of course, but I prefer to concentrate my energies on my degree and enjoying my time here."

"That's what I intend to do too. So you're in your second year?"

"Yes, and for all that Andrea says about the boys ribbing us, I thoroughly enjoyed my first year. It probably helped that I'm the only girl in a family of three brothers, mind you."

"I must admit I haven't thought much about the boys, just about my degree and coming to Cambridge." I looked round at the crowd. "I still can't quite believe I'm here."

"Well, it certainly is a surreal place, quite its own little universe, but I'm sure you'll get into the swing of things. Now, why don't we take a wander and see who else we can introduce ourselves to from your year?"

So we did, and as I shook hands with a clutch of young women, I realized that the majority of them were just as nervous as I was. Overall, they seemed like a nice crowd and as I finished my second glass of sherry, a calming warmth spread through me.

"Girls! May I ask you to gather round?"

I saw Miss Murray standing at the front of the dining room and moved forwards with the rest of the crowd.

"Firstly, I would like to welcome our new intake to New Hall. As I'm sure the original intake will agree, you can count yourselves lucky to be coming in a year on from the opening of the college."

"She means we've finally managed to get rid of the bed bugs from the mattresses," quipped Andrea and there was a chuckle from her friends.

"Quite," said Miss Murray. "Those and a number of irritating details that we had to sort out when we moved into our new home. However, sorted they are, and I really feel that, after a year of teething troubles, we as a college can really start to establish ourselves as a force to be reckoned with, academically of course, but also by the kind of women you are and intend to be in the future. As I explained to each of you in your interviews, being a female student at Cambridge in a minority ratio of one girl to every ten boys is daunting, even to the most confident woman. It would be very easy to be strident when faced with the continual banter that your male counterparts seem to find so amusing. And of course, each of you must deal with it in your own way. But let me say this: as females, we have our own unique strengths. And as an academic for the past twenty years, working in the world of men, I have often been tempted to give as good as I got, but I entreat you all to uphold your femininity, to use your own unique skill-set to your advantage. Remember, the only reason many of them react as they do is simply because they are frightened. Slowly, their all-male bastions are being infiltrated and let me tell you, this is only the start of our march towards equality."

"Golly, are the boys really that bad?" murmured one of the new girls nervously.

"No, but forewarned is forearmed," said Miss Murray, "and I do not wish to hear of any of our girls being involved in a fist fight, as happened at Girton last term. Now then, on a jollier note, I have decided that, whilst the weather is still warm enough to use the garden, we shall open our doors to the new undergraduates of St John's College—who own this property and have been kind enough to rent it to us—next Friday night for drinks. Which will give you girls a chance to meet a selection of your male counterparts in a relaxed social setting."

"The enemy safely in captivity, you mean?" Andrea chuckled.

Miss Murray ignored her comment and I had the feeling that if anybody was going to be involved in a fist fight with the boys, it was Andrea.

"Now I'm going to pass you over to our other resident tutor, Dr. Hammond, who will talk to you about the nuts and bolts of the academic side of things, but before I do, I'd like to propose a toast to New Hall and its new residents."

"To New Hall," we all chorused, and the same warmth that had suffused me earlier filled me again, because I *knew* I was part of something very special.

And indeed, as I began to get to know my fellow students in the weeks that followed, I started to feel more and more that I was no longer a fish out of water, that for the first time in my life I actually belonged. Every girl I met was frighteningly bright and—more to the point—they were all here simply because they were passionate about their subjects. As the nights drew in, conversations around the fire in the comfortable common room ranged from pure mathematics to the poetry of Yeats and Brooke. We lived and dreamed our chosen subjects, and, perhaps because of the fact we all knew how lucky we were to be here, there were few complaints when it came to the heavy workload we were given. I thrived on it, and still had to pinch myself every time I walked through the door of the Botany School.

The building was very unprepossessing, being a square, many-windowed building on Downing Street, but at least it was only a short bicycle ride across the river from New Hall. I got used to seeing the same faces on my morning commute over the rickety cobblestones, the old bicycle I had bought second-hand squealing in protest with every turn of the pedals.

Nothing could have prepared me for the sheer excitement of entering the laboratory for the first time: the long benches, the modern equipment my fingers were itching to touch, and the collections of seeds and dried plants at my disposal in the herbarium (with a permission slip, of course).

As Andrea had warned me, I was one of only three women on the course. Enid and Romy—the other two females—sat determinedly apart from each other during lectures, each seeking out their own territory amongst the men. We would often meet at lunch break at our favorite bench in the Botanical Garden, sharing notes on lectures and raising a communal weary eyebrow at the boys' antics. The three of us had passionate debates about the future of botany whenever we took a table at The Eagle. The pub was always busy, partly because every scientist at the university seemed to be hoping to catch a glimpse of Watson and Crick, who had discovered the structure of DNA only two years earlier. The night that I spotted the back of Francis Crick's head at the bar, I had sat frozen in my seat, so in awe at being close to genius. Enid, who was far more confident than me, had gone straight up to him and talked his ear off until he had beaten a swift but gracious retreat.

"Of course it was Rosalind Franklin who did most of the work," Enid had said fiercely when she had come back to our table. "But she's a woman, so she'll never get credit for it."

I hadn't had the time or the inclination to join any societies, wanting to concentrate all my energies on my studies. Both Celia and Andrea, who had become my firm friends at New Hall, flitted about each weekend from one event to the next, Celia with the chess club and Andrea with the Footlights, the renowned drama troupe. I spent every spare moment in the gardens and in the greenhouses, and Dr. Walters, one of my professors, had taken me under his wing in the Tropical House, a beautiful glass structure where the air was thick with humidity. There were nights when I didn't arrive back until curfew, making my way up to my chilly bedroom and sliding between the sheets, exhausted but content.

"Golly, you're a dull sort," Andrea said to me one morning over breakfast. "You hardly venture out if it hasn't to do with seeds and mud. Well, tonight, there's a Footlights bash and if I drag you there with my own bare hands, you're coming with me."

Knowing Andrea was right, and besides, that she wouldn't take no for an answer, I let her add one of her bright scarves to the red dress I'd worn for my eighteenth birthday. I knew within a few seconds that it was going to be as grim as I thought it would be. The cacophony of loud voices and music as we entered the rooms of the head of the Footlights warned me that I would be a fish out of water. Nevertheless, I grabbed a drink from the table to help my nerves and entered the fray. Andrea pushed through the crowd to find the host of the proceedings.

"That's Freddie there. Isn't he dreamy?" She smiled in a most un-Andrea-like way.

I followed her pointed finger and saw a young man surrounded by a crowd of acolytes, all listening attentively as he held court. As I looked at him, I had the strangest sensation of time standing still. I watched his full lips open and close in slow motion, his hands gesticulating as he spoke. His dark hair was thick and wavy and fell to his shoulders like the paintings of the romantic poets I'd seen. His eyes were big and expressive and the color of a young fawn, his cheekbones high and his jaw chiselled like a sculpture. He would make a very beautiful woman, I thought to myself as Andrea pulled me into the milieu and I extracted myself from my reverie.

"Freddie, darling, may I introduce you to Posy Anderson, a great friend of mine."

I felt a jolt like a thousand bolts of lightning run through me as he took my hand in his and kissed it, his eyes upon me as if I were the only person in the room.

"Delighted," he said in a deep, melodious voice. "And what do you do to keep you occupied here in Cambridge?"

"Botany," I managed, feeling my wretched blush sweep up my neck. In my red dress, I imagined I must resemble an overripe tomato.

"Well now, we have a scientist amongst our aesthetic ranks!" he said to the crowd, and I couldn't help but feel as though he was making a joke of me, even though his eyes—which were still locked to my own—were kind.

"So where do you hail from, Posy?"

"Suffolk originally, but I was brought up in Cornwall."

"Suffolk?" Freddie smiled. "Well, that's something we have in common. It's where I was born too. Let us talk later, Posy. I'm fascinated to hear why a beautiful woman such as you"—I felt his eyes sweep down my body—"has ended up in a white coat staring through a microscope."

I nodded and grinned like an idiot—I literally couldn't speak and was only glad when someone else took Freddie's attention away and his eyes finally left me.

Of course we never did get to "talk later"; Freddie spent the night surrounded by the kind of sophisticated women that I, in my plain red dress with my untamed curls, could not begin to compete with. Andrea soon got lost in the crowd and forgot about me, so I left an hour later and made my way home to dream about Freddie and the fact he had called me "beautiful."

Winter in Cambridge was an unexpected joy. The ancient stone buildings were smothered in a blanket of sparkling white frost, and venturing into the greenhouses in the Botanical Garden felt like being in a giant igloo. It was nearing the end of the Michaelmas term, and dinner conversations in New Hall all revolved around one subject— the Christmas Ball at St John's college.

"I shall wear trousers," Andrea had declared. "I'll be like Marlene Dietrich, and any man who dares approach me will have to prove his mettle."

Celia and I spent a Saturday morning shopping for the perfect outfit, and I had parted with some of my allowance to buy a blue velvet dress, cinched in at the waist with a bow at the front of it. I thought ruefully of all Maman's beautiful evening dresses at Admiral House and wondered if they had found a new home in her palazzo.

Celia persuaded me to buy a pair of high heels to go with it, as I owned none. "Don't you dare go digging for plant samples in them," she'd warned me with a grin.

"I'm far more worried I'll topple over and make a complete fool of myself," I told myself as I practised walking in them around my tiny bedroom.

On the last day of term, I ran out of the Botany School, sliding over the icy steps then fumbling to unlock my bicycle. I was already late to meet Celia, who had promised to help me style my hair into some semblance of fashion for the ball that night. It was already six o'clock as I hopped onto my bike and pedalled towards Silver Street, ignoring the honks of irritated drivers as I steered around the potholes.

Suddenly, the world toppled upside down, and I came face to face with gray slush on the cobbled street, my bicycle a few inches away from me, the wheels spinning.

"I say, are you all right?" came a voice from above me.

Shaken, I staggered up from the ground. "I...yes, I think so."

"Come and sit down and collect yourself. That was quite a fall you took," the young man said. I felt him put a reassuring arm around me as he led me off the road. He settled me on the bench at a bus stop, then went back to fetch my bicycle, deftly kicking out its stand with his foot before settling it next to me. He had kind blue eyes and a smile below his neat moustache, and I could see wisps of blonde hair under the brim of his hat.

"Thank you," I said, pulling at my skirt to make sure it hadn't ridden up. "I've never had a fall like that, I'm usually very careful—"

"It's unavoidable with the roads this icy," he said. "The council haven't got round to gritting the streets on time. Typical. I'm Jonny Montague, by the way."

"Posy Anderson," I replied, taking his outstretched hand and shaking it. I stood up. "I'm so sorry, I must be getting on, my friend is waiting for me—"

"I can't let you get back on your bicycle after a fall like that," he said. "Where were you going? I'll escort you."

"Really, I'm fine."

"I insist." He took hold of the handlebars of my bicycle, which admittedly looked rather bent. "Lead the way, m'lady."

As we walked towards New Hall together, I discovered that Jonny was reading geography at St John's College.

"...But I'll be going into the army after university, just like my dear old pater," he said. "What about you?"

"I'm doing botany...plant sciences," I said. The word 'science' had the expected effect on him.

"A scientist?" he said, looking down at me in surprise. "My, my, what kind of science do you do on plants?"

Before I could explain to him about grafting and taxonomy and ecosystems, we had arrived outside the college.

"You need someone to take a look at that bicycle before you get back on it. It's been lovely to meet you, Miss Anderson, despite the dramatic circumstances."

"Yes," I said, "and thank you again. It was very kind of you to stop."

"The least I can do." Jonny nodded, then with a doff of his hat, walked off into the night.

Slightly dazed, I went up to my room where Celia was waiting for me, tapping her foot impatiently and wielding a frightening-looking set of curling irons.

"But my hair is already curly," I protested.

"Not the right kind of curly," she said. "Now sit down. Oh Posy, what on earth have you done? Your hair is a fright!"

An hour and a half later, trying not to walk too unsteadily in my heels, a group of us New Hall girls approached St John's College. The darkness was kept at bay by candles and tapers set into the frost-covered lawns, illuminating the ancient stone towers and neo-Gothic façade, and we could hear the sound of a swing band coming from inside the Great Hall and the murmur of voices already well lubricated with alcohol. In one smooth move, my coat was taken from me by an attendant and a glass of champagne was placed in my hand.

"Come along, Posy." Celia took me by the arm and led me into the Great Hall. She had managed to smooth and curl my hair into delicate waves, then pin them back from my face with diamanté clips. She'd also done my makeup, and I was scared to move my lips in case the bright red lipstick smudged.

The hall was full to the brim with men in black tie, their voices echoing up to the high ceiling above us.

"Cheers, girls," Andrea toasted us. "Here's to a happy Christmas."

"Hello, darling. Glad I've found you in this crush! Want to come and dance?"

Matthew, Celia's beau, appeared beside us. They'd been walking out with each other since October.

"Of course."

They floated away and I was left with Andrea.

"She'll probably end up married and pregnant in a couple of years" time," Andrea snorted. "And her degree will simply go to waste. God, this kind of thing is so not my scene. Come on, let's go and find some grub. I'm starving."

The two of us pushed through the crowd over to the long trestle table heaving with food. I wasn't hungry, my stomach churning with nerves, but Andrea piled her plate high.

"Only reason I've come," she smiled, tucking in.

"Hello there," said a voice from behind me.

I turned round and saw Jonny, my knight in shining armor from earlier, standing beside me.

"Hello."

"Golly, you look different," he said admiringly.

"Thank you."

"Have you recovered from your fall?"

"I have, yes."

"Enough to join me for a dance?"

"I...yes," I replied, feeling the usual blush spread up my neck.

He held out his hand and I took it.

"Another one bites the dust," I heard Andrea say under her breath as we moved towards the dance floor.

Later, we moved outside to get some air and smoke. (I had started the habit because everyone smoked all the time and I didn't want to look square.) We sat companionably on a bench in the courtyard.

"So where are you heading for the Christmas holiday?" he asked.

"Cornwall. I live with my grandmother."

"Really? What about your parents?"

"My father died in the war. He was a pilot, and my mother lives in Italy," I found myself telling him. It was rare for me to open up to anyone at Cambridge about my home life, but he seemed to invite confidences.

"I'm sorry to hear about your father," he said gently. "I know I'm very lucky to still have mine after that wretched war. Your father must have been a hero."

"He was." I noticed that he had edged closer to me, and the sleeve of his dinner jacket was brushing my arm. I could feel his warmth and didn't move away.

"What about you?"

"My parents live in Surrey. I have two sisters, one cat and an aging Labrador called Molly, so that's me. Pretty standard all round, I'd say."

"So your father was in the army?"

"Yes. He was injured early doors at Dunkirk—he lost a leg, actually, so he sat out the rest of the war behind a desk. He always said losing the leg was a blessing. At least he kept his life. I'm sorry your father didn't."

"Thank you." I stubbed my cigarette out with one of my new shoes, then shivered. "Shall we go back inside? It's awfully cold out here."

"Then let's have a dance to warm up."

He took my arm and led me back into the Great Hall.

Over Christmas in Cornwall, I thought about Jonny endlessly. After the dance, he'd walked me home and given me my very first kiss. He'd said he would write to me, and every day I hurried to greet William the postman, feeling a thrill every time there was a letter addressed to me in Jonny's neat handwriting.

Granny raised an eyebrow and smiled, but didn't probe, for which I was grateful. When I returned to Cambridge for the Lent term in the new year, Jonny and I were soon officially stepping out together. It seemed to happen naturally and before I realized what was happening, I wasn't simply "Posy" any more, I was one half of "Jonny-and-Posy." We saw each other twice a week, once on Wednesday in between tutorials for a spot of lunch at a café and on Sundays at The Eagle. I discovered I quite liked kissing, even if his moustache tickled my skin, but I had not yet experienced any of the other things that the New Hall girls liked to whisper about in the common room in the evenings.

Andrea was less discreet. She had insisted on meeting Jonny and giving him a grilling in order to "approve" him.

"He seems sweet enough, Posy, but to be honest, he's rather dull, isn't he? All that talk of his ghastly suburban background—are you sure you don't want someone more exciting?"

I ignored Andrea, understanding she enjoyed being as rude as possible just for effect. After my unusual upbringing, I positively welcomed the description of his family, and hoped he'd take me to meet them one day.

Estelle, my old friend from school, who was now in the *corps de ballet* at the Royal Ballet in London, came to visit me one weekend, and we shared a bottle of cheap wine and confidences long into the night.

"So, have you, you know, done it with Jonny yet?"

"Golly no," I blushed. "We've only known each other for a few months."

"Darling Posy, you haven't changed a jot since school," she laughed. "I've slept with at least five men in London—without even thinking twice!"

The Easter break came, and I spent all my time at home in Cornwall studying hard for my first-year exams. Back at Cambridge, Jonny complained that he hardly saw me.

"After the exams are finished, you can see me as much as you want," I consoled him, wondering why he wasn't studying hard for his own exams.

Finally, the exams were over and I felt that I'd acquitted myself relatively well and could relax. The May Ball season was upon us, and Jonny and I debated which one to choose. Jonny managed to get four tickets to the Trinity College May Ball, the most popular ball at Cambridge.

"I'll invite Edward"—this was Jonny's best friend—"and why don't you invite Estelle? I know he's had a crush on her since he met her in February," Jonny suggested.

Estelle duly arrived and we spent the day together getting ready.

"Do remind me what this Edward looks like, darling," Estelle said as she twisted her flaxen hair into a practised knot on top of her head. "Is he a dish and worth getting dressed up for?"

"You must remember him, Estelle. We spent the evening in his rooms, drinking gin and toasting bread over his fire."

"Oh, that was eons ago, Posy. Do you like my dress, by the way?" she asked, twirling in a shimmering creation of white satin and tulle. "I stole it from the costume department."

"It's very...floaty, and suits you perfectly," I said, feeling like a great lumpen elephant next to my dainty friend as I asked her to fasten the buttons on the back of my gown. Granny had come to the rescue and had her dressmaker (who she said cost a snip compared to city seamstresses) make me a beautiful periwinkle-blue dress with a full skirt that swished around my ankles.

When we were both satisfied with our appearances, we walked outside in the warm June air to meet Jonny and Edward.

"You look utterly beautiful, darling," Jonny smiled, taking my gloved hand in his and kissing it.

We joined other revelers walking towards the ball, and Estelle and I fell behind the men by a couple of paces.

"No wonder I didn't remember him, but I suppose he'll do for tonight," she whispered.

"Estelle, you are perfectly awful," I muttered back.

During the champagne reception held in Trinity Great Court, Estelle pointed out gowns that she recognized from *Vogue*. Then we sat down to a delicious five-course meal before the dancing began.

I was content to sway in Jonny's arms as Estelle pirouetted around Edward and generally showed off to the admiration of the crowd. After the fireworks display and the survivors' breakfast, the four of us sat on the Backs to watch the dawn. There was a gentle mist over the river, and the sleepy beginnings of birdsong heralded the arrival of another warm day.

"I could stay at Cambridge forever," Edward mused, looking up at the approaching sunrise.

"Not me," said Jonny. "I'm looking forward to my officer training at Mons when I leave. I'm only here because Pater insisted I should get a degree in case I wanted to bail out of the army early. I can hardly wait to travel, see the world." He squeezed my hand and turned to me. "You'll like that too, won't you, Posy?"

"I...well, yes," I said, taken by surprise, because up until that minute, I hadn't really thought about the future, or at least not one with Jonny...

"Right." Estelle came to my rescue, slipping off her shoes. "Let's go and see if we can break this famous Trinity Great Court record. Race you!" She dashed off, leaping like a sprite, and before Jonny could hold me back, I was running after her.

That summer, I was finally to meet Jonny's family. I took varying trains from Cornwall to Surrey, with jams and pickles that Daisy had given me to present as a gift. Jonny met me at Cobham Station in a smart racing-green Ford sedan.

"Sweetheart! How wonderful to see you." He greeted me with a kiss and I slid into the leather seat, watching in fascination as he drove the car along lush leafy lanes, past pleasant houses with manicured lawns. We finally pulled into the drive of a house with symmetrical hornbeam hedges that looked like they had been trimmed with the aid of a spirit level. Jonny bounded out of the car and opened the passenger door for me. I stepped out onto the gravel, my stomach turning with nerves.

The front door opened, and an old Labrador ambled out first, followed by a pretty woman in her early forties with a smooth blonde bob and a sweet smile. Behind her was a tall, slim man with a walking stick and a moustache like Jonny's.

Jonny took my hand and pulled me forward. "Posy, these are my parents."

Mr. Montague shook my hand first, his touch dry and firm. "Wonderful to meet you, Posy. Jonny's told us so much about you."

"It's a pleasure to meet you," added Mrs. Montague. "Welcome to our home."

I followed them inside, the Labrador panting at my feet, and I noticed that Jonny's father, despite his wooden leg, had a very smooth gait.

"Jonny, darling, take Posy's case up to the guest bedroom, please."

"Of course, Ma."

Jonny obediently went up the stairs whilst his mother led me through the hall and into a clean white kitchen. A Victoria sponge was sitting resplendent on the sideboard. "I hope you don't mind, I thought we'd take tea outside in the garden, it's such a beautiful day."

"I'd love that," I smiled. I followed her out of the kitchen door and onto a terrace lined by a border full of sweet-smelling gardenias. Two young women were setting china teacups onto a table and looked up at me with a smile.

"This is Dorothy and Frances," Mrs. Montague said, and the two girls came over to greet me.

"Please call me Dotty," one of them said, giving me the same firm handshake as her father.

Both of them shared Jonny's smooth blonde hair and light blue eyes, and were just as tall as I was, which made me glad not to tower over other women for once.

"Jonny's never brought a girl home to us before," giggled Frances, whom I guessed was the younger of the two sisters and around sixteen. "Has he proposed yet?"

"Frances!" Jonny had appeared behind me. "You really are the end!"

Over tea, I observed Jonny's interactions with his family and felt a warm affection for him. I wasn't used to the affable teasing between him and his siblings, nor the gentle but amused rebukes from his mother, but as I watched clouds of yellow butterflies flitting above the purple verbena in the immaculate garden, I felt relaxed and at ease.

"Jonny's told me that you live with your grandmother in Cornwall. It must be a quiet life down there," said Mrs. Montague as Frances and Dorothy argued vociferously about something on the other side of the table.

"Yes, it's peaceful," I said, taking a restorative sip of my tea, "but very wild, especially in winter."

"Jonny also said that you are studying botany. Perhaps you and I could take a turn around the garden tomorrow, and you could give me some advice."

I looked into her kind blue eyes, and felt a confusing mixture of emotions: joy at being welcomed so generously by Jonny's family and envy at the fact that he had grown up with so much love from his parents and had a mother who took such an interest in his life.

"That would be wonderful," I said to her, swallowing the lump in my throat.

Over the next few days, I helped Mrs. Montague, who insisted that I should call her Sally, in the kitchen and gave her tips on slug prevention in the garden. I chatted with Mr. Montague about his days in the army and went shopping in the pretty village of Cobham with Frances and Dotty. Every night I fell into my bed in the guest room and pondered whether perhaps this was what it was like to be normal, and I was the last person in the world to receive the script.

On our final evening, before I was to return to Cornwall for the rest of the summer, Jonny borrowed his father's car again and took me to a restaurant in Cobham. He seemed conspicuously nervous, picking at his braised beef casserole, whereas I tucked into mine hungrily.

Over pudding—a lackluster apple crumble with congealing custard—Jonny took my hand in his and gave me a shy smile.

"Posy, I just wanted to thank you for being utterly wonderful with my family."

"It's been a pleasure, Jonny, really. They are simply delightful."

"The thing is, Posy, we've been together now for seven months, and I...well, I want you to know that my intentions towards you are honorable. I'm hoping...I mean, I hope that one day, I will be able to formally ask you to be mine forever, but it wouldn't be right until I've left Cambridge and am starting to earn my living as an officer. So," he continued, "I've been thinking that perhaps we could promise ourselves to each other unofficially, be engaged to be engaged. What do you think?"

I took a sip of my wine and smiled at him, the warmth of the time I'd spent with his family flooding through me.

"Yes," I answered.

When we returned to the house, the lights had already been switched off and the family were tucked into their beds. Jonny took my hand and we tiptoed up the stairs so as not to wake them. Outside my room, Jonny cupped my face in his hands and kissed me.

"Posy," he whispered into my neck, "would you...will you come with me to my room?"

If we're engaged to be engaged, then it has to happen sometime, I suppose, I thought as I let him lead me down the corridor to his bedroom, which was conveniently at the other end of the house to his parents'.

Inside, he led me over to the bed and kissed me some more, then his hands unzipped my dress, tracing a path gently across my skin. Together, we lay back on his narrow bed and I felt his heavy weight on me, skin on skin for the first time. I shut my eyes tightly as he sat up suddenly, opened his bedside drawer and pulled out a small, square package, whispering that he must protect me. A few seconds later, I stifled a yelp of pain as he pushed himself inside me.

It was all over far more quickly than I expected. Jonny rolled off me, then wound his arms around my naked shoulders and held me to him.

"I love you, Posy," he said sleepily, and not long afterwards I heard him snoring gently next to me.

I wriggled back into my underwear, then stood up and collected my dress and shoes before tiptoeing back into the guest bedroom. I lay awake until the first faint glimmer of dawn appeared at my window, wondering what on earth the fuss was all about.

We returned to Cambridge that autumn and settled back into our old routine—with one significant change: once a month or so, we would spend the night together in a bed and breakfast on the outskirts of Cambridge. Due to the penalty of being immediately sent down for undergraduates found with a male or female in their college rooms, the bed and breakfast did a roaring trade, and I often saw faces I recognized sneaking in and out of it.

"Golly, you're so desperately straight, Posy," Andrea had said dismissively when I returned from one of my overnight forays. "Only last night I saw Arabella Baskin climbing out of George Rustwell's window at King's."

"Well, she's lucky that her beau has rooms on the ground floor, and besides, I'm hardly going to chance messing up my degree, am I?" I'd retorted.

I kept quiet about my engagement to be engaged and threw myself into my work with Dr. Walters. I had joined his prestigious research project on the cytogenetics of plants in the Asteraceae family, and was one of the few undergraduates, and certainly the only woman, working on the project. Under his tutelage, my confidence grew and I found I was no longer afraid of voicing my opinions during tutorials. I'd also developed a reputation around the Botany School for having a knack at bringing plants back to life. My small room in New Hall was now filled with the earthy scent of growing plants as I was gifted ailing spider plants, cacti, and at one point, a gingko bonsai tree.

"Apparently it's fifty years old," Henry, one of the lab technicians, had said as he'd handed me the dwarf tree, its leaves drooping miserably. "It belonged to my grandfather and I can't be responsible for killing it after all this time, Posy, my family would never forgive me."

In the mornings before breakfast, I would tend to my motley nursery in my room, then cycle to the Botany School. I counted the weeks, months and seasons at Cambridge not by terms or essay deadlines as my friends did, but by the natural rhythms of the flora that grew around me. I made detailed botanical drawings of all the unusual and exotic plants that were collected in the herbarium, and was never happier than when my fingers were digging in the moist, soft earth as I repotted seedlings that had outgrown their original cradles.

After my second-year exams were over, I had a message from Dr. Walters to attend a meeting in his rooms. I didn't sleep the night before, wondering what on earth he wanted to see me about; dark visions assailed me of some unknown misdemeanor resulting in me being sent down in disgrace.

"Come in, Miss Anderson," he smiled at me as I entered the elegant oak-panelled room. "Sherry?"

"Umm...well, yes, thank you."

He handed me a glass, then gestured for me to sit in the cracked and faded leather chair on the other side of his desk. On the walls hung his many intricate botanical drawings, and I wished I could inspect them more closely.

"Miss Anderson, it goes without saying that you've made a great contribution to our project," he said, leaning back in his chair, folding his hands over his stomach and regarding me over the rim of his glasses. "Have you given any thought to what you might do after you leave Cambridge?"

"Well," I began, my mouth suddenly feeling very dry, "I love working with plants, nurturing them, so perhaps if there was a chance to do some post-graduate research for you..."

"I'm flattered, Miss Anderson, but I have something else in mind for you." He took a sip of sherry. "You'll have noticed that our research has become ever more focused on the minuscule—the genetic level—but you have a way with nurturing plants that should not be wasted in a laboratory. Have you ever been to Kew Gardens in London?"

The mention of Kew sent a thrill down my spine. "No, but I've heard wonderful things," I breathed.

"My good friend Mr. Turrill is the Keeper of the Herbarium, as well as the various other plant houses," he said. "I think you would be a perfect candidate to work there."

I was speechless. "I..."

"Of course it would help to finish with a First," he continued, "but from what I've seen of your marks, I'm sure that will be easily manageable for you. So would you like me to put in a good word for you with Mr. Turrill?"

"Golly," I said, completely overcome, 'that would be marvellous!"

I was bereft when Andrea and Celia, who had both been a year ahead of me, left Cambridge. On their graduation, they both looked resplendent in their black gowns, the fur-lined hoods draped neatly at their backs. Celia had become engaged a few months ago and I was looking forward to her wedding to Matthew in Gloucestershire in August.

"Do you think you will ever work?" I asked her as I watched her pack her possessions away into suitcases.

"I've applied for two teaching jobs, so until the babies come along, yes, I certainly will. We'll need the money—Matthew has Bar School to get through," she said, then hugged me tightly. "Keep in touch, darling Posy, won't you?"

After that, I went downstairs to say goodbye to Andrea.

"Goodness, I'll only be in London at the British Library, Posy," she said to me when tears threatened my eyes. "And by next year you'll be at Kew, so we'll see each other all the time." She looked up at me seriously. "Promise me you won't marry your Jonny Army too soon? Live your life a little first, will you?"

"I do hope I will, yes. See you in London." I smiled as I left to go and pack my own suitcase for a summer in Cornwall.

My last year at Cambridge felt as if I was speeding through a tunnel with only one destination at the end of it: to work at Kew. In April, just before my finals, Dr. Walters sought me out in the herbarium.

"I've heard from Mr. Turrill at Kew, Miss Anderson. An interview has been arranged for you there next Monday at ten thirty a.m. Do you think you could manage that?"

"Of course!" I said eagerly.

"I will let Mr. Turrill know. Good luck, Miss Anderson."

The morning of my interview, I dressed carefully in my best skirt and blouse and pulled my hair back into a chignon for some semblance of professionalism. Then I slid my botanical drawings into a smart new leather portfolio that Jonny had given me for Christmas. I hadn't told him about the interview, wanting to wait until I knew if I had the position before I broached the subject of The Future. So far, we'd done an awful lot of talking about *his* career and almost none about mine.

I arrived at King's Cross in the middle of the commuter rush, squeezed onto the Circle Line tube, and then changed to the District Line for Kew Gardens station. It was a bright, fresh morning and the cherry trees that lined the roads were in full glorious bloom. Ahead of me was an impressive wrought-iron gate with decorated white pillars on either side. I walked through a little side gate and found myself in a grand park, the centerpiece a lake that reflected the blue sky above it, and winding paths that led to various Victorian buildings and greenhouses. Consulting the directions that Dr. Walters had given me, I set off for the main reception.

Inside, I went up to a young woman wearing fashionable cat-eye glasses and sitting behind a desk.

"Hello," I said, wishing my mouth didn't feel so dry. "I'm Posy Anderson, and I have an interview with Mr. Turrill at ten thirty."

"Please take a seat with the others and your name will be called shortly," she said in a bored voice.

I turned and saw three young men in dark suits—all with leather portfolios similar to mine—sitting in a small waiting area. Sitting down amongst them, I felt even more aware of how *female* I was.

An hour passed as, one by one, the men were escorted into a little office, then returned and departed the building without so much as a nod of goodbye. When the last man had left, I sat clutching my portfolio in sweaty hands, wondering if they had forgotten about me.

"Miss Anderson?" called a deep voice.

A tall man in a tweed suit emerged from the office and I saw kind blue eyes twinkling from behind a pair of thick round spectacles.

"Yes." I stood up hastily.

"I'm rather parched after all that talking. Would you like to come for a cup of tea with me?" he asked.

"I...yes, please."

He led me out of the building and we walked companionably through the park, the sun warming my face pleasantly.

"Now, Miss Anderson," he said, putting his hands in his pockets. "Dr. Walters has told me quite a bit about you."

I nodded, too nervous to speak.

"I have been Keeper of the Herbarium since just after the war," he continued, "and I have seen it change a great deal."

"Yes," I said, "I've read all of your work, sir, and your leaf-shape classification system is ingenious."

"Do you think so? Well, I am glad. I'm actually retiring this year, and I shall be sad to leave Kew. We are a family here, you see, and choosing a new member to join the clan is a serious task. Dr. Walters says that you are quite adept at botanical illustration."

"Yes; although I haven't been to art college, I have been drawing specimens since I was a little girl."

"That is the best way to learn," he said. "We need someone who is artistic and scientific in equal measure. Both the Herbarium and the Jodrell Laboratory will be expanding significantly in the next few years, and we require a staff member who can liaise between them. Ah, here we are."

We had arrived at a Chinese pagoda that sat amidst a manicured garden. Small tables had been arranged outside it to catch the sunshine, and Mr. Turrill indicated I should sit down. A young woman in an apron arrived from within.

"Your usual, Mr. Turrill?" she asked.

"Yes, dear, and perhaps some cake for Miss Anderson and me," he nodded at her. He turned to me. "Now, let's have a look at your illustrations."

I fumbled with the latch on my portfolio, then spread out the drafting paper on the table. Mr. Turrill took off his glasses to inspect the drawings carefully.

"You have an excellent eye, Miss Anderson. They rather remind me of the work of Miss Marianne North."

"I admire her greatly," I said, flattered. Marianne North was indeed a woman I looked up to enormously—a Victorian pioneer who had dared to travel by herself to collect specimens from all over the world.

"Now, working here at Kew would be varied. You would mainly be at the Herbarium, drawing and cataloging new specimens, and you would occasionally help at the Jodrell Laboratory with the research into cytogenetics. And we all pitch in at the greenhouses. Dr. Walters tells me you have a knack for breathing life into any plant that comes your way."

I blushed. "I simply respond to the needs of the plant and do my best."

"Jolly good. We receive a lot of exotic plants from all over the world here at Kew. And more often than not, we don't have a clue what their ideal growing conditions are, hence the need for experimentation...and a large portion of luck!" He chuckled and regarded me more closely.

At that moment, a woman with tanned skin and short curly brown hair approached the table. She was dressed in a practical trouser suit and had a vasculum—a leather carrying case for plants— slung over her shoulder.

"William, who are you courting today?" she called merrily.

"Ah, Miss Anderson, this is Jean Kingdon-Ward, one of our renowned plant hunters," Mr. Turrill said, standing up to greet her. "She is just returned from Burma."

"And covered in insect bites," she laughed and shook my hand. "A pleasure to meet you, Miss Anderson."

"Miss Anderson will soon be a Cambridge graduate, and we are considering her for a position at Kew."

"It's the best place in the world to work, Miss Anderson," said Jean. "William, shall I take the sample straight to the Herbarium?"

"Yes, but this time do a thorough check for any of our insect friends before you settle it in," he said, raising an eyebrow. "Need I remind you of the caterpillar infestation we dealt with last year?"

"Always a stickler," said Jean and gave me a smile before walking towards the Herbarium.

"Are you a keen traveller, Miss Anderson?" Mr. Turrill asked me as our tea and cake arrived.

"I can be, yes," I said, taking a sip of my tea and thinking that to work here at Kew, I could be anything they wanted me to be.

"Jonny, darling, I have something to tell you."

We were lying in bed in the bed and breakfast, smoking after our lovemaking.

"What is it, darling? You look awfully serious."

"I've been offered a job at Kew Gardens in London. I'll be working in the Herbarium cataloging the plants and sketching them."

"Well, that's just wonderful news!" Jonny replied, turning to me with a genuine smile. For some reason, I'd thought he might be cross, so relief poured through me when he offered me his congratulations.

"I'll be down at Mons in Aldershot, which is only an hour and a half's train ride from London, so we should be able to see each other regularly once I get leave after my initial training. Where will you stay?"

"Oh, Estelle says I can move in with her. Her flatmate is off to a ballet company in Italy next month, so I can take her room."

"That sounds perfect, although Estelle is rather wild, Posy. You won't be tempted to follow her lead, will you?"

"Of course not, darling. We'll hardly see each other anyway, with me working all day and her dancing all night."

"At least it will keep you out of trouble until I've completed my training, and then"—he squeezed me tight—"we're off to see the world."

I decided not to continue the conversation further. The fact that

Jonny simply assumed I would leave my longed-for job the moment he said I should was a subject for another time.

My last May Ball was bittersweet. Jonny and I and a group of St John's and New Hall undergraduates leaving Cambridge danced until dawn, downing champagne until I collapsed on the Backs against Jonny's shoulder, feeling tearful from too much alcohol as I watched the sun rise over the Cam for the last time.

"Posy, I love you," Jonny murmured.

"Mmmph, I love you too," I said drowsily, shutting my eyes and wanting to sleep, but Jonny moved from under me so I put my head against the soft, sweet-smelling grass.

"Posy?"

I dragged my eyes open and saw Jonny was on one knee in front of me, holding a small jewelry box in his hands.

"I know we've been engaged to be engaged for quite some time now, so before we go our separate ways, I thought I should make it official. My mother gave me her grandmother's ring when I went home for Easter, you see, and I've been carrying it around in my pocket waiting for the perfect moment. It's been such a wonderful night, and we're both leaving Cambridge, and...what I mean to say is"—he took a deep breath—"Posy Anderson, will you marry me?"

He opened the box to reveal a ring made up of three sapphires surrounded by tiny diamonds and slipped it onto my finger.

"I...yes," I replied, watching the way the ring glittered in the first rays of the sun. And even though, when he drew me to him to kiss me, I didn't feel the excitement I perhaps ought to at the prospect of being an engaged girl, I kissed him back.

Common Poppy
(Papaver rhoeas)

Chapter 21

Admiral House
November 2006

Over the weekend, Amy's emotions had lurched between guilt and euphoria. The morning after the night with Sebastian, she'd risen early, unable to sleep, woken her children, and they'd crept out of the house so as not to disturb him. She'd driven straight into Southwold, drawn some money out of the bank and been the first in the queue at the post office to pay the electricity bill. Arriving back home to their chilly house, she saw that the fridge-freezer had started to defrost, leaving a big puddle on the kitchen floor, which meant that most of the food inside it would be ruined. Salvaging what she could to eat in the next twenty-four hours, Amy cleared up the mess and at noon, the fridge had started whirring once more and the bare bulb in the kitchen had lit up.

When Sam had arrived home, she'd told him in a matter-of-fact way about the electricity being cut off and that they'd all had to ship out to Admiral House for the night. If she'd wanted to cover her tracks and lie about where they'd been, it was pointless. The children would tell him anyway.

Sam had been full of remorse, saying it must have slipped his mind and how could she ever forgive him? Far too exhausted for an argument and hardly feeling she held the moral high ground anyway, Amy said she forgave him, that it was one of those things and she was prepared to forget it. Obviously relieved he'd been let so lightly off the hook, Sam announced that he'd been paid yesterday, that he'd like to take Amy out to supper that night and could she get a babysitter at short notice? She had thanked him but refused, the thought of spending a couple of intimate hours across a table from her husband too much for her, and had taken herself off for an early night. Sam had followed her to bed and proceeded to try and make love to her. She had feigned sleep, and he'd taken her rejection as a sign that underneath, she was still cross with him about the electricity bill. He'd been in a bad mood for the rest of the weekend and Amy had done her best to keep out of his way.

She was glad when Monday arrived and she could escape to work. She bought herself a sandwich at lunchtime and went down to the sea front to eat it on a bench. The day was fresh, but not cold. Amy closed her eyes and for the first time, allowed herself to remember what it had felt like to have Sebastian making love to her, the words he had spoken, the way he'd caressed her body, her face, her hair, so gently. Having little with which to compare the experience other than a few university romps and the early days with Sam, she wondered whether the loving way Sebastian had been and the things he'd said were par for the course when a man got a woman into bed: was she just another notch on his bedpost, or had it meant more?

Amy had felt the tingle in her lower stomach as she remembered, and knew for her, it was definitely the latter.

She walked back towards the hotel, wondering if Sebastian contacted her, whether she would want it to happen again. And despite trying very hard to think of her marriage, her children and the dire consequences of being discovered, Amy knew she would.

However, in the following few days, as she heard nothing from Sebastian, any romantic thoughts began to disappear. It was obvious that he was not interested in pursuing the relationship any further. Why else wouldn't he have contacted her?

She tried to remember that she was a consenting adult, that he had not dragged her into bed, that she'd gone of her own free will for her own pleasure. Therefore, she must not feel used by Sebastian. That was old-fashioned. These days, it was perfectly acceptable for a woman to sleep with a man without having to label herself a tart.

Nevertheless, as the week passed, her spirits sagged further as still she heard nothing from him. Even Sara and Jake noticed their mother's short temper. Sam imaginatively asked her whether it was the time of the month as she slammed their supper onto the table.

"Mum called whilst you were out shopping," he said as they sat down to eat.

"Really?"

"Yes, she wanted to know if we'd like to go round to Sunday lunch this weekend."

The thought of going anywhere near Admiral House was anathema to Amy. Sebastian would be there, probably gloating over his conquest as she suffered the humiliation of rejection.

"I don't think so, thanks," Amy stood up and tipped her bolognese into the bin. "I've got a heap of washing and ironing to do and to be honest, at the moment, I can't think of anything worse."

"Keep your hair on, darling! I thought you liked going to Mum's."

"I do...I did...I'm just not up to it at the moment, that's all. Now if you'll excuse me, I'm going up to bed."

Amy climbed the stairs, fell onto the unmade bed and sobbed her heart out into the pillow.

By Monday, over a week had passed and it was becoming impossible for Amy not to hate Sebastian. She realized she must try to forget all about him and what had happened. For all she knew, Sebastian spent his life sleeping with women and not giving them another thought. And because of him, she'd been rotten to the kids, and it wasn't their fault she'd made a total fool of herself.

That evening, as she was leaving the hotel to walk to the car, a hand was placed on her shoulder.

"Amy."

"Hello, Sebastian." She did not look at him as her heart banged against her chest.

"How are you?" he asked as she carried on walking towards the car park, looking nervously from side to side in case anyone saw them.

"Fine," she lied.

"Why did you leave that morning without saying goodbye?"

"I..." She was shocked that, after over a week of hearing nothing from him, he could somehow twist the blame to her. "You were asleep. I had to go and pay my electricity bill."

"Oh. I presume you now regret what happened?"

She stopped and turned to look at him. "You obviously do, or maybe you've just forgotten all about it by now."

"What?!" He looked amazed at her anger.

"Let's face it, you've hardly made a big effort to contact me in the past week, have you?" she said.

"Amy, last Monday morning, I came to the hotel. You weren't in yet, and I was rushing to catch a train for London, so I left a note for you with someone on reception. Didn't you get it?"

She shook her head. "No, I didn't."

"Well, I swear to you I did. Check when you get back to the hotel. It was heavily coded, of course, and brief, but it told you I was off to Oslo for a literary festival. It gave you my mobile number and said to call whenever you could."

"Oh."

"Yes, oh," he repeated. Then he smiled. "So there was me in Oslo, miserable as sin because you didn't call, and you here, thinking what a complete and utter bastard I was."

"Something like that, yes," Amy agreed, allowing a small smile to cross her own lips as relief flooded through her.

"Amy..." He grasped her fingers in his hand. "I'll ask you again, and please tell me honestly: Do you regret what happened?"

"Do you?"

"God, no." He shook his head vehemently. "I'm worried you do."

"No," she said quietly, "unfortunately I don't. I wish I did."

"And I wish I could hold you," he muttered under his breath. "I've missed you so much. All I thought about in that hotel room was you. When can I see you?"

"I really don't know."

"Do you get any time off during the week?"

"Wednesday afternoon," she said.

"Posy is now working until five at the gallery on a Wednesday because of Christmas. Could you come to Admiral House? Please?"

he urged her.

Amy rubbed her forehead. "God, Sebastian, this is wrong. I—"

"We just need to talk, that's all," he said gently.

"I have to pick the children up at three-thirty from school, unless I asked Marie to collect them for me...oh dear...I really shouldn't...I..."

"*Please*, Amy."

She took a deep breath and exhaled. "Okay." She got inside the car and smiled wearily up at him. "Bye, Sebastian."

"See you on Wednesday," he whispered.

The following day, Posy arrived at Ferry Road as Amy was feeding the children their supper.

"Sara, darling, what a lovely hug," Posy said as the little girl flung herself around her legs. "Amy, you look well. Better than last time I saw you, anyway." She extracted herself from Sara and bustled into the kitchen. "And there was Sam saying you weren't feeling well enough to come over for lunch on Sunday. Here, I made a trifle for the children's pudding." Posy put it down on the kitchen table and stared at her. "Have you had your hair cut?"

Amy blushed. "Yes. I popped into the hairdresser at lunchtime for a quick trim. I haven't had it cut for over a year, and it needed it."

"Well, it looks splendid. In fact, my dear Amy, *you* look splendid." Posy's eyes crinkled with mischief. "By the look of you I'd say things were going much better with Sam. Am I right?"

"Yes," Amy nodded vehemently, "yes, they are."

"It's amazing how it shows. You have that sparkle back in your eyes and it's wonderful to see."

Amy busied herself with spooning out the trifle so Posy wouldn't see her flushed cheeks, then shooed the children off into the sitting room.

"I heard about the electricity bill debacle, by the way." Posy sat herself down at the table. "Sam was mortified for forgetting to pay it. And of course, it's typical I wasn't at home. Still, I'm sure Sebastian looked after the three of you."

"Yes, he did."

"He's such a nice chap. I'll miss him when he leaves for good."

"He's leaving?" Amy couldn't help herself asking.

"Not until Christmas, as far as I know. I'm just saying I've got used to him being around, that's all. But, of course, so much will change in the new year," Posy sighed. "However, the sight of you looking so much better cheers me enormously and makes me feel it was the right thing to do, to give Sam his chance at Admiral House."

"Yes, thank you again, Posy."

"Anyway, I popped in because there were a few things I wanted to ask you. Number one, I wondered whether you'd do me the honor of designing me some Christmas cards? I thought it might be a nice idea to have a last sketch of Admiral House on the front. I'd pay you, of course."

"Don't be silly, Posy. I'll do it for nothing. I'd love to."

"Thank you, dear. That would be marvellous. And I also wanted to know whether you'd be able to come and see some houses with me this coming weekend? Marie has popped some details in to the gallery and a couple look quite interesting."

"Of course I would. I'll see if Sam will mind the children."

"I think at present, Sam would walk over burning coals to be forgiven for his misdemeanor. Saturday it is, then. We could go for that lunch we keep promising ourselves. Now, the other thing is, I presume the two of you are still going to Tammy's launch party next week in London?"

"To be honest, I'd forgotten all about it," said Amy truthfully.

"Well, I think it's very important for you and Sam to go. Every couple needs the occasional night to themselves. I'll have the children."

"Thank you."

"Oh, and the other thing is that, in readiness for the big move, I actually went upstairs into the bedroom wardrobes to begin to clear things out," explained Posy. "And I found racks of my mother's old evening dresses. I'm sure a lot of them are far too moth-eaten to be salvageable, but there are a few, including a beautiful black Hartnell, that are definitely worth you trying on. My mother was about your size and the Hartnell in particular would be perfect for the party. The ones you don't like can go to Tammy for her boutique. Anyway, I shall leave them out, and if you're passing, pop in and have a try."

"Actually..." A thought jumped into Amy's mind. "I might pop in sometime tomorrow afternoon, if that's okay with you."

"Fine by me, dear. I'll be at the gallery, but I'll leave the kitchen door open."

"So how was Amsterdam?"

"Delightful."

"And when do we get to meet your Freddie?"

"He's not 'my' Freddie, dear, just a very pleasant companion. Now, I really must be off. I'll give you a buzz when I know what time the viewings are on Saturday, but why don't we say I'll pick you up here at twelve?"

"Okay. Bye, Posy."

Amy watched her mother-in-law head for the sitting room to say goodbye to the children and thought she wasn't the only one who apparently had a sparkle in her eye these days.

On Wednesday afternoon, hardly believing her good fortune at having found a genuine reason to be at Admiral House, Amy left work and drove the ten minutes out of town, butterflies fluttering round her stomach. She parked her car at the front and made her way round to the kitchen door. Before she could open it, Sebastian appeared and enveloped her in his arms.

"God, I've missed you." He pulled her inside and kissed her almost roughly. Amy found herself responding with similar fervor. Managing to break away and draw breath, she looked up at him and smiled.

"I thought I'd come here to talk?"

"We can, yes," he replied, kissing her neck and removing her coat at the same time. "But first, please, come to bed. It's much more pleasant to talk with no clothes on." His hands slipped underneath her shirt and her body tingled with desire. She let him lead her up the stairs to his room and insisted he lock the door just in case Posy returned early.

"Darling, she just might notice your car parked right outside, but never mind," he teased her as he ripped the clothes from her body and began to make love to her.

An hour later, she was propped up in bed, leaning against his chest as he stroked her hair.

"This may sound corny, but has it ever been like this for you before?" Sebastian asked.

Amy stared into the distance. "I suppose I should say that, yes, I've had great sex with lots of men, so if you dump me, I won't feel you were just getting an ego boost—"

"Amy, stop it, I know you spent a week thinking I was a total bastard, but you have to trust me. I'm just not that kind of man. In fact, the last time I had sex was..." He thought about it. "Over a year ago."

"Oh, so you're just desperate, are you?" She turned to him and played with the wiry hair on his chest.

"Sometimes a man just can't win," he sighed.

"Well the truth is, I have never, ever had anything like what we just had then." She kissed his chest. "Okay?"

Sebastian was silent for a while before he said, "Amy, the way I feel for you, it's not just about sex, you know. It's something much deeper than that. And it frightens me. The last time I felt this for someone, she went and died on me."

"Well, I'm not intending to do that," Amy promised.

Sebastian shook his head. "But you are married to someone else. Morally, you are not mine to love."

"And vice versa," she sighed. "I'm a wife and a mother."

"What I'm trying to say is that it might actually be better if it was just a strong physical attraction, a mutually beneficial arrangement between the two of us with no strings attached. I mean, where on earth do we go from here?" he pondered.

"Sebastian, we hardly know each other, and—"

"I feel as though I've known you for a very long time," he interjected.

"Well, you haven't."

"No." Sebastian was silent for a while. "Amy, this is a ghastly question to ask you, but I have to know the answer. Do you still love Sam?"

She bit her lip and stared out of the window. "I've been asking myself the same question for the past few weeks; I mean, before you and I...He's the father of my children, and that's a huge bond that can never be broken, whatever happens. As to whether I love him...well, if I'm brutally honest, no. I'm not in love with him anymore."

It was the first time Amy had actually admitted the truth to herself, let alone anyone else. The statement brought tears to her eyes and she sat up.

"God, what a bitch I am. Sitting here in bed with another man, telling him I no longer love my husband."

"It happens, to millions of couples the world over." Sebastian stroked her back gently. "And I've heard from Posy what a fantastically supportive wife you've been to him."

"And what a fantastically dramatic fall from grace I've just taken," she muttered miserably.

"The big question is, of course..." Sebastian paused, obviously thinking about how to word his sentence. "Will you suffer in silence and stay with Sam for the sake of the children, or will you accept the relationship is over and be brave enough to move on?"

"I don't know. I really don't know."

"No, of course you don't, and it's unfair of me to ask. We must both accept that I have an obviously biased view of the situation, so perhaps it's better if I don't comment. All I will say is that I know I love you and want to be with you. It would be better if you were free, from my point of view—to put it mildly—but I promise I will try to be patient and not rush you into a decision."

She turned to face him. "Sebastian, how can you be so sure about me after such a short time?"

"I don't know. I just am. But then it's much easier for me. I am completely unencumbered. So I just have to wait and hope that one day you will be too."

She kissed him goodbye twenty minutes later, with a promise to call him the following day, and set off to collect the children. As she drove towards Southwold, her heart bursting with conflicting emotions, she realized she'd completely forgotten to try on the vintage dresses.

The following Saturday, Sam said he'd look after the kids for the afternoon whilst Amy went out house shopping with Posy.

"It'll do you good to have a break for a change," he announced. "And don't worry what time you get back. We'll be fine here."

"Thanks, Sam. The shepherd's pie should be ready in half an

hour. Make sure both of them eat all of it before you offer them any pudding."

"I will. Bye, sweetheart. Have a good time," he said as he heard his mother hooting the horn outside. He made to kiss her on the lips, but she turned away and he only managed her cheek.

As she walked down the path to Posy's waiting car, Amy almost wished Sam wasn't trying so hard to make up for his misdemeanors. It only increased her guilt.

"Hello, dear, how are you?" said Posy.

"I'm very well," said Amy as she settled herself into the passenger seat.

"Good. This is a treat, just you and I, isn't it? I thought we'd drive to Walberswick for lunch at that nice pub. The first house we're looking at is in Blythburgh at two o'clock, which should time just nicely."

"I'm in your hands, Posy," nodded Amy as they set off, skirting round the main street and along the sea front.

"That's where Evie Newman lives." Posy pointed to a large Victorian house as they turned a corner into a wide, tree-lined road, a stone's throw from the pier. "Far too big just for her and her daughter, but very impressive," she commented. "By the way, did you manage to try on those evening dresses last Wednesday? They didn't look as though they'd been touched."

"Er, yes. They were all too big, I'm afraid." It was the first lie Amy had told and she hated herself for it.

"Really? I'm surprised. My mother was a slip of a thing. We obviously need to feed you up, Amy."

Over fresh mussels in the pub, Amy managed to keep the conversation confined to Posy, who, with a little encouragement, began to talk about her trip to Amsterdam with Freddie.

"It made me realize that one can become very parochial living in a small town. When I was married to Sam's father, we moved across the world from one army base to the next and I never thought twice about it." Posy took a sip of her wine. "Perhaps, once Admiral House is sold, I might take myself off on a Scandinavian cruise. I've always wanted to see the Norwegian fjords."

"And will Freddie go with you?"

"Who knows? As I've told you, we are just good friends. *Really*," she emphasized. "Although it's far more fun doing that kind of thing with someone else. Now, we'd better get a move on or we'll be late for our first appointment." Posy put her coat on and gazed out of the window at the drizzle. "A gray and miserable November day—perfect for seeing houses at their absolute worst."

The first two houses were non-starters, due to Posy's obsession with having a south-facing garden.

"I know I asked Marie for something with 'character,'" said Posy, fastening her seat-belt, "but to be quite honest, I just wonder whether a low-ceilinged cottage wouldn't send me bonkers, after all the space I've been used to. Just one last place to see, and it's a three-story townhouse near the lighthouse. I have to admit I quite fancy living right in the center of town, after so many years of making the journey in and out of it."

The townhouse turned out to be the hit of the day: newly refurbished, with plenty of light, a modern kitchen, and a small but definitely south-facing garden. Amy followed Posy around jealously, thinking how she'd kill for a house like this.

"It couldn't be more different to Admiral House, could it?" Amy commented as they stood in the rain whilst Posy calculated exactly where the sun would fall during the day.

"I have to admit I'm rather taken with it. I know it should appeal more to a thirty-something swinger than an old granny like myself, but I like it a lot. It's light and airy because of the windows and the high ceilings, and there are enough bedrooms for friends and family to come and stay."

"It's very expensive, Posy. I mean, nearly half of what you'd get from Admiral House." Amy studied the details as Roger, the viewings agent, locked the door behind them.

"Ridiculous, isn't it?" Posy agreed. "However, you can't take it with you, and as what gets left behind will be split between Sam and Nick, I'd say a house like that would make a jolly good long-term investment," she commented as they drove though Southwold. "I must speak to Sam and ask him how things are going on Admiral House, and then I might be very tempted to put in an offer."

As they passed Evie's house, both women stared at the unmistakably familiar red car parked against the curb outside it.

"That's Nick's car, isn't it, Posy?"

"Yes, it is."

"Did you know he was down in Southwold this weekend?"

"No." Posy cleared her throat. "Mind you, he is a grown-up and doesn't tell his mother every move he makes."

They drove on in silence, neither of them wishing to pursue the conversation further.

Chapter 22

On the morning of the launch party of 'Reborn,' Tammy woke up sweating with nerves. Even though everything was absolutely as organized as it could be, she had a hundred things to do before this evening. She jumped out of bed, showered, made herself a quick coffee, then drove round to the shop. Meena was already there, vacuuming the carpet.

"Though why I am bothering, with a hundred pairs of feet about to tread all over it, I do not know," she sniffed.

Tammy glanced at her watch. She had an interview at ten with a daily newspaper, the flowers for the window were arriving at noon, and the caterers at three.

"Where they're going to store the canapés, I just haven't a clue," she fretted. "We'll need the office table to pour the champagne into glasses." Tammy slumped into a chair. "God, I don't think I have ever been so bloody nervous in my life. Even more than going down my first runway at the Paris collections."

"Oh, Tammy, remember these people who are coming tonight are your friends. They all want you to succeed. Try to enjoy it. Days like today don't come along often, you know. When is Nick arriving?"

"Not until later on. He's up to his eyes too. We've hardly seen each other in the past three weeks. Hopefully, once tonight is over, we can spend more time together."

"Yes. He is a nice man, your Nick. I like him," Meena declared.

"Right, I will go to rinse out the hundred champagne glasses they sent round yesterday. I am not happy with their cleanliness."

The flowers arrived and Tammy spent an hour fiddling with the window display and thinking about Nick. She missed him when she didn't wake up next to him. With that thought, she dialed his mobile number as she clambered out of the front window. He answered immediately.

"Hello, darling, it's me."

"How are you feeling?" he asked her.

"Sick with nerves, to be honest."

"Of course you are. I'm waiting here at the shop for a delivery, but once it's unloaded, I'll come across and offer you some moral support."

"Thanks, darling, I appreciate it. I miss you," she said shyly.

"I miss you too. I'll see you later."

As Tammy stuck the mobile in her back jean pocket, she realized how much she'd wanted to replace "I miss you" with three far more powerful words.

"Shit, Tammy," she muttered to herself as she went to help Meena set out the glasses. "You're in deep."

Amy was thankful Posy was working at the gallery that morning, which meant she could drop the children's overnight bags there rather than run the risk of seeing Sebastian at Admiral House.

"Hello, Amy," Posy smiled. "All set?"

"Just about, apart from the fact that Jake seems to have got that nasty cough and cold Sara had a few weeks ago. He doesn't have a temperature and he's gone to school, but I gave his teacher your number here at the gallery, just in case. I hope you don't mind."

"Of course I don't."

"I've put some Calpol in his bag." Amy handed it over to Posy. "If he does seem hot, a couple of teaspoons should calm him down. Maybe he shouldn't have a bath tonight, either."

"Amy, please try not to worry. I promise I'll look after them. I did bring up two of my own, you know," Posy responded patiently. "Now, what time are you meeting Sam?"

"He's at the architect's in Ipswich, so I'm driving to Ipswich station and meeting him there. Right, I'd better be going. And you know we'll be at Tammy's tonight if you need us," she confirmed.

"Yes, Amy, I know you will. Now, you go and have a splendid time. Goodbye."

Amy sat on the platform at Ipswich, nervously checking her watch. The train to London was due in two minutes and there was still no sign of Sam. She'd called his mobile over and over, but it was switched off.

She saw the train approaching the station and tried Sam again. This time he answered. "Hello?"

"It's me. Where are you? The train's here!"

"Sweetheart, I'm afraid I've been held up at the architect's and I'm not going to make it. I'm sorry, Amy, I really am. You go and have a good time."

"Okay, bye then."

Her anger at being stood up was tempered by guilty relief that she wouldn't have to spend the evening with him. But could she really go without him? *Yes, dammit, I can.* Before she could question her decision, Amy leapt onto the waiting train as the doors began to close.

She arrived at Tammy's boutique just before six, knocked on the door, and was greeted by a glamorous Indian lady with an amazing set of white teeth.

"You are Amy, yes?"

"I am. Is Tammy here?"

"No, she has nipped home to have a bath and get changed. I am Meena, her right- and left-hand woman. She said I was to expect you and your husband."

"No, it's only me, as it happens. My husband couldn't make it."

"Ah well," Meena shrugged. "Can I get you a cup of tea?"

"Oh I'd love one," breathed Amy, following Meena into the shop, admiring the cream damask which Tammy had fashioned on the high ceiling to create a tented effect. "This sounds very silly, but where are the clothes?" she asked.

"We have locked the stock downstairs in the basement to give more room. The gowns will be worn by Tammy's model friends, and as many pretty female guests as she could persuade to do so. Tammy has left a dress out for you, if you wish to wear it."

"That's very kind of her, but I'm not exactly a model type," said Amy.

"Toosh!" said Meena. "You are very beautiful. You remind me of Princess Grace of Monaco in her youth. Why don't you go into the changing room and try on the dress that is hung there for you?"

"Why not?" Amy agreed, thinking of her old little black dress from Topshop lying crumpled in her overnight bag. She went into the curtained changing room and looked at the shimmering midnight-blue satin sheath, the front decorated with hundreds of tiny sparkling beads.

"Wow!" she said as she looked at the label inside and saw it was a Givenchy.

"Amy!" Meena clasped her hands together in delight when she emerged. "You look perfect."

"Amazingly, it fits me like a glove," acknowledged Amy, giving a twirl.

"And shows off your beautiful figure. You should wear your hair up in a chignon, like this." Meena piled Amy's hair onto the top of her head. "You have a wonderful long neck. Shall I style it for you?"

"If you have time, yes please."

"I have time, and there is nothing I like better than dressing someone up for a party. In my culture, we take hours to get ready. Now, sit down in front of the mirror and I'll fetch my hairpins."

Twenty minutes later, after Meena had not only expertly fastened Amy's hair into a chignon, but applied her makeup too, Amy stood up.

"Breathtaking," Meena exclaimed.

"Just one little problem," said Amy. "I haven't got any suitable shoes."

"Ahhah!" cackled Meena. "What are fairy godmothers for?" She took Amy's hand. "Follow me, Cinders, to my daughter's shop next door, and you shall go to the ball!"

Chapter 23

"How do I look?" Tammy asked Nick as she walked down the stairs into the sitting room.

"Absolutely stunning, darling," Nick said, admiring the opulent green off-the-shoulder dress that matched Tammy's eyes perfectly. "I'm sure you'll make all the gossip columns looking like that." He took her by the shoulders and kissed her. "I'm very, very proud of you. Here." He offered her a small velvet box.

"What's this?" she asked.

"A present, to mark the occasion."

"Thank you, darling." Tammy opened the box and found a delicate antique peridot necklace inside. "It's beautiful," she breathed, "and it goes with my dress perfectly. You are clever."

"It's about a hundred and fifty years old," Nick smiled as she turned round so he could do up the clasp. "There."

She turned back into his arms and kissed him. "I love it. And I love you," she added quietly.

"Do you?" He tipped her face up to his and looked into her eyes. "Really?"

"Yes, really."

He stroked her neck and let his hand trail down to her cleavage. "How about we forget all about your party and just stay in for the night?"

"I wish, but I think we'd better be getting a move on. Right." Tammy took a deep breath. "Let's go."

By eight o'clock, the party was in full swing. Paparazzi were stationed outside, marking the arrival and departure of the guests, and a camera crew was interviewing Tammy on the pavement.

Amy was having a wonderful time. Everybody was very friendly and kept telling her how lovely she looked. She'd made a new friend called Martin, a freelance photographer, who was plying her with champagne and compliments in equal measure.

"You know, you could have a career in photographic modeling any time you wished."

His hand was caressing her shoulder as she suddenly became aware of a pair of eyes staring at her from the entrance. Her heart skipped a beat.

"Excuse me, Martin. I think I need a breath of fresh air." She extracted herself from his grasp and headed towards the door where he stood.

"Do I know you?" he asked sardonically.

"What on earth are you doing here?" she asked.

"I was in London for lunch with my editor. I wasn't going to come to the party even though Tammy had kindly invited me, because it isn't really my scene. But my flat is literally round the corner, so I thought I'd wander past on my way for some milk and bread. Then I saw this vision in the window being pawed by some sweaty male. Who's the gorilla?" Sebastian asked, indicating Martin.

"Some fashion photographer," Amy shrugged.

"And where's the husband?"

"At home. He didn't make it."

"So you mean to tell me," Sebastian whispered into her ear, 'that you are in town alone for an entire night?"

"Yes."

"Well, with you looking..." Sebastian shook his head as he tried to find the right words, "utterly astonishing, and by yourself in the big city, I feel it is my duty to protect you from hairy-arsed predators like that prat over there." He kissed her gently on the neck. "I want you, now."

"Excuse me, chaps." Tammy squeezed past them and Amy blushed to the roots of her hair. "How are you, Sebastian? Lovely to see you."

"Very well," answered Sebastian smoothly. "May I offer my congratulations on an obviously triumphant evening?"

"You may," nodded Tammy happily. "It is going rather well, actually. Everyone seems to have turned up, and I should get some column inches in the press. Listen, if I don't see you later, a few of us are going out for supper afterwards to La Famiglia, just off the King's Road. I'd love you to come, both of you."

"Tammy!" a voice called from somewhere within.

"Coming!" She raised an eyebrow. "Sorry, bye, both."

"Oh Christ," whispered Amy as she watched Tammy make her way through the crowds, "she must have seen."

"Amy, my dear, this is not Southwold and Tammy is not your friend Marie. She is a cosmopolitan, intelligent woman who could not give a shit if we're having a fling or not," countered Sebastian.

"You make me sound so...provincial," breathed Amy.

"I have never seen anyone who looks less provincial than you tonight, my darling. Now, let's seize the chance whilst we've got it and enjoy our evening."

Amy knew she had drunk far too much champagne, but she was at a glamorous party in the heart of London, in a gorgeous dress, and best of all, Sebastian was at her elbow.

An hour later, Sebastian whispered in her ear, "Okay, can we go now, please? I've had enough."

"But I'm having a lovely time and I don't want it to end just yet. Another ten minutes," she pleaded.

Finally, he managed to drag her to the door and onto the pavement outside. "Come on, you need something to eat," he said.

"I'm fine," she said as she hiccupped, then kissed him on the cheek...just as a flashbulb went off in their faces.

"Mr. Girault, can we take the name of your companion for the caption?" asked the photographer.

"No, you bloody well can't!" replied Sebastian grimly, pulling a giggling Amy off down the street before they could take any more. "Well, that's just peachy, my dear. That picture could end up in a bloody column!"

"Does that mean we'll be in *Hello*?" Amy jigged down the street unsteadily and Sebastian couldn't help but smile at her.

"Well, I'm glad you're so happy about it. I'm not so sure your husband will be."

"He never reads *Hello*, and to be honest, tonight, I couldn't give a damn who sees it."

"You might in the morning," Sebastian muttered, steering her into the local all-night shop to buy some carbohydrates to sober her up. Then he marched her towards Sloane Gardens and unlocked the door to his flat. Amy danced in and fell onto the sofa. "Oh, I've had such a wonderful time," she sighed, and reached out her arms to Sebastian. She hugged him to her. "And I do love you."

"I love you too, you drunken hussy. Right, you stay there and I'll go and make some coffee and toast."

When Sebastian returned to the sitting room, Amy was fast asleep. Sighing, he found a blanket, covered her up gently, and went alone to his bedroom.

Chapter 24

Tammy woke to the smell of brewing coffee. Still half-asleep, she opened her eyes as Nick came into the bedroom with a breakfast tray piled with fresh croissants and a selection of the morning newspapers.

"Urgh, what time is it?" she asked, her voice husky from far too many Marlboro Lights the night before. These days, she only smoked socially and it didn't agree with her.

"Almost ten."

"Christ, I said I'd see Meena at nine to help tidy up the mess from last night." Tammy sat up and brushed her tousled hair out of her face.

"I called her and said you were still asleep and she said not to worry, that she'd make a start on things. Meena is the kind of person who absolutely loves feeling useful."

"I know." Tammy giggled. "She got chatted up last night by an ancient male model in a toupée. She was loving it."

Nick sat on the bed next to her and spread out the newspapers. "Right, madam, I only purchased the ones you're in, of course," he grinned.

She made her way through four papers, all of which had varying sizes of photo and caption, of Tammy with different guests.

"'Tammy Shaw celebrates the launch of her new boutique, Reborn. Ex-model Tammy, pictured here with her successful antiques dealer boyfriend, Nick Montague, played host to a clutch of celebrities.' Darling, you look very suave." She kissed him on the neck, then leafed through the other papers.

"I think you've arrived," said Nick.

"Well, thank God that's all over. Now I can get down to the serious business of making money." Tammy reached for Nick's hand. "Thank you so much for all your support last night. You were fantastic."

"Don't be silly. I shall expect the same from you when I open my own doors in the next month and invite the local vagrants for some lemonade and a Spam sandwich to celebrate," Nick laughed, kissing her forehead. "As a matter of fact, before you go to the boutique, there's somewhere I want to take you."

Nick drove Tammy over the Albert Bridge, negotiated the traffic, and pulled the car to a halt in front of a Victorian house, situated in a wide leafy road which overlooked Battersea Park.

"What do you think?" he asked her.

"Of what?"

"Of the house we are sitting in front of."

Tammy studied it. "I think it looks...big."

"Absolutely. Come on, I've got the keys. Let me show you round."

Having pulled Tammy through the three spacious floors of the house, Nick opened the back door, which led onto a large garden.

"So, what do you reckon?"

"I think it would make the most fantastic family house," said Tammy, looking confused.

"Absolutely. That's the reason I like it. So, Miss Shaw, can you see our sprogs racing round this at a rate of knots as we sit on the terrace enjoying our sundowners?" Nick looked straight ahead of him as he spoke, hands thrust deep into his pockets.

"I...Nick, what are you saying?"

"I suppose I am asking whether, rather than me buying a bachelor pad, you might, in the fullness of time, consider filling some of the space this house has to offer. And possibly helping me to provide some of those sprogs to race around the garden." He finally turned to her and smiled. "I can't think of anyone else I'd prefer to do it with."

Tammy shook her head. "Neither can I," she said quietly.

He walked towards her and held her. "Good. Tammy?"

"Yes?" She looked up at him.

"There are some things I have to sort out before I can genuinely commit fully to you, but I want you to know now that it's what I intend to do."

"You mean getting the business going? I understand, Nick. There's no rush."

"That, and something else, which I'll explain as soon as I possibly can. But if you would be happy in principle to think about being in this house with me, I shall put in an offer and see if we can get the ball rolling. I really think it has great potential and we could turn it into something special."

"Yes," Tammy agreed, feeling overwhelmed. "I think we could."

Amy had the sensation that she was trying to sleep on a carousel and needed to get off immediately so she could be sick. She sat bolt upright as bile rose to her throat. The room was in complete darkness and she could not for the life of her remember where she was.

"Help," she whimpered, staggering off the sofa she'd been lying on and searching ineffectually for a light, bumping into something and hurting her shin.

"Ouch!"

A door opened and Sebastian stood there, bathed in light from the hallway. "Morning."

"Bathroom, I need the bathroom," she managed to blurt, heading towards him.

"In there," he pointed, and Amy made a run for it.

She only just made it before throwing up. Washing her face in cold water, she studied her reflection in the mirror. Last night's makeup was no longer round her eyes, but underneath them. Her chignon was hanging down and the beautiful evening dress was crumpled and stained.

"Oh God," she groaned as she opened the bathroom door and teetered along the corridor. Images of last night were beginning to come back to her. Sebastian was in the kitchen and she could smell coffee brewing. It made her gag and she rushed back to the bathroom again.

"Poor old you," Sebastian commented as she returned to the kitchen a second time. "Feeling a bit rough, are we?"

"Dreadful," Amy admitted as she slumped into a chair and leant her elbows on the narrow table. "Did I make a complete fool of myself last night?"

"Not at all. You were the belle of the ball. Can I get you something?"

"Water, please, and a couple of aspirin if you have them."

"Okay." Sebastian produced a glass of water and some tablets and Amy swallowed tentatively, hoping her stomach would accept them.

"I'm so sorry." She shook her head. "I don't understand why I got so drunk. I can't remember drinking that much."

"One doesn't at these kind of dos," said Sebastian. "You empty one glass, then another arrives by magic and you lose count. I presume you'd had nothing whatsoever to eat either."

"No, not since breakfast-time yesterday," Amy agreed.

"Well then, what did you expect?"

She looked up at him. "Are you cross with me?"

"Only selfishly, I suppose. Our one possible night together and you fall asleep on the sofa. Anyway, at least I was able to tell Tammy the truth when she rang here looking for you last night."

Amy looked up at him in horror. "How did she get your number?"

"She called Posy."

"Oh God," Amy groaned. "So Posy knows I'm here too."

"Yes, but don't worry, I've phoned her, explained what happened, and she said to tell you the children are absolutely fine. I suggested that, given your current condition, it might be best if I drive you back with me to Admiral House and she'll collect the children from school. We'll all rendezvous there later."

"Sebastian, I'm so sorry to put you to all this trouble. I feel terrible about it."

"No problem, really, Amy."

"But what if they think...?" She bit her lip. "That you and I...?"

"Given the state of you this morning, I don't think anyone would have any difficulty believing the explanation. Now why don't I run you a bath and you can freshen up?"

"Oh!" Amy put her hands to her face. "My clothes are still at Tammy's shop."

"Good point. I've got to go out and get a paper anyway, so whilst you have a bath, I'll retrieve them. I'll also return the shoes and pop that lovely dress Tammy lent you into the dry cleaners and give her the ticket so she can collect it, okay?"

Amy nodded gratefully. "Please send her my apologies and tell her thank you for the dress and the party."

When Sebastian left the flat, she lay in a lavender-scented bath, feeling horribly guilty for her behavior, but actually rather enjoying the fact that Sebastian, without being told what to do or say by her, had taken charge. So very different from Sam, who looked to her to organize their lives.

By the time Amy emerged, wrapped in Sebastian's dressing gown, which smelt deliciously of him, he had returned and was frying sausages, bacon and eggs. Croissants were warming in the oven. "You might not think you want food, but the best thing you can do is eat." He put a glass of orange juice in front of her. "Drink, please, madam. Get some Vitamin C down you."

"Thank you." Amy sipped the juice as she watched Sebastian move around the kitchen. "You're very domesticated."

"When you've been by yourself for as long as I have, you have no choice."

"It's a long time since someone cooked me breakfast," she said wistfully.

"Then enjoy it whilst you can," he said, dishing up the food onto two plates and putting one in front of her. He sat down on the other side of the table.

"Er...where exactly are we?" she asked, tentatively putting a piece of bacon to her lips.

"If you mean where is my flat located, it's just two minutes from Sloane Square," answered Sebastian, "and about five minutes from Tammy's boutique."

"How lovely to be so close to everything."

"To be honest, at the time I bought it six years ago, I wasn't sure I'd like it. My wife and I used to live in a small country village in Sussex. I loved it there. We were very much part of the local community and I'm really a country boy at heart. But after she died I wanted somewhere I could be anonymous, where no one would bother me and I could live without any reminders of her."

"A completely fresh start."

"Yes," he agreed. "I knew my friends thought I was running away, and maybe I was, but my belief is that you have to do whatever you feel is best for *you* when you're grieving. And this was what was best for me."

"I can't imagine how you coped. Losing a wife and a child all at once."

"The hardest thing was the expectation of happiness before she died. By that I mean the contrast between expecting new life and all the joy that brings, and then actually experiencing the complete opposite: the end of two lives. No one knows what to say to you. They either ignore it and try to jolly you along, or go overboard and treat you like an emotional basket case." He shrugged. "Everyone meant well; it's just that nothing could bring me comfort."

"Except your writing."

"Yes. I suppose, given the wreck of my real life, I felt it was the one thing over which I could have control. I played God: I decided who lived, who died, who was destined for happiness or misery. It was writing that kept me sane."

"But you must wish every day that things had happened differently, surely? That your wife was still alive?" Amy questioned.

"I've become much more fatalistic about it. If she had lived, we would probably still be in that Sussex village and I might have made it to editor of the newspaper I worked for and never written the novel. Tragedy either makes or breaks you and in retrospect I think it made me. I'm far less shallow than I was and it's definitely made me a better person. Also, Amy, if life hadn't taken the painful twists it has, then you and I wouldn't be sitting here having breakfast together." Sebastian reached for her hand across the table. "And I'd have hated to miss meeting you."

"Even after my behavior last night?"

"Yes. Even if it was only temporary, I enjoyed imagining we were together; a proper couple, enjoying an evening out. I felt enormously proud to be with you."

"Before I got drunk, obviously," she countered.

"Actually, it was lovely to see you so happy and observe your obvious capacity for fun. You're not like that in Southwold."

"I don't usually have the time or the wherewithal to have fun. In fact, I'd forgotten what it felt like and now..." Amy shook her head as tears came to her eyes. "It's so awful, but I really don't want to go home."

Sebastian reached for her hand and squeezed it. "Then don't."

"God, if only life was that simple. But it isn't. It never is when you have children."

"Of course it isn't, but maybe you should take me out of the equation and ask yourself whether, with or without me, you'd want to stay with Sam?"

"There's no doubt that before you and I became...close, I'd considered leaving him. The trouble is that he's on a high at the moment, due to buying Admiral House. I can't say he's being awful to me, because he's not. In fact, he's trying hard to be better."

"Maybe he's rumbled something is up."

"God, no! How could he?" Her heart began to pound. "If he ever found out, I..."

Sebastian rose from his chair. "Anyway, let's forget about your husband and enjoy the precious little time we have left, shall we?" He pulled her to standing, kissed her, then led her off in the direction of the bedroom.

Amy was very quiet on the drive back to Southwold. She clutched Sebastian's hand tightly and closed her eyes. Of course she wanted to see the children, but the thought of going back to that dreadful house, and, worst of all, Sam, was horrendous.

Could I do it? Could I leave him? she asked herself.

Perhaps she could rent a small house in Southwold to give herself some breathing space whilst she considered her options. Running straight into Sebastian's arms was wrong, even if he wasn't currently residing with her mother-in-law at Admiral House. He had to get to know the children and vice versa before they made any long-term plans.

Amy studied him surreptitiously. He was concentrating on the road in front of him and humming to Classic FM on the radio. It wasn't just the lovemaking, which got better on each occasion; it was the fact that the more she discovered about him, the more she liked him. He was kind, funny, gentle, completely straightforward, and eminently capable. It made her feel cherished, protected and loved.

In essence, he was the complete opposite of Sam. And Amy knew, even after this short time, that she wanted to be with him.

Sebastian brought the car to a halt just before they turned in to the drive of Admiral House. He reached for her and she nestled into his arms.

"I just want you to know that I love you, and that I want to be with you, but that I understand how difficult the situation is for you. And that I will wait as long as I can whilst you decide what to do."

"Thank you," Amy murmured. She took a deep breath. "Right, let's face the music."

Sara and Jake were sitting in the kitchen eating the cupcakes they had just made with Posy.

"Mummy, Mummy!" They threw themselves at Amy as she and Sebastian walked in.

"Hello, darlings, have you been good?"

"I don't know, but we've had a lovely time," said Jake. "And Daddy's here too."

Amy's stomach turned over. "Is he?"

"He's in the morning room with Granny. Daddee! Mummy's back!" Sara shouted.

The door to the morning room opened and Sam and Posy emerged, Sam holding a file of papers and a roll of plans.

"Darling." Sam walked over to Amy and kissed her. "I'm so sorry I didn't make it last night, but when I explain why, you'll understand."

Posy, following Sam into the kitchen, saw Sebastian watching her son embrace Amy. The expression on Sebastian's face told her something she really didn't want to know. "Hello, you two, good drive back?"

"Yes, thank you, Posy," replied Sebastian. "Now, if you'll excuse me, I think I'll go up and get on with some work."

He made to leave the room, but Sam stopped him. "Before you go, come and see what I've just been showing Mum." He steered Amy towards the table and unrolled the plans, with Sebastian following him reluctantly. "Look, darling, do you recognize where this is?"

Amy stared at what was obviously an architect's plan for a house. She shook her head. "No."

"You know the derelict barn about three hundred yards from the back of Admiral House, right on the edge of the land, hidden behind the pine trees?"

"Er, vaguely," nodded Amy.

"I know where you mean. I walked down there last weekend," said Sebastian. "It's a lovely spot."

"Exactly," said Sam. "Well, I've had a word with the architect who's working on the design for the apartments, and he thinks we may well be able to get planning permission to turn the barn into a dwelling. If we can do it, sweetheart"—he smiled up at Amy—"this is going to be our new home. You can see he's drawn a big galleried sitting room, large kitchen, a playroom for the children...and four bedrooms upstairs. So what do you think? How would you like to live in it?"

Amy forced a smile onto her face and nodded. "It looks great," she said.

"See, I told you that one day I'd get you a lovely home. What do you think, Seb?"

Sebastian shuddered at the shortening of his name. "I think it looks great. Now, if you'll excuse me, I really must go and lock myself away. Bye, Sam. Bye, Amy." He nodded and left the room.

"Right, who's for a nice cup of tea?" asked Posy, trying to ease the obvious tension.

"I've got to pop in to the office and make a few phone calls." Sam checked his watch. "Don't forget the surveyor's coming at ten tomorrow morning, will you, Mum?"

"Of course I won't," said Posy.

"And if there are no major hitches, we should be all set to exchange contracts next week."

"Yes, Sam, you've said, three times," nodded Posy patiently.

"I suppose I just worry that you'll change your mind at the last minute, that's all. You won't, will you, Mum?"

"No, Sam, I won't."

"Right, I'll come back for you in an hour shall I, Amy?" said Sam.

She nodded, wishing he'd never come back for her at all. As her husband left, Amy felt weary and low. She sat down heavily at the kitchen table and both children immediately climbed onto her lap. Posy, seeing the expression on Amy's face, suggested she put the TV on in the morning room, and the children followed her out.

"You look shattered, my dear," Posy said as she returned and put the kettle on to boil.

"I am," sighed Amy. "I'm not used to late nights and alcohol. I'm ashamed to say I had far too much and ended up passing out on Sebastian's sofa."

"He said as much. Ah well, sometimes it does one the world of good to let one's hair down."

"I'll try not to make a habit of it, Posy. I am a mother, after all. So," Amy swiftly changed the subject, "how are you feeling about letting go of Admiral House?"

"I'm thinking positive. If we exchange next week, I can go ahead and put an offer in on that darling townhouse we saw last weekend. So, that's quite exciting, isn't it?"

"Is it?" Amy watched Posy as she poured hot water into a teapot. "Are you absolutely sure you want to sell Admiral House?"

"Of course not, but that doesn't mean I don't know it's the right thing to do, because it is." She looked across at her daughter-in-law. "Sometimes, even when your heart is telling you to go one way, you must follow your head. We all have to make hard decisions at some point in our lives, don't we?"

Amy could feel heat rising to her cheeks, even though she knew Posy was referring to her own dilemma. "Yes," she managed.

"Besides, I really do feel I could be happy in that town house. I'll miss the garden here, of course, but it's getting to be far too much for me to manage. So, how would you feel about living in the old barn if Sam does manage to get planning permission?"

"It looked...great." Amy did her best to feign enthusiasm. "But I don't want to get my hopes up."

"I rather like the thought of a Montague still being on the land and bringing up their children here. It makes the parting less absolute, and of course it means I can come back for a visit," Posy smiled.

"Of course you can," agreed Amy. "*If* it happens."

"I understand your faith in Sam's business ventures has been sorely tested, but I've never seen him so enthused. It must make life easier for you, having a happy husband."

Amy could not help feeling Posy was probing, and she couldn't cope with it just now. "Yes, of course it does." She stood up. "If you don't mind, I'll go and watch some TV with the children."

Posy watched Amy disappear out of the kitchen and sighed. For once, she wished age had not brought with it such wisdom.

Chapter 25

With a big helping hand from Meena, Tammy had worked hard to get the shop into some kind of shape to open properly for business. There had been a list of phone calls to return, consisting of enquiries from the media and potential customers wanting to know her opening hours.

"Tomorrow, we really begin," said Meena, as they made another trip downstairs to retrieve the last of the stock from the basement.

"Yes. Right, if that's the lot, I'm off to Nick's shop. He's taking me out to dinner." Tammy turned to Meena and smiled. "You've been such a superstar. Can I take you out to supper next week to say thank you?"

"There is no need, but yes, that would be most enjoyable, Tammy."

"Well, I couldn't have done it without you." She gave Meena a warm hug.

"And you have given back some purpose to my life, so we are both happy. Have a nice evening and I will see you tomorrow."

Tammy arrived at Nick's shop twenty minutes later and stood in front of it looking in the window. A pair of round art deco mirrors were suspended by invisible wires and an exquisite chandelier made of tiers of delicate Murano glass hung between them over a chaise longue upholstered in its original cream leather. A wave of love and pride washed over her as she entered the shop. She heard loud hammering from downstairs in the basement.

"Darling, it's me!" she shouted over the banister.

"Okay! Up in a minute," Nick shouted back as the hammering resumed.

Tammy wandered round the showroom, which was filling up with the pieces Nick had so painstakingly collected over the past two months. From somewhere in the showroom, a mobile rang. She stood up to find it and located it on the satinwood table that Nick was using as his desk.

"Nick, phone!" she called down the stairs, but the hammering did not stop, so Tammy answered. "Hello, Nick Montague's phone."

There was a pause on the line, then the caller rang off. Tammy checked the caller log and saw the number of the most recent call had come up as "EN." She also saw that the number below was "Mum" and noticed that Posy's area code was the same as "EN." so it was obviously a caller from Southwold.

The hammering finally ceased downstairs and Nick emerged at the top of the stairs, sweaty and dusty.

"You missed a call," said Tammy. "I answered it, but the person put the phone down on me. It was someone called "EN.""

"Oh yes, that would be a mate of mine who's checking out a couple of spectacular marble lamp bases for me," said Nick, shrugging on his jacket.

"Does he live in London?" asked Tammy lightly.

"Yup, he lives in London. Right, darling, shall we go?"

"Hello, Sebastian," Freddie said as he opened his front door. "Thank you so much for coming."

"Absolute pleasure," he replied as Freddie led him through to the sitting room, where a fire burned brightly in the grate. "To be honest, I'm grateful for any excuse to part me from my laptop."

"Hard going, is it?"

"Yes. I'm currently right in the middle of the story. For me, writing a book is rather like swimming the Channel: you start off full of energy and anticipation, then by the time you're halfway across and can't see land behind or ahead, you realize it's too far to go back, but you're nowhere near the finishing line. If that makes sense," Sebastian added as he sat down in the chair Freddie had indicated.

"Beer, or wine perhaps?"

"A beer would be great, thanks."

Freddie came back with two bottles, handed one to Sebastian and sat down. "Cheers."

"Cheers."

They both took a swig, then Sebastian waited for Freddie to explain why he wanted to talk to him. It was some time before Freddie took his eyes from the fire.

"I wanted to discuss a couple of things with you, actually. I need what one might call an unbiased opinion. You know Posy, and I believe you care about her, but you aren't emotionally attached. I also know from your biography in the book that you're an ex-newshound so you're unlikely to be shocked by what I have to say."

"I understand. And of course, nothing you tell me will leave this room."

"Thank you. It's difficult to know where to start." Freddie scratched his head. "Well, the first thing is that I'm rather concerned about this son of Posy's buying Admiral House."

"Right. You don't think he's trustworthy?"

"It's not so much him, rather his business partner and backer; a gentleman called Ken Noakes."

"And?"

"Posy gave me some paperwork to look over and I noticed that this Noakes chap isn't named as a co-director on the company notepaper or the legal documents. Having been a barrister for over forty years, I've come across more dodgy characters from the property business than you can shake a stick at. And if this man is the one funding the entire enterprise, which he must be, as we both know as Sam doesn't have a bean to his name, the fact he isn't named as a director immediately roused my suspicions."

"Right. Well, I can certainly get a friend on my old news desk to take a look at him, see what his track record is like. He can nose out dirt at a few paces."

"That would be most kind of you, Sebastian. I would so hate to see Posy fleeced over the sale of Admiral House. Between you and me, even though I've only met him briefly, I can't say I'm much of a fan of Sam, but one couldn't ever say that to a mother, could one?"

"No, one couldn't."

"Have you met him?" Freddie asked.

"Yes, a couple of times actually and I'm afraid I agree with you."

"I do feel so sorry for that dear wife of his. He strikes me as rather an aggressive character. And Posy has told me often how Amy is so very gentle."

"She is, yes."

Another silence ensued as Freddie stood, stoked up a fire that didn't need stoking then turned to Sebastian. "Darn it! I'm going to need a whisky for this. Want to join me?"

"No, thank you. The afternoon would be a write-off, literally," he smiled. Freddie left the room and when he returned with the whisky, his expression was grim. Sebastian realized immediately that all Freddie had said so far was peripheral and only now was he about to hear whatever it was he really wanted to tell him. He watched Freddie sit down and take a great gulp of his drink.

"Well, well," he sighed, then looked at Sebastian. "Forgive me for procrastinating. You'll understand why when I tell you. And it will be the first time the information has ever left my lips. I hope I can count on you to keep your own sealed tight."

"You can," agreed Sebastian.

Freddie took a great shuddering breath, then drained his glass. "Right, I shall begin..."

An hour later, Sebastian had joined Freddie in a couple of whiskies and the bottle stood half-empty on the table.

"I seriously don't know what to say."

"No," agreed Freddie. "What can one say?"

"I mean, I'm a writer and I don't think I could ever dream up such a...tragic situation."

"Well, I can assure you that every word of what I've told you is true. Sadly," Freddie added. "If you look hard enough, you'll find it all there on the internet."

"And you're sure Posy still doesn't know?"

"She doesn't, no. I mean, I have to say when I met her again after all this time, I presumed that she would by now. That someone would have told her. But she was away from Admiral House for over twenty-five years."

"I *can* believe it, actually," said Sebastian. "People don't like to mention unpleasant things to the hurt party. When my wife died, even my closest friends wanted to avoid the subject, let alone strangers."

Freddie looked at Sebastian, then at the dying embers of the fire. "You do understand why I had to leave her the first time around?"

"I do. You were in an impossible situation."

"When I realized who she was, and that she didn't know, I really had no choice. I..." Freddie's voice cracked and tears appeared in his eyes. "It nearly broke me, but I knew it would break her."

"From what you've told me, at the time, it would have done."

"The question I've asked myself over and over is..." Freddie poured himself more whisky. "Will the truth break her now?"

Sebastian tried to empathise, to think how *he* would feel...something he'd learnt to do when in a quandary about a character.

"I just...don't know how she would react, Freddie. With utter shock and disbelief, I expect. Having said that, at least she would understand why you left her."

"And why I've been unable to commit to her. She must wonder what on earth is going on. And the ridiculous thing about it is that, after fifty years, all I want to do is go down on bended knee, tell her I love her, and finally make her mine." Freddie reached in his pocket for a handkerchief and blew his nose loudly. "Maybe I should just walk away, Sebastian, sell up—"

"And join the Foreign Legion?"

That at least made Freddie smile. "I'm even too old for that! What would you do in my shoes?"

"I think...I think I would probably try to find a way to tell her, but that's just me, because of the life I've had. When I lost my wife I realized that one has to seize the day, especially when it comes to love."

"I agree of course, but once something is said, it can never be unsaid, can it?"

"No, but remember that you were *both* innocent victims of something beyond your control. I know you have tried to protect her because you care for her so deeply, but you suffered too. She will understand that, I'm sure."

"I did suffer, yes, and you're right. Well now, I've taken up enough of your time and I'm deeply grateful for your wise words. Perhaps...perhaps I should leave telling her until after she has moved out of Admiral House and is embarking on a new life. I feel it might soften the blow—she wouldn't be living in it, so to speak."

"I think you're correct. Let her make the move, which is going to be traumatic in itself, and allow some time for the dust to settle." Sebastian stood up and Freddie walked with him to the door. "Goodbye, Freddie, let's keep in touch."

"Absolutely, and I'm glad you're there with Posy. I worried about her in that big house all alone."

"Honestly, if it helps, I think Posy is one of the strongest people I've ever met," replied Sebastian. "I'll get my mate on the news desk to check out this Ken Noakes too and let you know."

Posy was not sleeping well, disturbed by the thought of everything she had to do between now and the move. That morning, Nick had called to apologize for his initial reaction to selling the house and tell her he had asked his old school friend Paul to take a look at the paintings. "He's hoping I've missed a Van Gogh," her son chuckled.

"Darling boy, you know very well the paintings in the house are daubs that need to end up in the rubbish, rather than at Sotheby's."

"At worst, it's an excuse to visit Southwold, Mum. You know how fond Paul has always been of you, and Admiral House. He'd like to come to say goodbye."

"To me or the house?!"

"Very funny. So Paul will be with you around ten on Saturday, and I'll be there too at some point this weekend."

"Wonderful. I'll cook some lunch. Will you bring that lovely lady friend of yours?"

"No, Tammy is very busy at the boutique just now."

"Well, she needs to come here at some point and decide what she wants from your grandmother's gown collection. Do ask her for Christmas, won't you? It will be our last one here, and I'd like as many bodies here as possible to make it a jolly one."

"I...yes, of course."

"Everything all right between the two of you?" Posy queried.

She knew her son inside out and that slight pause before he'd answered had alerted her.

"They're fine, Mum. We're both just very busy, that's all—talking of which, I have an auction to get to in Lots Road. I'll text you the number of the local Southwold auctioneer I know so he can come in and value the contents of the house. I'm warning you, don't expect to get a lot for it. Brown furniture is almost worthless these days unless it's something really special. I'd pick out anything of sentimental value and put it to one side, then hire a couple of skips and get rid of things like beds and sofas that way. You won't get anything for them."

"I'm not expecting to, darling."

"So the sale is definitely happening?"

"As far as I know, yes."

"And you're still okay with it?"

"Whether I'm 'okay' or not is immaterial. I really don't think I have a choice, Nick, unless I can magic up a million or so to restore it."

"No, you're right of course. I wish I could spare the cash, but all my funds have been spent on setting up the business."

"Which is as it should be, Nick. It's time to move on, however hard it is. It's the garden I'll miss most, but at least Sam has told me that a property management company will come in to service the apartments and take good care of the grounds. Besides, I quite fancy some modern furniture and double glazing."

"Yes, well, I'd better shoot. Speak to you tomorrow. Love you, Mum."

"Love you too." Posy put the receiver down and sighed, then contacted the local auctioneer Nick had recommended to come and value the contents of the house. They made an appointment for a couple of days' time.

As she wandered from room to room doing as Nick had suggested, Posy realized that there was very little she wanted to take with her into her new life. The odd painting, the jade art deco clock that stood above the fireplace in the drawing room, her father's desk with its battered leather top...

Posy sat down heavily on the well-used mattress in one of the spare rooms. She saw herself in the old, heavily foxed gilt mirror, which had reflected back the images of generations of Andersons. What would they all be thinking as she threw away three hundred years of family history, she wondered. If one 'thought' any more beyond the grave, which these days, she often doubted. And yet, in these past weeks since she had agreed to sell, she had felt her father's presence around her more strongly than she had for years.

"Posy, it's time," she told her reflection.

"I was wondering, Sebastian, whether you would have half an hour to spare to come with me to the Folly in the garden. It was my father's eyrie, you see, and when I was younger, I was never allowed in. My father—whom you know I utterly adored—would take me round the grounds and teach me to net butterflies. He'd then take them into the Folly to 'study' them, and after that he told me he set them free. I managed to sneak inside once, and what did I find but a large collection of framed and very dead butterflies hanging on the wall. It broke my heart at the time, but of course he was simply a collector. It was perfectly normal in those days and he was preserving them for posterity—there are probably some specimens that are extinct now."

Sebastian's hand, which was holding a slice of toast dripping with homemade jam, paused on its way to his mouth. "Well, they're probably worth something, at least."

"Probably, but I'd never want money for them. If they're of any value, I'd donate them to the Natural History Museum. Anyway, I have to admit that I'm not relishing the thought of entering the Folly. I haven't been inside it for over sixty years. After my father died, I went off to live with my grandmother in Cornwall, and when I eventually came back here with my husband and children, well, I simply couldn't face going in."

"I can quite see why not, Posy," Sebastian replied neutrally.

"And I don't think I can face it now, alone anyway; but of course, I simply must, because it needs to be cleared out before the move."

"Of course I'll come with you, Posy. Just let me know when."

"How about this afternoon? I really must tackle it and what with Paul, Nick's art dealer friend, coming this weekend, I thought it might be a good idea to show him the butterflies."

Sebastian watched Posy leave the kitchen with a heavy heart and wondered why she wasn't asking Sam to accompany her. As her elder son, he was the obvious choice. He rose to wash his plate and mug in the sink, thinking that perhaps he was biased, but even if he wasn't in love with Sam's wife, he was pretty sure he'd still find the man obnoxious and arrogant.

"You never can tell with genes," he murmured as he walked up the glorious turned staircase, hoping Posy wouldn't mind that he'd stolen its beauty to use as a central motif for his book.

"So can you spare me that half an hour to go the Folly?" Posy asked him once they had finished lunch.

Sebastian put his knife and fork together. "That beef and dumpling stew was the best I've ever tasted and I'd accompany you to the moon if you'd make it again for me at some point. Right, I'll just go and fetch a couple of flashlights. I doubt there's electric light in there."

Posy managed a weak smile, but as Sebastian stood up, he could sense her tension.

As they walked through the gardens, heavily hung with autumn mist that hadn't cleared all day, Sebastian saw the Folly sitting behind the row of bare chestnut trees. He shivered involuntarily; given what he knew, he was feeling perhaps as much trepidation as Posy.

They approached the door, made of once-sturdy oak that had now partially rotted away after so many years of negligence. Posy lifted the heavy bunch of keys to the lock. Her hand was shaking so much that she couldn't slide the correct key into the keyhole.

"Here, let me."

As Sebastian used all his strength to release a lock that he realized had not been opened for over sixty years, he felt his own heart rate rising. Who knew what was in there, what was left behind from the tragedy that he knew had occurred within these walls...

The key finally turned and before he had further time to speculate, Posy was pushing the door open. They entered a darkened room; Sebastian saw the window was covered with cobwebs on the inside and a tangle of ivy on the outside. They both switched on their flashlights and shone them around.

"This is where my father kept all his sporting paraphernalia," Posy announced as she stepped over a collection of sticks covered in green mould. "Cricket stumps," she said, "and look at this." She picked up a wooden object and waved it at him. "A croquet mallet. I remember we used to play when my parents had their parties."

Sebastian shone his flashlight on a large cupboard. The door hung ajar and as he pulled it open, he saw a collection of guns lined up in a neat row, the shiny metal now rusted to a deep brown. His heart missed a beat as he saw one was very obviously missing.

"My father's hunting guns," said Posy. "I used to hear a gun going off sometimes at night. Daddy said it was the local farmer shooting rabbits, but the farm is quite a long way away and the sound of the gun was very close, so it was probably him."

"This is a Purdey, and if it was cleaned up, it's probably quite valuable," he said as he pulled out one of the guns.

"Do you shoot?"

"God no, I only know about Purdeys because I had to research guns for my last novel," he smiled. In the gloom, he saw Posy shining her flashlight up a flight of stairs.

"Shall I go first?" he asked her.

"If you wouldn't mind. Be careful, they twist round quite sharply, from what I remember."

"Okay."

The sound of their footsteps on the old stone steps echoed around the turret as they climbed. The smell of damp was palpable and Posy had a fit of sneezing as they reached the narrow landing at the top.

"Goodness me," she said, burrowing in her Barbour pocket for a handkerchief and blowing her nose. "We're probably breathing in wartime air!"

"So—" Sebastian studied the door in front of him—a miniature version of the oak front door but in much better condition. "Here we are."

"Yes." Posy studied the door as a hundred memories seemed to fly out of the wood itself.

"Shall I open it?"

Posy handed him the big iron key ring, which reminded her of an oversized bracelet, the keys of different sizes masquerading as charms.

Sebastian tried the handle to check it was locked in the first place—which it was—then tried three keys before he found the right one.

"Ready to go in?"

"Can I wear a blindfold so I don't have to see all those poor dead butterflies?"

"Yes, but it would make this rather a pointless exercise."

Sebastian held out a hand and Posy took it, breathing deeply to try to calm her fluttering heart. Behind this slab of wood was the very essence of her beloved father. She followed Sebastian inside, eyes fixed on the floor, which was covered in decades of dust.

Sebastian shone his flashlight around the circular room, illuminating the large number of framed dead butterflies hanging lopsidedly against the walls. He noted a desk, a leather chair, and a bookcase still full of its paper tenants. Then behind it, his flashlight caught a large stain on the wall. It was copper-colored with tiny splatters surrounding it, as though a modern artist had haphazardly thrown paint at a canvas.

It took time to make sense of it, but when he did, he had to take in a large gulp of fetid air to steady himself. He looked round at Posy and saw her back was turned towards him as she studied a particular framed butterfly.

"I remember this one—it was me who caught it and Daddy was thrilled, as Large Blues were very rare. In fact, it was probably the last one I ever did catch," she sighed. "Perhaps I'll ask Amy to paint it so I can remember its beauty, but not have to witness its demise," she said as she turned to him with a sad smile.

As her eyes scanned the room, Sebastian's instinct was to hurry her out of it before she noticed, but it was already too late. Posy was shining her flashlight directly onto it.

"What on earth is that?" She walked towards the wall to examine the stain more closely.

"Maybe it's something that's dripped from the ceiling."

Even he heard the hollowness of his own lie.

"No..." Posy virtually put her nose to the stain. "It looks like dried blood to me, Sebastian. In fact, it looks as though someone has been stood in front of the wall and shot."

"Maybe it was one of your ancestors involved in some derring-do or other?"

"That's a thought, yes, but I'm pretty sure I would have noticed it when I sneaked in here as a child. I mean, one can hardly miss it. And it's right opposite the door."

"Perhaps there were more framed butterflies hanging over it last time you came."

"Maybe you're right. In fact, I'm sure Daddy's Red Admiral collection hung there. If I remember correctly, those were the first butterflies I saw when I opened the door, because then I simply fled back down the stairs. Yes, that would explain it."

Sebastian felt weak with relief as Posy turned and walked towards the desk. She picked up a big magnifying glass and blew on it. Thousands of dust motes flew into the air, the light of the flashlight making them shine like glitter.

"I suppose this was one of his instruments of torture. What lies adults tell children to protect them," she sighed. "We all do it, of course, but in the long run, I do wonder if it's actually for the best."

Again Sebastian had to take a deep breath. "Should I collect the butterfly frames and bring them all over to the house?" he said.

"Yes please, Sebastian." Posy indicated the books on the shelf. "Apart from these, I think everything else can go into the skip." She shivered. "I don't like it in here at all. It has an odd atmosphere. And there was me as a child imagining Daddy in his shiny bright throne room; the King of the Fairies sitting atop his castle. Well," she shrugged, "it was only a game, wasn't it?"

"Yes, it was. You go ahead, Posy. I'll bring the butterflies across to the house."

"Thank you, Sebastian," she replied.

Chapter 26

Tammy lay in bed next to Nick and watched as he read through a sale catalog.

"So you're up in Southwold this weekend?" she asked.

"Yes, like I mentioned, Paul's coming to take a look at the paintings at Mum's and there's an auction I want to attend in Lavenham on Sunday. I'll drive up to Admiral House on Friday night and I should be back late Sunday afternoon."

"Can I come with you? I'd love to see your mum, and she said she has some gowns for me to look at."

"I'd have thought you'd want to be at the shop on Saturdays. You said it's your busiest day of the week."

"I do have Meena, remember, and she's a far better saleswoman than I'll ever be!"

"Yes, but she's not you, and anyway, haven't you arranged lunch with Jane?"

"I had, but I can always cancel. I'd like to see your mother again," said Tammy.

"I think she's got a lot on her plate at the moment, to be honest. Perhaps another weekend, when things are clearer with the house sale, okay?"

"God, Nick, that's what you always bloody say!" All Tammy's uncertainty and frustration welled up. "I can't remember the last time you and I actually spent a weekend together. You're always disappearing off somewhere or other by yourself."

"Yes, to enable me to buy some good stock to get my business off the ground. I'm very sorry all my attention hasn't been with you, Tammy," he said coldly, "but I thought we understood and respected each other's work."

"We do, I do," said Tammy, "but surely, even in the midst of all this chaos, it would be possible to find the odd twenty-four hours to spend together? Isn't life meant to be about balance?"

"Tammy, I don't wish to sound churlish, but it seems to me that now your business is up and running, you're resenting that I've got to spend time on mine."

"That is so unfair! I've always made time for you so we could be together."

Nick slammed the sale catalog onto the floor and got out of bed. "I've got a hundred things on my mind, all of which need my care and attention, and the last thing I need is hassle from you. I'm going back to Paul and Jane's to try and get some peace!"

Tammy heard the door slam behind him. She buried her head in her pillow and burst into tears.

Two days later, having heard nothing from Nick, Tammy left the boutique at noon to meet Jane at Langan's in Beauchamp Place, their usual Saturday lunchtime haunt.

"You look radiant," said Tammy as she sat down opposite her friend.

"Thank you, I feel it. Now I've had the first scan and, cross fingers, everything seems to be fine with the baby, I can relax a little. Glass of wine for you, Tam? You look as though you could do with it." Jane studied her. "Are you feeling okay? You look very pale."

"I've not been sleeping very well, that's all."

"What? Too busy counting up all the takings in your head?" Jane smiled as she ordered mineral water and wine from a passing waiter.

"No, although things have gone really well in the past few days, and this morning we were heaving. In fact, I really can't stay for too long. I've left Meena to cope by herself."

"Well, I'm sure she's more than capable, but if things continue to go well, you'll have to get an assistant to help both of you."

"I know. I'll think about it," agreed Tammy.

"Tam, come on, you should be jumping up and down with excitement. Everyone is talking about you and your fabulous gowns and you look miserable. What is it?"

Tammy reached for her glass of wine and took a big gulp. "I had a row with Nick a couple of nights ago and I haven't heard from him since. Janey..." Tammy took another gulp of her wine. "I think Nick might be having an affair."

Jane looked at her in complete amazement. "What?! No, never!"

"Well, I reckon he is."

"But when I saw you together at the party, you looked blissfully happy." Jane shook her head. "I'm sorry, but I just can't believe it. Not of Nick, of all men. He's just not the type."

"Janey, something happened recently and I know for a fact Nick lied to me about it."

"What?"

Tammy told Jane how she'd taken the call on Nick's mobile and how the phone had been slammed down. Then how she'd seen the initials "EN" and noticed that the area code was the same as Posy's in Southwold.

"Nick told me this 'EN' lived in London. Why would he lie?"

"Perhaps 'EN' does live in London some of the time. That's hardly proof of infidelity, Tammy."

"No, I know, but I just have a feeling..." Tammy fingered her wine glass. "Besides, he actually told me he had something to sort out before he could fully commit to me. You once mentioned a girl he'd known who lived in Southwold?"

"Yes, but...I don't think it was serious or long-term. If I remember rightly, she had a live-in boyfriend."

"But there was definitely someone?" Tammy confirmed.

"Yes."

"What was her name?"

"I think it was Evie somebody. Evie Newman, that's right."

"Oh my God! 'EN'!" Tammy felt tears burgeoning in her eyes. "I knew it!"

"Please, Tam, try and keep calm..."

"How can I?! It's obvious he's seeing her again."

"It was ten years ago, and you have absolutely no proof whatsoever he's involved with her now," Jane placated her.

"Okay, so why did she call him and why didn't he want me to go with him this weekend?"

"Because he thought you'd be bored and had better things to do, like see me for lunch?"

"No, Jane, we both know why he's there, and if I look back, almost every weekend over the past month, Nick has been away, ostensibly at an auction."

"So what? He's an antiques dealer, that's what he does," shrugged Jane.

"And he never asks me to go. In fact, if I suggest it, he finds some reason why I can't."

"Look, Tammy, I understand why you're suspicious. I would be too. But I'm absolutely sure Nick loves you—he's even confessed it to Paul. So before you ruin the best thing that's happened to you in years, you need to confront Nick and have it out. There may be a perfectly legitimate reason why he's in Southwold. Now, we'd better order if you've got to get back to the shop. I'll have the monkfish."

"I'm not hungry. I'll have the rocket salad and another glass of wine."

As Jane ordered, Tammy fiddled distractedly with her napkin.

"What makes it even weirder is that he took me to see a house in Battersea recently and asked what I thought of it; whether I could picture our children running around the garden."

"There you are then! What more proof do you need?"

"None, I suppose," said Tammy, dipping a breadstick into the olive paste, "but it still doesn't explain 'EN.'"

"Look, I've known Nick for years. He isn't a game-player, Tammy, I swear. Paul and I were only saying the other night that we both thought this was it for him. Do you love him?"

"Yes. I'm horribly afraid I do."

"Then as a married woman, my advice is never to let these arguments fester. Is Nick at his mother's in Southwold tonight?"

"Yes, at least that's what he told me."

"Well, if I were you, I'd get in your car, drive up there this evening and see him. It's pointless going through all this agony for a moment longer than you need to. Go and sort it out."

"Maybe," shrugged Tammy, "but I've never run after a man in my life."

"This isn't any man, Tam. It's the man you want to spend the rest of your life with. So swallow your pride and go and talk to him. That's my advice anyway," said Jane. "Now, let me be completely sad and show you the picture of the baby they gave me at my scan."

Tammy arrived back at the shop and found Meena valiantly fielding four customers at the same time. They were manic for the next couple of hours, then, at four o'clock, the shop suddenly emptied and by a quarter to five, not a soul had walked in since.

"I'm going to close up early, Meena," Tammy yawned. "I feel completely exhausted."

"You have been working too hard. Now you make sure you have a good rest tomorrow, young lady. It's been a busy time for you."

"It sure has," Tammy replied as she switched off the till and began to help Meena count the takings.

Half an hour later, pacing around her house, Tammy couldn't settle.

"Bugger it!" she said, then stuffed a wash-bag and a change of clothes into a holdall, left the house, and headed towards her car. On the journey to Southwold, she dialed Nick's mobile, which, as usual, was on voicemail. Gritting her teeth, she left a message.

"Hi, it's me. Just to say I'm sorry about the other night. I was being selfish. I'm driving to Southwold now because I want to see you and sort things out. I'll be there at around eight. Let me know if it's not convenient. Okay, bye."

As Tammy finally steered up the drive towards Admiral House, her heart beat hard against her chest. She was terrified of what she might discover. At least someone was in, as she could see the lights on. She walked to the front door and knocked on it loudly.

"Hello, Tammy, what are you doing here?"

It was Amy who opened the door, not Posy.

"I...well, I came to see Nick."

"Nick?" Amy frowned. "But he's not here, Tammy."

"Oh."

"Come in, anyway, it's lovely to see you," Amy smiled as they walked across the entrance hall towards the kitchen. "I've been here working on the drawing of the house that's going on the front of Posy's Christmas cards."

Sebastian sat at the kitchen table, a glass of wine in hand.

"Tammy, what a pleasant surprise. Would you like a glass of wine? I was just keeping Amy company whilst she finished up."

The fact it had been dark for at least three hours, not to mention the over-explanation from both of them, confirmed what Tammy had suspected on the night of her party.

"Yes, I'd love a drink," she said, slumping into a chair and feeling completely drained. "Where's Posy?"

"Out to supper with her gentleman friend, Freddie," said Amy. "You've only missed her by ten minutes or so." Amy poured her a large glass of wine and handed it to her. "There."

"Right, I'm back up to work," said Sebastian. "I'll leave you girls to it. Nice to see you again, Tammy, and thanks for the invite to the party, I enjoyed myself. Bye, Amy," he added with a nod.

"Bye, Sebastian."

Tammy tried not to smile at their exaggerated formality. She took a hefty gulp of her wine.

"So Posy wasn't expecting Nick here tonight?"

"She didn't say so, but he's probably got a key and might have told Posy he'd let himself in." Amy glanced at the stove, knowing that if someone had been coming to stay, however late he or she was arriving, something would have been cooked by Posy and left for them to heat up. The top of the stove was empty.

"Nick told me he was staying here last night."

"He might have been, Tammy. I didn't arrive here until after lunch. That art dealer friend of his, Paul, was here and left about three. I'm so sorry, but it looks like you've had a wasted journey."

"Yes," she grimaced. "I've obviously got my wires crossed."

"Never mind. It's lovely to see you anyway, and I'm sure Posy wouldn't mind a bit if you stayed the night."

"Oh no, I think I'll head straight back to London."

Amy could read the misery in Tammy's expressive green eyes. "Look, I don't mean to interfere, but would it help to talk about it?"

"There's nothing to talk about, really. I thought Nick said he was coming here for the weekend. I clearly...got it wrong." The emotion of the past few days was catching up with her and she felt a lump rise in her throat and tears well in her eyes. "Shit! I'm sorry, Amy. I've no right to pour my troubles onto you."

"Don't be silly. Here." Amy passed a box of tissues to Tammy, who blew her nose. "I'm just going to call Sam and say I've been delayed, then we can talk, okay?"

Whilst Amy spoke to Sam, Tammy tried to gather herself together.

"So I presume the two of you have had an argument of some description?" Amy sat back down at the table.

"Yes."

"Can I ask what it was about?"

"Nothing really," Tammy replied with a shrug. "I mean, it was caused by me getting suspicious about something, which led to insecurity, which inevitably led to the argument."

"Well, I'm amazed you'd be suspicious of Nick. He adores you."

"That's what everyone says," sighed Tammy. "Amy, I need to ask you something. Do you know someone called Evie Newman?"

"I know her, yes, but not well. I'd just started going out with Sam, but I was still living in London. By the time I married him and moved permanently to Southwold, Evie had upped and left."

"But now she's back."

"Yes."

"Was Nick in love with her?"

"From what I've heard, yes, he was," Amy confirmed. "I'm so sorry, Tammy."

"It's okay, my friend Jane has already told me. Doesn't it strike you as strange that Evie appears back in Southwold just at the same time as Nick returns from Perth?"

Her heart sinking, Amy remembered driving past Evie's house with Posy and seeing Nick's car parked outside. "I...well, I suppose it is, yes."

"I think he's seeing her again. A couple of days ago, I took a call on his mobile from someone whose initials were 'EN.' When I said hello, the caller rang off, but I noticed it was a Southwold number. It has to be her, doesn't it?"

"Well, it is a coincidence, yes."

"So you don't think I'm being paranoid?"

Amy shook her head sadly. "No, I don't."

"And then Nick told me he was staying here at Admiral House this weekend. Why? Why did he lie to me?"

"I honestly don't know."

"It must be because he's with her."

Amy couldn't reply as she had to agree. It must have shown on her face because Tammy said, "Please tell me if you know anything. It's much better I find out now than go on in the dark and end up looking like a complete idiot."

"I...well, a couple of weeks ago, Posy and I drove past Evie's house and we both saw a red Austin Healey parked outside. But that doesn't mean it was Nick, does it? It might have been a coincidence..."

"Well," Tammy's eyes filled with tears. "We both know it's not. How many bright red vintage Austin Healeys are likely to be hanging around Southwold?! Christ! How could he do this to me?!"

"You don't know for certain, please. You must talk to him— there might be a reason why he's had to see her, to do with his business or something," pleaded Amy.

Tammy was up from the table. "Amy, I want you to do me a big favor; will you come with me into Southwold and show me where Evie Newman lives?"

"If you really want me to, yes."

"I do," Tammy said firmly and walked out of the kitchen, leaving Amy to follow in her wake. They got into Tammy's car and she turned the engine on, then sped out of the drive.

"Turn right, here, then first left," directed Amy. "Okay, it's the house on the corner, just there."

Amy could hardly bear to look as Tammy slowed down and they crawled towards Evie's house. She breathed a sigh of relief when the road in front of it was empty of cars.

"You see? It was probably a coinci—"

"There!" Tammy was pointing to the other side of the road, thirty yards along from the house. She drove past the car slowly, reading the number plate to double-check. "That's Nick's car, all right."

Tammy pulled the car to an abrupt halt further along the road and the two women sat in silence.

Eventually, Amy spoke. "I'm so sorry, Tammy. I still think you must speak to Nick. There could be some innocent explanation for this. Nick just isn't that sort of a ma—"

"Would everybody stop telling me what kind of man Nick is, when it's patently bloody obvious he's a complete SHIT!" Tammy thumped the steering wheel and burst into tears. "Sorry for shouting, Amy. It's not your fault."

"Don't worry, please. I completely understand. Let's drive back to Admiral House and have another glass of wine and a chat."

"No, thanks." Tammy reached for a tissue from the glove box and blew her nose. "Just now, I never want to enter any premises that Nick Montague's feet have crossed before me. I'll drop you off there and then head straight back to London."

They drove back to Admiral House in silence, Amy knowing it was pointless to try to offer any trite words of comfort. Tammy pulled the car to a halt.

"Are you sure you'll be okay driving back?"

"Fine."

"I'm so sorry, Tammy."

"So am I."

"Can I call you in the next couple of days to see how you are?" Amy said quietly as she opened the door to climb out.

"Yes, of course. And thanks for being so great. Bye."

Amy watched the car do a U-turn and screech back down the drive. She then glanced up and caught Sebastian standing at his upstairs window, looking out at the disappearing taillights of Tammy's car.

Having just witnessed the pain moral deceit such as hers could cause, Amy wasn't up to going inside to explain. She took her car keys out of her handbag, climbed into her own car and drove home to her children and her husband.

Chapter 27

Posy arrived home from dinner with Freddie feeling exhausted. Even though she was used to his mood swings—at one moment warm and effervescent, the next, distant and almost secretive—tonight he'd been unusually monosyllabic and she'd had to drag conversation out of him.

On top of that, Paul Lyons-Harvey, Nick's friend, had been to look at the paintings in the house. Even though she'd thought she was resigned to the sale, hearing him talk of their value—or in most cases, the lack of it—had been the first real manifestation of the enormity of what she was about to do.

She was surprised to see Nick's car parked in the drive. She hadn't been expecting him until tomorrow morning and for once, she didn't relish her son's presence. All she wanted to do was to make herself a hot water bottle and climb into bed.

"Mum!" A wild-eyed Nick was pacing round the kitchen. "Thank God you're back. Has Tammy been here tonight?"

"I've been out, Nick, but why should she have been?"

"Because she left me a message on my mobile earlier saying she was coming here to see me, that she'd arrive about eight. I only listened to it about fifteen minutes ago and came straight here."

"I see. Well, Amy was here, and Sebastian. You'd better go up and ask him if Tammy arrived."

"No, Mum, I don't like to disturb him."

"He rarely sleeps before one or two," said Posy.

"That's me, the vampire who comes out at night," chirped Sebastian, entering the kitchen with his mug. "I came down for some cocoa. Hello, Nick. Blimey, it's like Piccadilly Circus in this kitchen tonight."

"Sebastian, was Tammy here earlier?" Nick followed him to the stove as he heated some milk in a saucepan.

"Yup," he nodded. "She got here just after eight."

"Was she okay?"

"I'm not sure. I left Amy talking to her and scarpered upstairs to do some work. She did seem pretty surprised to see you weren't here, though. I think she was under the impression you would be."

"Shit! How long did she stay?" Nick ran a hand distractedly through his hair.

"Oh, about fifteen minutes. Then both she and Amy went tearing off in her car. They arrived back here half an hour later. I'm afraid I snooped from my window and saw Amy get out of Tammy's car, then get into her own and they both left separately. That's all I know."

"How very odd," mused Posy.

Nick looked at his watch. "It's ten o'clock now. Amy will still be up, won't she?" he asked no one in particular as he walked over to the telephone, leafed through Posy's address book and began to dial. "Amy? Yes, it's Nick. I hear you saw Tammy tonight. Would you mind if I just popped round to yours now to have a word? Okay, thanks. See you in a few minutes." Nick slammed down the phone, grabbed his keys and headed for the door. "Bye, Mum, I'll be in touch about tomorrow, but under the circumstances, I may have to drive to London tonight so don't wait up for me."

"I won't. Just keep in touch."

"I will, Mum. Bye."

Sebastian raised an eyebrow as they both heard Nick's car fly over the gravel as it sped back down the drive. "And here's me trying to make up fiction whilst the real-life plot thickens around me."

"Do I want to know what has happened?" asked Posy tentatively.

"I couldn't say, I'm as much in the dark as you. Want some cocoa? You look frazzled."

"Yes please, and I am," agreed Posy.

"Want to talk about it?" suggested Sebastian.

"Not tonight, no, but thank you for asking." Posy filled her hot water bottle. "Honestly, you'd think that when one got older, life would become less complicated."

"It doesn't?" he said, handing Posy her cocoa.

"Unfortunately, it doesn't. Goodnight, Sebastian."

Amy answered the door to Nick in her dressing gown.

"Hi, Amy, sorry to drop in so late. Is Sam in?" he asked.

"No, he's still out at the pub. He had to look after the kids until I got back here so I said he could go. Come in," she said, and he followed her into the tiny sitting room. "Sit down, Nick."

Nick did not sit down. He paced the room. "Amy, what happened with Tammy tonight?"

"I don't think it's up to me to tell you. I think you'd better talk to Tammy."

"Where is she?"

"She said she was going back to London, so I presume she went home."

"Christ! How was she when she realized I wasn't at Admiral House?"

"Upset. Very."

"Did you go looking for me?"

Amy nodded silently.

"And did you find me?"

"Yes, Nick, we did. I'm sorry."

"But how...?" he shook his head. "You didn't tell her, did you?!"

"No, I didn't! The reason Tammy came down to Southwold was because she suspected something was up beforehand. She knew about Evie. She'd taken a call on your mobile from her and put two and two together."

"So I presume Tammy asked you to show her where Evie lived? Where she suspected I might be?"

"Yes, she did, and she—we—saw your car. What could I do? I had no idea whether you'd be there or not." Amy was beginning to feel upset and more than a little angry. "This situation is nothing to do with me and I really don't want to be blamed or involved."

"No, of course not." Nick slumped into a chair. "I'm sorry I shouted at you. Oh Amy, what on earth do I say to her? How do I make her understand?"

"I don't know, Nick. I thought you loved Tammy."

"I do, I do. But there's a situation...oh God..." He shook his head helplessly. "There's nothing I can do."

"Look, it's absolutely none of my business what you do in your private life, but it's obvious that you were with Evie tonight. Perhaps if you try and explain the reason you were there, Tammy will understand. I know she loves you very much, but you've hurt her, badly."

Nick stared into the distance. "Maybe it's for the best. I mean, how did I ever think I could have it all? It would never have worked. How could it?"

Amy watched him, confused. "Nick, you're not making any sense."

"No, I'm sure I'm not." He stood up. "Sorry to bother you, Amy. It's late. I'd better go. Thanks for telling me."

"Are you going back to London now?" she asked as she led him to the front door.

Nick shrugged. "There's no point. I can't even begin to explain, and as I said, there's absolutely nothing I can do. See you."

Amy let him out of the front door, not understanding why, when it was obvious what he had done, she felt a wave of sympathy for him.

Chapter 28

On Monday morning, Sebastian knocked on the door of Freddie's cottage.

"Hello, Sebastian, what are you doing here?" Freddie asked as he led him into the sitting room.

"I thought I'd drop by on the off-chance to tell you that my contact on my old news desk has come up with some very interesting stuff on Ken Noakes. He ran his surname through his computer and past his sources." Sebastian pulled some sheets of paper from his pocket and unfolded them. Then he searched for his reading glasses and put them on. "Kenneth Noakes was the sole director of a property company in the late nineties. He was building a few smart houses on some land he'd bought from a local school in North Norfolk. He took the deposits but then, a few months later, declared himself bankrupt. The properties were only at foundation stage and the creditors received little or nothing in recompense."

"I knew it." Freddie shook his head. "What happened to our Ken next?"

"It turns out that at least three—or possibly four, but he's still checking—other 'Noakes' have been registered since as directors of various companies. And they are all related to him. We have the ex-wife, the current wife, a brother and possibly a daughter too, but that, as I said, is to be confirmed."

"The usual story—he himself is barred from becoming a director but uses his family on paper, and runs the company as he would normally, but behind the scenes."

"Exactly."

"Were these other companies property development too?"

"Out of the four he ran, one was, yes, but the other three were property rental companies."

"I see. Pray continue," said Freddie.

"Well, listed here we have..." Sebastian read from the printout. "'Trimco Ltd,' trading as 'Westway Holiday Cottages,' 'Ideal Ltd,' trading as 'Hedgerow Holiday Homes,' and 'Chardway Ltd,' trading as 'St. Tropez Blue.'" Sebastian removed his glasses. "My mate's contact at the DTI explained that unfortunately the holiday rental scam is surprisingly common. You rent an office with a couple of phone lines, produce a nice glossy website and advertise on the usual outlets. Then you cream in the deposits and six months later, when you have a nice pile of checks laundered into a bank account on the Isle of Man, you declare the company insolvent and scarper with your winnings. Then you start again somewhere else."

"Leaving the poor old punters with a lost deposit and no holiday," finished Freddie.

"Absolutely. My mate's feeling is that this is only the tip of the iceberg. He's only managed to trace these companies because Mr. Noakes used relatives with the same name. But he'll have used other mugs as well. Sam, for instance, is the sole director of Montague Property Development Ltd."

"Yes." Freddie sighed heavily. "Dearie me."

"Quite," said Sebastian.

"Where does this Noakes chap live?"

"My mate didn't get that far, I'm afraid, but I'll guarantee you that it's out of the jurisdiction of British law."

"So what to do?"

"James is going to do some more digging—he has a contact in the police and is going to find out if Mr. Noakes is a 'person of interest' to the fraud squad. Chances are he is, but of course, if he's scarpered abroad, given the lack of funding in the police at the moment, he's not a big enough fish to warrant the cost of extradition. Anyway, James said to leave it with him. He's happy—it's a good story for his paper."

"I know he's been back in the country—Posy told me Sam had

gone to meet him in Norfolk recently."

"Right."

"Shouldn't we tell Posy? I mean, if this Noakes is going to play the same game again—advertise Admiral House 'retirement apartments' and take what will be hefty deposits, then send the company into liquidation—then she should know. And what about Sam?...Do you think he knows?"

"I have no idea. I presume he would have checked out his backer's history, but..."

"Perhaps he didn't want to know." Freddie mirrored Sebastian's thoughts. "From what Posy has told me of her son, he isn't a businessman. And he's obviously desperate to prove himself. To his wife and his mother. What a mess."

"I'm afraid it is. I think the best thing to do is to wait a while whilst James investigates further. When we have more information, we can decide what's best to do. There's no contracts signed yet, are there?"

"No, although Posy's solicitor has just sent the contract through," said Freddie. "She's asked me to take a look at it."

"Good. Then get it from her and hold on to it until we know where we are."

"I will, although if it all falls through, it rather puts paid to me telling her about the other subject we discussed. It could be months...years even, before a buyer turns up for her house and I'm not sure how much longer I can continue to see her without telling her the truth. It's burning inside me...Forget Noakes," Freddie sighed, "it's me who feels like a fraud."

"I understand, Freddie, but let's give James a few days to see what else he can find out. Now I must get back."

"Of course." Freddie rose with him and they walked to the front door. "I can't thank you enough for your help, Sebastian."

"No problem. Bye, Freddie, I'll be in touch as soon as I hear anything."

Sebastian walked away from the cottage, pondering that, if any reviewer commented that the plot of his novels couldn't happen in reality, he might punch them.

Chapter 29

Amy stood looking out to a gray, angry sea. The clouds were scudding overhead, pushed across the sky by an angry wind, which was also attacking her hair and making it fly all over the place. Her ears were ringing and the newspaper she'd bought was flapping in her hands.

She walked towards the bus shelter, which smelt of all sorts of nefarious, unpalatable substances, and sat down on a bench to try and think.

Yesterday evening, when he'd come home, Sam had laid out the plans for the barn conversion on the kitchen table.

"I had a meeting with my surveyor, and he's pretty confident that the planning officer will approve the change of use. The only complaint they may receive is from Admiral House, and as I'll own it, that's obviously not a problem.," he'd grinned. Then he'd waxed lyrical yet again about the architect's plans for the vast sitting room, with its vaulted ceiling and old roof beams, the inglenook fireplace and the state-of-the-art kitchen they'd have put in.

Amy had done her best to look and sound interested and excited, but she knew she had failed miserably, which had left Sam extremely irritated.

"I don't understand you," he'd said. "I thought a beautiful home was what you wanted. I thought it would make you happy."

Later that night in bed, Sam had attempted to make love to her. Just his touch made her skin crawl. He'd obviously noticed her reticence, which had angered him, and had then resulted in him pinning her to the bed, his hands holding her wrists above her, his weight on top of her making it impossible to move.

She had screamed at him to stop, and he had, swearing profusely as he'd left the bedroom and disappeared downstairs to take solace in what was left of the bottle of whisky he'd bought earlier.

Amy looked down at her wrists and saw the tender skin on the inside had now turned a vague purple from where he'd gripped them.

She pulled down the sleeves of her shirt to cover the marks and felt tears pricking again at the back of her eyes as she thought of the tender, gentle way Sebastian had made love to her.

She realized Sam had always been aggressive in bed, especially after a few drinks—what she'd mistaken for passion back then just wasn't.

It's not normal if he hurts you, Amy...

She only wished she had someone to confide in about Sam's temper and the things he'd done to her over the years, but who could she tell? And besides, it was usually only when he'd had too much booze. But...this morning something had happened to really worry her. She'd been getting Sara ready for school upstairs, then she'd heard a crash from the kitchen and Sam shouting. Hurrying down, she'd arrived to find a broken butter dish on the floor and Sam shaking Jake as though he was a rag doll. She'd screamed at Sam to let go and had taken her little boy in her arms, feeling him shiver with fear at his father's sudden outburst.

In the car on the way to school, she'd gently asked Jake if Daddy had ever done anything like that before.

"Not like that, Mummy, though he does whack me sometimes if you're out and I'm naughty."

"And me," Sara piped up from the back seat. "Daddy gets really cross."

Amy rubbed her fingers distractedly up and down her forehead.

"Oh God, oh God," she murmured to herself desolately. She could take it, but if he was starting to take out his angst on the children...

She realized it had nothing to do with where they lived, or in fact, how much money they did or didn't have. She didn't want to be with Sam anywhere. The simple truth was that she didn't want to be with him at all. His anger was getting out of control and after this morning, she knew she had to do something about it.

Amy stood up from the bench and headed for work, knowing one thing for certain. For the sake of her children, they had to leave.

Later that afternoon, she looked through the rentals page in the *Gazette*. There were a number of furnished holiday cottages whose owners wanted winter rentals, most at a very reasonable amount per month. It wasn't perfect, because they'd have to move on at Easter when the holiday season got into full swing, but at least it would take them from where they were now—and away from Sam.

As for Sebastian...yes, she loved him, but she was not leaving Sam for Sebastian; she was leaving him for the safety of all three of them.

She waited until the reception was quiet, then dialed the number she'd copied down from the paper.

"Hello, I'm enquiring about your advert in the *Gazette*. Is the house still available?"

"It is indeed," said a rich male voice.

"I have two children, would that be a problem?"

"Not for me, no, but you might find the space a bit limited."

"I'm really not looking for anything very big. Could you tell me a little about it?"

"There's a good-sized twin bedroom with an en-suite shower room, a small kitchen and bathroom, and a sitting room which has a small galleried landing above it. I've put a sofa bed there, but if it was going to be in more permanent use, I'm sure I could find you a proper bed."

"It sounds perfect," breathed Amy. "Could I pop along and see it?"

"Of course you may. When would you like to come?"

"Are you in this evening at about half past five?"

"I am indeed." He gave her the address and she wrote it down. "My name is Lennox, and you are?"

"It's...Amy." She didn't want to say her surname. The Montagues were famous in Southwold. "I look forward to seeing you later—goodbye, Mr. Lennox."

Freddie had just put down the phone to Amy when it rang again almost immediately.

"Hello, Sebastian. What news?"

"My mate James from the news desk has just called me. It seems the fraud squad are indeed interested in talking to Kenneth Noakes."

"Right."

"As James suspected, Noakes left the country before they could nab him. I've just had a call from one of the fraud squad officers. They want to know if Mr. Noakes is likely to be in England any time soon."

"And how will we discover that?"

"Amy will probably know. So we need to find out."

"And how, pray, are we meant to do that, Sebastian?" Freddie chuckled. "I came to Southwold for a quiet life away from crime, not to become an undercover agent for the fraud squad!"

"No, of course not. It's simply a case of keeping one's ear to the ground. If Posy mentions anything about the date of exchange to you, for example."

"Why on earth don't they simply bug Sam's mobile?"

"The officer I spoke to says they want to try the 'soft' approach first, see if they can catch Noakes unawares whilst he's here in the UK. Even though they'll nab him if they can, I get the feeling that Noakes is not the top of their hit list. He's a small-time crook to them."

"But a major one to those he's swindled and of course, our beloved Posy." Freddie grunted in irritation. "I'm afraid I've been there many times before in my career as a prosecuting barrister. The police are understaffed and underfunded; often, an obviously guilty suspect would get off on a technicality."

"Well, we'll do what we can. I'll keep in touch. Bye, Freddie."

"Bye, Sebastian."

Amy arrived outside a pretty cottage which was within easy walking distance of the hotel. She thought how convenient the location would be for her. The cottage was tucked away at the end of a narrow lane, and even though she thought she knew Southwold like the back of her hand, she would never have known the property was there. Built of local stone, it was immaculate, the courtyard swept of leaves and its brass knocker freshly polished, as she tapped to alert the occupant she was outside. The door opened and a pair of bright eyes peered around it.

"You must be Amy, I presume?" he asked.

"Yes, and you must be Mr. Lennox."

"Indeed, but please call me Freddie. Now then, I have the keys right here, so what say you we take a look at the Hophouse?"

Amy nodded and followed Freddie across the cobbled courtyard to the converted building opposite. "Now, I did warn you on the telephone that the Hophouse was not the most spacious of residences. I think you might find it a little small for your needs," he said, unlocking the front door.

It took Amy approximately two minutes to walk around the little house. Freddie was right, it was small, but Amy loved it. It had obviously been carefully restored, every available inch of space imaginatively used, and because of the vaulted ceiling in the sitting room, she didn't find it claustrophobic.

"Is there an area of garden that comes with it?" she asked.

Freddie shook his head. "Unfortunately not, but I can't see why you shouldn't use mine if you need to once the weather cheers up."

"I presume this would only be a short-term rental anyway, until the holiday season begins?"

"I would prefer to take it on a month-by-month basis, if you were interested. See how we all rub along together. We will be living in rather close proximity, as you can see," he smiled.

"Really, Freddie, I think it's perfect for us, but please say if you would prefer a tenant without children. I'd like to say my two are as quiet as mice and never any trouble, but unfortunately they're—"

"Just children," he finished for her. "Personally, I've no problem with little ones at all. Shall we go back to my cottage and have a cup of tea?"

Amy checked her watch. "A very quick one, yes," she agreed, as she followed him outside and back across the courtyard.

"Do you have family of your own?" she asked as he handed her a cup of tea and they sat down in the sitting room.

"Sadly not. As I was saying to a friend of mine the other night, I have no one to think of but myself."

"So, Freddie, when could I move in and what kind of deposit will you require?" Amy asked.

"I believe the usual terms are a month in advance. And you can move in whenever you wish."

"Would the day after tomorrow be too soon? If I paid you the first month's rent and the deposit first, of course."

Freddie saw the desperation in her eyes. "That would be acceptable, yes. How about you just pay me for the week in advance? Call it a trial run to see how we all get on? We could consider it a holiday let, if you will."

"Really?" Amy's eyes shone with tears. "That's so kind of you, Freddie."

"Do excuse me for prying, but I presume the children's father will not be moving in with you?"

"No. We're, well, we're separating, actually, but I work at the Feathers Hotel as a receptionist, so I can obviously provide references for you from there."

Finally, the penny dropped. "Amy, are you by any chance related to Posy Montague?" Freddie asked her.

"Er, yes. I'm her daughter-in-law."

"I thought so," he nodded. "You're Amy Montague, married to her son, Sam. You have two children, and you work like a Trojan as a hotel receptionist to keep the family body and soul together. Posy's always saying what a miracle you are."

"And you must be Freddie, Posy's friend," said Amy slowly, everything falling into place. "Oh dear." She looked up at him in panic. "How embarrassing. The thing is, Freddie, that absolutely no one knows I'm leaving Sam. Not him *or* Posy."

"My dear, before you even say it, let me promise you that not a word shall pass my lips."

Amy stood up, feeling flustered and comforted at the same time. Freddie seemed such a nice man—it took all she had not to burst into tears on his shoulder and tell him everything. "Can I pop round tomorrow with the first week's rent?"

"There's no hurry, Amy, my dear. I'm sure you have a lot on your mind at the moment."

"And Freddie?" Amy turned to him at the front door, her eyes begging him for secrecy.

He put his finger to his lips. "Mum's the word, I promise."

"I..." Amy paused on the doorstep. "Do you know if Posy is home at the moment?"

"She isn't, no. She's working late at the gallery. There's a private viewing tonight, though if you need to see her, I'm sure she could spare you ten minutes."

"I...no, it's fine. Goodbye, Freddie."

Freddie closed the door behind him and went into the conservatory to pour himself a large whisky.

"What to do?" he muttered to himself, feeling the threads of the Montague family once again tightening around him. He'd seen those bruises on Amy's wrist as she'd lifted her arm to drink her tea. Yet how could he ever tell Posy her son was obviously a violent brute? The fact that he was offering her daughter-in-law sanctuary from Sam might well be seen by her as a betrayal.

"Darling Posy," Freddie whispered to the clear night sky above the conservatory. "Are we destined never to be together?"

On the way home with the children, knowing Posy was at the gallery, Amy drove to Admiral House. She needed to see Sebastian, feel the security of his arms around her for a few minutes as she told him about her momentous decision. Parking in front of the house, she turned and saw Sara was asleep in her car seat.

"Jake, I've just got to go in and see Granny for a few seconds. Will you wait here? I promise I won't be long."

Jake nodded, his eyes glued to the comic she'd bought him. She dashed round the side of the house and let herself in, then chased up the stairs to the bedroom where Sebastian worked.

"Amy!" He turned from his computer and stood up.

"I can't stay long. The kids are in the car outside."

Sebastian walked towards her, then pulled her to him. "Darling, I've missed you," he whispered into her neck.

"Something happened this morning and I've made a decision. I've found a place for me and the kids to live, and I'm leaving Sam. I'm going to tell him tomorrow."

Sebastian stared down at her in shock and surprise. "Is it too insensitive to tell you how happy that makes me?"

"Probably, but I think I need to hear it."

"Well, I am." He squeezed her tightly to him. "And I promise I'll be there as much as you want me to be."

"Which won't be a lot to start off with," she sighed. "The place I've found to live in is owned by Freddie, Posy's gentleman friend. He lives next door."

Sebastian raised an eyebrow. "Well, that's just peachy. I live with the soon-to-be-ex mother-in-law, and you go and rent a place slap bang under the mother-in-law's boyfriend's nose." He smiled down at her. "We might just as well put a front-page advert in the *Gazette*."

"I know, but I really think Freddie is the kind of decent chap who will offer discretion. Besides, it's cheap, very nice and available immediately."

"Yes, Freddie is indeed a decent sort, and you know I'll help financially if necessary. All you have to do is ask."

"Thanks, Sebastian, but I really need to do this on my own. And I want you to know this has nothing to do with you."

"Nothing?"

"It's...well, I've been left with no choice."

"I see."

"I'd have had to do it, even if I'd never met you."

"Right."

"Please don't breathe a word to Posy, will you? Not yet."

"Of course not."

As Amy swept a hand distractedly through her hair, Sebastian saw the bruise on her wrist.

"How did you get that?" he asked her.

"I tripped and fell and my wrist took the brunt of it. I must go— Sam will wonder where we are."

"Amy, please be careful, won't you? Sam might get...upset when you tell him."

"I will, don't worry. Sam's away tonight. He's meeting his backer in that Victoria Hotel place in North Norfolk. The backer is handing over the cash for the deposit so they can exchange contracts on this house in the next few days."

Bingo!...thought Sebastian.

"So I'll pack our stuff up tonight," Amy continued, 'then put it in the car. After I've told him tomorrow morning, I'll be ready to leave."

"Amy, please tell me; are you afraid of Sam?"

"Afraid? No, of course not. I just know he'll be upset when I tell him, that's all. I'll call you as soon as I've done the deed."

"Amy?"

"Yes?" She stopped and turned back to him.

"Just remember, I love you, and if you need me, I'm here, okay?"

Sebastian watched from his upstairs window as Amy climbed into her battered car, started the engine and disappeared up the drive. Then he grabbed his mobile and dialed the number the fraud squad had given him to tell them about Mr. Noakes's whereabouts tonight. If all went well, Amy wouldn't have to tell Sam at all...

Chapter 30

Once the children were in bed, Amy packed a holdall full of her clothes and gathered together some of the children's toys, stowing them beneath a blanket in the back of her car. Then she climbed into bed and did her best to fall asleep, but in the end, she gave up trying and went to make herself a cup of coffee, which sent her beating heart pounding even faster.

"Keep calm, Amy, you must keep calm for the children," she whispered to herself as she watched a dove-gray dawn struggling to emerge from night.

She tried to focus on the fact that tonight, she and the children would be safely in the cosy sanctuary of the Hophouse. She wanted to cry with relief that she'd found it. Even though she hadn't told Freddie, the fact that it was so tucked away was a huge bonus. So if Sam *did* manage to find her, all she'd have to do was scream and Freddie would hear her.

She woke the children at seven and fed them breakfast, trying to keep everything as normal as she could. On the way to drop them at school, she listened to Jake read his book and Sara chatter about her angel costume for the Nativity play.

Back home, she went to their bedroom and stuffed their clothes into two bags, adding them hurriedly to the collection in the boot of her car. Then she sat at the kitchen table, beside herself with tension. She even looked at the dregs of a bottle of red wine on the table and considered drinking it. The clock on the wall told her it was nearly nine o'clock—another hour until Sam had said he'd be back. She was just considering going out for a walk when her mobile rang.

"Oh God," she breathed as she saw it was Sam.

"Hello?"

"Amy, thank God! I need you to come and get me."

"Have you broken down?"

"No, I...I'm at Wells police station in Norfolk. Oh God, Amy..." Sam's voice broke, "They've arrested me."

"I...but why?"

"I can't talk now. My solicitor's arranged bail and I need a thousand pounds. Can you go to Mum, tell her what's happened and beg her to lend you the money? I have to go now. Bye, darling, I love you."

The line went dead. Amy stared at her mobile, her mind going blank with shock. When she recovered her senses she found she was shivering from head to toe. She dialed Posy's number and told her briefly about the call from Sam and what he needed.

"I'll drive into town and go to the bank immediately to get the cash, then I'll come to you. Try not to panic, Amy, I'm sure there's been some mistake."

Whilst she waited for Posy, Amy knew instinctively there'd been no mistake. She sat at the kitchen table focusing on a crack that zigzagged all the way down the wall.

"Oh my dear." Posy arrived on her doorstep, white with shock. Amy led her into the sitting room. "What did he actually say to you?"

"That he's been arrested and is at Wells police station in Norfolk," Amy answered robotically.

"Amy, whatever can he have done?"

"I have absolutely no idea," she said dully.

"Perhaps it was drunk driving?"

"Maybe."

"What if he's hurt someone...?"

"The best thing I can do is to go and find out."

"Would you like me to come with you for moral support?"

Amy thought about all the stuff in the car boot and shook her head. "I'll be fine, thank you."

"Right, well, here's the thousand in cash." Posy pulled an envelope out of her handbag.

"Thank you," said Amy as she put the money into her own bag. "I'll be in touch as soon as I know anything."

Posy gave Amy a fierce hug. "Anything you and the children need, I'm here for you."

Amy did not allow herself to think during the hour's drive to Wells. She played Classic FM very loudly and concentrated on the road.

At the tiny police station, she filled out a form and handed over the thousand pounds. She was told to sit in the waiting area, which was thankfully empty.

Finally, Sam appeared. He looked dreadful; chalk-white, his hair standing on end like a toddler's. She stood up and he sank into her arms. "Thank God you're here, darling, thank God."

"Come on, let's get out of here, shall we?" she said gently.

As they made their way outside, Sam hung on to her arm as though he didn't have the strength to walk by himself.

"My car's still at the hotel," he said as he sank into the passenger seat and Amy started the engine.

"Okay. Tell me where to go."

"Head for the coast road and the Victoria is about ten minutes away, on the left. You remember."

As she navigated the car through the narrow streets of the town and eventually found herself on the coast road, Amy *did* remember the last journey she'd made to the lovely hotel, over ten years ago now. The excitement she'd felt as Sam had driven her along the coast, hoping she was right and he was going to propose. He hadn't, but it had still been a wonderful night. Back then, the sun had been making a sparkling guest appearance. Today, gray clouds, heavy with the promise of rain, hung low over the land. They arrived in the car park and Amy drew up next to Sam's Fiat.

"Are you going to be okay to drive home?" she asked him.

"I...yes."

"Well, I'm not, until I know what it is you're meant to have done."

"Oh God, Amy." Sam shook his head, unable to look at her. "I've let you and the kids down so badly. I really thought that this time, I'd do it, make you proud of me. Now everything's gone, everything. What are we going to do?"

"I don't know until you tell me what's happened."

"It's my business partner, Ken Noakes. Apparently, he's a crook and a fraudster of the first order. In a nutshell, he's been ripping people off for years. Basically, the money used to fund the development on our property company is technically stolen. Or at least, owed to creditors. We were sitting in the bar having a drink— Ken had brought the hundred grand in cash with him so we could exchange on Admiral House today—and these two plain-clothes policemen suddenly appear and ask us both to come with them to answer questions in relation to 'fraudulently obtaining money from...'" Sam shook his head. "I can't remember the exact words. I was too shocked. One of them put me in his car and Ken went with the other officer. I haven't seen him since."

"Okay, but if this is to do with Ken Noakes's past, why did they arrest you?"

"Because I'm the sole bloody director of his company! Ken's just my backer, his name's not even on the company notepaper! Christ! How was I supposed to know his money came from some dodgy dealing?! The fraud squad just didn't believe I didn't know."

"Oh Sam..." Amy bit her lip. "Had you really no idea?"

"Of course not! Christ, Amy," he swore angrily. "I might be many things, but I'm not a crook. Okay, so I may have some failed businesses behind me, and believe me, they'd dug up any dirt they could find on those. They accused me of trading whilst insolvent on the last company I ran, which is also a criminal offence. They might have me for that as well, but the solicitor who was with me thinks he can probably get me off all charges in return for giving evidence against Ken. The problem is, I know nothing, nothing at all." Sam looked at her. "Amy, you do believe me, don't you?"

Despite everything, Amy did. Her husband wasn't a criminal, just desperate and not very bright.

"Of course I do. Let's talk when we get home."

"Oh God." Sam put his face in his hands. "How am I ever going to face Mum? The sale of Admiral House is up the swannee, that's for sure. I'm such a bloody failure. Nothing I've ever done has succeeded and I really have tried so hard. I'm so sorry, Amy. I've let you down yet again." Suddenly he clutched her arm. "Promise you won't leave me. Without you and the kids, I'm...I just...well, I couldn't go on."

Amy couldn't reply.

"Promise me, Amy, *please*. I love you. I really do." Sam began to sob. "Don't leave me, please don't leave me..." he begged as he reached across the gear-stick and clung to her like a child.

"I won't leave you, Sam," Amy heard a dull voice that didn't sound like her own reply.

"Promise?"

"I promise."

When they arrived home, Amy told Sam to go upstairs and take a shower. He came down twenty minutes later looking more like himself.

"I'm going to drive over to Admiral House and see Mum. At the very least, I owe her an explanation."

"Yes, you do." Amy continued to fold clothes from the airer into a laundry basket.

"I love you, Amy, and I'm so, so sorry. I'll get us out of this mess somehow, I promise. Bye, sweetheart."

When Sam had left the house, Amy waited five minutes, then went to her car and lugged everything from the boot inside. She emptied the contents back into the drawers of both her own and the children's rooms. Then she walked back down the stairs, took the piece of paper with Freddie's number out of her purse and dialed it on her mobile.

"Hello?"

The deeply comforting sound of his voice threatened to disturb the strange calm that had descended on her. She took a deep breath.

"Hello, Freddie, it's Amy Montague here. I'm just calling to tell you that something's come up and I'm not going to be able to move in today after all."

"Right. Well, that's not a problem. Just let me know when is convenient, Amy. No hurry."

"The problem is, I'm not sure when that will be, so it's best if you let the Hophouse to someone else."

There was a pause on the line.

"I see. Is everything all right, Amy?"

"Not really, no, but I'm sure Posy will tell you what's happened. I...I need to go now, Freddie, but thank you so much for your kindness. Bye."

She ended the call before she burst into tears. Then, knowing Sam could be back at any moment, she dialed Sebastian's number. It went straight to voicemail.

"It's me, Amy. Please meet me in the bus shelter on the sea front at five today."

Amy dropped her mobile into her handbag and went upstairs to put on her uniform for work.

Sebastian was already there when Amy arrived. He stood up from the bench and made to hold her, but she drew back.

"Amy, I know what's happened. Posy told me after Sam had left."

"Yes." Amy's voice was a monotone. "I'm here to tell you that I'm staying with Sam because I'm his wife, the mother of his children, and because he needs me."

Sebastian did his best to choose his words carefully. "I understand that today has been a shock, and obviously you feel you should support him just now. You need to let the dust settle, of course you do."

"No, it's more than that, Sebastian. What we did—what I did—was wrong. I'm Sam's wife, I took vows in a church. I'm the mother of his children and...I can't leave him. Ever."

"Are you telling me we—*this*—is over?"

"Yes. I made my bed and I have to lie in it. Sam's in a terrible state, and whatever I feel, I have to stand by him. If he knew about us, I think it would finish him. He virtually threatened suicide in the car this morning."

"I understand, but maybe in time..."

"*No!* Sebastian, there won't ever be a 'time.' Please believe me. I will never leave my husband, so it's not fair to string you along. Go and have a life with someone who is free, please," she begged him.

"I don't want a life with anyone else. I want it with you. I love you!"

"I'm sorry, Sebastian, but as I said, it's over. I've got to go. Bye."

Amy turned and began to walk away from him.

"Amy! Wait! I know what he does to you!"

She shook her head as she continued to walk swiftly towards the High Street. Sebastian watched as she turned a corner and was gone. He swore heavily under his breath, knowing this was all of his doing. If he hadn't alerted the fraud squad to Ken Noakes's whereabouts, Amy and the children would now have been safely in Freddie's cottage. By trying to protect Posy, he'd managed to destroy his own chance of happiness—and ultimately Amy's.

Sebastian sat down on the bench on the sea front, put his head in his hands, and sobbed.

Peacock butterfly
(Inachis iois)

Posy

London
Summer 1958

I stood on the bus, crushed on one side by a woman with a pushchair, on the other by a youth who stank of stale sweat. Even though the windows were open, it was hotter than any greenhouse I'd ever worked in. I was glad when I saw Baron's Court appearing round the corner. I rang the bell and squeezed through the crowd to step off the back of the bus.

London in August was extremely unpleasant, I thought to myself, remembering with a pang the beautiful summer days I'd enjoyed in Cornwall at the same time of year. The city wasn't built for the few days a year it experienced serious heat, I realized as I walked along the pavement to my block of flats. Estelle and I were on the top floor of the building, which meant six flights of stairs to reach it. I was sure the exercise was good for me, but not when the temperature was in the high seventies. I unlocked the front door, dripping with perspiration, and went straight to the tiny and rather grim bathroom to run a lukewarm bath. As usual, the sitting room smelt of cigarette smoke and I opened the window as wide as I could to release it, then set about clearing the coffee table, which was littered with empty beer bottles, gin glasses and overflowing ashtrays.

Taking them into the kitchen and dumping their contents into the sink and the bin respectively, I wondered whether it really had been a good idea to share a flat with Estelle. We had such totally different lifestyles; whereas I was out bright and early every morning in order to arrive at Kew Gardens for a nine o'clock start, Estelle could sleep in much later—her daily class at Covent Garden wasn't until eleven. In the afternoons, she would come home to rest before leaving for a performance just as I was on my way home. I would have peace from then until eleven or so, by which time I was in bed, exhausted from a day's work. Just as I was dropping off, the front door would open and Estelle would arrive with an array of bohemian friends, fresh from the bars around the theater, to continue the party. I would lie there sleepless as the music was turned on full-blast—I'd once loved Frank Sinatra, but now he felt like my torturer as his mellow voice sang out to me into the small hours.

Having cleared up the sitting room and wondering why Estelle never thought of doing it herself before she went out to the theater, I undressed and climbed into the bath, which was so small that I had to keep my knees bent into my chest.

I'll go to bed at eight tonight, I thought as I soaked myself, then stepped out and towelled myself dry. Dressed in my robe, I made myself some cheese on toast and sat on the sofa eating it. *Am I boring, preferring seedlings to non-stop partying?* I asked myself. When I'd complained about the noise a few days ago, Estelle had told me I was getting old before my time.

"You can sleep when you're in your forties, Posy darling. Enjoy your youth whilst you have it," she'd said nonchalantly as she took another drag of a joint she'd been passed by a young man who was very obviously wearing lipstick. I had skulked back to my bedroom and stuck cotton wool in my ears.

At least I adored my job. Mr. Hubbard, the new Keeper of the Herbarium, seemed to like me and was very encouraging. Every morning, we received new plant samples at Kew from all over the world: some delivered by the plant hunters in special cases to keep the specimens alive after months of travels through mountains and jungles, and some in boxes sent over from botanical gardens in Singapore, Australia or the Americas. After carefully checking the plants for little travellers such as lice or flies, I would begin to study them, make scientific illustrations at my tiny desk, and take photographs, then develop them in the darkroom.

I learnt to press the samples on archival paper in the mounting room, then marked the origin, the collector, the family and genus numbers on small labels. Deciphering the notes from various botanists all over the world took the longest time, but ultimately gave vital information on the care and upkeep of the plant. Once dried, I would put the pressed plants in the tall cupboards in the center of the Herbarium, a two-storied room that was already overcrowded with samples. I asked my colleague Alice how many there were in total, and she chewed on her pencil thoughtfully before replying, "Perhaps four and a half million?"

I could not ask for a more glorious place to work; the garden around me provided a much-needed contrast to the bustle of the city.

I'm a country girl at heart, I acknowledged as I yawned, washed up my plate and cutlery and headed for bed. "I miss Cambridge, and Jonny," I murmured as I lay uncovered on the hard mattress—it was far too hot for a sheet. Still sweating, I then divested myself of my nightie too and lay there naked. I reached for the book on my bedside table and attempted to read, but I was so exhausted I soon fell asleep, lulled by the lightest touch of a breeze coming from the open window.

I came to a few hours later, hearing the front door slam and the sound of laughter in the narrow hall.

"Oh God," I groaned as I heard Frankie blaring out from the gramophone. Reaching for the glass of water on my bedside table, I drank thirstily. Lying back down, I closed my eyes and wished I too could fly to the moon like Sinatra was begging a girl to do. At least there would be silence there.

"Won't be a tick, just going for a..."

My bedroom door was suddenly opened. I gave a small scream and fumbled for a sheet to cover my modesty as the hall light was switched on.

"Go away!" I called as I looked at the figure in the doorway. There was a man silhouetted in the light behind him. I couldn't see his features in the gloom, but with a jolt, I realized exactly who he was.

"God, do excuse me, I was looking for the lavatory," said my intruder, pushing a hand through his thick wavy hair. I could feel him staring straight at me. I blushed, pulling the sheet tighter around me.

"That's okay," I gulped. "The lavatory's on the other side of the corridor."

"Of course. And I do beg your pardon." He squinted at me again. "Are you sure I don't know you? You look awfully familiar."

"I'm sure you don't," I said, wishing he would just go away.

"Were you by any chance at Cambridge?"

"Yes," I sighed, "I was."

"And you had a friend called Andrea?"

"Yes, I did."

"I never forget a face," he smiled. "She brought you to one of my parties—I remember it vividly. You were wearing a red dress."

"Yes, it was me," I said as my eyes adjusted to the light and I saw his big, fawn-colored eyes.

"Well, well. Isn't it a small world. I'm Freddie Lennox. It's very nice to see you again, er...?"

"Posy Anderson."

"Of course, I remember now. May I ask why you're in here like Cinderella whilst the party goes on around you?"

"Because unlike most of the guests, I have a job to do."

"That sounds serious," Freddie smiled. "Well, I'll leave you to your beauty sleep. It's been very nice making your acquaintance again, Posy. Goodnight."

"Goodnight."

As he switched off the light and closed the door behind him, I lay back on my bed with a sigh of relief. I remembered accompanying Andrea to the party—and I remembered Freddie vividly; I'd thought at the time he was the most handsome man I'd ever seen, way out of my league with his looks, his confidence and the fact that he was a third year. I was amazed he remembered me—I'd only spoken briefly to him.

As the music played next door, I thought about Freddie standing only a few feet away from me, probably nursing a drink and talking to one of Estelle's extremely pretty ballerina friends. Reaching for the cotton wool I kept in my drawer, I broke off two pieces of fluff and stuffed them in my ears.

The following morning, I emerged from my bedroom and sighed at the detritus in the sitting room. There was a body on the floor and one on the sofa, but I ignored them as I went to the kitchen to make a cup of tea and some toast. I was just spreading jam on the latter when a familiar voice spoke from behind me.

"Good morning, Posy. And how are you this fine day?"

Freddie stood in the doorway, watching me.

"I'm very well, thank you," I said politely as I cut the toast in two.

"That looks just the ticket," he said, indicating the toast. "May I have a slice?"

"Help yourself," I said. "I'm afraid I'm in rather a hurry." Taking my tea and plate, I walked to the kitchen door. He stepped back to allow me through and smiled at me.

"Thank you."

"I must say," he whispered as I passed him, "I much prefer you with no clothes on."

I hid my blushes as I stalked through the sitting room to my bedroom. Sitting down on the bed, I ate my toast and drank my tea, swearing I'd speak to Estelle about the situation. Having strange men accost me as I was trying to make breakfast was really not on. Gathering up a handbag and my leather case, I applied some lipstick and left my room.

"Where are you headed?" Freddie asked me as I opened the front door.

"To Kew Gardens."

"How very...botanical," he replied, following me as I began the endless descent down the stairs. "Is that for pleasure?"

"No, I work there."

"You're a gardener?"

"No, I'm a scientist."

"Yes, yes, of course you are. I remember you telling me. How very impressive."

I wondered if he was teasing me, and he must have felt he was because he added a 'really" to the end of his sentence. "I studied law at Cambridge."

"Did you?" I said as we finished the long walk down the stairs and I opened the front door.

"Yes, but I really wanted to be an actor, so I thought I'd try my luck in London."

"Right," I said as we stepped out onto the pavement and he walked amiably by my side.

"I've done some radio and had a bit part in a TV drama, but that's about it."

"The life of an actor seems to be more about luck than talent, from what Estelle's friends have told me."

"That is very true," Freddie agreed. "I met Andrea through the Footlights, if you remember."

"I do, yes."

"It was the main reason why I agreed to go to Cambridge. I do miss it, do you?" he asked me as we arrived at my bus stop.

"Yes, I do. Now, if you'll excuse me, this is my bus and I really must go."

"Of course, Posy. And I must go home to my flat and have a wash and brush up. I have an audition later."

"Good luck with that," I said, stepping onto the bus.

"What time do you get home?" he called to me as the bus conductor dinged the bell to let the driver know it was safe to pull off.

"Around six usually," I called back.

"Bye-bye, Posy, I'll see you soon!"

That day, I was not as attentive to my drawings as usual. Despite myself, I couldn't help thinking of Freddie's gorgeous eyes and the thick head of shiny hair my fingers ached to touch...

"Really, Posy," I chided myself as I ate my lunchtime sandwiches in the gardens, "you're engaged to be married and he's a penniless actor. You need to get a grip, my girl."

On the bus on the way home, I couldn't help fantasising that he would be waiting at the front door when I arrived home, and gave myself another stern talking to as I walked towards it. But, to my utter shock, there he was in reality, lurking outside, looking conspicuous (and utterly dreamy) in a blue velvet smoking jacket and a paisley cravat.

"Good evening, Posy. I came to apologize for barging in on you last night." He proffered me a wilting bunch of flowers and a brown paper bag. "I brought some gin and some sweet vermouth. Have you ever had a Gin and It?"

"I don't think I have, no," I said, unlocking the front door.

"Then tonight, you will have one, my dear Posy. We are celebrating."

"Are we?"

"Most definitely, yes. My audition was successful!" he said as he followed me up the stairs. "I have a walk-on part in a Noël Coward play opening at the Lyric on Shaftesbury Avenue. A whole four lines, Posy! Isn't that wonderful?"

"It is," I replied as I began to mount the stairs, feeling...well, not sure what I was feeling, if I was truthful. I couldn't understand why he was here, because he just couldn't be interested in a girl like me, could he...?

We reached the tiny top landing and I opened the door to the flat. Freddie followed me inside and surveyed the sitting room, still not cleared from last night's antics.

"Goodness, it's a mess in here. I'll help you clear up."

He did so, which I thought was awfully sweet of him, and then he made us both a Gin and It.

"Cheers," Freddie toasted. "Here's to me following in the footsteps of Olivier."

"Here's to you," I said and took a swig of the drink, which really was rather nice.

"I seem to remember you came from Suffolk originally, like me. Do you get back there often?"

"Never," I sighed. "I left when I was nine."

"Lovely county," Freddie said, "but of course I much prefer the Smoke, don't you?"

"Not really, no. I like wide open spaces."

"Do you now?"

"Yes. When I have the money, I think I'll move out to Richmond, which is very near Kew and has the most wonderful park."

"I've never been. How say you we take a picnic there tomorrow?"

"I...well," I blushed, not knowing what to say.

"Are you desperately busy? Or are you trying to tell me to bugger off and leave you alone?"

I knew that I really should tell him now that I was engaged to be married. It would have been perfectly obvious and so much easier if I had a ring sitting on my finger. But the fact I spent so much time with my hands in soil meant that I kept my beautiful engagement ring safely in a box in my bedside drawer. I stood in an agony of indecision, the "good" Posy encouraging me to say the words I should, and the "bad" Posy refusing to let me open my mouth and say what I needed to.

"Well?" Freddie gazed at me steadily.

"No, I'm not busy," I heard a treacherous voice that just happened to be mine saying. "That would be lovely."

After my second Gin and It, Freddie announced he was hungry and would pull something together from the meager stores in the cupboard. We ate sardines with buttered bread as Freddie entertained me with his life in London and the famous actors he'd met.

"Right," he said eventually, "I suppose I must be going or I'll miss my last bus home to Clapham."

I looked at my watch and could hardly believe it was past eleven.

"It really has been the most pleasant evening," he said as he stood up.

"Yes, it has," I said as I stood up too, my head spinning a little from the gin.

"And I have to say, my dearest Posy, you are utterly, utterly gorgeous."

Before I knew it, Freddie had pulled me into his arms and was kissing me. And it felt like heaven. My body responded immediately, in a way it had never done with Jonny. And I was disappointed when he pulled away.

"Now I really must dash, or I'll be on a park bench for the night," he smiled. "I'll be here at noon tomorrow. You bring the food, I'll bring the booze. Goodnight, darling girl."

"Goodnight."

After he'd left, I floated into my bedroom, divested myself of my clothes and lay on the bed in a gorgeous haze of gin and lust. I imagined Freddie's elegant fingers creeping down gently over my breasts, my stomach...When Estelle arrived with her usual gaggle of friends, I hardly minded, and at least I could sleep in a little tomorrow morning.

"Goodnight, darling Freddie," I said as I closed my eyes.

Even though I woke up the following morning with a blistering headache and a heart full of guilt, I'm ashamed to say that neither made me cancel the picnic in the park with Freddie. We sat on the parched grass, drinking wine on a blanket, my head resting on his shoulder.

I simply couldn't believe how natural it felt—I remembered how it had taken months for Jonny and me to relax physically with each other. There was an awful lot of kissing and not much talking, and eventually both of us fell asleep. We caught the bus back to the flat, and he came upstairs with me. As usual, the mess was there from the night before, but we ignored it and did some more kissing.

"Posy," he said as he nuzzled into my neck, "you know that I would absolutely love to take you into the bedroom and—"

"No, Freddie!" I sat upright, bleary from too much wine and sun, and looked at him sternly. "I'm simply not that kind of a girl."

"And I respect that," he nodded. "I'm just saying that I want to—am desperate to. Every time I close my eyes, I have visions of you sitting there on your bed like an alabaster statue of Aphrodite, with only a sheet to hide your modesty." He smiled.

"Why do you want me, Freddie? Surely you'd prefer some glamorous actress, not a dowdy scientist like me."

"Goodness, Posy, you're hardly dowdy. Part of the reason I'm so attracted to you is because you don't know how gorgeous you are. You're so natural," he said, his lips moving towards mine. "Such a breath of fresh air from the girls I usually meet..."

I moved away from him. "Well, I'm not like them in all sorts of ways. Are you after me purely for my body?" I asked him boldly.

"I'm definitely after that, yes, as I've freely admitted to you. But no, it's more than that. Under this vacuous actor's façade, I happen to be rather a serious person, you see. So many of the women I meet are facile, without a brain in their head. After the initial attraction has disappeared, one needs to be able to hold a conversation, doesn't one?"

"Yes, I think one does."

"And you're so very bright, Posy. I love hearing you talk about polytunnels and compost. It turns me on."

374 / *Lucinda Riley*

I allowed him to kiss me again, pacified by what he'd said. And, I thought when he'd left, the worst thing that could happen was that he'd have his wicked way with me and then leave me broken-hearted. And if I was to be married to Jonny for the rest of my life, surely it was all right to have an adventure before I did so...?

Summer turned to autumn in a flash, and still my affair with Freddie continued. Jonny wrote to me every week from his officer cadet training base in Aldershot, telling me he'd soon get leave and would be able to come up to town to visit me for a weekend. He sounded happy, talking of which regiment he would join—the 7th Gurkha Rifles—and of where "we'd" be based when he finished his six months' training. He was hoping for somewhere exotic like Malaya.

It suddenly struck me that I hadn't really thought the future through; and now here I was *in* it, with Jonny training for the army and me having achieved my dream of working at Kew. If I went ahead and married him, I'd have to go wherever he was, which would mean giving up all my goals and ambitions for the future. Whereas, with Freddie, I could stay in London and pursue my career...

Freddie's play had opened, and I'd been to see him say his four lines and given him a rousing cheer as he'd bowed. We saw each other less because of his evening performances, but we always spent Sunday together.

"Have you slept with him yet?" Estelle asked me as I readied myself to meet him for lunch at the Lyon's Corner House on Charing Cross Road.

"Of course not, Estelle," I said as I applied lipstick in the mirror that hung above the sofa in the sitting room.

"I'm surprised, you certainly look as though you are to me."

"What do you mean?"

"Just the way you're so familiar with each other."

"Well, we haven't."

"You must have been tempted. He's a total dish," said Estelle, still fishing. "What are you going to do about Jonny Army?"

"I...don't know."

"Does Freddie know about him? That you're engaged?"

"Er, no, he doesn't."

"Honestly, Posy," Estelle giggled. "And there was me worrying about my morals, when you're two-timing your fiancé!"

On the way to meet Freddie for lunch, I thought about what Estelle had said. I knew she was right. In my mind, I'd conveniently managed to sanction my affair with Freddie simply because we hadn't yet been to bed together, but I knew I was lying to myself as well as to Freddie. I had fallen madly in love with him, and that was the truth of it.

I had to tell Jonny it was over. It was only fair.

But what if Freddie leaves you...?

If he did, I thought, I thoroughly deserved losing Jonny. He was so good and kind and steady—the perfect husband-to-be. He would be devastated if he knew his fiancée was behaving as she was.

After lunch I told Freddie I had a headache, took the bus home and sat down in my bedroom to write to Jonny. It took at least six drafts, because it was so difficult to find the words I needed, but eventually I folded the letter in two and put it in the envelope. Then I took my engagement ring out of its box, wrapped it round with cotton wool and Sellotape and placed it inside with the letter. Sealing it with my tongue, I addressed it to his base, then stuck a stamp to the front. Before I could change my mind I went out to the postbox and, taking a deep breath, dropped the envelope inside.

"I'm so terribly sorry, Jonny. Goodbye."

Three days after that, I went to bed with Freddie. And if any part of me had been worried that breaking off my engagement was the wrong thing to do, my fears were blown away by how he made me feel. The event took place at Freddie's flat in Clapham. Afterwards, we lay there smoking and drinking Gin and It, which had become our favorite tipple.

"So you're not a virgin." Freddie let a hand stray across my breast. "I thought you might be. Who was the lucky man?"

"Freddie, I have something to tell you," I sighed.

"Spit it out then, darling. Have I got a rival for your affections?"

"You did have, yes. I was...engaged when we met, you see, to someone called Jonny. He's away training for the army, and well, anyway, I wrote to him a few days ago to say that the engagement was off. That I couldn't marry him."

"Was it to do with me?"

"Yes," I replied honestly. "I mean, please don't feel frightened or anything, will you? I'm not thinking that you and I will get engaged, but I felt it was only right to tell him."

"You dark horse, you," Freddie smiled. "And there was me thinking you were so sweet and innocent, and all the time there was someone else."

"Yes, I know I've been awful, and I'm sorry. I haven't seen him since you and I met because he's training. So I haven't been unfaithful to you, Freddie."

"So that was why you wouldn't sleep with me?"

"Yes."

"Well, for my part I'm awfully glad he's gone and your morals are no longer holding you back." He reached for me and held me tight. "Shall we do it again to celebrate?"

I was only glad that Freddie didn't seem at all perturbed by my confession. I'd worried he'd feel that I was putting pressure on him, which of course I wasn't at all. I told myself there were other reasons for breaking off my engagement; not least, the thought of leaving my beloved job behind to travel abroad with Jonny. But if I was truthful with myself, I knew that if Freddie asked me to, I'd travel with him to the ends of the earth without a second thought.

After that first, wonderful time in bed, I virtually moved in with Freddie. I'd wait for him after the show, and we'd make love till the small hours before I fell asleep in his arms. The odd thing was that even though I was existing on very little sleep, I'd feel as fresh as a daisy when I woke and left for Kew. I'd read endless romantic novels when I was younger, and only now did I understand what the writers had been expressing. I'd never been as happy in my life.

Mid-October, I made my weekly trip back to Baron's Court to get a change of clothes and collect my post. Waiting for me in my bedroom was a thick vellum envelope with an Italian postmark on it.

Maman, I thought as I tore it open.

Ma chère Posy,

It is a very long time since I last wrote, and I hope you will

forgive me for that. Life has been very busy with the marriage of one of Alessandro's sons. Congratulations on your First at Cambridge. I am proud to have such an intelligent daughter.

Posy, myself and Alessandro are flying to London at the beginning of November and I would very much like to see you there. We will be staying at the Ritz between the 1st and 9th, so please telephone me to tell me when you can come. It has been too long, so please, say you will see your Maman and meet her husband.

With all love,

Maman

I sat there staring at the letter, thinking it had been over thirteen years since I had last set eyes on Maman. Whichever way one looked at it, my mother had deserted me. And even though the adult, sensible side of me realized that it had been the right thing to have the stability of Granny and Cornwall, rather than being dragged around Europe as I grew up, the emotional part of me was as hurt and angry as any child whose mother had abandoned them.

On the bus back to Clapham, I mulled over whether I should discuss it with Freddie and decided against it. I couldn't bear the thought of him pitying me so I said nothing. When I got home, he noticed that I was distracted.

"What is it, darling girl? I can see there's something wrong."

"Nothing, Freddie; I've got a headache, that's all."

"Then come here and let me mop your fevered brow." I went into his arms and felt comforted there.

"You know, I've been thinking about whether you and I should consider getting a flat together. This single bed is becoming rather too irritating, don't you think?"

I looked up at him. "You're suggesting we live together?"

"Don't look so shocked, darling. We live together now, just unofficially."

"Golly, Freddie, I'm not sure what my grandmother would say if she knew. I mean, it's a bit risqué, isn't it?"

"It's the 1950s, Posy, and lots of people do it, I promise you. I want you to have a decent kitchen where you can make all these scrumptious meals you keep telling me about," he smiled.

"Can I think about it?"

"Of course you can." Freddie kissed me on my cheek.

"Thank you."

One way and another, as the Christmas of 1958 approached, my life could not have been fuller. It felt as though there wasn't one part of me that didn't feel sated; I had my wonderful job, and I had Freddie, who filled my every waking thought, my body and my heart. I was almost frightened at the happiness I felt, because surely it could not last forever, could it?

Buoyed up on my cloud of happiness, I decided I should see Maman when she came to London, out of courtesy if nothing else. So, the week she said she was in town, I phoned the Ritz hotel and was put through to her maid. I told her I'd be able to meet Maman for tea this coming Saturday. Then I went to Swan & Edgar in Regent Street and bought myself a smart suit that I could reuse for any upcoming occasion.

When I entered the Ritz a few days later, my legs felt as though they were made of cotton wool and my heart beat hard against my chest.

"Can I help you, Madam?" asked the maître'd who stood guard over the sumptuous lounge where tea was being served.

"Yes, I'm looking for the Count and Contessa d'Amici."

"Ah, yes, madam, they are expecting you. Follow me."

As the maître'd led me through the well-dressed guests sipping tea and eating dainty sandwiches, my eyes flitted to get a forward glance of my mother. And there she was, her blonde hair worn up in an elegant chignon, her makeup perfect. She looked exactly the same, apart from a triple string of creamy pearls around her neck and an array of diamonds sparkling on her fingers and wrist. She was sitting next to a diminutive, bald-headed man, who to my eyes looked double her age, but then perhaps Maman was just exceptionally well-preserved.

"My dear Posy, I'd like you to meet Alessandro, your stepfather."

"*Cara mia*, you are even more beautiful than your Mama told me. I am honored to meet you." Alessandro stood up and clasped my hands in his, and I was surprised to see tears in his eyes. I had been determined to dislike him, but his kindness was palpable, and I saw how clearly he doted on my mother.

As I nibbled on cucumber sandwiches and drank glass after glass of champagne, Alessandro regaled me with stories of their life in Italy, of their palazzo and their summer cruises along the Amalfi coast.

"Your mother, she is—what is the word?—marrrrvelous! She bring light and joy to my life!"

I looked down at my tea as he gave her hand a kiss. Maman beamed back at him, and I realized I could never remember her smiling like that at Admiral House.

"You must come to visit us!" Maman said once the waiters had cleared away the plates. "Christmas at the palazzo is so beautiful, and next summer, we will take the boat along the coast and show you the wonders of Italy."

"I'm not sure when I'll be able to get away from work," I hedged.

"But you must surely have some holidays," she said. "I..." Maman turned to her husband. "*Amore*, can you give me a moment alone with my daughter?"

"*Si, certo.*" With a final kiss of Maman's hand, Alessandro wandered out of the tea room.

Once we were alone, she leant closer to me. "Posy, I know I have missed much of your life—"

"Maman, I understand, you don't have to—"

"No, I do," she said fiercely. "You have grown into a beautiful, clever and strong woman, and I regret that I have had little to do with it." Her breath caught in her throat. "There are so many things that I wish I could explain to you, but..." She shook her head. "Time has passed and there is no use looking back." She patted my hand. "*Chérie*, please consider coming to Italy at Christmas, won't you?"

I walked away from the Ritz feeling a little squiffy after the champagne and wondering if I had indeed misjudged my mother; she'd put on such a good show that I had genuinely felt sorry for her. It took the bus ride home for the gloss to wear off and for me to realize that she was yet again manipulating me, and I'd fallen for it.

She had asked almost nothing about *my* life apart from the basics of where I lived and worked. Even though I'd been ready to tell her about Freddie and my love for him, the subject had never come up. She had been far too busy describing her own glamorous life, as she flitted around Europe with Alessandro to some glittering event or other. Needing a night alone, I telephoned Freddie at his flat to say I'd be staying at mine tonight and sat in my bedroom drinking tea to try to sober up and think.

And when I did, my heart began to harden all over again. I decided there would be no spending Christmas at the palazzo, or joining them in Italy next summer...Maman wasn't trying to make it up to *me*, she was trying to make *herself* feel better for the way she'd abandoned me.

"You survived the past thirteen years without her, Posy—you can survive the next," I said, brushing my tears away harshly.

There was a knock on my door and Estelle poked her head into my room.

"You okay, Posy?"

I shrugged.

"Anything I can help with?"

"Yes. Do you think you can ever stop loving a parent? I mean, even if they do terrible things to you, is that love still there?"

"Golly, Posy, that's a deep one." Estelle came to sit next to me on the bed. "Andrea and her English degree might be able to help you more."

"Love isn't technical though, is it? It's not something that you can quantify. It just...*is.*"

"Yes, you're right of course, and as to your question, I really don't know, Posy. I mean, I adore my parents, so it's not something I've ever had to think about, but at the end of the day, I suppose you can choose your friends, but not your family. You don't *have* to like them, though when it comes to love, especially with a mother, perhaps it is simply there forever, however badly they behave towards you. It's unconditional, isn't it?"

"Yes, I suppose it is, which is a shame actually, because I'd much prefer not to love her."

"So the meeting was difficult?"

"No, it was perfect," I smiled. "And that was the problem. I just don't want to be let down by her again. And if she thinks she can come waltzing back into my life after all these years...She asked me to go shopping with her tomorrow!"

"Well, that might be worth doing, Posy. From what you've said, she has plenty of money."

Estelle, ever the pragmatist, gave me a small smile.

"I don't want to be bought, Estelle, and that's what she would be doing. And then she'd think that we'd made up and that everything was fine."

"I understand. Well, the good news is that she lives in Italy and is not going to darken your doorstep very often. Out of sight is out of mind, after all."

"So you don't think I'm being churlish?"

"Not at all, no. She abandoned you when when you'd just lost your father. A few pretty dresses thirteen years on can't make up for that."

"Thank you, Estelle," I said, turning to her. "She made me feel so guilty for not immediately saying yes to her offer of me visiting."

"Well, don't feel guilty, Posy. *She* is meant to be the grown-up, not you. Right, I must be off. I have a date!" Estelle said, her eyes shining.

"You look excited. Is he the principal dancer at Covent Garden?"

"No, and that's why I *am* excited. Believe it or not, he has a proper job. He does something in the City with stocks and shares. He wears a suit, which of course I'm dying to rip off him, but I get the feeling he's awfully proper."

"You're saying he's normal?"

"Deliciously so," Estelle giggled as she walked towards the door. "I'm off to dig out my most decorous dress."

"Tell me all next time I see you," I called.

"Will do!"

"So, what are your plans for Christmas, Posy?" Freddie asked me as we drank tea at a cafe in between his Saturday matinee and evening performance.

"I'll be going home to my grandmother's in Cornwall as always,"

I told him. "What about you?"

"Oh, I suppose I'm on my way back to Mother's for our usual miserable couple of days. I've told you she suffers from her nerves, haven't I? And Christmas and New Year just happen to be a particularly bad time for her. At least this year, I have a genuine excuse! I'll only have to get through three days there, as we have performances right up to New Year."

Freddie never said much about his home life, or his childhood (which I'd gathered had been difficult from the little he *had* said), so even though I'd waxed lyrical to him about Daddy and how wonderful he had been to me before he died in the war, I'd refrained from enlarging on my own childhood. If we ever touched on it, he would always tell me that the past was irrelevant and we should both look to the future, which suited me fine.

"So you wouldn't have time to come to Cornwall?"

"Sadly no, though I would love to. Your Christmases sound utter bliss."

"Oh, they're not grand or anything, Freddie, just very...Christmassy, I suppose. And I really would love you to come and meet Granny."

"I promise I will as soon as this blasted run is over," Freddie sighed. "I'm sick of it, Posy, really I am. Hanging around in my dressing room for hours just to say my four lines. And I'm sure that damned actor I'm understudying has decided not to get sick on purpose. Everyone else has caught the cast cold except for him. I was hoping to bring agents in to see me play the role."

"Well, at least you're employed, which is something."

"Yes, and earning next to nothing," he added morosely. "Seriously, Posy, I'm thinking of throwing in the towel and going to Bar School next September if nothing happens in the next few months. I mean, man—and woman—can't live by sardines alone, can they?"

"I have my salary, Freddie, and we get by, don't we?"

"Yes, we do, but even though I like to pretend I'm all for equality and it doesn't matter which of the two of us earns it, I'm not sure I'm comfortable with being a kept man."

"Oops," I smiled at him, "there's that whiff of the traditionalist about you again."

"Yes, and I freely admit it. I've had my foray into the acting world and at least I can say that I've tried. But I was thinking only this morning, that actually, what is being a barrister, other than standing up and performing in front of an audience? The difference is that you get awfully well paid for your troubles, and might even do some good in the world to boot. Acting really is the most vacuous profession, isn't it? I mean, it's all about oneself."

"I suppose it is, yes, although it does give a lot of pleasure to other people; lifts them out of the grim reality of their own lives for a few hours."

"You're right, of course," he agreed. "Perhaps I'm just getting old, but one day, I'd like to provide you with a nice home and enough money to have a couple of children."

I lowered my eyes so he could not see them fill with pleasure. I couldn't think of anything I wanted more than to marry Freddie and spend the rest of my life with him. I'd even caught myself looking at bridal gowns in women's magazines.

"We'd do all right together, wouldn't we, you and I?" I looked up and he smiled at me.

"I think so, yes. You...wouldn't ever stop me working though, would you?"

"Of course not! I mean, I'd obviously hope that you'd take a week or two off if we ever had children, and I'd have to be earning far more than you, of course, but..."

I thumped Freddie playfully on the arm, knowing he was teasing me. He looked at his watch.

"Right, I'd better get back to my prison cell of a dressing room before the half-hour call. Bye-bye, darling girl, see you later at the flat."

I watched him thread his way through the tables and saw a couple of females glance up at him as he passed. He really was extraordinarily handsome and I wondered for the umpteenth time how on earth I'd managed to have him as mine.

"He's just perfect," I murmured to myself as I decided to walk along Regent Street and look at the department stores' Christmas window displays. The street was crowded with people doing the same thing as me, and the hot-chestnut sellers were attracting a roaring trade.

"Tonight, I love being alive," I said to the chestnut as I popped it into my mouth, then ran for the bus that would take me back to Freddie's flat in Clapham.

The night before I was due to catch the train home to Cornwall was a bittersweet one. Even though I was looking forward to seeing Granny and Daisy, I realized that Freddie and I had barely spent a night apart in the past four months. Freddie arrived home from the theater and joined me in bed, making love to me with what felt like extra passion.

"God, I'm going to miss you desperately," he said, stroking my hair as I lay in his arms afterwards. "Posy, darling girl, will you marry me?" he whispered into my ear.

"I...are you being serious?" I moved my head so I could look at him in the flickering light of the candle.

"Of course I am!" Freddie looked affronted. "I'd hardly jest about something like that. Well?"

"Is that it, then? No going down on bended knee?" I teased him, my heart simply bursting through my skin with excitement and love.

"If that is what madam requires, then so be it."

I watched as he sighed, climbed out of bed, then sank to one knee in front of me. He took my hand in his and looked up at me sitting on the mattress. "Darling Posy, I—"

"As this is a formal proposal, I feel you should use my proper name."

"What proper name?" He frowned at me.

"The one that's on my birth certificate, of course. Posy is only a nickname, you see."

"Right. So, what is the name on your birth certificate?"

"Adriana Rose Anderson."

"Adriana Anderson?" His eyes flickered away from me, seemingly confused.

"I know, it's hideous. I'm afraid I was named after my mother. Anyway, you only have to use it twice—once now and then on the wedding day. So...?"

Freddie turned his eyes back to me, then gave me what seemed like a rather desolate shrug.

"I...well, I think that you're right, Posy. I should do this properly. With some clothes on, you know?" he chuckled nervously as he stood up.

"Oh Freddie, I was only teasing. You don't really need to call me by my proper name or anything."

"No, when you come back in for the New Year, I'll...arrange something."

He climbed in beside me and I blew out the candle as I snuggled into his arms.

"You seem upset, darling," I whispered.

"No, no, not at all. I'm just tired after two shows, that's all."

"Posy?" he asked, just as I was starting to drop off. "What was the name of the house you lived in as a child in Suffolk?"

"It was called Admiral House," I murmured sleepily. "Goodnight, darling Freddie."

It was wonderful to be home with Granny in Cornwall, and Christmas passed in the traditional manner it always had.

"So when am I to meet this Freddie of yours?" Granny asked me after I'd turned the conversation back to something he'd said or done for the umpteenth time.

"When he's finished his play in London. He told me to tell you he's really looking forward to it."

"Well, it's obvious that you're totally smitten. Of course I can't help but worry a little that he's an actor and all that entails. It's hardly the most reliable of professions, is it?"

"Freddie has already said that he'll almost certainly go to Bar School in September. He wants to provide for me properly, so please don't worry about that, Granny."

"So you think he will make an honest woman out of you, Posy?"

"Oh yes, we've talked about it already. Underneath it all, he's awfully traditional, you see."

"And you've never regretted breaking off your engagement to Jonny?"

"Oh no, Granny, not once."

"He was a very nice man, Posy. He would have made you an excellent husband."

"So will Freddie."

"If he asks you."

"Granny, he already has, unofficially, at least."

"Forgive me, Posy, I just worry a little that you might have said goodbye to Jonny and live to regret it. I fully understand the thrall of newfound passion, but in my view, slow and steady often wins the race."

"Granny, just because Freddie is trying his hand as an actor does not make him a flighty bohemian. When you meet him, you'll understand, I promise. Now, I must go to bed before Father Christmas arrives." I smiled as I stood up and went to kiss her. "Goodnight, darling Granny."

I spent all of Christmas Day waiting for Freddie to make his promised phone call, though for some reason it did not come. I put it down to a glitch at the telephone exchange, knowing there must be a barrage of calls going backwards and forwards between households across the land, and our line had never been the most reliable.

"He'll phone tomorrow, I'm sure he will," I comforted myself as I went to sleep that night.

I was out on Boxing Day morning to visit Katie in the tiny cottage that she shared with her husband and two children.

"They are utterly adorable." I smiled as Mary, the toddler, climbed onto my knee for a cuddle while Katie fed the newborn Jack. "I just can't believe you have two already. I don't feel old enough to be a mother."

"Well, comes with the territory, doesn't it?" Katie shrugged. "Judas, it's hard work though. All I long for is a night's sleep."

"Does Thomas help you with the children?"

"You jesting me?" She rolled her eyes. "He's down at the pub most nights."

As I left to walk back home, I thought that Katie wasn't exactly a walking advertisement for motherhood. Usually so immaculate, her greasy hair had been scraped back in an elastic band and she'd still been in her dressing gown at eleven o'clock.

I hope I never let myself go like that when Freddie and I have children, I thought as I entered the Manor House and went into the kitchen, where Daisy was making her traditional leftovers stew.

"Anyone telephone for me while I was out, Daisy?"

"No, Miss Posy, sorry."

"Oh, right. Anything I can do?"

"No, it's all under control, thank you."

Granny had the vicar and his wife over for lunch, but I was distracted, wondering why on earth Freddie hadn't telephoned me to wish me a belated Happy Christmas. Then I started to worry that some accident had befallen him, that he could be lying in hospital somewhere, in pain and alone...

"Granny, would it be all right if I telephoned Freddie's flat in London? I'm rather concerned that I haven't heard from him."

"Of course, my dear," Granny agreed.

I went up to retrieve my address book, then dialed the number with shaking hands. It was a communal phone, which serviced the three flats in the converted house and sat in the hallway.

"Please someone answer," I whispered, just wanting to know that he was all right.

"Hello, Clapham 6951."

"Hello, is that Alan?"

"It is, yes."

"Alan, it's me, Posy," I said to Freddie's flatmate. "Is Freddie there?"

"No, Posy, I thought you knew he was going home to see his mother for a couple of days. He should be back after the show tonight, though."

"I see. It's just that I was a little worried that something had happened, because I hadn't heard from him. Would you leave him a message to telephone me as soon as he gets in tonight? Tell him it doesn't matter how late it is."

"Will do, Posy. And I'm absolutely sure he's fine. You know what Christmas can be like."

"Of course I do, yes. Thank you, Alan, and see you soon."

"Bye now, Posy."

I came away from the phone feeling rather silly. Of course nothing had happened to Freddie; he'd probably been busy with his mother. At least now I'd hear from him later. Feeling relieved, I went to join Granny for a game of cards.

Even though I stayed awake long past midnight, sitting on the bottom stair opposite the table on which the telephone was placed so I would not miss the call, it remained resolutely silent.

As I walked miserably back upstairs, dark and terrible thoughts filled my head. Freddie had never yet not returned a call. After a sleepless night, I knew there was only one thing to be done. By the time Granny came down for breakfast, I was packed and ready to go to the railway station.

"I'm dreadfully sorry, Granny darling, but one of my friends has been taken into hospital in London, and I really must go back to see her. She's at death's door, apparently," I lied.

"Really? I didn't hear the telephone ring last night or this morning."

"Then I'm glad it didn't disturb you, Granny."

"Will you return to see in the New Year here or not?"

"I think it depends how my friend is. I'll let you know as soon as I can. Now, I must dash if I want to catch the nine o'clock. Bye-bye, darling Granny, and I hope to see you soon."

"Safe journey, Posy dear," she called to me as I ran out of the front door, where Bill had already got the old Ford running and my suitcase stashed in the boot.

Granny didn't believe me, I knew, but it couldn't be helped. Whatever had happened to Freddie, I simply couldn't bear to spend another five days here not knowing.

When the train eventually pulled into Paddington station, I caught the underground to Baron's Court and staggered up the many steps to the flat to deposit my heavy case and freshen up before going to Freddie's. Estelle had obviously had a party last night, for there was the telltale detritus in the sitting room. I ignored it, used the bathroom and then went into my bedroom.

There, sitting on my pillow, was an envelope. I recognized Freddie's writing immediately. My fingers were shaking so much that I could hardly tear the envelope open. With tears blurring my eyes already, I began to read.

My dearest Posy,
I'll keep this short and sweet. When I proposed to you just

before you left for Cornwall, you may have seen that I was in rather a queer mood afterwards. Perhaps saying the words for real made me realize that you and I are simply not destined to be. Even though I had thought I was ready to settle down and commit to marriage and domesticity, I find that I am not. Dearest Posy, it is all me, not you, I promise, but for your sake, I want you to believe that there can be no chance of any kind of future for us.

Sorry to sound harsh, but I want to make sure that you put me from your thoughts as soon as you can and find someone else who truly deserves you. Equally, I won't ask for your forgiveness, because I don't deserve such a thing.

I wish you a long and happy life,

Freddie

I felt my breaths coming in short sharp bursts, my heart pumping madly to provide enough oxygen to accommodate them. I put my head between my legs to try and stem the dizziness before I fainted clean away.

Surely, this was some kind of malevolent practical joke? Not a single word of it sounded like the Freddie I'd known and loved. It was as if an evil imposter devil had inhabited his soul, forcing him to write the cold, callous words down onto the page. I could read it a hundred thousand times over and I knew I would find no warmth contained in it. He might just as well have written *I don't love you any more* and left it at that.

Once the dizziness abated, I lay down weakly on my pillow, too shocked to cry. I just didn't, *couldn't* understand what had happened in the brief few minutes from our lovemaking and his proposal, to his strange behavior afterwards. The only explanation was that saying the words out loud had indeed made him realize it wasn't love. *Unless*, I thought, another surge of pain ripping into my tortured heart, *he'd met someone else...*

Yes. That was the only explanation for his total change of heart. Could it be that young, attractive actress in the play? I'd been sure I'd seen her shooting admiring glances at Freddie when we'd gone out en masse with the cast for a drink after the show. Or maybe the props girl, with her jet-black hair, her eyeliner and red lipstick...

"Stop it, Posy," I moaned to myself, shaking my head backwards and forwards on the pillow. Whatever the reason, the words that lay on the page told me our affair was categorically over, and the future that had been mine three days ago hung about me in shreds.

I stood up, grabbed the letter and rolled it aggressively into a tight ball. Then I carried it with the tips of my fingers, as though it might wound me further, into the sitting room. I threw it into the fireplace, took a match to it, and watched it burn to ash in the grate.

Perhaps I could pretend I hadn't received it, turn up tonight at the stage door as if nothing had happened...

No, Posy, then you would just have to hear him say the same words he wrote, which would make the pain worse...

I walked into the kitchen to see what I could salvage from last night's party. Picking up a glass, I poured a large measure out of the gin bottle and added what was left of the vermouth, then swallowed it down in one. I poured myself some more—anything to numb the pain—and some more after that. An hour later, I collapsed on my bed, my head spinning, and not long after I leaned over the side of my bed and vomited all over the floor. I didn't even care because nothing mattered any longer. My golden future with the man that I loved would never happen. And nothing would matter ever again.

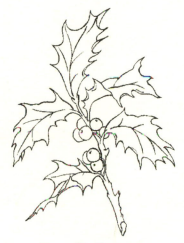

Holly
(Ilex aquifolium)

Chapter 31

December

When Posy arrived home the evening after Sam's arrest, exhausted from a sleepless night of thinking about her son and a busy day at the gallery, she found an envelope lying on the kitchen table underneath a bottle of champagne. She sat down wearily to open it.

Dear Posy,

The first draft of the book is finished, so I've completed what I came to Admiral House to do. I apologize profusely for leaving without saying goodbye in person, but unfortunately, my schedule demands it. Enclosed is my rent until the end of December, with a little more for all those bottles of wine you've so kindly shared with me. I have put my address and telephone number at the top of this letter. Please, if you ever find yourself in London, look me up and I'll take you for a slap-up lunch.

Posy, you are a very special lady. You deserve great happiness and your family are extraordinarily lucky to have you. Just remember to put yourself first sometimes, will you?

Much love and thanks,

Sebastian

P.S. I will send you a proof copy of the novel. You might recognize parts of your beautiful house!

Posy drew the money out of the envelope and saw Sebastian had enclosed at least double what he owed her. Tears pricked the backs of her eyes. Apart from the fact she'd miss him dreadfully, she was surprised at the way he'd left so hurriedly, with no warning at all.

As Posy put the kettle on the stove, she could feel the atmosphere in the house had changed already. Even though Sebastian had spent much of his time upstairs, the presence of another person had been palpable. She was back to being alone. Ordinarily, she would have been fine—after all, she'd lived in this house for many years by herself. But tonight, what with Sam and the bloodstains she'd seen on the wall in the Folly, she wasn't just alone, she was lonely. And she needed someone to talk to. Making a quick call, then taking the shepherd's pie she'd made for Sebastian's supper earlier and grabbing the bottle of champagne, Posy left the house, walked to her car, and set off to see Freddie.

"Come in, come in," Freddie said as he ushered her in through the door.

"Thank you, Freddie. I brought a shepherd's pie. It just needs warming through in the oven."

"What a treat," he smiled, taking it from her. "I was about to have scrambled egg on toast."

"I'm not disturbing you, am I?" Posy asked him as she followed him through to the kitchen.

"Not at all." Freddie glanced at the champagne bottle. "Are we celebrating?"

"Unfortunately not, no. That was a parting gift from Sebastian. He's upped and left out of the blue."

"Really? That surprises me. He seemed such a steady sort of a fellow, but I suppose one can never tell with these artistic types. Should we open it?"

"Why not?" Posy sighed. "I'm sure it's just as good for commiserating as celebrating."

"Well, I shall open it while you put the pie in the oven. Then you can tell me what's happened."

"It's Sam, Freddie. He was arrested last night at the Victoria Hotel in Norfolk and charged with fraud."

"I see," said Freddie, hoping his face didn't betray the fact he'd already heard this from Sebastian. He retrieved two champagne glasses from the cupboard.

"He's out on bail," Posy continued, "and his solicitor thinks if he's prepared to give evidence against his former partner, he may not be charged, but it's up to the CPS to decide."

"I wouldn't hold your breath, Posy. Certainly when I left, the backlog on criminal cases such as this was months. This partner of his—dodgy, was he?"

"Obviously. I don't know the details, but the point is that, as well as my son being arrested this morning, the sale of Admiral House is down the drain. Thank you, Freddie," she added as he handed her a champagne glass. "I'm not sure what to toast to."

"To life perhaps? To the fact that despite everything, no one died last night and from the sound of it, Sam will hopefully walk away with a ticking off from the judge. There simply isn't room to put all the petty criminals away, Posy."

"My son, a criminal," Posy shuddered. "Will he have a record?"

"He might, yes, but there's no point in thinking about that now. There's a long way to go yet. To you, Posy," Freddie toasted and took a sip of champagne.

They ate the shepherd's pie at the table in the conservatory, and Posy noticed Freddie seemed quieter than usual.

"Coffee?" he asked her.

"Thank you."

They took their cups into the sitting room and sat down in front of the fire.

"Are you all right, Freddie? You seem...unlike yourself."

"Yes, I do, don't I? Well, perhaps that's because I am."

"Can you tell me why?"

He looked at her, his eyes full of sadness. "Posy, I...Well now, how does one put this? I have something I need to tell you. I've delayed and delayed, waiting for the right moment, but I really feel I can't hold it in any longer. Something that perhaps I should have told you fifty years ago, but now is hardly a good time."

"Goodness, Freddie, you look dreadfully serious. If it was to do with another girl back then, please don't worry. It was an awfully long time ago."

"No, Posy, unfortunately for both of us, it's nothing like that."

"Then please, spit it out. One way and another, it seems to be all bad news at the moment, so I doubt more will make any difference."

Freddie stood up and walked over to Posy. He offered his hand to her. "I'm afraid that I think this might. And before I tell you, because there really is no good time, I want you to know that I loved you then and I love you now. But I simply can't keep this dreadful secret to myself any longer."

"Please, Freddie, you're scaring me now. Just tell me, will you?" Posy urged him.

"All right." Freddie went back to his chair. He took a sip of brandy before he said, "It's about your father, Posy."

"My father?" Posy frowned. "What about my father?"

"Posy, my dear, I'm afraid there's no other way to say this; your father did not die flying his Spitfire as you were told. He..." Freddie struggled to find the words. "He, well, he was found guilty of murder and..." He paused and gave a long, deep sigh.

Posy's head was spinning as she stared at him. "What, Freddie? Just tell me, for goodness' sake."

"He was hanged for his crime. I am so terribly, terribly sorry, but believe me, it's the truth."

Posy closed her eyes for a moment, feeling breathless and dizzy. "Freddie, dear, I think you may have your wires crossed here. My father was killed in his Spitfire. He was a hero, not a murderer. I promise you."

"No, Posy, that is what you were told when you were a little girl, but it was a lie." Freddie stood up, went to the small desk that sat under the window and took a file from one of the drawers. "It's all in here." He opened the file and pulled out a photocopy of a newspaper cutting. "Here, Posy, take a look."

Posy grabbed the sheet of paper and saw her father's face, then the headline above it.

LAWRENCE ANDERSON FOUND GUILTY OF MURDER!

"Oh my God, oh my God..." Posy let go of the piece of paper and it fluttered to the floor. "No! I don't believe it. Why would everyone lie to me?"

"Here, have some brandy." Freddie proffered her a glass, but she refused it.

"I don't understand, Freddie. Why did no one tell me?" she

repeated.

"Because they were trying to protect you. You were only eight years old, and from everything you've told me, both back when I first met you and now, it was obvious that you adored him."

"Of course I did, he was my father! He was the most gentle man, we used to collect butterflies together...he wouldn't murder another human being. My God!" Posy wrung her hands. "Why did he?"

"It was a crime of passion, Posy. He got leave for the New Year of 1944 and went home to surprise your mother. When he arrived at Admiral House, he found her with...another man upstairs in the Folly, in flagrante. He took out one of his hunting guns from the cupboard downstairs and shot the man against the wall at point-blank range."

Posy looked down at the black-and-white photograph lying on the floor beneath her. It showed her father obviously being led away from the court in handcuffs. She couldn't speak, or begin to think straight.

"I'm so desperately, desperately sorry to tell you this, Posy."

"Then why did you?" She looked up at him. "Why on earth did you?!"

"I had to, you see. The man he murdered—his name was Ralph Lennox—he was my father."

Posy closed her eyes, trying to keep calm and take deep breaths. She could not, *would not* take this in.

Ralph...the name spun around her mind as it scudded back over sixty years to her childhood. And there he was. Uncle Ralph, her father's best friend, the man who used to bring her chocolate when he visited her mother...Freddie's father.

"Posy, are you all right? Please, I know how dreadful the shock must be. But don't you see? I had to tell you if we were to take this relationship any further. I didn't...*couldn't* tell you all those years ago. Perhaps in retrospect, alarm bells should have rung when I heard your surname and that you originally hailed from Suffolk. But I was so enchanted by you, they simply didn't. I only realized who you were when you told me what your real name was in bed that night, when I proposed to you. I knew how you adored your father, and that you thought he'd died flying his plane during a sortie, so I had no choice but to walk away. I knew the shock of how and why your father really died would break you, and I simply couldn't bear to be the one to tell you. Which makes me either cowardly or over-protective...I'm not sure which," Freddie sighed. "But I couldn't have married you without you knowing. Please, Posy, say something."

Posy opened her eyes and looked at him.

"I wonder how you can bear the sight of me. The daughter of the man who shot and killed your father."

"Good Lord, Posy! That was nothing to do with you, nor did I think it was, either then or now. It was just a twist of fate that we would find each other in the future. I...loved you then as I love you now, and I beg you to forgive me for telling you the truth after all these years. When I met you again, I presumed you knew; that living back here in Suffolk in the house in which it all happened, someone local would have mentioned it to you, but they obviously didn't."

"No, they didn't." Posy stood up abruptly. "Excuse me, Freddie, but I must go home now. Thank you for telling me, and I understand why you did. But really, I must go."

"Of course. Can I drive you there, Posy? You're in no fit state to—"

"No, I'm quite capable of driving myself."

"Here, please take the file. Perhaps once the shock has worn off, you'll wish to confirm what I've told you." Freddie followed her to the hallway, where she was already putting on her coat, and handed the file to her. "I'm so desperately sorry, Posy. I wouldn't upset you for the world. I hope you know that. But I had to—"

"Yes." Posy had already opened the door. "Please leave me alone. Goodnight, Freddie."

Chapter 32

Tammy woke up on the second Saturday in December and realized it had been three weeks since she'd found out about Nick's deception. It felt like months. Even though she was snowed under at work, and had just hired an assistant to be in the shop whilst she hunted for stock, she'd managed to take little, if any, joy out of the burgeoning success of her business. She was also aware that she needed to go to Southwold to retrieve the vintage dresses at Admiral House. But how could she face going back there?

"It's business, Tammy, and you'll just have to," she told herself firmly. Wardrobes of vintage clothes did not appear every day, and even though she had put an advert in *The Lady* magazine to attract women of a certain age wanting to sell their old gowns for cash, the response had been patchy. Last night as she'd lain sleepless, trying to divert her thoughts from Nick, she'd come up with what she thought was a rather good idea: the one gown women usually kept was their wedding dress. What if she started a bridal section in the boutique, choosing only the best vintage gems?

"Marriage—hah!" she muttered as she took a sip from the now lukewarm tea Meena had brought her earlier.

Despite herself, Tammy was astounded there had been no word from Nick. Even though she didn't want to see him—of course she didn't—she'd thought at the very least she might have the satisfaction of telling him to his face what a bastard he was. The fact he'd not even bothered to contact her had only compounded the situation, making her feel angry and devastated in equal measure.

She also felt animosity toward anyone who had ever told her what a great guy Nick was, feeling in some way that they had helped to lead her further up the garden path. Subsequently, she had hidden away, not answering calls from anyone who had colluded in the deception. She'd packed up Nick's clothes and the general clutter that had collected in her flat over the past couple of months and stuffed everything into bin bags. Even though she felt like burning the contents, Tammy had decided to bring the bags to the boutique and drop them off on Paul and Jane's doorstep afterwards, ringing the bell to alert them, then beating a hasty retreat.

In the same spirit, Tammy took a deep breath and dialed Posy's number on her mobile. The line rang and rang, and there was no answering machine to leave a message. So she gritted her teeth and tried Amy's mobile instead.

"Hello, it's Sara," said a high voice.

"Hello, Sara, is your Mummy in?"

"Yes, but she's washing cos I dropped ketchup on my dungarees and—"

"Hello?"

"Is that Amy?"

"Yes, who's this?"

"It's Tammy."

"Oh, hi." Amy's voice sounded dull and monotone. "Did you get my messages?"

"Yes. Sorry, Amy, it's been busy here and—"

"There's no need to explain. I just wanted to let you know that I saw Nick that night after you left Admiral House. He knows you know about his car being parked outside Evie's house. If it makes you feel any better, he was in a terrible state."

"Not really, no, but thanks."

"Have you heard from him?" Amy asked quietly.

"No, and I really don't want to talk about it."

"I understand."

"Actually, I was just calling as I need to get in touch with Posy about collecting her mother's clothes. She must be moving out soon."

"No, she's not. It's all off, Tammy. The sale's fallen through."

"Oh dear—what happened?"

"It's...a long story."

Tammy heard Amy sigh down the line. She sounded as low as she felt herself.

"Are you okay?"

"Not really, but never mind."

"Well, if I manage to get in touch with Posy and arrange a time to collect the vintage dresses, why don't you and I have lunch?"

"I'd like that," Amy answered feebly.

"Is Posy at Admiral House?"

"I think so, yes. What with one thing and another, I haven't been to see her in over a week. I'll give her a call too and if I don't get any reply, I'll pop round to check she's all right."

"Thanks, Amy. Let's keep in touch anyway. Bye now."

"Bye."

"Fresh cup of tea for you?" Meena poked her head round the office door.

"Please," Tammy replied, and watched as the older woman left the office. Tammy had told Meena immediately that she and Nick were over to prevent his name being mentioned in the future. Meena had not broached the subject since, but Tammy knew she cared for her in other ways: she'd arrived with a fresh bunch of flowers for her one morning, appeared with cakes to tempt her appetite at tea-time, and had given her an exquisite scarf she'd embroidered herself as she said it matched her eyes.

Tammy received the cup of tea gratefully and spent the next forty-five minutes on the computer looking at the finances. Even though the takings had been up on her original forecast, budgeting for the extra stock she'd need, coupled with employing Meena *and* a part-time shop assistant, was proving a drain.

"Speculate to accumulate," Tammy muttered. Then she left the shop to make the ten-minute drive round to Paul and Jane's house. She noticed the Christmas lights had been placed on the trees in Sloane Square. It looked idyllic, and she wanted to tear down every single bulb with her bare hands.

She parked the car and took the bin bags out of the boot. She dumped them on the doorstep, rang the bell and was walking away swiftly when Paul opened the front door.

"Hi, Tam. Not stopping to say hello?" Paul raised an eyebrow as he eyed the bulging bin bags. "What on earth is in all these? A dead body?"

"I wish. It's Nick's stuff."

"I see. Why are you bringing it here?"

"Because this is where he lives, isn't it?" she said, still hovering from a safe distance.

"Alas, no longer. He packed up his goods and chattels a couple of days ago when Jane and I were away in the country. He left a note saying thank you and a rather good bottle of brandy, and I haven't seen him since. I have to say, we both presumed he'd taken the plunge and moved in full-time with you."

"No, he hasn't."

"Oh." Paul looked bemused. "Where is he, then?"

"I have absolutely no idea."

"I see. Drink? I promise the Nick-coast is clear. And Janey's out on a night shoot."

"Go on then," Tammy sighed, feeling in sudden, urgent need of one. She followed Paul down the hallway to the kitchen.

He opened a bottle of wine and poured them both a glass. "What's happened, Tammy?"

"Do you mind if I don't go into it?"

"If you don't want to, that's fine," Paul agreed. "I must admit in retrospect that it was all rather strange. I tried to call in at his shop yesterday, and the place is locked up. I could swear he said he was opening this week."

"Yes, he was," agreed Tammy.

Paul took a slug of his wine. "Well, if he's not with us or you, and the showroom is closed up, one can only presume he's gone away."

"Probably."

"Well, I do hope the old boy's all right."

"Personally, Paul, I hope he rots in hell."

"So, I presume the two of you...?"

"Are over, for good." Tammy drained her glass. "Anyway, thanks for the wine. Is Janey well?"

"Blooming," smiled Paul.

"Tell her I'm sorry I haven't spoken to her recently, and I'll call her tomorrow," Tammy said as she walked back down the hall towards the front door.

"Tammy?"

"Yes?"

"Take care of yourself. And keep in touch."

"I will. Thanks, Paul."

Chapter 33

Amy put the phone down after speaking to Tammy and thought that at least a lunch with her offered a bright spot amongst the pall of gray that currently hung over her life. She went back into the sitting room where Jake and Sara were excitedly hanging decorations all over the bottom branches of the tatty fake Christmas tree Amy had taken down from the loft earlier in the day.

"Maybe I could put some decorations on a little higher up the tree, chaps?" she suggested, trying to garner some enthusiasm for their sakes.

"No, me and Sara like it like this," said Jake firmly.

"Okay, okay," nodded Amy. It hardly mattered what the tree looked like anyway. They were not exactly entertaining at home over Christmas.

"I'm going to cook some lunch," she told them.

"After, can we make my angel costume like you promised, Mummy?" said Sara timidly.

"Of course we can." She kissed Sara on the top of her golden curls and left them to the tree. She put the sausages under the grill, then tried to reach Posy again, but both her landline and mobile went to answering machines. Amy slumped into a kitchen chair and rested her head on her arms. Even though the children were demanding, noisy and totally unaware of their parents' travails, Amy thanked God she had them. They kept her busy and took her mind off other things. She really thought that, without them, she couldn't have gone on.

The past two weeks had undoubtedly been the worst of her life. Sam had taken up residence on the sofa, watching TV morning, noon and night, silent most of the time and only answering her with a "yes" or "no." She'd tentatively suggested he go to the doctor to get some tablets to ease his obvious depression, but he'd completely ignored her.

When she'd eventually plucked up the courage to suggest that he could try looking for a job—which might help take his mind off his problems, not to mention ease their financial situation—he'd looked at her as if she was mad.

"Do you really think anyone would take me on, with a court case coming up and the state I'm in?!"

"Sam, you know your solicitor has told you they're almost certainly not going to press charges. They've accepted you knew nothing about Ken Noakes and his past."

"They could still change their minds, Amy. Bloody CPS—I've just got to sit here for what could be months and wait until they decide."

"Lunch!" she called to Sam and the children from the kitchen. Sara and Jake bounced in and sat up at the table.

"Bring mine in here on a tray, Amy," Sam called back from the sitting room.

Amy did so, then sat with the children, listening to them chatter on about Father Christmas and what he would bring them.

She swallowed the lump in her throat, knowing there was simply no money for expensive presents. She'd had to delve into her hidden stash just to keep them all fed. Having done the washing up, she went into the sitting room, where Sam was still sprawled on the sofa as the children squabbled over who would hang the last bauble.

"Sam, have you heard from your mum recently?"

"What?!" He looked up at her. "Are you completely crazy, Amy? After what I've done, I doubt she'll ever speak to me again."

"You know that's not true. She was very understanding when you went to see her after you'd been arrested."

Sam shrugged morosely and took a swig from his bottle of beer.

"I just tried both numbers again, and she still wasn't picking up.

I'll try the gallery," she said, walking back into the kitchen. "See if she's working an extra shift because of Christmas."

Amy did so, and after a brief conversation with the gallery owner, went to get her coat from the peg on the wall.

"Mr. Grieves says your mum called in sick ten days ago, and he hasn't heard from her since. I'm going round there now. Can you mind the children for a bit?"

She got the usual shrug, and before she burst with fury at his lack of concern for his mother—or in fact, for anyone but himself—she left the house.

She drove along the High Street, trying to take pleasure from the pretty lights framing the shop windows and the bustle of excitement on the crowded pavements. It was simply a relief to get out of the house, even if she was deeply concerned about Posy. It was so unlike her mother-in-law not to call to check in or answer her mobile. And, buried deep in her own problems, Amy realized she hadn't noticed.

"Please be okay, darling Posy," she begged the darkening skies.

When she arrived at Admiral House, Amy saw Posy's car sitting in the drive. She walked round to the kitchen door, hoping her sense of dread was manufactured from stress and not real. The kitchen was in darkness and the radio—which was permanently tuned to Radio 4 and normally talked to itself in the background—was unusually silent.

"Posy? It's Amy. Where are you?" she called as she went into the morning room to find that deserted too.

Having searched all the downstairs rooms—including the loo—Amy continued to call Posy's name as she walked up the stairs. The master bedroom door was shut and as she tapped on it, her imagination conjured up visions of what she might find behind it. Receiving no answer, she garnered some courage and pushed it open, almost crying with relief to see the bed empty and neatly made. She then made a sweep of all the other rooms, pausing in the bedroom Sebastian had used when he'd been here and made love to her so gently...

"Stop it!" she hissed to herself, then turned and left to check the attic floor above. That too was deserted, and it was clear that Posy wasn't at home. Yet her car was...

Running back down the endless flights of stairs, Amy tore along the corridors towards the kitchen, her head full of images of Posy having collapsed days ago in the garden, lying there alone and in pain, or even worse...

"Hello, Amy," a familiar voice said as she entered the kitchen. The lights were now on and Posy stood by the stove in her Barbour, warming her hands and waiting for the kettle to boil.

"Oh my God! Oh my God, Posy!" Amy panted and sat down heavily on a chair. "I thought you were, I thought you were..."

"Dead?" Posy looked at Amy and smiled, but it didn't quite reach her eyes.

"Yes, to be honest. Where have you been? You haven't been answering the phone, you haven't been at work..."

"I've been here. Tea?"

"I'd love one, thank you."

Amy studied Posy. She looked the same physically, but something about her was different. It was as if all her joie de vivre—which encompassed not only her zest for life, but her kindness and concern for those around her—had been sucked out.

"There." Posy put the mug down in front of Amy. "I'm afraid I only have biscuits from a shop. I haven't done any baking recently."

"I'm fine, really."

She watched as Posy poured her own tea, but didn't move to join Amy at the table as she usually would. "Have you been ill?" she ventured.

"No, I'm in my usual fine fettle, thank you," Posy replied.

Amy realized she'd never had to "lead" a conversation with her mother-in-law before, and she was struggling. Posy was normally so interested in hearing her news.

"What have you been doing?"

"I've been in the garden mostly."

"Right."

A silence fell between them and Amy didn't know how to fill it.

"Posy, is it about Sam and what happened?" she asked eventually. "I'm so sorry, I mean, I'm sure you'll get another buyer and—"

"It's not about Sam, Amy. For once, it's actually about me."

"Oh, right. Is it anything I can help with?"

"No, dear, but thank you for asking. I've just had something I needed to think about, that's all."

"About the house?"

"I suppose that is part of it, yes."

Amy sipped her tea, realizing that she wasn't going to get any further information out of Posy.

"Tammy's been trying to contact you about coming to collect your mother's old clothes."

"Actually, I've boxed them all up and put them in the stables. Tell her she can collect them any time."

Amy saw Posy give a sudden strange shudder.

"Right, I will. I like Tammy a lot, actually, and it's just a shame that...well." Unable to stand it any longer, Amy stood up. "I'd better be getting back, but if there's anything I can do, please tell me, Posy."

"Thank you, dear. Send my love to Sam and the children."

"I will."

Amy put her cup in the sink and walked to the back door. She turned and looked at Posy.

"We all love you very much. Goodbye, Posy."

"Goodbye."

Driving home, Amy stared mutely ahead. Up until now, she hadn't realized what a huge cradle Posy had provided over the years with her endlessly positive outlook and practical but sensitive advice. She stopped at the supermarket to buy pasta and baking potatoes, which would hopefully take the family through until her salary came in next Wednesday. With the last of her money, she added a six-pack of beer to her basket and went to the checkout to pay.

As she stood waiting to be served, Amy pictured Posy's expression in her mind's eye.

And realized she had looked broken.

Posy stood in the morning room and watched the taillights of Amy's car disappear down the drive of Admiral House. Twinges of guilt that she had not been the usual Posy plagued her, but just now, she simply couldn't be. In fact, she wasn't even sure whether the "usual" Posy was really "her" anyway, or merely a persona she had developed and worn like a favorite cardigan, tightly wrapped around her to hide the fearful, confused soul who lived inside it.

Well, the cardigan had been well and truly stripped away in the past ten days, moth-eaten as it was after all these years. After Freddie had told her and handed her the file, she'd somehow driven home, let herself in, then climbed up the stairs to bed. And there she'd lain for almost three days, only rousing herself to use the bathroom and drink some water from her tooth mug. Somewhere in the background, she'd heard the telephone ringing, but she hadn't answered it.

She'd spent a lot of time staring at the ceiling but not actually seeing it as she went through the endless algorithms of her brain to try to make sense of what Freddie had told her. Realizing it was an impossible task, she'd slept a lot instead—perhaps, she thought, it had been her body's way of protecting her, because the pain and shock were so dreadful. She was grieving all over again for a father she realized she'd never known and a mother whom she had known all too well.

A crime of passion...a brutal murder...

Posy had realized it was both.

What hurt the most was the betrayal of everything she had believed about her father for over sixty years. And there was not the slightest doubt that Freddie was telling the truth. When she'd eventually dared to open the file, she'd seen the headlines splashed all over the newspapers.

BUTTERFLY ROOM MURDER LATEST!!...WIFE AND LOVER CAUGHT IN FLAGRANTE BY SPITFIRE PILOT HUSBAND!...WAR HERO ANDERSON TO HANG!!

At first, she'd snapped the file closed quickly, knowing the salacious details could bring her nothing but further pain. Freddie had handed it to her as proof because at the time, she simply couldn't accept what he was telling her. Subsequently, she'd realized everything made perfect sense. She knew her darling grandmother must have done all she could to protect her: stuck out in the middle of Cornwall for all those years, there was little chance of her hearing that her beloved father was in prison and subsequently being tried for the murder of Uncle Ralph.

"Freddie's father," she murmured, still incredulous at the thought.

And of course, she'd been named in the newspapers as "Adriana Rose"—the very thing that had alerted Freddie to who she really was the night he'd proposed to her. There had been nothing to connect

"Posy," the little girl who lived in a tiny village near Bodmin Moor, to the terrible thing happening far away on a gallows in London.

Posy only wished she could have asked her beloved grandmother how *she* had borne the ignominy and pain of her son being tried for murder and subsequently hung for his crime. Images of Granny's pale, strained features floated back to her...that day when the telegram had arrived a few hours before her mother—come to tell her that her father was dead—and all the times she had gone away to London, probably to visit and then say a final goodbye to her son...

"How would she have coped with Maman?" she'd muttered to the ceiling. The wife of her son, whose actions had pushed him to kill another human being.

She'd subsequently read in the old newspapers that her father's defense had pleaded that, after years of risking his life to protect his country, Lawrence had not been of sound mind. They'd begged for leniency, for a war hero whose nerves had been stripped raw by the lottery of possible death he'd been subjected to day after day as he flew across Europe. Apparently, the trial had divided the country and provided the media with plenty of fodder to fill their pages as public opinion swung backwards and forwards.

And what if he had lived? Been sentenced instead to life imprisonment? she'd thought. *Would they have told me then...?*

What burnt in her heart the most was the way her mother had left the country almost immediately and moved swiftly on, as if her old life was an unwanted dress; she'd cast it off and quickly acquired a new one.

"And leaving *me* behind," she'd added out loud, further tears coming to her eyes. "Oh Granny, why aren't you here to talk to?"

Eventually, she'd roused herself from her bed and taken sanctuary in the only place she could find comfort. For once, she'd been grateful for the weeds that sprang up in the flower beds no matter what the season. As she'd tugged them from the earth, her senses had begun to clear, but so many questions filled her thoughts that she nearly went mad with frustration. Granny and Daisy were both gone, and the one person who could help her make sense of these thoughts was the person she could never see again. Her father had murdered his father, destroyed his childhood, as she had floated through hers unaware.

Posy had shuddered as she remembered the many times she'd waxed lyrical about her father to Freddie, especially in the early days, and realized it was *Freddie* who was the real victim in this. No wonder he had left her when he'd discovered who she really was. Not Posy, the woman he'd once said lit up his life, but Adriana Rose, the daughter of the man who had taken his father away forever.

Of *course* he'd presumed she'd known, that fifty years on, *someone* would have told her, but they hadn't. Posy had thought back again to the moment she'd returned to Southwold and Admiral House with her young family and husband. She'd searched her mind and vaguely recalled some strange looks from one or two of the locals. She'd assumed at the time that they were to do with a stranger arriving in the midst of their small community, but in retrospect, the real reason was clearly something different.

She felt so ashamed—tainted by the past her father had created for her, a past that had haunted her to this day and, through the irony of life, changed the course of her own. Without his actions, Freddie and she would have been married as they had planned, had children together, a happy life...

"Do I hate my father?" she'd asked the gardening fork as it burrowed beneath the frost-hardened soil to find the roots of a weed.

It was a question she'd asked herself over and over again, but her heart still refused to offer a verdict. She almost expected it to send her one of those "out of office" emails that so irritated her; she only hoped it would return from its break soon and give her an answer.

Posy sipped the rest of her tea, listening to the silence in the house and shivering. To top it all, any chance of moving away from the very building that had witnessed the tragedy and making a fresh start in some purer air was now on hold. No wonder Freddie had been eager for her to move on. How he could bear to come near a house where his father had been slaughtered in cold blood, she just didn't know.

Now, having licked her wounds for the past ten days, Posy realized the only way she could survive was to think of the future. She could put Admiral House on the open market, sell it, and maybe move away completely from Southwold. But what of her beloved grandchildren, her job and her life here? She'd seen a number of her contemporaries retire and move away to the sun, but she was single and alone; and besides, if she knew one thing for certain, it was that the past went with you, however much you tried to run away from it. And maybe this house and all that had happened here was her destiny: like Miss Havisham and her lost love, she would sit here until she died, slowly rotting away with Admiral House...

"*Stop* it, Posy!"

Amy's visit had broken the spell. The one thing that horrified Posy more than anything else was the thought of being seen as a victim.

"Enough of your self-indulgence—you have to pull yourself together," she told herself. The thought of Amy running home to tell her son his mother was losing it was enough to fire her up.

That begged another question: would she tell her boys what she had just discovered about their grandfather...?

No, was her brain's instinctive reply.

"Yes," she said out loud. Look where protecting one's children had got *her*. Besides, they were both grown adults and had never even known their grandfather. Yes, when the time was right in the future, she *would* tell them.

She walked over to the radio and firmly switched it back on. Then she gathered together the ingredients to make a cake, which she would take over to her grandchildren tomorrow.

Posy began to sieve the flour into a bowl. Order was restored. For now...

"And where have *you* been?"

Amy looked at Sam, swaying menacingly in the doorway of the sitting room. She could see he was drunk, but where he'd got the money to buy more alcohol, she'd no idea. There was no way he could have found her secret stash, was there...?

"At your mother's, Sam. I'm worried about her. She's not herself at all."

"Bitching about me, were you?"

"No, of course not. I just told you, I'm worried about her," she repeated. "Have the kids had anything to eat?" She took the shopping through to the kitchen and dumped it on the table.

"There wasn't anything to eat, Amy, as you well know."

She watched Sam's eyes light up when he saw the beers. He grabbed a bottle, popped the top off and took a deep swig. Biting her tongue to prevent herself from saying he looked as though he'd already had enough, she went into the sitting room, where Jake and Sara were glued to a video.

"Hi, you two," she said, kissing them both. "I'm going to put on some pasta for tea. It won't be long, promise."

"Okay, Mummy." Jake barely looked away from the screen.

She walked back into the kitchen to begin preparing supper.

"What is it?" Sam asked her.

"Pasta."

"Not more bloody pasta! It's all I've had for the past two weeks!"

"Sam, there's no money for anything else!"

"Oh yes there is. I found some cash in the bottom of the wardrobe."

"That's for the kids' Christmas presents, Sam! You haven't taken it, have you?"

"You haven't taken it, have you?" he mimicked her cruelly. "Don't trust me, then? Thought I was meant to be your husband," he said as he opened another bottle of beer.

"You're my husband, Sam, and you're also a father. Surely you want the kids to have some presents?"

"'Course I do, but why does it always seem that my needs come last, eh? Eh?" Sam came up behind her, leaning over her as she took the boiling kettle to pour the water into the pan.

"Careful, Sam, I'll spill the water."

Amy was aware from his breath at her shoulder that he was very, very drunk. He must have found her stash and gone out to the off-licence whilst she was out. She walked to the hob and filled the saucepan with boiling water, then added the pasta.

"I know that's not the only cash in the house, Amy."

"Of course it is. I only wish there *was* more stashed, but there isn't."

"I know you're lying."

"Really, Sam, I'm not."

"Well, I'm not prepared to have any more bloody pasta! I want a takeaway and a decent bottle of wine, so you'd better tell me where it is."

"There's no more money anywhere, Sam, I swear."

"Tell me where it is, Amy."

Sam swiped the bubbling pan from the hob.

"Put that down before you spill it, please!" Amy was frightened now.

"Not until you tell me where you're keeping the rest of the cash!"

"No, I can't because there isn't any, really!"

Amy watched the boiling water splash out onto the kitchen tiles as he walked towards her.

"Sam, I promise, there isn't—"

"You're lying!" Sam hurled the pan in her direction. The contents came at her like a small tidal wave, and she gave a cry as she felt searing hot agony hit her legs before the pan clattered to the floor.

Sam then lurched towards her and grabbed her by the shoulders.

"I just want to know where you've hidden the money."

"I—I haven't," she cried out. She wrenched herself out of his grasp and staggered to the hallway, but felt his hand grip the back of her shirt to spin her around and pin her against the wall. She tried to push him away, scratching and clawing at him, but he was too strong.

"Sam, *stop* it! *Please!*"

His hands were around her throat now and she felt herself being lifted up against the wall, her feet struggling for purchase.

"Amy, just tell me where the money is, just tell me..."

But she had no breath to speak, her eyes bulging and her mouth open as she desperately tried to take in precious oxygen. Her head was spinning and she knew she was about to black out.

Then there was a shout from close by and the grip around her neck suddenly loosened. She slid down the wall to the floor, gulping in air hungrily. She blinked and looked up, the world swimming back into place. Above her stood Freddie Lennox, with Sam struggling in his arms.

"Mummy, what's happening?"

Through blurred vision, Amy saw Jake standing with his arms around Sara at the door to the sitting room.

"Darling, Mummy will come to you in a minute," she panted hoarsely.

Freddie saw the children, then threw Sam to the floor and in a few long strides was beside them. He took Jake and Sara firmly by the hand, then returned to bend over Amy.

"Can you stand, my dear?"

"I think so." Amy tried but her legs wouldn't obey.

Sam stumbled towards them.

"What the hell are you doing?!" he slurred at Freddie.

"Don't you dare go near her," Freddie said icily. "Lay a hand on Amy or your children and I will dial 999 immediately. Right. Jake, you take Sara's hand while I help Mummy to the car, okay?"

"Amy, stop! Where are you going?" Sam whined as Freddie ushered the children through the front door and half-carried Amy behind them.

"Amy! I—!"

Freddie pulled the door closed behind him and then guided them towards his car.

"Now," Freddie said once they were all settled inside. "Let's get you to hospital, young lady."

Amy shook her head. "N-no, I'm fine. R-really. It's just my legs—he threw boiling water at them," she managed, her teeth starting to chatter from shock.

"Then we need to get you checked out," said Freddie firmly, starting the engine. "Okay, kids?" He turned and saw two frightened pairs of eyes.

"I think so," said Jake.

"Good chap," he nodded as he pulled away from the curb and Amy closed her eyes in utter relief.

Chapter 34

The landline rang just as Tammy was about to leave the shop the next night.

"It's Jane," said Meena. "She sounds odd."

"Okay." Tammy took the receiver. "Hi, Janey, are you okay?"

"Sort of, but I need to talk to you urgently. Could you come over?"

"Of course I can," Tammy agreed, even though she felt completely drained.

"Thanks, Tam. Bye."

Tammy left the shop, then drove round to Gordon Place, hoping against hope that it wasn't another miscarriage. She rang the bell with trepidation.

The door was opened immediately. "Hi, lovely, thanks for coming."

Tammy thought that, for someone who'd just told her she was in deep trauma, Jane looked very relaxed.

"What's up?"

"Come through to the kitchen. Glass of wine?" Jane offered.

"Thanks." Tammy took it. "How're you and the baby?"

"We're very good." Jane proudly smoothed down her shirt to reveal the smallest outline of a bump. "So what are you doing for Christmas?"

"Sewing." Tammy looked at her suspiciously. "Janey, what's going on?"

"Nothing, nothing at all, really..."

The front door opened and shut. Tammy heard the sound of male voices approaching the kitchen and her heart began to thud slowly against her chest. "Janey, *no*...please!" She glanced around the kitchen like a cornered animal seeking escape.

"I think that it's actually a very good price and you should advise your mother to take it," said Paul as he entered the kitchen.

With Nick.

Their eyes locked on each other. Then they both spoke at once.

"Christ, Paul!" raged Nick.

"Thanks a million, Janey! I'm leaving." Tammy pushed past him, looked down and for the first time, registered a young girl of nine or ten who was holding Nick's hand.

"Well?" said Paul. "Am I going to make the introductions, Nick, or will you?"

Nick sighed resignedly. "Tammy, this is Clemmie. My daughter."

"Excuse me, everyone, but goodbye." Tammy pushed past them all and headed for the front door, the blood pumping so fast through her veins she felt dizzy. Once outside, she began running away from what she didn't want to know, or to hear.

"Who was that, Daddy? She's very pretty," said Clemmie.

"For God's sake, man, get after her!" urged Paul as he saw Nick staring after Tammy. "Don't you think at the very least she deserves an explanation?" Paul virtually pushed him out of the kitchen. "We'll look after Clemmie here. Now GO!"

Nick stepped outside onto the pavement and saw Tammy legging it along the road. He dawdled for a while, keeping her in sight, still uncertain; then he started to pick up speed. Paul was right. Tammy did deserve an explanation. Now that the cat was out of the bag, the least he could do was talk to her.

Tammy ran blindly on, heading for Kensington Gardens, needing air and space around her. Entering the park, she sank onto the bench and screamed in frustration as Nick appeared beside her a few seconds later.

"Please, go away!"

"Tam, I understand you never want to set eyes on me again, and I'm sorry we were both set up so crudely. I swear it wasn't my idea."

Her head was bowed and she could only see his shoes and the

bottom of his jeans. She closed her eyes tightly, because she didn't even want to see those.

"Look, I'll tell you what's happened, then I'll go," said Nick. "Okay, here it is: eleven years ago, I employed a young woman called Evie Newman in my shop in Southwold. She was eager and willing to learn. We got on very well, and even though I knew she had a long-term boyfriend, I...fell for her, but never once did she give me any indication that my feelings were reciprocated. Then we went on a buying trip to France. We went out to a bar and got outrageously drunk, and that night, we slept together. At the time, I thought it was all my dreams come true. I confessed my feelings to her and told her I loved her."

Nick began pacing backwards and forwards as he talked.

"The next day we came home, me assuming it was the start of a wonderful, all-encompassing love affair, but she spent the next couple of weeks doing her best to avoid me. Then, a few weeks later, she told me she was pregnant. Brian, her boyfriend, had got a new job as a lecturer in Leicester and they were leaving Southwold."

Nick kicked a stone with his shoe and it scudded across the ground.

"It's difficult to explain the kind of love I felt for Evie to anyone. In retrospect, I've realized it wasn't love in a healthy form, it was obsession. After she'd told me she was leaving, I realized I couldn't live in a place that would hold a constant memory of her, so I sold up and moved to Australia. Can I sit down?"

Tammy shrugged, and he sat down on the bench some distance away from her.

"The next time I saw Evie was a couple of months ago when I went to visit my mother in Southwold. She'd written me a letter, you see. I went to her house and she explained why she'd decided to contact me. Are you still with me?"

"Yup," Tammy whispered.

"Well, the issue she'd written to me about was Clemmie. Evie told me that after they'd moved to Leicester, her relationship with Brian had run into problems, but she didn't know why. Soon after Clemmie's birth, Brian had confessed to her that he'd had a vasectomy five years before. He was a good fifteen years older than her, and he already had a divorce and two kids who lived with their mother behind him. In other words, he couldn't possibly be Clemmie's father. He'd thought he'd be able to cope with Evie's betrayal and bring Clemmie up as his own, but apparently, he couldn't. So he moved out soon after and Clemmie grew up with no idea who her father was."

Nick studied Tammy's face for a reaction. It was expressionless, so he continued.

"Evie asked me that night in Southwold whether I'd be prepared to take a paternity test to prove I was definitely her father. So I took the test—to be honest with you, praying that it would be negative. I'd just met you—we were making plans for the future, I..." Nick shook his head and sighed. "Anyway, the result was a positive match with Clemmie's DNA. I am her biological father."

Tammy breathed in slowly, trying to keep calm. "Why weren't you happy? You just said you loved Evie. Surely it was all your dreams come true?"

"Once upon a time, it would have been, yes. But as I said, it was an obsession, not real love. Not like the love I feel for you. And besides..."

"What?" Tammy prompted him, just wanting to get this whole gut-wrenching nightmare over.

"Evie's dying of leukemia. She asked me to take the paternity test so that it might be possible for Clemmie to have one natural parent at least. And a possible extended family when she was gone. That's why she moved back to Southwold."

"Oh my God." Tammy stared at Nick in utter shock. "That is...dreadful."

"Yes, it is. She's only thirty-one—the same age as you."

They both sat in silence for a while.

"Nick," Tammy said softly. "I totally apologize for asking this after what you've just told me, but are you...with her again?"

"No. I swear I'm not. I told her all about you, that I loved you and wanted a future with you."

"But..." she eventually managed to gulp, "if Evie was well, would you want to be with her?"

"Believe me, I've thought about that endlessly, Tammy. And the answer is no. I love you, whether or not Evie had reappeared in my life. You broke the spell. I've never been so happy, I swear, and then all this happened and I...I..."

Nick put his head in his hands and Tammy saw his shoulders were shaking. Despite herself, her heart forced her hand to move towards his and she squeezed it gently.

"I'm so sorry, Tammy, so sorry for this mess."

"Nick, why on earth didn't you tell me sooner?"

"Because I needed to be there for Evie, and also, have some time to get to know Clemmie, establish the relationship and find out whether it was going to work before I presented the situation to you. Also, as has been proved by what subsequently happened, I didn't think you'd believe I wasn't still having an affair with her mother. I honestly thought you'd leave me if you knew the truth. We haven't known each other long. How could I ask you to cope with me visiting my ex-lover and my daughter on a regular basis?"

"I saw your car outside her house the night Amy and I drove by."

"I know. Amy told me. I was there with Evie and Clemmie. I've spent most weekends with them. If it makes any difference, Evie said that when the time was right, she wanted to meet you."

"Why on earth would she want to meet me?"

"Because," Nick sighed, "she knew the possibility was that you would become Clemmie's stepmother one day."

"Right." The thought brought a lump to Tammy's throat. "Well, it might have helped if you'd told me the facts instead of slinking around leaving me to come to the obvious conclusion. You didn't trust in me, or my love, Nick," she whispered.

"I know I didn't, and I'm so, so sorry."

"So where have you been for the past two weeks?" she asked him. "Paul said you'd moved out of Gordon Place."

"I have. I dumped my stuff at the new house in Battersea, then I took Clemmie out of school early and we flew to Verbier together to ski. We needed some time alone, not to mention Clemmie needing a little lightness in her life. She's having to watch her mum fade away in front of her."

"It must be heartbreaking for her."

"It has been, yes. Evie found out she had leukemia a couple of years back. Clemmie was pretty much her primary carer as she went through treatment. Then she was in remission for a year, but in June, it was back with a vengeance and Evie was given a terminal prognosis."

"So Clemmie knows her mum is going to die?"

"She does, yes. She's a lovely little girl, Tammy, and so incredibly brave. She's heartbroken about her mum, of course. I can't change that, but at least I can be there for her, distract her while Evie..." Nick gave a shrug. "Since we arrived back from Verbier, we've been choosing furniture for her bedroom at the house in Battersea. It's important she feels she has a home."

"The home you asked me to live in with you a few weeks ago?"

"Yes."

Tammy looked at him and sighed. "Wow, it's a lot to take in. Were you ever going to tell me?"

"I...don't know. With the past literally exploding into the center of my present, all I've been able to do is take it day by day. I had to be there for Clemmie, and I just didn't know how to begin to explain it to you."

"I understand."

"Do you?"

"Yes."

Nick turned to her, his eyes wet with tears. He took the hand that lay on top of his and clasped it.

"Thank you."

They sat like that for a long time, Tammy doing her best to compute what he'd told her.

"Nick?"

"Yes?"

"Please can you tell me now, honestly, if you still have feelings for Evie?"

"I...care for her, Tammy, of course I do. She's dying and she's so young, and life is so cruel, but do I love her like I love you? No, I don't."

"Honestly? Please, Nick, you have to be honest," she begged him.

"Honestly." He turned to look at her once more and smiled. "And tonight, the way you've reacted to what I've told you, I love you even more. You're beautiful, inside and out. Truly. The question is, whether you could cope with being with a man who, out of the blue, has suddenly acquired a nine-year-old daughter?"

"I've never seriously thought about having kids," she admitted.

"Ironically, nor had I until I met you." Nick smiled. "But now I have a ready-made one who isn't yours by birth, and I'd totally understand if you felt you couldn't cope. Clemmie's going to need a lot of love in the months ahead. I'll have to be there for her, Tammy."

"Of course you will."

"And it goes without saying that I'd love you to be there for her too."

"I...oh God, Nick, I just don't know. I'm not sure I'm maternal and besides, Clemmie would probably hate me because I can never, ever be her real mum."

"I'm sure she wouldn't, Tam. I promise you, she's incredibly sweet-natured. Before you and I...broke up, I told her about you, that I hoped one day we'd get married. And she said she wanted to meet you."

"Did she really?"

"Yes."

Tammy looked at him and knew she believed him. She also realized she was freezing.

"Nick, I think I need some time to process everything you've told me."

"Of course."

"I mean, I'd hate to walk into Clemmie's life, then find out I couldn't cope and walk out of it. Do you understand?"

"Completely." Nick smiled at her weakly. "Please know that I love you and I want more than anything to make this work. But I'll understand if you feel you can't do it—that it's just too much."

"Thank you." Tammy stood up and jabbed her hands into the pockets of her leather jacket to warm them up. "I'll let you know as soon as I can. Bye, Nick."

"Bye."

Nick watched her walk off—her hair catching the light as she walked beneath a lamppost. He sent up a fervent prayer, then stood up to return to his daughter.

Chapter 35

"Hello, Sam. I brought a cake round for the children."

Posy surveyed her son as he held open the door for her. He looked utterly dreadful. His eyes were red-rimmed, his skin pallid with a slight sheen of sweat on it, even though, as he led her inside, she felt the temperature of the house. It was freezing. Sam slumped back onto the sofa, the cushions at one end indicating he'd probably spent the night there. Beer bottles crowded like skittles on the coffee table and a half-empty bottle of whisky stood beside them.

"Is Amy in?"

"Nope."

"Where is she?"

"Don't ask me, Mum."

"The children?" Posy asked.

"With Amy. They left last night with that fancy-man of yours."

"Freddie?"

"That's the one."

"He's hardly my fancy-man, Sam, and why on earth was he here?"

"Search me."

"Are you trying to tell me that Amy has left you?"

"Maybe, yes. I mean, look at me, and this." Sam waved his arm round the room. "Would you want to stay?"

"Amy loves you, Sam. She'd never just walk out." Posy realized she was still holding the cake and cleared some bottles away so she could put it down on the table. "Have you been drinking?" she asked pointlessly.

"Drowning my sorrows, more like."

"I'm going to put the kettle on, get you some coffee. Then you can tell me exactly what happened."

In the kitchen, Posy found a saucepan on the floor, congealed pasta oozing out of it like innards. The floor was still wet around it and Posy took a cloth to wipe it up. Then she scooped the pasta back into the saucepan and dumped the contents in the bin.

"So what has happened?" she asked as she returned to the sitting room and put the coffee down in front of her son. "From the state of the kitchen, it looks like you two had a falling-out."

"Yeah, we did, and then she left with the kids."

"To stay where?"

"Ask your fancy-man. He's the one who took her and the kids away. Accused me of attacking her!" Sam looked at his mother and tears filled his eyes. "You know I'd never do anything like that, Mum. It was just an argument."

Posy's head was spinning. Sam wasn't making sense. She took a sip of her coffee, trying to interpret what he was saying.

"Freddie accused you of attacking Amy?"

"Yup," Sam nodded. "Ridiculous, isn't it?"

"Then why haven't you gone after them?"

"I don't know where he lives, do I?" Tears appeared again in his bloodshot eyes. "I love Amy, Mum, you know I do. I'd never do anything to hurt her, or the kids."

"I think you'd better pull yourself together, Sam. Drink that coffee then go upstairs and take a cold shower. You smell like a brewery and so does this room. While you do that, I'll go and try to find your wife and your children."

"She'll just tell you a pack of lies, don't you understand? Yes, I'd had a few, and things got a bit heated but..."

"Enough, Sam." Posy stood up. "I'll see you later."

"Mum! Don't go! Come back!"

Posy slammed the door behind her, thinking how Sam's pleading reminded her of when she'd left him at boarding school for the first time. It had broken her heart then and she'd sobbed all the way home. But Sam was thirty-eight now—a husband and a father.

As she climbed into her car, she gave a shudder. His continual selfishness and self-pity—not to mention his fetid, hungover state this morning—had not brought out her usual maternal sympathy. She was horrified to realize that her own son disgusted her.

She tapped her fingers on the steering wheel, knowing she was faced with a dilemma. The only person who Sam had indicated knew where Amy and the children were, and what had happened here last night, was the one person she could never see again.

Should she walk away? Leave Amy and Sam to sort this out between them? Their marriage was none of her business, after all.

But your grandchildren are...

Something very bad must have happened to necessitate Amy and the kids leaving the house with Freddie. And whatever it was, Posy knew she needed to find out, or she would have no peace. She started the engine and drove slowly towards the town center. Surely, *surely*, Freddie was wrong and Sam had not attacked Amy? Sam might be many things, but she'd never witnessed him violent. She wondered if he was on the verge of a breakdown, would do something stupid now he was alone...

"No," she said out loud. Whatever Sam was, he was a survivor, and probably too much of a coward to harm himself. She parked on the High Street, then walked briskly along it and into the lane that led to Freddie's house. Before she could turn away, she rang the bell. A few seconds later, Freddie opened the door.

"Hello, Posy." He gave her a weak smile. "I presume you're here to see Amy and the children?"

"I am, yes, but before I do, I'd like to hear from you just what you saw last night." Posy could hear her own brusque tone. "If you don't mind," she added guiltily. None of this was Freddie's fault, after all.

"Of course, but I'm warning you, it won't make pleasant listening," he said as he led her into the sitting room.

"Are they here?"

"No, they're next door in the Hophouse, my little rental place."

"And are they...well?"

"The children are fine. They were in here decorating my tree earlier, to let Amy get some sleep. They're lovely kids, both of them," Freddie smiled.

"And Amy?"

"She'll be okay. I took her straight to A&E to see about the scalds on her thighs. Luckily, she had jeans on so it wasn't quite as bad as it could have been. They've dressed the wounds and given her some painkillers."

"He threw a pan of boiling water at her?"

"Apparently, yes. I didn't arrive until after that had happened."

Posy saw the pan still lying on the floor of the kitchen in her mind's eye and swallowed hard.

"So what did you see?"

"Posy, I...do you want a drink of something?"

"No thank you. What did you see, Freddie? Just tell me."

"I arrived on the doorstep and heard shouting coming from inside. I opened the door to find Sam in the hallway with his hands round Amy's throat."

"Oh my God." Posy dropped into a chair.

"Posy, I'm so very sorry. I...I shouldn't have put it so bluntly. Let me go and get you a brandy."

"No! I'll be fine, really, Freddie. I'm just...shocked, naturally. Was he trying to—" Posy swallowed—"kill her?"

Freddie paused for a moment. "I couldn't say. He was simply very, very drunk."

"Good God, Freddie, good God." Posy put a hand to her brow. "Does she have bruises on her neck?"

"I'm afraid she does, yes. The doctor at the hospital wanted to call the police, but Amy refused point-blank. She reiterated to me this morning that she doesn't want to press charges."

Posy could not find words, so she sat silently, her hands clasped tightly in her lap. Freddie moved hesitantly towards her.

"I'm so dreadfully sorry. This is all you need, on top of what I had to tell you. Please, darling Posy, tell me what I can do to help."

She looked up at him and gave a small shake of her head. "Freddie, don't apologize. None of this, my...messy life, is your fault. Now, can you take me to Amy?"

"Of course."

Posy followed him out of his cottage and across the courtyard to the Hophouse. She knocked on the door and Jake answered it.

"Hello, Uncle Freddie." He gave a big grin. "Can we come and watch the Christmas channel on your satellite TV again?"

"'Course you can. Is Mummy sleeping? Granny's here to see her."

"Hi, Granny, Mummy's awake. I made her a drink of water. She got burnt by a saucepan last night and Daddy was a bit drunk and wasn't allowed to drive, so Uncle Freddie and us took her to hospital."

Sara had appeared in the doorway behind her brother, her mouth smeared with chocolate. "Hello, Granny, Uncle Freddie took us to the toyshop and bought me a new dolly," she said, then reached her arms out for a hug.

Doing her best not to cry, Posy pulled both her grandchildren to her and held them tightly, thanking God for their innocence. And for Freddie's kindness.

"Come along then, you two. Let's go and watch some television. I think *The Muppet Christmas Carol* starts in ten minutes. It's my favorite," Freddie added as he reached out a hand to each child. After Sara had collected her new doll, Posy watched as Freddie led them both back across the courtyard to his own house. Then she stepped inside. Amy was sitting on the sofa, with a tiny blanket barely bigger than a flannel across her thighs.

"It's Sara's new doll's blanket. She thought I should keep warm," Amy commented as she removed it, revealing three big white surgical dressings, and put it back inside a small wicker cradle that lay on the floor at her feet. Then her eyes moved up nervously to meet Posy's.

"Oh my dear, I'm so terribly, terribly sorry." Posy walked towards her and sat down on the sofa next to her. She reached for Amy's hand. "How are you feeling?"

"Okay. The doctor says I probably won't scar, which is good, and I have some nice strong painkillers." Amy stifled a yawn. "The trouble is, they're making me very sleepy. I'm so sorry, Posy."

"What on earth have *you* got to be sorry for? Freddie told me what he saw last night." Now she was close, Posy could see the dark smudge of bruising round Amy's neck. She shuddered involuntarily.

"I..." Amy shook her head and her teeth bit hard on her bottom lip. "You mustn't blame Sam. He's had such a difficult time and he'd just had too much to drink and—"

"No, Amy, please do not excuse his behavior. It is completely unacceptable. He may be my son, but goodness me, attacking his wife like that, I..." Posy shook her head. "He's a disgrace, and let me tell you, if you want to press charges, I'll come to the police station with you. Please Amy, you must tell me the truth; is this the first time or has it happened before?"

"I...never as badly as last night," Amy sighed.

"So it has."

After a long pause, Amy nodded, the movement obviously hurting her, because she winced and her hand moved to her neck.

"Well, I want to apologize to you for not seeing what was under my very nose."

"It didn't happen very often, Posy, really, only when he was drunk, but recently..."

"It should never have happened at *all*, Amy. Do you understand? There are no excuses for beating up a woman. None."

"But I..." Amy's eyes filled with tears. "I haven't been a very good wife, Posy. I...met someone."

"Sebastian?"

Amy looked up at her mother-in-law in shock. "Yes. How did you know?"

"It was written all over the both of you, I'm afraid. Did Sam know?"

"No, or at least I don't think he did. He was so caught up with his new business, but...you see? It's not all his fault."

"Yes it is, Amy, and you must believe that," Posy said vehemently. "From what you've said, this started long before you met Sebastian, didn't it?"

"Yes."

"And you mustn't blame yourself for seeking comfort elsewhere. It's absolutely understandable given the circumstances. You're only human, Amy, and after what you've endured, well..."

"So you don't hate me?"

"Of course I don't."

"But...I loved, *love* him, Posy. Sebastian was so kind to me, so gentle, I, oh dear..."

Amy sobbed then and Posy put her arms carefully around her daughter-in-law and held her to her, stroking the blonde hair gently. When she had quietened, Posy dug in the pocket of her jeans and handed Amy her handkerchief. Amy blew her nose and lifted herself into a more comfortable position.

"I'm so sorry, Posy."

"Please stop apologizing, my dear. Life is a harsh and messy business. We'll sort this out, I promise."

"It's my mess to sort out, Posy. You have enough on your plate."

"My 'plate,' as you put it, is my family, and that means you and my darling grandchildren." While Amy had cried, Posy had been thinking. "Sam needs help urgently, and perhaps he always did..."

"What do you mean?"

"Just that a mother's love can sometimes blind her to reality. Anyway, would you all like to come back with me to stay at Admiral House?"

"If it's okay with you, Freddie said we can stay here for a while. I'd feel safer, as Sam doesn't know where we are. I couldn't face seeing him just now, I'm afraid. Freddie is such a lovely man, Posy. He's been so kind to us, and the children love him already. You're very lucky."

"Yes, he's a very good person."

"He obviously cares about you so much. That was why he'd come to see me last night, to check how you were. He was worried about you and so was I. Are you all right, Posy?"

"I'm fine, Amy, and only concerned with making sure that you are too. I must say, this place of Freddie's is awfully cosy."

"I adore it." Amy smiled properly for the first time. "It's...sanctuary," she added.

"And that is just what you need. Now I have to ask you one last time; are you absolutely sure you don't want to press charges against Sam?"

"Absolutely. I just want to forget about it, not drag it out into some long process that ends up with Sam and me in court."

"Well, it's your decision, Amy, but something has to be done about him. Currently, he's a danger to other women who might cross his path. You do know you can never go back to him, don't you?"

"Maybe if he stopped drinking, Posy, I could think about it. He is the children's father, after all."

"Exactly, and for the sake of your children, you must stay away from him. If he's been violent with you, how long before he turns on

Sara and Jake?"

Amy stared into the distance, as if debating something. She turned back to Posy. "It's terrible, but the truth is, even if he did get sober, I don't love him any more. I feel so guilty about it."

"You must understand, Amy," Posy said slowly, "that after that first flare of passion, love has to be earned if a relationship is to survive the test of time. Even without knowing what I know now, I could see that Sam wasn't doing that."

"God, Posy, how can you be so honest about your own son? Most mothers couldn't be."

"Because I've learnt the hard way that you can choose your friends, *and* your partner, but not your family. I'll always love Sam, of course I will, and yes, I will try to help him as much as I can—*if* he'll accept my help—but that doesn't mean I like him at the moment. Truth be told, I'm thoroughly ashamed of him and have been for years. And I accept that part of who he is is down to me. There," Posy breathed, "now that's my confession for the day."

They both watched the fire flickering for a while before Posy turned to Amy and smiled. "I blame the 'Perfect Family' scenario: we all feel that we are failing because our lives never seem to live up to the films, or more importantly, the front that so many of us present to the world. One can never know what goes on behind closed doors and I guarantee you, behind them, most families are as complicated as ours. Now, I think we could both do with a nice cup of tea."

She stood up and walked towards the small but beautifully fitted kitchen.

"Posy?"

"Yes?"

"Thank you. For everything. I think you're the most amazing person I know and I love you very much."

"Thank you," Posy replied, tears pricking at the backs of her eyes as she switched on the kettle. "I love you too."

Fifteen minutes later, Posy left the Hophouse. As she walked across the courtyard, Freddie opened his front door and walked towards her.

"How is she?"

"Calm," Posy replied. "We talked about where she goes from here."

"And?"

"She eventually admitted that she doesn't want to go back to Sam, even if he does manage to sort himself out, but she's frightened of telling him."

"She mustn't go near him, Posy. I'm sorry to say it, but you didn't see what I saw last night."

"Of course not. She said you'd offered her the Hophouse for a while. I said she was welcome to come back with me to Admiral House, but she'd prefer to stay here for now. She says she feels safe."

"Good. That's the most important thing. She and the children are welcome to stay as long as they wish."

"Thank you, Freddie, you've been so kind. And now," Posy sighed, "I must go and see Sam and collect some clothes and toys for Amy and the children."

"I'll come with you, Posy, you can't go by yourself."

"I understand your concern, but really, I know my own son. He's in the 'woe is me' stage today and not at all dangerous."

"Please let me at least drive you."

"I think you've done enough for my family already."

"And you, Posy? How are you?"

"Getting on with what I have to do. Now I really must go." She turned to walk away, but Freddie caught her arm.

"We need to talk."

"I know, but not now Freddie, please. I can't cope. Later." Posy gave him a whisper of a smile and headed off along the lane.

There had been no answer when she'd knocked on the door of Amy and Sam's house, so Posy had let herself in with the spare key she kept. Calling her son's name, then checking the downstairs and moving up to the bedrooms, she saw he was obviously not at home. Taking a couple of holdalls, she stuffed in as many of Amy's and the children's clothes as she could find. Then, after filling a box with toys, she took them out and placed them in the boot of her car. Just as she was closing it, she saw Sam walking towards her along the pavement.

"Hey Mum, how's Amy and the kids? Where are they?"

Posy was pleased to see he wasn't drunk, at least. "Shall we talk inside?"

She led the way and they went into the sitting room. Posy sat down, Sam did not.

"So? Where are they?" he asked again.

"I'm not telling you."

"Not telling me where my wife and kids are?!"

"You attacked Amy last night, Sam. You're very lucky she has decided not to press charges. The A&E doctors said she should."

"A&E?" Sam looked amazed. "Honestly Mum, it was just an argument that got a little out of control."

"Amy has a number of serious burns on her legs and bruising to her neck where you attacked her. There was also an eyewitness who is very happy to stand up in court and say what he saw. There is little doubt you would be charged with assault and most probably end up in prison. So." Posy pointed to the chair opposite her. "I suggest you sit down and listen to what I have to say."

Sam did so, his face deathly pale.

"Amy and the children are moving out. I have their clothes and toys in my boot."

"Are they staying with you?"

"No, they are in a safe place and I warn you, Sam, if you even try to approach Amy or the children at work or school, Amy will go to the police, so I suggest for now that you stay away."

"But what about the kids? I have every right to see them."

"I'm sure, in time, something will be worked out, but firstly, I want to talk about you."

"And tell me how disappointed you are in me for the umpteenth time?"

"I've never said those words and you know it, Sam. I've supported you to the hilt, even to the point of giving you first refusal on Admiral House, so please don't give me that self-indulgent rubbish. This—what happened last night—was in another league, and yes, I freely admit that I'm shocked and ashamed by your behavior. However, I'm still your mother and I love you. I'm here to tell you that you need help. It's obvious you have an alcohol problem, which makes you violent enough to assault your own wife."

"Truly, Mum, I never meant to hurt Amy. I love her."

Posy ignored his remark and continued, "What I suggest is that I pay for you to go into one of those rehab centers, where they can help get your alcohol and anger issues under control. What I won't do is subsidize you continuing to live like this. You won't get another penny out of me, and without Amy's salary coming in, I assume you would have to go on the dole, or whatever they call it these days. So, what is it to be?"

Sam stared at her as though she was mad. "Mum, please, stop! I know what happened last night was wrong, but I don't need to be sent to a bloody funny farm to dry out! I'm not drunk today, am I? Look at me! I'm fine."

"I'm sure you are, but when you drink you obviously have a tendency to become violent, Sam. You could have killed Amy last night if Freddie hadn't arrived. You had your hands round her throat, for God's sake!"

"I honestly can't remember, Mum."

"Which makes it all the more important you go and get help. Otherwise, you really could kill someone one day. Sam, you must accept how serious this is. Someone else *saw* what you did, and the A&E doctors too. You could even be charged with attempted murder, so Freddie said."

"And what does he know?"

"He's an ex-criminal barrister, Sam. He knows a lot, I'm afraid. Anyway." Posy stood up. "I can only advise you, offer you the help I think you need, but I'm not going to force you. Right, I must go." She began to walk towards the door.

"Mum! Where are you going?"

"To take Amy's and the children's things to them. Should I add an apology from you to that? I haven't heard one from you so far."

"I...well of course I'm sorry, but—"

"No 'buts,' Sam. It's about time you started taking responsibility for your actions. Give me a call when you've decided what you want to do. Goodnight."

Posy climbed into the car and slammed the door behind her. As she sat behind the wheel, she heard her breath coming in short, sharp bursts and saw that her hands were shaking. Sam was standing on the doorstep staring at her. Before he could jump in his car and follow her to Freddie's, she started the engine and drove off.

Chapter 36

"You look done in, dear girl," Freddie said as he opened the door to Posy.

"I am. Sorry to bother you yet again, but Amy and the children weren't in the Hophouse and their clothes and toys are sitting on the doorstep."

"That's because they're in here with me. We've just finished supper."

"Right. Well, if you could tell Amy that I brought..."

Posy swayed suddenly and for the second time that day, thought she might pass out.

Freddie grabbed her arm and half carried her into the sitting room. "You stay there. I'll get you a brandy and tell Jake and Sara their toys have arrived. That will send them running back to the Hophouse."

"Thank you. I can't face them just now."

Freddie closed the door behind him and Posy looked round the wonderfully cosy room, the fire burning brightly in the grate, the lights of the Christmas tree twinkling in the window. Her heart began to slow down, her eyelids became heavy, and by the time Freddie walked in with her brandy, she was almost asleep.

"All clear. They've gone back to the Hophouse. There," he said. "Drink that."

"Actually, I can't, because it would go straight to my head. I haven't eaten a thing since breakfast."

"Then I'll get you a bowl of my lamb hotpot—Amy and the children devoured it—and swap that brandy for a glass of white wine. Two ticks and I'll be back."

It was such a very long time since anyone had looked after her—brought her a drink, cooked for her—that whilst she waited for Freddie, she felt very emotional.

"There we go, dear Posy." Freddie placed a tray—which also contained a linen napkin and tiny salt and pepper pots—on her knee. He lifted the glass of wine from it and handed it to her. "I'll go and clear up the kitchen. Nothing worse than being watched whilst one is trying to eat."

He's so thoughtful, she thought again as she spooned up the hotpot, *and so kind...*

When she'd finished, she carried the tray into the kitchen.

"Feeling better?" Freddie asked as he dried up a saucepan.

"Much, thank you. That was delicious."

"Thank you. Mind you, don't get too carried away. My wife always teased me that I only had two recipes—a barbecue in the summer and that hotpot in the winter! Shall we go and sit down?"

Posy supposed she should go home, but it felt so warm and cosy here compared to the vast and chilly Admiral House that she agreed. Freddie stoked the fire and sat in the armchair opposite her, nursing a brandy.

"How did it go with Sam?"

"I really don't know. I made him my offer—to pay for treatment for his alcohol addiction at a clinic—but he's still in denial."

"Bullies always are, I've found. It's always someone else's fault, they did nothing, et cetera et cetera."

"That's interesting. Sam was always telephoning me from school, complaining about how he'd fallen out with his friends. Anyway," she sighed, "would you mind if we didn't talk about it any more? For tonight at least, Amy and the children are tucked up safely next door and I've done all I can. Thank you again, Freddie. You should have called me on my mobile last night. I would have taken Amy to A&E."

He looked at her quizzically. "Would you have answered it when you saw it was me?"

"No, probably not." She gave him a small smile.

"Then you're still angry with me for telling you what really happened all those years ago?"

"No, not angry. How could I be? I just needed some time to take it all in. Readjust the view of my father after over sixty years of placing him on a pedestal."

"If I hadn't walked back into your life, you might never have known."

"And would that have been right? To go to my deathbed never knowing the truth? No, in retrospect, now I've calmed down, I'm glad you told me."

"You do understand why I had to leave you all those years ago?"

"I do. I hardly think your mother would have been pleased with your choice of bride." Posy sighed. "The daughter of a man who murdered her husband."

"The husband who had betrayed her for years with your mother," Freddie added quietly. "You know, after I realized who you were, I remembered that you and I did meet once when we were much younger."

"Did we?"

"Yes. I was about five and you were no more than three. Your parents came to stay with us and brought you. I remember waking up in the night and hearing the most almighty racket from my parents' bedroom. My mother was crying hysterically, and my father was trying to calm her. In retrospect, I reckon she had discovered something was going on between Father and your mother."

"Even I remember Uncle Ralph appearing at Admiral House regularly when Daddy was away. The affair must have gone on for years. And I recall Daisy, our maid, saying something about Maman wanting to get us away from the house for Christmas when we were both packed off to Granny's. Were your parents still together when...it happened?" she asked him.

"By that time, I was away boarding at prep school, but yes, they still shared the same house, if not the same bed or conversation. The marriage was obviously over, but my mother was completely dependent on Father financially, as most women were in those days. Perhaps she had just accepted the situation because she had no other choice. And because," Freddie sighed, "she loved him. She was heartbroken when he...died. She never got over it, led the rest of her life as a widow, lonely and bitter. I remember telling you how miserable our Christmases were. New Year's Eve in particular, as you can imagine."

"Oh, I can, yes," Posy agreed. "I wonder if my father knew before he...caught them together?"

"We humans have an incredible capacity for ignoring things we don't wish to see, Posy."

"You're right. Look at me with my son. My father worshipped my mother. And if he didn't know, to find them there, in his special butterfly room, in flagrante, I...well, I can understand why he did what he did, however wrong."

"Especially given he'd been risking his life flying Spitfires for the past five years. What that must have done to his state of mind, well," Freddie shuddered, "many never got over it."

"Still, it's no excuse for cold-blooded murder."

"No, but it should have been taken into account at the trial. I don't believe he should have been hanged and nor did many others."

"And what about you, Freddie? Did they tell you what had happened?"

"Not at first, no. I just remember a knock at the door and two policemen appearing. I was told to go up to my room and few moments later, I heard my mother screaming. The police left and my mother came into my bedroom. She was hysterical, as well she might be. She ranted that my father was dead over and over again until our maid called the local doctor. He virtually dragged her from my bedroom and must have given her a sedative to calm her down. The next day I was back at school. Subsequently, my fellow pupils filled me in on all the gory details from the newspapers."

"Oh, Freddie, I'm so very sorry. You were only ten. It must have been quite dreadful for you."

"In truth it was, but you hardly need to apologize, my dear Posy. It really was a case of the sins of our fathers," he smiled weakly. "And at least I *knew* the truth, however brutal, and had no choice but to come to terms with it. The most tragic part of it for me was when I realized who *you* were. And that you didn't know. I'd heard you talk about your father so often, and with so much love...I knew I couldn't break your heart by telling you the truth."

"I wish you had."

"Do you, Posy? Well, perhaps it's easy in retrospect to say that, but I doubt you would have been able to marry me once you knew. It would have been all too much. Wouldn't it?" Freddie prompted her.

"Yes." Posy gave a deep sigh. "I was utterly heartbroken when you left me. I...hated you."

"I can understand why, but what else could I do?"

"Nothing, I know that now. I decided then and there that true love was a fantasy and that I'd live my life alone as a spinster." Posy looked up at Freddie and gave him a sad smile. "And in fact, my wish almost came true. I've spent the vast majority of my adult life alone, apart from the twelve years I was with dear Johnny."

"How did you come to marry him, Posy? I mean, after telling him about me and breaking off your engagement?"

"We met at a party Andrea threw a few months after you'd left me. Jonny was on leave—he'd finished his training—and was just about to be posted overseas. He asked how I was, whether you and I were still together, and I told him it hadn't worked out. He invited me out for supper a week or so later and for want of anything else to do, I accepted. He was so very calm and kind to me, Freddie. He said he forgave me about you—that it was understandable given the amount of time he'd been away. Which it absolutely wasn't— understandable, I mean." Posy blushed. "He asked me out again, and after grieving for you for months, it was a relief to at least smile at one of his stories. It felt comfortable to be with him, as it always had done, and he made me feel loved and wanted when I needed it, so when he asked me if I'd reconsider marrying him, I said yes. I wanted to get away from the memories of you, so I left my job at Kew Gardens, got married in rather a hurry, and went with Jonny to his first posting in Cyprus."

"And were you happy with him?"

"Yes, I was. It was a good life," Posy reminisced. "I lived in some very interesting places, including Malaysia. Even though I wasn't working any longer, the flora and fauna in the jungles was breathtaking." She smiled. "I was able to continue with my botanical drawings."

"Did you love him?"

"I did. Not in the all-consuming, passionate way I felt about you, but I was certainly devastated when he died. He was a very good man, and a wonderful father to Sam. It was so terribly sad he never met Nick or had a chance to enjoy life on civvy street at Admiral House, but as we've both learnt to our cost, life can be terribly cruel. I've certainly learnt that one must do one's best to seize the day."

"Yes, and talking of which..." Freddie leant forward and reached for Posy's hand, "can you forgive me, Posy?"

"Goodness, Freddie, there's nothing to forgive."

"Then can you...can *we* try again? I mean, you know now, so it seems to me that for the first time in our relationship, there's nothing stopping us being together."

"No, there isn't," Posy agreed.

"Well?"

"I...yes, we could certainly try. If you want to, that is." Posy could feel herself blushing.

"I do, desperately. I love you and I always have. I don't want to waste any more time than we already have. Who knows how long we have left? Surely we owe it to ourselves to take some happiness now whilst we can?"

"Oh Freddie, you already know how complicated my family is and—"

"*All* families are complicated, Posy, and better that than living a solitary, empty life. We both know how that feels, don't we?"

"We do, yes." Posy yawned suddenly, the stress of the day catching up with her.

"You're exhausted, dear girl. How about you stay here overnight?"

She eyed him silently, and he chuckled.

"Goodness, what do you think I am?"

"I know exactly what you are, Mr. Lennox," she replied as she gave him a wry smile. "And I remember rather enjoying it."

"Well now, for tonight at least, I have a perfectly comfortable guest room which you are welcome to use, and I promise your honor will not be compromised." He stood up and held out a hand. "I'll take you up and show you the facilities."

"Thank you. I really am too weary to drive home."

Posy took Freddie's hand and he led her up the stairs and onto a narrow landing. "There now, this is your room," he said, opening a door and switching on the light.

"It's utterly delightful," she said, taking in the restful colors and the smell of paint and new carpet as he shut the thick curtains. "And so warm."

"I'm glad you like it. Now, can I offer you a T-shirt of mine to wear in bed?"

"That would be most kind," she agreed.

"Back in a tick," he said as he left the room.

Posy sat down on the bed, noticing how comfortable the mattress was compared to the old horsehair one on her own bed at home, and equally, how comfortable she felt here in Freddie's home.

"Could we really have a future together after all that's happened?" she whispered to herself. Well, there was nothing to stop them trying, and what did she have to lose? Posy experienced a tingle of what felt a little like happiness running through her.

There was a polite tap on the door before Freddie entered with a T-shirt and a mug.

"I made you some cocoa. It might help you sleep," he said as he put the mug down on the bedside table.

"You are sweet, Freddie. Thank you."

"Well now, sleep well and pleasant dreams." He leant forwards, cupping her face in his hands and planting a light kiss on her lips. Then, as she didn't move away, he kissed her again, properly, and as his arms wound round her body, Posy felt the heady feeling of arousal sweep over her.

"I'd better be off before I misbehave," he smiled as he stood upright. "Goodnight."

"Goodnight, Freddie."

Posy switched off the light and lay in the comfortable bed, a hundred thoughts spinning around her head. It had been quite a day.

"As Scarlett O'Hara once famously said, I will think about it tomorrow," she told herself as she settled down to sleep.

Chapter 37

"Hi," Tammy said tentatively as she opened the door to Nick's shop. "Thought I'd pop in on my way home to see how you're doing."

"I'm getting there, slowly," he smiled at her as he heaved a 1930s mirrored dressing table across the showroom.

"That is heavenly, Nick. I wish I had enough money to buy it."

"Well, if I sell it at a good profit, I'm sure I can find a similar one for you."

"Have you decided when you're going to open?"

"I'm going to leave it until Clemmie has gone back to school after Christmas. She needs all I can give her just now."

"Of course she does."

A silence hung between them. Eventually, Nick walked over to her.

"How have you been?"

"Okay. Yes, okay. I've been doing a lot of thinking."

"Right. And...?"

Tammy looked at the hope in Nick's eyes. "*And*...I thought I should meet Clemmie."

"Really?"

"Yes. No promises, Nick, but just to see how we get on."

"Okay. Well actually, I really need to go and see my mother, try to explain everything. She needs to know she has a granddaughter and what has happened to Evie before it's too late. She was very fond of her."

"Yes, you must, Nick."

"I was thinking of going this Wednesday. So would it be possible for you to look after Clemmie for the day?"

"I don't know, Nick." Tammy frowned. "I'll be at the shop. What will I do with her?"

"I'm sure you'll find something to keep her amused, Tam. If not, she can stay with Jane and Paul."

"Surely, if you're going to Southwold, Clemmie will want to see her mother?"

"Evie's been taken into hospital in Ipswich. She's very ill, I'm afraid. She has a kidney infection and they're trying to stabilize her. I'll obviously go to see her, but she doesn't want Clemmie to visit just now."

"I...okay. How bad is she? I mean—"

"Is this it?" Nick said the words for her. "Who knows? She may well pull through this, but sadly, it's only a matter of time until she doesn't."

"God, Nick, it's so dreadful. I just can't imagine how she must feel. And of course I'll look after Clemmie," Tammy agreed.

"Thank you." Nick gave her a tight hug. "Right, I'll go and ring Mum and then I'd better be off to collect Clemmie from Jane and Paul's. She's been out on a photo shoot with Jane today. She was very excited—it's a video for some boy band's latest single. I'd never heard of them, but she has."

"Blimey." Tammy rolled her eyes. "Being at the boutique will be a bit of a comedown."

"I'm sure it won't. I'll see you on Wednesday, then."

"Okay. Bye, Nick."

Tammy kissed him, then left the shop. Climbing into her car outside, she sighed heavily. "What have I got myself into?" she asked herself as she turned on the engine and headed for home. Committing to Nick had been one thing, but being presented with his child was another. She didn't know whether she had a maternal bone in her body.

"What if she doesn't like me?" Tammy bit her lip as she sat at a set of traffic lights. "What will I do then? Besides, I have my business, and I can never replace her real mum, and..."

Arriving in front of her house, Tammy parked, then opened the front door. She poured herself a large glass of white wine from the fridge and took a hefty slug. There was no point in panicking about it. She would just have to see how Wednesday went.

"Hi, Tam, here we are."

Nick walked into the boutique holding Clemmie's hand.

"Hello, Nick—hi, Clemmie." Tammy smiled down at the little girl and received a shy smile in return.

"Hi, Tammy."

"I hope you're going to help me out today."

"I'll try," Clemmie said, "but I've never worked in a shop before."

"Right then, I'll be off. I'll give you a call when I'm leaving but I should be back by six."

"No problem, Nick. Send my love to your mum," said Tammy.

"Will do. Bye, Clemmie." Nick kissed his daughter on the top of her silky head. "Be a good girl."

"I will. Bye, Daddy," she said as Nick gave her a wave and left.

"And who do we have here?" Meena appeared from the office and bustled across the shop towards them.

"I'm Clemmie. It's nice to meet you."

"And I am Meena. What beautiful manners you have, Clemmie. Now then, how do you feel about coming downstairs with me and making a necklace for your mummy for Christmas? I have many different colored beads, and you can choose which ones she would like."

"I'd love to, thank you."

Tammy watched them go downstairs and sighed. Meena was a natural with children, having had so many of her own, whereas she, well, she didn't know where to start.

Thankfully, the boutique was busy and Tammy was kept occupied with customers all morning. With the party season about to arrive, she sold more stock in one morning than ever before.

Meena and Clemmie appeared upstairs at lunchtime. "We are going out to the deli. Anything you would like, Tammy?"

"My usual salad would be great, thanks. And a Coke. I need the caffeine," she said as she watched Clemmie wandering along the rails of clothes.

"Your dresses are so beautiful, Tammy," she breathed.

"Thank you, Clemmie. I...well, I will see you when you're back."

Tammy turned away and walked into the office, kicking herself for sounding so insincere. *She* was the adult, yet she felt completely tongue-tied, her head emptying of anything to say to Clemmie.

The two of them were back ten minutes later with lunch, and they all took the food into the back office and sat down to eat.

"I love Coke, but my mum doesn't let me have it. She says it rots your teeth," said Clemmie as Tammy took a sip from her can.

"Your mum is right, it does," Tammy agreed.

"Well, your teeth look perfect, Tammy," Clemmie said, eyeing the can.

"Would you like some? A small amount won't hurt, I'm sure."

"Yes please, but don't tell Daddy or he might be cross."

"I won't, promise," Tammy said as she poured some into a glass. The bell tinkled to inform them a customer had just come in.

"I'll go," said Meena. "You two eat your lunch."

"Meena's so nice," said Clemmie. "She said she'll make me a curry next time I come. I love curries, but I've only ever had them from a takeaway, not from a home."

"Prepare to have your head blown off, then. She makes them very spicy." Tammy smiled, and Clemmie giggled.

"Daddy said you were a model before you had a shop."

"I was, yes."

"You have beautiful hair, Tammy. I wish I had hair like yours. Mine's boring."

"No it isn't. It's thick and shiny and straight, which is what I've always wanted."

"I bet you had your hair done loads of times when you were a model."

"I did, yes, and I hated it."

"Did you enjoy being a model though?"

"Bits of it, yes. I liked traveling and seeing new places, and some of the clothes I got to wear were gorgeous, but it's actually really hard work."

"I thought models married princes." Clemmie took a sip of her Coke, then looked at Tammy apprehensively. "So why are you with

Daddy?"

"Because I love him," she shrugged.

"I love him too. I didn't know whether I would when Mummy told me about him, but I'm really glad he's my dad now. Have you met Posy?"

"Yes, once. I really liked her. Do you?"

"A lot. She's very young for an old person." Clemmie took a bite of her baguette. "Did you know she's my granny for real?"

"I did, yes."

"Daddy's gone to tell her about me today. I wonder what she'll say."

"I am absolutely sure she will be thrilled. Your mum and her used to be very good friends, so your Daddy told me."

"I know. Daddy said I have cousins and an aunt and uncle too. I've never had a family before. It was just me and Mummy."

Clemmie gave a long sigh and her eyes filled with sadness. Instinctively, Tammy reached for the small hand and took it in hers. "And they, and Daddy, will all be there for you."

"I think she might die quite soon, Tammy. I heard Daddy speaking on his mobile to the doctor. I hope I can see her before she does. I want..." Clemmie bit her lip as tears filled her eyes, "I want to say goodbye."

"Of course you do. Come here." Tammy reached for Clemmie and sat her on her knee. She stroked her dark hair gently, feeling a lump lodged in her own throat. "You know what, Clemmie? I think you are about the bravest person I've ever met."

"No, Mummy's the bravest."

"Well I haven't met her, but if I had, I'm sure she would say you were too."

"It's quite hard to be brave sometimes, but I'm trying for her."

"She must be so proud of you, Clemmie. I would be if you were my daughter."

"Well, I will be your daughter when you marry Daddy, won't I?"

"I...yes, and I'll be the proudest stepmum ever, promise," Tammy said, gulping back tears and realizing she meant it. "I know I can never be your real mummy, but I so hope we can be friends."

"Yes." Clemmie took one of Tammy's hands in hers and looked at her fingernails. "I really like that color, Tammy. Can I paint mine the same?"

"'Course you can. I have the nail varnish in my handbag." Tammy pointed to it. "Can you get it out? I'll paint them for you now."

"But you have customers."

"Meena's looking after them. Close the door and I'll tell Meena we're in a meeting."

She winked at Clemmie conspiratorially as the child climbed off her knee to reach the handbag and then, with a grin, pushed the door closed.

"Hi, Mum, how are you?" asked Nick as he walked into the kitchen at Admiral House.

"Nick, darling boy! How are *you*?" Posy asked as she put down the wooden spoon she'd been stirring soup with and walked over to embrace her son.

"Yes, I'm okay, Mum, I just...needed to talk to you, that's all."

Posy saw the serious expression on her son's face. "Should I open the bottle of wine that's sitting in the fridge?"

"I'll open it, though it'll just be a small one for me. I'm driving back to London later."

"Really? I was hoping you might stay for the night."

"I'm afraid I can't," said Nick as he pulled the bottle of wine from the fridge.

"Is Tammy expecting you?"

"Yes. Mum, shall we sit down?" Nick brought the bottle to the table and poured it into the two glasses Posy had already set for lunch.

"Right, well, you go first, because I have some things to fill you in on too," said Posy. "Where have you been for the past couple of weeks? You weren't answering your mobile."

"I'm sorry, Mum. I should have said where I was, but...unfortunately I had other things on my mind. Are you all right?"

"Yes, I am now, but I'll save mine for later. Tell me about what's happened to you, Nick." Posy took a sip of wine to steady her nerves. She only hoped it wasn't more bad news—she wasn't sure how much more she could take.

"You remember Evie Newman?"

"Of course I do. You know how fond of her I was. She's moved back here and I took her daughter out once—such a sweet little thing—but Evie doesn't seem inclined to be friendly."

"No, well, I hope that after what I've told you, you'll understand why, Mum." Nick took a gulp of his wine and did his best to gently explain what had happened.

"Right." Posy's brain was struggling to compute what Nick had told her. "Goodness." She looked up at her son. "Are you trying to tell me that Clemmie is your daughter?"

"I am, Mum, yes."

"Which means that she's my granddaughter?"

"Yes, she is."

"I...How long have you known?"

"Only since I came back here to England."

"Is that why you came home?"

"No, it was pure coincidence. Evie had written to me in Australia—she'd found me through my business—but then you told her I was home, so she dropped in that letter for me to the gallery, asking me to contact her."

"I see, I think. But why now, Nick?" Posy frowned. "Why did she wait ten years to tell you?"

"Mum, I'm afraid this is where it gets painful. The reason she contacted me is because she's very, very sick. She has leukemia, and there's a very good chance she won't make it until Christmas. I'm so sorry, Mum; I know how fond you were of her." Nick reached a hand across the table towards his mother and took hers in his.

"Oh dear, oh dear, such a beautiful little thing, and so young..." Posy dug for a handkerchief in her pocket and blew her nose. "When I'm sitting here at almost seventy, as hale and hearty as you like. Life is just so damned unfair! Mind you, I should have known something was up. She looked utterly terrible when I called round to take Clemmie out."

"I know, Mum, it's completely tragic."

Mother and son sat together in silence for a while, lost in their own thoughts.

"So, Evie contacted you because of Clemmie," Posy said eventually. "Because you are her biological father."

"Yes."

"And of course Evie has no other family...she herself was orphaned young. How is Clemmie?"

"Amazing under the circumstances, but that's partly to do with the way that Evie has handled it. She's been so brave. They both have."

"And do you and Clemmie get on?"

"We more than get on, Mum. I was so nervous to meet her, but from the start it felt completely natural, as if we'd always known each other. I know I can never replace Evie and I'm not even going to try, but I'll be there for her every step of the way."

"And what about Tammy? How does she feel about the situation?"

"I'm afraid I didn't handle that very well at all," Nick shrugged. "I was so scared of losing Tammy that I didn't know how to tell her about Clemmie, so I just cut and ran. It was only because of Jane and Paul getting us together that I ended up telling her the truth. She's been fantastic about it and in fact, she's looking after Clemmie at the moment. It's weird, Mum, I've been by myself for over ten years—longer if you count the time I was in love with Evie—and suddenly I seem to have got myself a family."

"Both Clemmie and Tammy are very special, Nick. I hope you count yourself lucky."

"Oh, I do. Tammy was very nervous about spending time with Clemmie today. I just hope it all goes well."

"I'm sure it will. It shows just how much she loves you, Nick."

"I know, and I swear I'm going to do everything I can to show her how grateful I am."

"Do you love her? Seeing Evie again must have stirred up a lot of feelings."

"Yes, it did—*does*—but I think I put her on a metaphorical pedestal. What I feel for Tammy is very different. It feels"—Nick searched for the right word—"*real*. She feels real."

"And Evie? Who is caring for her, Nick?"

"She's in hospital at the moment, in Ipswich. But when she's at home, there's a round-the-clock nurse with her."

"I only wish I'd known—I could have helped—but she made it very clear to me that she didn't want to see me."

"She was embarrassed and ashamed at what she'd done, Mum, but now that you know, I'm sure she'll be happy that you can officially play a role in Clemmie's life."

"Absolutely, Nick. Well, please assure her that I'll be there for Clemmie. Now." Posy cleared her throat and stood up. "I think we should both have something to eat. Soup?"

"Lovely, Mum."

Posy filled two bowls and added some warm bread from the oven.

"So," Nick asked, "what's been going on here?"

"A lot, I'm afraid, and some of it not good."

"Sam?" Nick took an educated guess.

"Yes," she replied as she sat down. "Let's eat first before the soup gets cold. It doesn't make pleasant listening."

Over coffee afterwards, Posy filled Nick in on the aborted sale of Admiral House.

"I'm sorry to say, but it's bloody typical of him. So will the police charge him?"

"If he'll testify against this Ken Noakes, which I'm sure he will, he'll probably get off with a caution. But I'm afraid that there's something else, Nick, something far more serious."

With a heavy heart, Posy told Nick about his brother's abuse of his wife.

"And he's still refusing to go to a clinic to sort out his problem. He doesn't believe he has one."

"Well, he does, Mum," Nick said firmly. "I could have told you about it years ago. He bullied me for most of my childhood."

Nick watched his mother's face drain of color.

"I'm so sorry, Mum. Hearing this must make you feel dreadful, but you need to know that what happened to Amy isn't a one-off. I know he also bullied other boys at school, but somehow, he always managed to wriggle out of punishment."

"Nick, I don't know what to say. Did he hurt you badly?"

"All brothers fight, but you know I wasn't the aggressive type, so I didn't want to fight back. Anyway, it all stopped when I got to thirteen and grew taller and stronger than him. I'm afraid I landed some punches he'll never forget. He left me alone after that."

"I should have seen...Why didn't you tell me, Nick?"

"I was too scared of retribution. That's how bullies get away with it. Amy should press charges. Sam certainly deserves it, that's for sure. Are you all right, Mum?"

"To be honest, no. How could I be? I mean, when you were growing up I sometimes worried that Sam's unruliness was the result of him losing his father so young, but I never believed him capable of such malice. And knowing that *you* spent your childhood in fear of your brother? It all makes me feel like a terrible mother. I should have recognized the signs and protected you, Nick, and I failed to do so."

"Seriously, my life was never in danger and you were—*are*—a wonderful mother and grandmother."

"Goodness!" Posy reached for her hanky again. "What a few weeks this has been, one way and another. Anyway, I won't sit here feeling sorry for myself—Evie's situation puts everything into context, doesn't it? I can only say how sorry I am that I didn't realize what Sam was doing to you."

"Listen, Mum," said Nick, "why don't you leave Sam to me? I'm going to pay him a visit on my way to the hospital. Help persuade him he needs to go to rehab."

Posy eyed him. "That sounds ominous. You won't hurt him, will you?"

"God, Mum, of course I won't! He's far more likely to hurt me. You've done enough. Let me handle this."

"Thank you, Nick. Please tell him it's for his own good."

"I will. Right, I'd better be on my way." Nick stood up. "I was thinking that perhaps I'd bring Clemmie up to stay here at Admiral House for a while, if you don't mind. That way, we're closer to the hospital in case anything happens."

"I'd love that, Nick, of course. But what about your work?"

"All on hold until the new year. For once I'm getting my priorities in order," he smiled.

"Well, I'm happy to be here for Clemmie as much as she needs me. And Evie too. Please send her all my love, won't you?"

"Of course I will, Mum. And when we have more time, we need to talk about Admiral House."

"Yes, we do. I'm certainly back to square one with it, but that's the least of your worries at the moment. And just to end on something positive, Nick. I...have someone I'd like you to meet," she said as she walked him to the back door.

"Really? Is the 'someone' a man?" A glimmer of a smile played on Nick's lips as he watched his mother blush.

"Yes, he's called Freddie, and he's the dearest person I know."

"It sounds serious, Mum."

"Maybe it is," Posy agreed. "I met him when I was much younger, and then again recently when he moved to Southwold."

"Does he make you happy?"

"Yes," Posy nodded, "he does."

"Then I'm thrilled for you, I really am. You've been by yourself for far too long."

"And so have you." Posy kissed him warmly. "Bye, Nick, and please telephone me once you've seen Sam."

"I will. Bye, Mum."

Three hours later, on his way back to London, Nick called his mother as she'd asked. The call was picked up on the second ring. "Hi, Mum, are you okay?"

"Yes, and how are you?"

Nick could hear the anxiety in her voice.

"I'm fine, and so is Sam. We had a chat and he's agreed to go into rehab. We looked up a clinic, gave them a call and I'm going to drive back up, collect him and take him in tomorrow."

"Oh, that is good news! Was he...I mean, how did he take it?"

"I think that after a few days alone in that dreadful house he's been renting, with no money to buy booze, he's come to his senses," Nick replied diplomatically, wanting to spare his mother the initial aggression Sam had shown him and what it had taken to convince him to agree.

"What about the cost? I did take a look at a clinic on the internet and it is terribly expensive."

"Don't worry about that, Mum. I'm paying."

"Thank you. I've been so terribly worried about him. Now, more importantly, how is Evie?"

"Very weak, I'm afraid. She's on lots of medication so she slept most of the time I was there. I did tell her you sent her love and if it's okay with you, I'll definitely bring Clemmie up to Admiral House next week. I think we need to be nearby. Evie also said she wanted to meet Tammy, so she might come with us too."

"The more the merrier, if you'll forgive the expression, darling boy. Oh, I can hardly bear it for all of you."

"No. Anyway, I'll let you know when we'll be arriving as soon as I can."

"Okay. Drive carefully, Nick, and thank you for everything."

"I will. You take care of yourself too, Mum. Bye."

Nick allowed himself a small smile as he switched off the call. He'd probably be a pensioner and his mother would still tell him to drive carefully. He felt awful for telling her about Sam—he'd known how upset she would be, but at least now she understood why there had been a lack of closeness between the two of them.

As he approached Chelsea, Nick turned his thoughts back to Tammy and Clemmie. Tammy had texted him just as he was leaving the hospital to say that she was taking Clemmie back to her house and they were getting takeaway pizza, which boded well, he thought.

"Hi, darling," he said as Clemmie answered the door to Tammy's house.

"Hi, Daddy," she replied, and he saw her eyes were sparkling. "We're just waiting for the pizza to arrive. We ordered you one too."

"Thanks," he said as he walked inside and saw Tammy getting out some plates in the kitchen. "Have you had a good day?"

"Very," Clemmie said, sticking out her hands to show him her nails. "Tammy painted them. What do you think?"

Nick looked down at the vivid turquoise color and nodded. "Lovely," he agreed.

"Isn't this house the nicest house you've ever seen, Daddy?" said Clemmie. "It's like a doll's house but for grown-ups. Can we live here instead of Battersea?"

"I think it's a bit small for the three of us, but yes, it is lovely. Hi, Tammy." Nick kissed her chastely on the cheek. "How are you?"

"I'm fine," Tammy smiled. "We had a lovely day, didn't we, Clemmie?"

"Yes. We were going to watch Tammy's old Barbie videos while we ate the pizza, but I s'pose you won't want to watch them, will you?"

"I don't mind, Clemmie, whatever you'd like."

"Don't worry, 'cos Tammy says I can come for a sleepover one night. How's Mummy?"

"She's okay, she sent her love," he added as Tammy indicated the glass of wine she was pouring for herself and he nodded. "I saw Posy, your grandmother, today. She was wondering if we wanted to go and stay with her for a while. Then we'd be nearer to Mummy."

"Can Tammy come too?"

"Of course she can. If she can spare the time away from the boutique."

"I'm sure I could leave Meena in charge for a few days," said Tammy, handing Nick a glass of wine.

The doorbell rang and Clemmie went to collect the pizzas.

"How was it today?" Nick whispered to Tammy.

Tammy shook her head. "Your daughter is truly incredible, Nick. I love her already."

Her words brought involuntary tears to Nick's eyes and he swallowed them back hard. "Do you?"

Tammy reached for his hand. "Yes, I really do."

Chapter 38

"So, Amy, Nick took Sam in to the clinic yesterday. How do you feel about that?" Posy asked her as they sat drinking a cup of tea in the Hophouse.

"Relieved, to be honest, Posy. At least I know he won't be paying me a visit when I go back to work tomorrow. I was scared he might."

"I also wanted to tell you that I saw Nick at the weekend. He told me that Sam bullied him badly when they were both younger. It's important that you know that it isn't just you, that Sam has been violent with others before. You can imagine how mortified I am that I never saw what was happening right under my nose—to you or to him."

"I promise you, Posy, Sam was always very good at making sure no one would notice," Amy sighed.

"Are you going to see a solicitor about divorcing him?"

"I will eventually, but maybe I'll leave it until after he's finished his treatment. It won't be a messy divorce anyway. We have nothing to argue over, apart from the children."

"Well, you're going to have to handle that very carefully indeed when the time comes, Amy. Unless there are some drastic changes, it wouldn't it be safe to leave Sam alone with them."

"I know, but I *am* hoping he'll be a changed man when he comes out. Do you know how long he's going in for, by the way?"

"Nick said six weeks at minimum, and then the doctors will assess him to see how he's doing. Now then, I must be off—I have Nick arriving with Tammy and Clemmie in a couple of hours' time."

"Clemmie? You mean Evie's daughter?"

"I do indeed, yes. And Nick's child, as it happens. It seems Sara and Jake have a new cousin."

Amy stared at Posy, her eyes wide. "Clemmie is Nick's daughter?!"

"Yes. Sadly, Evie is very ill. She contacted Nick out of the blue a few weeks back to tell him."

"So that's why Tammy and I saw his car sitting outside her house. Tammy was convinced they were having an affair. She was in a terrible state when she left. But if she's coming today, they've obviously sorted things out."

"They have, yes, and I'm very happy for all of them, although they're staying with me to be nearer the hospital. Evie doesn't have much time left. Now, I really must go. Perhaps you and the children would like to come round for supper in the next few days?"

"That would be lovely, Posy, and thank you for being so amazing."

"Nonsense, if I *had* been amazing, none of this mess with Sam would have happened. Anyway, I must run now."

Posy left the Hophouse and was walking across the courtyard when Freddie's front door opened.

"Posy, my dear, have you time for a cup of tea?"

"I'm sorry, Freddie, but I haven't, no."

"A hug, then?"

"I always have time for one of those," she said as Freddie drew her to him and she breathed out fully for the first time that day.

"I know your schedule is busy, but do you think it might be possible to book an appointment for lunch or supper with me some time this week?"

"Of course it would, Freddie, you know I'd love to see you. It's obviously busy, what with Nick bringing Clemmie and Tammy to stay, but you must come round to meet them all, too."

"Yes, I'd like that. Please, darling girl, don't overdo it, will you?"

"I'll do my best, Freddie, I promise."

"Good," he said as Posy extracted herself from his embrace.

"Do try and remember that you're well past the age of retirement and have every right to take it easy."

"I will," she said as she kissed him on the cheek. "Bye, Freddie, speak soon."

As Posy drove back to Admiral House, just for a few seconds, she allowed everything else to fade into the background as she focused on Freddie and the promise of happiness that he'd brought to her life. She only prayed that soon she'd have the time to enjoy it. Just now, all her thoughts were with Evie and her daughter.

Arriving home, she made up beds for her guests, then baked a cake for Clemmie and prepared a fish pie for supper. As dusk descended, Posy took herself out for a brisk walk around the garden to calm her mind and get some air. She hovered by the Folly, looking up at the turreted room at the top, its window partially covered by ivy.

Walking thoughtfully back to the house, Posy searched out her mobile from her handbag and scrolled through the numbers. Hesitating for a few seconds, she took a deep breath, then dialed.

"Hello, Posy," the deep, melodic voice answered after a couple of rings. "To what do I owe this honor? Is everything all right?"

"'Everything' is as complicated as always, Sebastian," Posy admitted, "but I'm surviving. How are you?"

"Oh, the same really. Using every trick in the book—including a lot of Christmas drinks parties I don't particularly want to go to—as an excuse for not sitting down at my desk and finishing the book, but I'm okay, thanks, yes."

"Sebastian, I was rather wondering whether you could help me with something."

"Anything, Posy, you know that."

"Freddie told me that he spoke to you about my...father."

"He did, yes. And subsequently, he's obviously told you too."

"Yes, he has. It was a terrible shock, as you can imagine, but I'm getting over it now. One has to, doesn't one?"

"Unfortunately, one does. And if anyone can do that, it's you, Posy. You're the strongest person I know. That's what I told Freddie when he asked my opinion on whether he should tell you. He was desperately worried about upsetting you. He adores you, Posy, truly."

"And I adore him. All is well between us now."

"That makes me very happy," Sebastian responded. "After all these years, you both deserve it."

"Thank you, dear Sebastian. One way and another, life has certainly been challenging recently. And as far as the business with my father is concerned, I've been trying to think of a way to put what happened—and him—to rest."

"You mean, you want closure, as our American friends would put it."

"Quite. And I've thought of a possible way to find it."

"Good. So tell me how I can help."

Posy did so.

"I see," said Sebastian after a pause. "Well, I can certainly put in a call to my contact at the Home Office. He helped me with research for *The Shadow Fields* and should be able to point me in the right direction. I've no idea if it's standard practice or not."

"Perhaps at least they could tell you where he is, Sebastian. Which would be something."

"Of course. I'll let you know if I get any joy, and you can take it from there."

"Thank you, Sebastian, I really appreciate it. Now, I must run over to the oven before my fish pie burns."

"I can smell it from here. Your cooking has ruined me, Posy. Takeaways haven't tasted the same since. I'll be in touch when I know more—bye now."

Posy clicked off her mobile and went to see to the fish pie.

"Nick, darling." Posy kissed her son warmly as he walked through the kitchen door.

"Hello, Mum. Something smells good, as always," he smiled, then turned to Clemmie, who was holding his hand tightly. "Your granny makes the best chocolate sponge cake in the universe."

"Hello, Clemmie," Posy said as she looked at the little girl's pale face, her features so like her mother's. "Can I give you a hug?"

"Yes, Posy...I mean, Granny," she blushed.

"I know, it is confusing," Posy said as she took the child into her arms and held her close. "But fun to be related, isn't it?"

"I think so, yes," Clemmie whispered shyly.

"Why don't you take off your coat and have a slab of that chocolate cake Daddy was talking about? You must be starving after your journey."

"Hello, Posy," said Tammy, bringing up the rear.

"Darling girl, how lovely to see you again. I'll put the kettle on." Posy walked over to fetch the kettle from the stove and filled it. "Good journey?"

"Not bad—at least we missed the rush hour," said Nick, his eyes glued to Clemmie as he took the knife to cut her a slab of cake.

"When you've eaten that, Clemmie, I'll have to show you your room. It's where your daddy used to sleep when he was younger," said Posy.

"This house is so big, Granny." Clemmie's eyes wandered round the kitchen. "It's like a castle."

"It is big, yes, and needs lots of people in it to fill it up," Posy smiled as the kettle boiled.

"You were very lucky to live here as a child, Daddy," Clemmie commented as she broke the cake into dainty pieces and popped some in her mouth.

"I was, wasn't I?"

"Now, shall we have tea in the morning room?" Posy suggested. "I've lit a fire."

Half an hour later, Tammy had taken Clemmie upstairs so that both of them could unpack and Posy sat with her son in front of the fire.

"Any news from the hospital?"

"The same, I'm afraid. I'm taking Tammy in tomorrow; Evie wants to see her. Can you look after Clemmie while I'm gone?"

"Of course I can. She can come to the gallery with me for a few hours. How is she?"

"She knows her mum's still in the hospital—Evie didn't want to see her until she was out, but I think it's too late for that," Nick sighed. "I just wish it wasn't Christmas—it all seems a lot worse when everyone else is full of festive cheer."

"Well, we'll do our best to make Clemmie welcome here. The Christmas tree arrives tomorrow afternoon, so she can help me decorate that."

"And maybe you could go and visit Evie too, depending on how she is."

"Of course, darling. Now I'd better put some vegetables on to go with that fish pie."

After supper, Nick took Clemmie up to get her ready for bed, and Tammy and Posy stood side by side doing the washing up.

"Amy told me that you found out Nick was visiting Evie," Posy said carefully.

"I did, yes."

"Well, it's all credit to you that you're prepared to support him and Clemmie."

"I love him, Posy," Tammy stated simply. "Admittedly, I did have my doubts about being a mother figure to Clemmie—before last week, I wasn't sure I was maternal at all, and I was worried how Clemmie would be with me. But she was so amazing, Posy. It was as if she understood how nervous I was, and she couldn't have made it easier for me to fall in love with her. She's just adorable, and it scares me how protective I already feel about her."

"Then that's what you must tell Evie when you see her tomorrow, Tammy."

"God, I'm dreading it, Posy," Tammy sighed. "Do you really think she'd want to hear that? She won't feel like I'm taking her child away from her, or anything?"

"I think it's exactly what she wants and needs to hear, Tammy; all that matters is that her little girl is loved and protected. At least, I know that's what I would feel if I were her."

"I don't think I'm very good in those kinds of situations," Tammy confessed. "I'll probably just break down and cry all over the place."

"You didn't think you'd be any good as a mum, Tammy, but it's obvious that you will be. All this is a lot to take on board and you can only take it one day at a time. For my part, I'm thrilled you'll be there for my son and granddaughter, and I'm sure Evie—once she meets you—will be too."

"Thanks, Posy, I really appreciate your support. Now then," Tammy said, drying her hands on a tea towel, "I'd better go and say goodnight to Clemmie."

Tammy felt nauseous as Nick led her down the ward towards Evie's room. She'd never been good in hospitals—was terrified of them, with all the machines that bleeped and buzzed constantly, monitoring the life they were attached to ebbing and flowing.

"She's just in there." Nick indicated the door.

"Oh my God." Tammy held on to him fast. "I'm not sure I can do this, Nick, I..."

"You're going to be fine, sweetheart, I promise. She's asleep most of the time now and I'll be with you, don't worry. Okay?" He tipped her chin up to look at him.

"Okay, sorry."

Nick pushed the door open and they walked into the room. Tammy gazed at the tiny, pale figure lying in the bed. Evie looked dwarfed by the machinery surrounding her—and hardly older than her daughter.

"Sit down there," Nick whispered to her as he pointed to a chair.

Tammy sat next to Nick, her eyes focused on the machine that showed Evie's steady heartbeat. It was just unthinkable that a woman who was the same age as her might be disappearing from the earth within days. Tammy swallowed hard. She had no right to cry, after all, because she was looking forward to the rest of her life with the man she loved and Evie's beloved daughter.

Eventually, Evie's long eyelashes fluttered and her eyes opened.

Immediately, Nick took Evie's hand.

"Hello, sweetheart. It's Nick here. Good sleep?"

Evie gave a ghost of a smile and the barest hint of a nod.

He dug in his jacket pocket and produced a card made earlier by Clemmie, covered in tiny red hearts. "Clemmie sent this for you." Nick put it in front of Evie so she could see it. "Shall I read you what it says?"

Again, another almost imperceptible nod.

"Darling Mummy, I miss you and I love you sooo sooo much. Tell Daddy when I can come in to see you. All my love, Clemmie."

Tammy watched a tear appear at the corner of Evie's eye. She heard her swallow.

"Evie, I brought Tammy to see you as you asked. She's just here."

Evie turned her head slowly towards Tammy and gazed at her

for a while. Tammy could feel herself reddening in embarrassment.

"Hi, Evie, I'm Tammy. It's lovely to meet you."

Evie smiled, then her small pink tongue came out to lick her lips. "You too," she whispered. She reached out a skinny arm towards Tammy and opened the palm of her hand. Tammy's own closed around it gently.

"You're very beautiful, like Nick said you were."

"He seems to have good taste in women," Tammy smiled as she squeezed Evie's hand.

"Yes." Evie was silent for a while as if garnering the energy to speak further. "Have you met...Clemmie?"

"I have, yes. She's just adorable, Evie. Honestly, you've done such a great job of bringing her up. I..." Tammy gulped the tears back down. "You must be so proud of her."

"Yes, very."

Tammy watched as Evie's eyelids began to close and a nurse popped her head around the door.

"Hello there, just checking Evie's stats and meds," she said cheerfully as she took a clipboard from the end of the bed. Tammy wondered how on earth the nurse could keep smiling, faced every day with this.

"Everything's fine," the nurse confirmed. "I'll leave you to it."

Evie continued to sleep once the nurse had left the room. Nick turned to Tammy. "You're doing great," he reassured her. "Fancy a cup of tea? I'll go and get a couple from the café while she's sleeping."

Tammy wanted to tell him to stay, that she needed him by her to do this, but she let him go. She wondered how Meena was getting on at the shop, thought about how stock was getting low and then looked down at Evie and realized that none of it mattered. All that *did* was represented right here in this room: caring for this woman's child as best she could.

"Tammy?"

Evie's voice brought her out of her reverie.

"Yes?"

"Where's Nick?"

"Gone to get some tea—he'll be back really soon, I promise."

"No, I'm glad we're alone. I...want to say that I'm happy you'll be there for Clemmie. Nick is"—Evie swallowed painfully—"good, but he's a man, you know?"

"I do know, yes," Tammy smiled.

"Clemmie needs a woman, a mother; are you...are you okay with that?"

"Oh Evie, completely. I was saying to Posy last night that I was worried I wasn't maternal. But then I met Clemmie and I...fell in love with her. I feel ridiculously protective already."

"That's good, I'm glad." Evie nodded. "I know...that I don't have long left. I need to see Clemmie. Say...goodbye." She bit her lip hard and nodded.

"When would you like to see her?"

"As...as soon as possible is best."

"Okay, I'll tell Nick."

"Look after her for me, won't you? Love her for me..."

"I promise I will, Evie."

"Thank you."

Evie's eyes closed once more just as Nick arrived back with the tea.

"You okay, darling?" he asked as he sat down and handed Tammy a tea in a styrofoam cup. Then he gently wiped away one of the tears that was rolling down her face.

"She just said she wanted to see Clemmie to...say goodbye. As soon as possible."

"Okay." Nick took a sip of his tea and they sat there in silence as Evie slept. Forty minutes later, she still hadn't woken, and Nick indicated they should leave.

"I saw the doctor on my way back from getting the tea," he said as they walked through the ward. "I'm going to drive you home and then bring back Clemmie tonight. Evie was right—she's running out of time."

"Okay," Tammy agreed.

"I'll have Mum come too so that she can drive Clemmie home afterwards, and then I can stay here with Evie," he added as they walked through the entrance doors and Tammy took great gulps of fresh air. "I don't want her to be by herself when..."

"Of course, Nick. Me and Posy are here for Clemmie, so you can be there for Evie," she said as they climbed into his car.

"You're sure you don't mind?"

"Mind? Oh my God, of course I don't mind."

"Some women would," Nick said as he started the engine. "After all, I loved her once and I'm aware that this whole scenario is hardly an ideal way to start our relationship."

"Please, Nick, no more. If I didn't want to be here for you and Clemmie, I wouldn't be, okay? Evie needs you now more than I do."

"Thanks, Tammy." He gave her a wan smile as they set off. "It was good you saw her today. What else did she say?"

"She said..." Tammy gulped. "She asked me to take care of Clemmie for her. I said that I'd do my best."

"You already are, darling, and I can't thank you enough."

Tammy was just pouring herself a large glass of wine, having waved Nick, Clemmie and Posy off to the hospital, when she saw the headlights of a car coming up the drive.

"Who on earth could that be?" she whispered to herself as the car pulled round to the back entrance.

Peering out of the kitchen window, she saw Amy walking towards the back door.

"Anyone at home?" Amy called as she opened it.

"Me!" Tammy walked over to kiss Amy warmly on the cheek. "How lovely to see you. I thought Posy had told you she was off to the hospital with Nick and Clemmie tonight."

"She did, yes, but I wanted to see you, and Freddie said he'd have the kids for a bit. He's really amazing—have you met him yet?"

"No, remind me who is he?"

"Posy's gentleman friend, as she calls him. But also my savior. He's a really special man, and I'm not joking. If Posy doesn't grab him, I think I'll marry him," Amy grinned. "Any wine going?"

"Sure," Tammy said, pouring her a glass. "Wow, Amy," she added as she handed it to her, "Nick told me what you've been through recently, but you look really well."

"Now I'm over the shock, I'm starting to feel it. It's just the relief, I suppose, knowing that Sam can't get to me, that I don't have to dread his key turning in the lock...Cheers."

They clinked glasses.

"You should have said something, Amy—you know I would have done anything to help."

"I know, but I was simply too scared of retribution. Sam would have denied it all anyway. You met him—saw what he's like. He can charm the birds out of the trees."

"Well, he certainly didn't charm me," Tammy shuddered. "I've met his sort before."

"Have you?" Amy eyed her as they sat down at the kitchen table.

"Unfortunately, yes. Luckily for me, I didn't have kids and was financially independent with a job that took me all over the world. I could escape, whereas you couldn't. So yes, I know a little of what you've been through. It's all about control, so my therapist told me after the event. Little men who can only feel big by controlling their women through anger and violence. Anyway, here's to him being gone."

"It's not for long. He might only be in the clinic for six weeks." Amy shivered. "Which brings me to why I wanted to talk to you. Posy told me how Sam had beaten up Nick when he was younger. Then I had a long chat with Freddie, who used to be a criminal barrister, and I'm...well, I'm going to press charges for assault."

"Right. And how do you feel about it?"

"Terrified, disloyal, guilty..." Amy shrugged. "But as both Freddie and Posy said to me, if I don't do it, it means Sam could do it again to someone else. And I can't have that on my conscience. What do you think?"

"I think, Amy, that it's an incredibly brave thing to do, *and* the right thing."

"What do you think Posy will say? I mean, she's been so kind to me and so supportive, but at the end of the day, Sam is her son."

"I know he is and I understand why you're concerned, but Amy, I'm sure Posy will agree that you should go ahead."

"Freddie said that it's unlikely Sam will get a long prison sentence; the fact he's already gone to a clinic to sort out his alcoholism and anger issues will go a long way to showing the judge he's accepted responsibility for what he did. He may even get off with a suspended sentence, but that isn't the point. I just want what he did to me to be on record, so that in the future, if he ever does it again, it's there in black and white. I'm dreading the process—the thought of standing up in court and giving evidence against my husband..." Amy shuddered. "But he could have killed me that night, and I can't be responsible for him doing that to someone else."

"No, you can't, and everyone will be there to nurse you through it, I promise. Seriously, Amy, I'm proud of you. So many women are understandably too scared to bring their abuser to justice, especially if it's their husband or partner. If more of us women did, then perhaps men would realize they can't get away with it." Tammy reached for Amy's hand across the table and squeezed it. "Do it for all of us, Amy, but most importantly, for *you* and your lovely children."

"Well, I'm going to leave it until after Christmas—one way and another, the Montague family have enough on their plate just now, but thanks so much for your support, Tammy." Amy's eyes glistened with tears and she took a large sip of wine. "Anyway, let's talk about something else, shall we? How's Evie?"

"Not good at all, I'm afraid. I went to see her today."

"And?"

"I spent most of the time trying not to sob all over her. It's just dreadful, Amy. Clemmie's gone to the hospital so Evie can say goodbye."

"My God, life is shit, isn't it? Poor Nick and poor Clemmie."

"I know. Nick is so good with her, so caring and kind."

"Nick is a good man, Tammy. And you mustn't worry that he and Evie..."

"Oh no, I don't any more, really, Amy. I'm just glad Evie has him there with her."

"How can two brothers be so completely different?" Amy sighed. "It looks like I picked the wrong one, anyway."

Tammy sipped her wine and eyed Amy. "Have you heard from Sebastian recently?"

"No, why should I have done?"

"Because at the party, you two looked...well, you looked as though you were together, to be honest."

"We...were, for a while anyway. As a matter of fact, I was about to leave Sam just before he got arrested over the Admiral House fraud. Then, when he got released on bail, I knew I couldn't. I told Sebastian to go away, that I never wanted to see him again."

"Right. And *is* it over? Even now that you've left Sam?"

Amy stared into the distance. "I keep telling my heart that it is, but it doesn't seem to want to listen. Anyway, I had my chance and I blew it. And besides, just now I need to focus on the children. Due to what's happened, they've just lost a father."

"So you're not going to tell Sebastian that you've left Sam?"

"No," Amy said firmly. "Anyway, I'm sure he's moved on since then. I was probably just a bit of entertainment whilst he was staying here."

"From what I saw, it was a lot more than that, Amy."

"Tammy, I'm really sorry to say this, but could we talk about something else?"

"Sorry, of course we can. How are the children?"

"They're great, thanks." Amy's face lit up. "They love their new house and their new babysitter, i.e. Freddie. He spoils them rotten. By the way, do you know what you and Nick are going to do for Christmas yet?"

"I think everything depends on Evie, to be honest. We haven't made any plans."

"Of course. I'm so glad the two of you managed to work it out, though, Tammy. And welcome to motherhood." Amy smiled and they clinked glasses again.

"I know. It's a bit sooner than I would have wanted, but Clemmie is such a lovely little girl, and besides, at least I've got out of the pain of giving birth to her."

"True," Amy giggled, 'though I'm sure that's all to come. Are you and Nick living together in London yet?"

"No, because I didn't want to rush Clemmie. But I think that after Christmas I'll move in with them to Nick's new house in Battersea."

"I so hope you two get married, Tammy. It would be nice to have a celebration to look forward to."

"One step at a time, but yes, I'd like it too, and it would probably be good for Clemmie. I'll have to wait for him to ask me, mind you." Tammy smiled. "We seem to have done everything back to front."

"That's modern families for you, isn't it? By the way, has Posy decided what she's going to do about Admiral House yet?"

"We chatted about it briefly this morning—I think she's going to put it back on the market in January."

"It's so sad—the house has been in her family for three hundred years. And it's so beautiful. Sebastian was completely in love with it, and so am I. I'll have to do a painting of it before it's sold. I was thinking I could give it to Posy as a seventieth birthday present."

"Posy is seventy?" Tammy looked amazed. "Wow, I'd put her at a decade younger."

"I know, she puts us all to shame with her energy. Well, I'd better head back and relieve Freddie from his twelfth viewing of *The Muppet Christmas Carol*. It's been lovely to see you, Tammy, and if you get the chance, why don't you pop round to see me? I'm just off the High Street, but if you call me before you come, I can give you directions. Bring Clemmie too, and she can meet her naughty little cousins."

"If there's time, of course I will. It's really wonderful to see you, Amy." Tammy stood up and kissed her. "Take care, won't you?"

"Now I can say that I most definitely will. Bye, Tammy."

Chapter 39

The following afternoon, Tammy was taking a walk around the gardens with Clemmie and Posy when her mobile rang in her pocket.

"Excuse me, you two, won't be a moment," she said, mouthing, "It's Nick," over the top of Clemmie's head. Posy nodded, then shooed Clemmie along so Tammy could take the call in privacy.

"Hello?"

"Tammy, it's Nick. Evie died twenty minutes ago."

She could hear the exhaustion and emptiness in his voice. "I'm so, so sorry, Nick."

"Thanks. I've got some paperwork to fill in here I'm afraid, but I'll be home once that's done. Don't say anything to Clemmie until I get back, will you? I should tell her."

"Of course. Take care, darling. I love you."

Tammy glanced across the mist-covered garden, smelling the comforting scent of wood smoke. Posy was cutting some holly from a bush while Clemmie held the ladder steady. Tammy walked towards them, and as she climbed down, Posy's eyes searched hers. Tammy gave a small shake of her head and Posy nodded.

"It seems that at last I have one member of the family who might share my passion for gardening, isn't that right, Clemmie?" Posy smiled.

"Oh yes, I love flowers and plants and Granny is going to teach me all about them when they start to come out in the spring."

"I am indeed. Now then, shall we go in for a nice mug of hot choccy and some cake? It's getting rather cold and dark out here."

As they walked back towards the house, Tammy looked up towards the sky and saw the first stars already twinkling in the heavens above them.

Godspeed, dearest Evie. And I promise I'll do the very best I can to take care of your daughter...

Nick arrived home an hour later, looking drawn and pale. He took Clemmie into the morning room where she and Posy had erected the Christmas tree, and shut the door behind him.

"I could do with a large glass of wine, and I'm sure you could too," said Posy grimly as she reached for the bottle from the fridge.

"Thanks, Posy."

The two women sat together at the table in silence, deep in their own thoughts.

"I was just a bit younger than Clemmie when I was told my father had died," Posy said eventually. "The difference being that I was unprepared; but still, however much her mother has done to help her cope with this news, it won't be easy for her. She'll be devastated. Up to this point it's just been imagined, and now it's real."

"How did your father die, Posy?"

"Now that, Tammy, is rather a long story." Posy gave a sad smile. "Recently something happened, and I felt I had lost him all over again."

Both women heard the door to the morning room open, and Nick emerged with Clemmie in his arms. Her head was buried in his shoulder.

"She said she wanted to see you, Mum," he said as he handed her over to Posy.

Tammy caught a glimpse of Clemmie's tear-stained face and felt her own heart lurch with love. Nick offered his hand towards her as Posy settled Clemmie onto her knee.

"Any of that wine going spare?" he asked.

Tammy retrieved the bottle and another glass, and the two of them left the room.

"How did she take it?"

"Very calmly, considering. She told me that Evie had said goodbye to her yesterday," he said as they sat down in the morning room in front of the fire. "But she's obviously devastated."

"Of course she is."

"I told her Mummy just drifted away peacefully up to heaven, which she did. Evie went to sleep and just didn't wake up. It was for the best, Tammy, she'd been in so much pain. I..."

Then it was Nick's turn to cry. Tammy drew him into her arms and he sobbed quietly on her shoulder.

"I'm so sorry, so very sorry," Tammy whispered.

Nick drew away from her and wiped his eyes on his sweater. "Sorry to cry on you, Tammy. I need to pull myself together for Clemmie. There's going to be things to sort out—Evie's funeral, for example—she just wanted something quiet at the local church. And then there's the house in Southwold—she's left everything to Clemmie, of course. She thought it was probably best to sell it and put the money away to use for her education and university."

"That can be organized over time, Nick. The most important thing now is for all of us to take care of Clemmie."

"Yes." Nick gave her a weak smile. "Thank you for being so fantastic. I'm so sorry, Tammy, I'm—"

"Hush, Nick. This is what love is, isn't it? Sticking together through the bad times."

"Well, let's hope there are some good times coming."

"There are, Nick. I promise," Tammy said with feeling.

Evie's funeral took place on a dank, gray Wednesday a week later. Afterwards, the few mourners went back to Admiral House for a glass of mulled wine and Posy's homemade mince pies.

"I'm so proud of her," Posy said to Nick as they watched Clemmie sitting on the floor in the kitchen with her two new cousins. "She seems to be adjusting very well. Have you decided whether she'll continue at her boarding school?"

"We've talked about it and Clemmie says she'd like to stay on for now, yes. She's made a lot of friends there, and at least it brings some normality, which I think is what she needs," replied Nick.

"Hello, Posy," said Marie, wandering over to them. "Hi, Nick."

"Hi, Marie, thank you for coming," he replied politely.

"Not at all. Evie and I were best friends at school. All those dreams we had..." Marie shook her head. "Who'd have thought this was Evie's future."

"I know, it's so very sad," Posy sighed.

"I'm aware this isn't the moment, but have you given any consideration to what you're going to do with Admiral House?" Marie asked.

"Not really, dear, no, but you'll be the first to hear when I do," said Posy, irritated.

"Well, I'll be coming in to see you about putting Evie's house on the market after Christmas," said Nick.

"Great, well, I don't think there'll be a problem selling it. Clemmie will probably be richer than any of us. Just give me a call whenever." Marie left with a nod.

Nick looked at the expression on Posy's face. "Life must go on, Mum," he said. "That's the way of the world."

"I know. It did when I lost my father." Posy turned to glance at Freddie, dapper in a dark suit. He was deep in conversation with Tammy.

"He seems very nice," Nick said with a grin.

"He is. I feel very blessed."

"It's about time you had someone to look after you."

"I hope we can look after each other," Posy smiled. "One day, I'll tell you all about him, and why we couldn't be together all those years ago. By the way, have you given any thought to Christmas, Nick?"

"I talked to Tammy and Clemmie about it last night, and we'd love to be here with you, if that's all right?"

"Of course it is, Nick. Freddie, Amy and the children will be here too. It's a difficult time for them as well—their first Christmas without their father. Anyway, we shall make it as jolly as we possibly can."

Posy heard her mobile ringing from within her handbag. "Do excuse me, Nick, I should answer that."

"Of course."

"Hello?"

"Posy, it's Sebastian."

"Hello, Sebastian dear."

"Is this a bad time?"

"No, not at all." Posy walked out of the kitchen and shut the door behind her in order to hear him. "Any luck?"

"As a matter of fact, yes. Your father was buried in an unmarked grave in the grounds of Pentonville Prison."

"Unmarked?"

"Well, he doesn't have a headstone, only a number indicating whereabouts in the grounds he was laid to rest."

"Right. And can I go to see him?"

"Well, it's not standard procedure, but my contact twisted an arm or two and yes, you can go. Will Friday suit you?"

"Even if it doesn't, I'll be there. Sebastian?"

"Yes?"

"Would you mind coming with me?"

"Of course not. But wouldn't you rather bring a family member?"

"No, most definitely not. My sons know nothing about all this yet."

"All right, then—I didn't think I'd ever be saying this to you, Posy, but I'll meet you at the gates of the prison at two o'clock."

"Perfect. Thank you from the bottom of my heart for organizing this."

"No problem, Posy. See you on Friday. Bye."

Posy took a moment to compose herself, feeling the irony of discovering her father's whereabouts just as they were burying another who had died before her time. She took a deep breath and walked back into the kitchen.

Chapter 40

"Hello, Posy. All set?" Sebastian smiled down at her.

"As much as I ever will be, yes."

"You're absolutely sure you want to do this? I mean, it's a bit grim," he said, indicating the austere building in front of them.

"Absolutely, yes."

"Right then. Here goes." Sebastian rang the buzzer, gave their names and the prison gates clicked open.

Fifteen minutes later, they were led into the garden by one of the prison clerks.

"Right, your father was buried just over here, according to the coordinates," she said as they walked over the grass—and, Posy imagined, endless bodies—towards a spot by the tall prison walls.

"Right," the clerk said, consulting the printout she'd brought with her. She pointed to a mound of grass just to their left. "That's him there."

"Thank you."

"Want me to come with you?" Sebastian asked her.

"No, thank you, I won't be long."

Posy approached the shallow mound the clerk had indicated and walked towards it, her heart drumming against her chest. She stood above it, her eyes wet with tears as she noted that there was nothing on the surface to mark who her father had been.

"Hello, Daddy," she whispered. "I'm so sorry you ended up in this terrible place. You deserved better."

As Posy stood there, it struck her for the first time that her father had been given licence to kill as he flew his Spitfire into the epicenter of war. For that, he'd been decorated, named a hero. But here he lay, amongst hundreds of other criminals, because he'd taken the life of a man who had so cruelly betrayed him.

"You shouldn't be here, Daddy, and I want you to know that I forgive you. And that I'll always love you."

She opened the canvas bag she'd brought with her and took out the small posy she'd made—ethereal white hellebore blooms, interspersed with berry-laden sprigs of glossy green holly.

She laid it on top of the mound, then closed her eyes and said a prayer.

Sebastian and the clerk stood watching her from a respectful distance.

"Does she know there are two other bodies buried in the same grave?"

"She does not, and neither does she need to," Sebastian whispered firmly as Posy crossed herself then walked back towards them.

"All done?" he asked her.

"Yes, thank you."

Leaving the prison, Sebastian turned to her. "Now that's over, how do you fancy jumping in a taxi and going for a slap-up afternoon tea at Fortnum's?"

"Sebastian, there is nothing I would like more," Posy smiled. "Now, let's get out of this terrible place."

Half an hour later, they were sitting in the festive atmosphere of the Fountain Room at Fortnum & Mason. Sebastian had ordered them both a glass of champagne.

"Here's to your father, Posy. And to you." He clinked her glass and they both took a sip. "How do you feel, having seen where he's buried? Better or worse?"

"Definitely better," Posy nodded as she helped herself to a cucumber sandwich. "However dreadful, there has been an end to what happened. I've said goodbye to him."

"It was a very brave thing to do, Posy."

"Well, I'm glad I have, and I can't thank you enough for organizing it. So tell me, how is the book going?"

"Oh, I'm getting there. I'll be handing it in at the beginning of February."

"So what are you doing for Christmas?"

"Nothing," Sebastian said. "Taking the time when everyone else is eating plum pudding to get some work done in peace."

"That sounds rather miserable, if you don't mind me saying."

"I suppose it is, but far preferable to spending it with my mother and the godawful man she married after my father died a few years ago. Christmas is for families, and I don't have one of my own, so that's just the way it is."

"Well now, would you consider coming to spend it with my family at Admiral House?"

"Posy, that's awfully kind of you, but I hardly think your family would want me there."

"Why?"

"Oh," Sebastian mumbled as he buttered a scone, "just because I'm an outsider."

"Actually, Sebastian, I think my family would love it. Especially one person in particular."

"And who would that be?"

Posy eyed him, then chose another sandwich. "Amy, of course."

She watched Sebastian blush to the roots of his hair.

"Please don't tell me you don't know what I'm talking about, Sebastian, because it would be a lie, and I've had enough lies for a lifetime just now."

"Okay, I won't." He reached for his champagne and took a deep gulp. "How did you know?"

"It was written all over both of you."

"It might have been, but Amy told me verbatim that she would never leave Sam."

"Which is the reason why you left Admiral House so abruptly."

"Yes. Forgive me, Posy, you must be utterly furious at me. Sam's your son, and—"

"Amy has left him, Sebastian. He had brutally attacked her, and thanks to Freddie, didn't do as much harm as he could have done. Sam is currently in a clinic in Essex trying to sort out his anger and alcohol issues."

"God, Posy." Sebastian shook his head. "I'm...well, I'm not sure what I am, to be honest. Horrified would come closest, I suppose."

"Did you ever suspect that Amy was a victim of abuse, Sebastian?"

"I...it did cross my mind, yes. There were bruises in strange places..."

"There's no need to be coy, Sebastian. I often wonder why the younger generation pussy-foot around the older when it comes to things like sex, when we've generally had far more experience of those things than they have. Anyway, the situation is that Amy will not be going back to Sam, even if he walks away from the clinic a reformed character."

"I have to say I'm relieved. She's such a good human being, and she's had a miserable time of it."

"She has indeed, yes. Sebastian, do you love her?"

"I do, Posy, and if I wasn't sure when I left, I certainly am now. Even though she told me I didn't have a hope, I've thought of nothing else in the past month. In truth, it's why I've not been able to write. I just...well," he sighed, "I think about her constantly."

"So, how would you feel about joining us for Christmas?" Posy repeated the question.

"I really don't know." He studied her hard across the table. "If I'm honest, I find it difficult to understand why you are encouraging your son's wife back into the arms of her lover."

"Because I'm a realist, Sebastian. It's not only Amy that's had a difficult time, it's you too. So many people don't get their happy endings—it took me fifty years to find mine, after all, and if it's in my power to make it so, then I'll do all I can. Amy needs you, and so do my grandchildren."

"And what about Sam?"

"No mother wants to admit that they've given birth to a bad apple, but I suppose that's what he is. And by ignoring it, I let Nick go through a terrible time as a child—and Amy, who I love dearly, came close to losing her life. I've been wondering in the last few days whether it runs in the genes. After all, my father was stirred to kill his best friend."

"Posy, that's completely different. It was a crime of passion. If it had happened in France, he'd probably have got an honorable pardon." Sebastian smiled. "Genes are genes, yes, but try to remember that each one of us has our own DNA, exclusive only to us. And in that exclusive bit can be all sorts of personality traits."

"I suppose you're right; I'd never thought about it like that. Of course I feel huge guilt for Sam's behavior. Was it something I did, or didn't do, was his bullying the result of losing his father so tragically young, and so on...but it's a road to nowhere."

"Yes, it is, Posy, but at least Amy and your grandchildren are safe."

"I'd also like them to be happy. Will you come, Sebastian? Freddie will be there, and my son Nick and Tammy."

"It's very kind of you, Posy, but do you think I could have some time before I answer?"

"Of course. Now, let me tell you the poignant story of how I found myself with an extra grandchild..."

"Alone at last!" said Freddie as he hugged Posy to him on his doorstep. "Come in, come in. I feel as though I haven't had you to myself for weeks," he said as he let her go and led her into the sitting room, where a tray containing a bottle of champagne and two glasses was sitting on the coffee table.

"Goodness, what's that in aid of?"

"Absolutely nothing, other than it's almost Christmas, and more importantly, our two hearts are still beating in our chests. One shouldn't need an excuse to drink champagne when one is our age, Posy."

"I had champagne yesterday too."

"Did you indeed? And where was that?" Freddie said as he popped the cork, poured some champagne into the glasses, and handed her one.

"At Fortnum's. I had tea with Sebastian."

"Well now! Do I have a rival for your affections?"

"If I were thirty years younger, then yes," Posy smiled. "Cheers."

"Cheers," Freddie toasted back. "How is he?"

"He's well, Freddie, and he sent his regards to you. I hear he took the role of listening ear in our melodrama."

"He did indeed, yes, and I'm grateful to him for his good advice. But more importantly, what were you doing meeting him at

Fortnum's?"

"I asked him to find my father's grave for me, and I went to visit it yesterday."

"I see. Where was it?"

"Pentonville Prison. And before you say anything else, yes, it could not have been more grim. But it served its purpose, and now I really feel I can move on."

"Then I'm happy for you, Posy, though if you'd have asked me, I'd have gladly accompanied you."

"It was something I needed to do by myself, Freddie. I hope you can understand that."

"Yes, I can."

"Actually, I've invited him for Christmas."

"Have you? Well then, I look forward to seeing him. We're rather short of men in your family these days."

"He and Amy were having an affair when Sebastian was living with me at Admiral House."

"Really? And you knew about it?"

"I certainly suspected as much, yes. And both of them have freely admitted it to me. He's such a lovely man, Freddie. Just what Amy needs."

"Quite the little matchmaker, aren't you?"

"After what has happened in the past few weeks, I think we can both agree that life is just too damned short. We missed out on a lifetime of happiness together, and I don't want that to be the case for Amy and Sebastian."

"Well, well," Freddie smiled at her, "it's a very generous gesture, considering Sam."

"Well, given Sam called me from the clinic a couple of days ago and said he'd met a woman to whom he'd become close, I doubt he'll be alone for long. She's called Heather, and she's in there for alcohol addiction. She knows all about Sam's anger and alcohol issues, apparently. Considering the circumstances, he sounded very upbeat. And of course, sober."

"Well, that's good news."

"It is, yes, and as far as Amy and Sebastian go, I've only issued an invitation. It's up to them to take it from here."

"Quite. Now, are you ready for something to eat? I'm afraid it's my hotpot again."

Freddie had lit the candles on the table in the kitchen and Posy sat down as he dished out the food.

"Posy my dear, I do have something to confess."

"Oh goodness, Freddie." Posy's heart began to pound. "I'm not sure I can take any more bad news. What on earth is it?"

"Well now, it's about Sam's arrest. A while ago, I had a conversation with Sebastian. I was concerned about this Ken Noakes and asked Sebastian if he had any contacts from his days as a newshound that could help us check out his background. And indeed he did. The fraud squad then contacted Sebastian to discover Mr. Noakes' whereabouts. Subsequently he was arrested, along with your son."

"I see. Well…" she replied after a pause. "At least it's not as bad as I expected. In fact, I should say thank you."

"Really?" Freddie studied her expression anxiously.

"Absolutely. Heaven knows what would have happened if you and Sebastian hadn't stepped in. Sam was on a slippery slope to oblivion and at least now he's getting the help he needs. And the thought of that ghastly man getting his hands on Admiral House…what you both did brought everything to a head. Painful, but necessary."

"So you forgive me?"

"There's nothing to forgive, Freddie. Really."

"Thank goodness. After all these years of keeping the terrible secret, I wanted nothing to be hidden from you. Now… how is Clemmie?" he asked, tactfully changing the subject as they ate.

"Doing well, and very excited about Christmas. They've gone back to London for a few days and will come up on Christmas Eve. I want to make it special for her if I can."

"I'm sure you will, Posy. And Admiral House?"

"Everything's on hold until after Christmas," Posy said firmly.

"Of course. Now, please, tuck in."

After supper, the two of them went back into the sitting room and sat with a glass of brandy in front of the fire.

"Let's hope we're sailing into calmer waters in the new year," said Freddie.

"Yes, and I just want to say thank you to you for all your

support, not just of me, but of my family. You've been so very kind, Freddie. Everyone adores you."

"Do they?"

"Yes. When I was introducing you to them, I felt like a child seeking approval from her parents. It's so very important, having approval from your family, isn't it?"

"Yes, it is, and I'm glad I've passed muster."

"I think you've done more than that, Freddie. And now I really must go. I'm exhausted from the last few days."

"Posy?" Freddie stood up and walked over to her. He took her hand and pulled her to standing. "Won't you stay?"

"I..."

"Please," he said. Then he kissed her and, as he eventually led her upstairs ten minutes later, she didn't mind at all that her body had seen almost seventy years, because his had too.

Tea rose
(Rosa odorata)

Chapter 41

"Amy, would you mind going to Halesworth Station to collect an old friend of mine? We're up to our eyes in mince pies, aren't we, Clemmie?"

"Yes," agreed Clemmie as she spooned out the mincemeat into the pastry shells.

"No, of course not. Who am I looking for?"

"Oh, he's called George. I'll text him to say to look out for a beautiful blonde," Posy smiled.

Freddie, who was sitting at the table, rolled his eyes at her in amusement.

"Okay, just keep an eye on the kids, will you? They're in the morning room, trying to guess all the presents under the tree."

"I'd better go and make sure they're not opening them, then," Clemmie said, wiping her hands on her apron and leaving the kitchen.

"George, eh?" Freddie said as he came to stand behind Posy and kneaded her shoulders.

"That's the name of the hero in Sebastian's book," she shrugged. "It was the first that came to mind."

"Right. Anything I can do?"

"You could certainly set the table, yes. Tammy and Nick are upstairs wrapping the last of the presents. The children are all going to be ruined this Christmas."

"Right-oh," Freddie said as he walked to the drawer to retrieve the cutlery. "I was wondering..."

"What about?" Posy asked, opening the door to the oven and sliding the tray of mince pies inside.

"Whether, after all this madness is over, I could whisk you away on holiday for a couple of weeks? You've certainly earned one, Posy."

"Well, that sounds wonderful, but..."

"No buts, Posy, I'm sure that everyone could manage to live without you for a couple of weeks. We deserve some time together, darling girl." Hands full of knives and forks, he planted a gentle kiss on Posy's cheek. "I was thinking the Far East. Malaysia, perhaps?"

"Golly, I'd love to go back there, Freddie."

"Good. Then we shall, while we're still fit and healthy enough to do so."

"You're right, yes," Posy agreed. "And I'd love to."

Then the three children arrived in the kitchen, and Posy's attention moved on to them.

Amy stood on the platform, clapping her hands together to keep warm. The train was delayed by fifteen minutes and it was freezing. Finally, it chugged into the station, disgorging passengers onto the platform, their hands full of bags containing Christmas presents. Amy scanned the crowd, hoping Posy's text had got through or she might never find George. Slowly, the platform emptied, and Amy was just about to turn back to retrieve her mobile from the car and call Posy when she saw a tall figure standing a few yards from her.

Amy gulped, wondering if she was having some kind of weird vision, but no, it was him. She watched as he walked slowly towards her.

"Hello, Amy."

"Hello—I'm afraid I need to run to the car because I'm meant to be picking up someone called George, a friend of Posy's, and..."

"That's me, yes," he smiled.

"But your name isn't George, and Posy hasn't invited you for Christmas, has she?"

"As a matter of fact, she has."

Amy stared at him in silence.

"If you don't believe her, give her a call."

"But why...?"

"Because she is one of the most amazing human beings I've ever met, but if you don't want me there, then I'll get the next train back to London. Do you want me, Amy?"

"For Christmas, you mean?"

"You know what they say about dogs being not just for Christmas," he said with a grin. "So maybe a bit longer than that."

"I..." Amy's head was spinning.

"If it helps, she's told me everything, and I'm so very sorry that you had to go through what you went through with Sam. I could throttle him with my own bare hands, to be honest, but I doubt that would be of much help, so I'll do my best to restrain myself. Now, before we both die tragically of frostbite, do you think you could come to a decision?"

Amy couldn't see him properly, because her vision was blurred with tears. Her heart, kept as it had been under lock and key since Sebastian had left, seemed to explode in her chest.

"Well," she swallowed. "You're Posy's guest and she asked me to bring you home."

"And you're sure you want to do that?"

"Yes, I'm sure."

"Then let's go." He held out a hand to her and she took it. And together, they walked through the deserted station to the car.

Chapter 42

Six months later

Posy sat in front of her dressing-table mirror and applied mascara to her eyelashes. Then she applied a new lipstick she'd bought especially for tonight, and immediately rubbed it off.

"Far too bright for an old biddy like you, Posy," she admonished herself.

Through the open window she could hear the small orchestra tuning up on the terrace. The caterers were busy in the kitchen and she had been banned by her family from entering it for the past three hours.

Rising from the stool, she went to the window and looked down. It was a gorgeous, mellow June evening, reminding her very much of the last big party that had been held here when she'd been just seven years old. She'd sat on one of the steps down to the garden, desperate not to be found and put to bed, and her father had joined her, smoking a cigarette.

"*Promise me that when you find love, you will grab hold of it and never let it go,*" he'd said.

His words rang in her ears, and she only hoped he'd approve of tonight.

Freddie and she had been married quietly at the registry office yesterday with only family in attendance. And tonight—on her seventieth birthday—they would celebrate.

Posy moved to sit on the edge of the bed and put on her shoes—they had a kitten heel and felt most uncomfortable, but she could hardly wear wellingtons on her special night, as Clemmie had pointed out when she'd taken her shopping to find a pair that matched her outfit.

Tammy had found the dress—a shimmering cream 1930s vintage piece that covered the lumps and bumps that age had brought, and didn't make her look like a ship in full sail.

There was a knock on the door.

"Who is it?"

"It's Tammy and Clemmie," Clemmie called. "We have the flowers for your hair."

"Come in!"

They did—Tammy looking utterly breathtaking in an emerald-green sheath, and Clemmie in bronze taffeta that set off her coloring to perfection.

"My goodness, don't you two look beautiful," Posy smiled.

"And you, Granny—I mean, you don't look like one at all," Clemmie giggled.

"Tonight, dear girl, I don't feel like one either," Posy agreed.

"Here's a glass of champagne to calm your nerves. Shall I pin the flowers into your hair?" Tammy asked.

"Thank you." Posy took a gulp of her champagne, then walked back to the dressing table and sat down. At Freddie's insistence, she'd grown her hair longer and it now fell in soft waves around her face.

"There," said Tammy as she fastened in the two creamy rosebuds, picked from the garden.

"How are the caterers getting on? Have they laid out the drinks?"

"Granny, stop fussing. Everything's taken care of."

"I promise it is, Posy," said Tammy. "Do you need anything else? The guests are starting to arrive and the boys are downstairs to greet them. We should go and mingle."

"No, I'm fine, thank you. Come here, my beautiful girls, and let me give you both a kiss." Posy put her hands out to pull Clemmie to her, but her granddaughter caught her left hand in her smaller one and held it out towards Tammy.

"Look, Tammy, Posy has two rings on her finger now and you

only have one."

"Cheeky monkey," Tammy admonished her. "You just want to wear another lovely bridesmaid's dress."

"I just want you and Daddy to get married for real so we can be a proper family."

"Soon, I promise, Clemmie, but we should let Posy enjoy her own wedding and birthday party first, shall we?"

Tammy rolled her eyes at Posy over Clemmie's head as Posy kissed her granddaughter. "Get on with you downstairs, miss. I'll see you in a while."

"Freddie will be up to collect you in fifteen minutes or so."

"Thank you, Tammy. I feel so spoilt."

"Well, you absolutely deserve to, Posy. You've done so much for all of us, now it's your turn."

The two of them left the room and Posy took another gulp of her champagne, then went to sit on the window seat, spying on the growing crowd of guests standing on the terrace below her.

There was another knock at her door.

"Come in."

This time it was Amy, looking lovely in turquoise silk.

"I just came to wish you luck for tonight, Posy."

"Thank you. You look like a dream, by the way. It really is a night of new beginnings, isn't it?"

"Yes, it is, but I promise, Posy, when Sebastian and I eventually move into Admiral House, you'll be welcome here any time."

"I know, darling, and thank you. The house needs a facelift and a family in it. I'm so grateful to Sebastian for wanting to take it on."

"Well, it'll be at least a year before we move in, because of the renovation, but I promise to care for it, if *you* promise to help us with the garden. I wouldn't know where to start."

"Then you will have to learn, and once I'm back from my honeymoon, I'll show you."

"You really don't mind, do you?"

"Of course I don't. After all, Jake and Sara are my grandchildren. They're Montagues, remember, so the bloodline essentially remains unbroken."

"I...Have you heard from Sam?" Amy asked timidly.

"Yes, he phoned me earlier to wish me a good evening."

"Right." Amy looked uneasily at Posy. "How did he sound?"

"In good spirits, considering. He's still staying with Heather—the woman he met in the clinic—at her house in Wiltshire. He told me that once the trial is over, depending on his sentence, they're thinking of moving abroad. Heather seems to have plenty of money, at least, and reading between the lines, is keeping Sam on the straight and narrow. He's certainly off the booze—Heather is teetotal since the clinic and drags Sam to AA meetings twice a week." Posy gave a sad smile.

"I'm so sorry he wouldn't come to the wedding or the party tonight," sighed Amy.

"It was for the best. Nothing in life is ever perfect, darling girl. Now." Posy stood up "Let's move on to happier things. I want you to enjoy tonight."

"I will. Oh, and I brought you this for your birthday present. It's from all of us. Open it when you have time."

"I will," Posy said as Amy indicated a big square package covered in brown paper leaning against the wall. "Thank you, darling."

"It's nothing, really, after all you've done for me." Amy walked over and gave Posy a hug. "You're amazing, you really are. Now, I'm off downstairs. Enjoy tonight."

"I will do my best, I promise."

Posy watched Amy leave, then walked over to the brown-paper-covered package. She sat down on the bed and held it on her lap for a while, thinking about Sam and mourning his absence. She only hoped he'd find contentment in his new life, but she somehow doubted it. One thing she'd learnt was that no one ever truly changed.

"Not now, Posy," she whispered to herself, and turned her mind to the parcel on her knee. She tore off the paper and saw the back of a canvas. Turning it over, she gasped as she saw the painting of Admiral House.

Amy had chosen the back aspect, with the terrace falling away to the garden Posy had created in the foreground. There was the butterfly garden, the parterre, the roses and the willow walkway, all beautifully depicted in full, glorious bloom.

Tears came to her eyes, and she swallowed hard in order not to disturb her makeup. This was *her* contribution to Admiral House, and she knew she had caretakers who would see it was nurtured into the future. She would suggest Sebastian and Amy find a good gardener—from the look of this painting, Amy was far too talented to spend her days knee-deep in compost.

There was yet a further knock at the door and Freddie entered, resplendent in black tie.

"Hello, darling girl," he smiled as Posy stood up. "Don't you look a picture?"

He held his arms open to her and she walked into them.

"How are you feeling?" he asked her.

"Nervous."

"And sad that this will be your last party at Admiral House?"

"Not really, no," she answered.

"I'm surprised."

"Well, I've learned something in the past few months."

"And what might that be?"

"That home isn't about bricks and mortar," she smiled up at him. "Home is right here, in your arms."

Freddie looked down at her. "Goodness, Mrs. Lennox, that's an awfully romantic thing to say."

"I must be going soft in my old age, but I mean it. Truly."

He kissed her on her forehead. "Well, I promise you will never have to leave these arms on my account, and also that, if you feel you want something larger to live in, and a garden to nurture, we can look after our honeymoon."

"No, your cottage is perfect, really, Freddie. It will provide a base when we're back from all the traveling we're going to do."

"We'll see about that. One distress call from a member of your family and you'll come running," he chuckled. "Which is the way it should be. I love you, Mrs. Lennox."

"And I love you too."

There was another knock, and Freddie and Posy jumped apart as Nick walked through the door.

"Honestly," he raised an eyebrow. "It's like finding two teenagers in the bedroom, doing something they shouldn't. Ready to go, Mum? Everyone is gathering downstairs in the hall."

"I think so, yes."

She turned to Freddie, her eyes shining.

"Life's coming back to this house, you know."

Freddie nodded. "I know, dear girl, I know." And with that, he led her gently out of the door.

Posy stood at the top of the stairs, flanked by her husband and her son. The chandelier glittered above her as she looked down to the hall below her. A sea of faces swam before her eyes. Amongst them was her beloved family—a new generation that she had given life to, their eyes full of hope for the future.

Someone started to clap, and the rest of the guests joined in until the hall echoed with the sound of cheering.

Posy held on tightly to both Freddie and Nick's arms and walked down the stairs to join them.

The Seven Sisters
AN EPIC BESTSELLING SERIES FROM LUCINDA RILEY
OVER 10 MILLION COPIES SOLD GLOBALLY

Book 1 - The beautiful recluse who must learn to love again - set in La Belle Epoque of 1920's Rio and Paris, and present-day Lake Geneva.

Maia D'Aplièse and her five sisters gather together at their childhood home of Atlantis—a fabulous, secluded castle situated on the shores of Lake Geneva—having been told that their beloved father, the elusive billionaire they call Pa Salt, has died. Maia and her sisters were all adopted by him as babies and, discovering he has already been buried at sea, each of them is handed a tantalising clue to their true heritage—a clue which takes Maia across the world to a crumbling mansion in Rio de Janeiro in Brazil. Once there, she begins to put together the pieces of where her story began…

Eighty years earlier, in the Belle Epoque of Rio, 1927, Izabela Bonifacio's father has aspirations for his daughter to marry into aristocracy. Meanwhile, architect Heitor da Silva costa is working on a statue, to be called Christ the Redeemer, and will soon travel to Paris to find the right sculptor to complete his vision. Izabela—passionate and longing to see the world—convinces her father to allow her to accompany him and his family to Europe before she is married. There, at Paul Landowski's studio in the heady, vibrant cafes of Montparnasse, she meets ambitious young sculptor Laurent Brouilly, and knows at once that her life will never be the same again.

In this sweeping, epic tale of love and loss—the first in a unique series of seven books, based on the legends of the Seven Sisters star constellation—Lucinda Riley showcases her storytelling talent like never before.

Read the spellbinding opening chapter now…

Chapter 1

I will always remember exactly where I was and what I was doing when I heard that my father had died.

I was sitting in the pretty garden of my old schoolfriend's townhouse in London, a copy of *The Penelopiad* open but unread in my lap, enjoying the June sun while Jenny collected her little boy from nursery.

I felt calm and appreciated what a good idea it had been to get away. I was studying the burgeoning clematis, encouraged by its sunny midwife to give birth to a riot of colour, when my mobile phone rang. I glanced at the screen and saw it was Marina.

"Hello, Ma, how are you?" I said, hoping she could hear the warmth in my voice too.

"Maia, I..."

Marina paused, and in that instant I knew something was dreadfully wrong. "What is it?"

"Maia, there's no easy way to tell you this, but your father had a heart attack here at home yesterday afternoon, and in the early hours of this morning, he...passed away."

I remained silent, as a million different and ridiculous thoughts raced through my mind. The first one being that Marina, for some unknown reason, had decided to play some form of tasteless joke on me.

"You're the first of the sisters I've told, Maia, as you're the eldest. And I wanted to ask you whether you would prefer to tell the rest of your sisters yourself, or leave it to me."

"I..."

Still no words would form coherently on my lips, as I began to realise that Marina, dear, beloved Marina, the woman who had been the closest thing to a mother I'd ever known, would never tell me this if it *wasn't* true. So it had to be. And at that moment, my entire world shifted on its axis.

"Maia, please, tell me you're all right. This really is the most dreadful call I've ever had to make, but what else could I do? God only knows how the other girls are going to take it."

It was then that I heard the suffering in *her* voice and understood she'd needed to tell me as much for her own sake as mine. So I switched into my normal comfort zone, which was to comfort others.

"Of course I'll tell my sisters if you'd prefer, Ma, although I'm not positive where they all are. Isn't Ally away training for a regatta?"

And as we continued to discuss where each of my younger sisters was, as though we needed to get them together for a birthday party rather than to mourn the death of our father, the entire conversation took on a sense of the surreal.

"When should we plan on having the funeral, do you think? What with Electra being in Los Angeles and Ally somewhere on the high seas, surely we can't think about it until next week at the earliest?" I said.

"Well..." I heard the hesitation in Marina's voice. "Perhaps the best thing is for you and I to discuss it when you arrive back home. There really is no rush now, Maia, so if you'd prefer to remain for the last couple of days of your holiday in London, that would be fine. There's nothing more to be done for him here..." Her voice trailed off miserably.

"Ma, of *course* I'll be on the next flight to Geneva I can get! I'll call the airline immediately, and then I'll do my best to get in touch with everyone."

"I'm so terribly sorry, *chérie*," Marina said sadly. "I know how you adored him."

"Yes," I said, the strange calm that I had felt while we discussed arrangements suddenly deserting me like the stillness before a violent thunderstorm. "I'll call you later, when I know what time I'll be arriving."

"Please take care of yourself, Maia. You've had a terrible shock."

I pressed the button to end the call, and before the storm clouds in my heart opened up and drowned me, I went upstairs to my bedroom to retrieve my flight documents and contact the airline. As I waited in the calling queue, I glanced at the bed where I'd woken up this morning to Simply Another Day. And I thanked God that human beings don't have the power to see into the future.

The officious woman who eventually answered wasn't helpful and I knew, as she spoke of full flights, financial penalties and credit card details, that my emotional dam was ready to burst. Finally, once I'd grudgingly been granted a seat on the four o'clock flight to Geneva, which would mean throwing everything into my holdall immediately and taking a taxi to Heathrow, I sat down on the bed and stared for so long at the sprigged wallpaper that the pattern began to dance in front of my eyes.

"He's gone," I whispered, "gone forever. I'll never see him again."

Expecting the spoken words to provoke a raging torrent of tears, I was surprised that nothing actually happened. Instead, I sat there numbly, my head still full of practicalities. The thought of telling my sisters—all five of them—was horrendous, and I searched through my emotional filing system for the one I would call first. Inevitably, it was Tiggy, the second youngest of the six of us girls and the sibling to whom I'd always felt closest.

With trembling fingers, I scrolled down to find her number and dialled it. When her voicemail answered, I didn't know what to say, other than a few garbled words asking her to call me back urgently. She was currently somewhere in the Scottish Highlands working at a centre for orphaned and sick wild deer.

As for the other sisters...I knew their reactions would vary, outwardly at least, from indifference to a dramatic outpouring of emotion.

Given that I wasn't currently sure quite which way *I* would go on the scale of grief when I did speak to any of them, I decided to take the coward's way out and texted them all, asking them to call me as soon as they could. Then I hurriedly packed my holdall and walked down the narrow stairs to the kitchen to write a note for Jenny explaining why I'd had to leave in such a hurry.

Deciding to take my chances hailing a black cab on the London streets, I left the house, walking briskly around the leafy Chelsea crescent just as any normal person would do on any normal day. I believe I actually said hello to someone walking a dog when I passed him in the street and managed a smile.

No one would know what had just happened to me, I thought, as I managed to find a taxi on the busy King's Road and climbed inside, directing the driver to Heathrow.

No one would know.

Five hours later, just as the sun was making its leisurely descent over Lake Geneva, I arrived at our private pontoon on the shore, from where I would make the last leg of my journey home.

Christian was already waiting for me in our sleek Riva motor launch. And from the look on his face, I could see he'd heard the news.

"How are you, Mademoiselle Maia?" he asked, sympathy in his blue eyes as he helped me aboard.

"I'm...glad I'm here," I answered neutrally as I walked to the back of the boat and sat down on the cushioned cream leather bench that curved around the stern. Usually, I would sit with Christian in the passenger seat at the front as we sped across the calm waters on the twenty-minute journey home. But today, I felt a need for privacy. As Christian started the powerful engine, the sun glinted off the windows of the fabulous houses that lined Lake Geneva's shores. I'd often felt when I made this journey that it was the entrance to an ethereal world disconnected from reality.

The world of Pa Salt.

I noticed the first vague evidence of tears pricking at my eyes as I thought of my father's pet name, which I'd coined when I was young. He'd always loved sailing and often when he returned to me at our lakeside home, he had smelt of fresh air and of the sea. Somehow, the name had stuck, and as my younger siblings had joined me, they'd called him that too.

As the launch picked up speed, the warm wind streaming through my hair, I thought of the hundreds of previous journeys I'd made to "Atlantis," Pa Salt's fairy-tale castle. Inaccessible by land, due to its position on a private promontory with a crescent of mountainous terrain rising up steeply behind it, the only method of reaching it was by boat. The nearest neighbours were miles away along the lake, so "Atlantis" was our own private kingdom, set apart from the rest of the world. Everything it contained was magical...as if Pa Salt and we—his daughters—had lived there under an enchantment.

Each one of us had been chosen by Pa Salt as a baby, adopted from the four corners of the globe and brought home to live under his protection. And each one of us, as Pa always liked to say, was special, different...we were *his* girls. He'd named us all after The

Seven Sisters, his favourite star cluster. Maia being the first and eldest.

When I was young, he'd take me up to his glass-domed observatory perched on top of the house, lift me up with his big, strong hands and have me look through his telescope at the night sky.

"There it is," he'd say as he aligned the lens. "Look, Maia, that's the beautiful shining star you're named after."

And I *would* see. As he explained the legends that were the source of my own and my sisters' names, I'd hardly listen, but simply enjoy his arms tight around me, fully aware of this rare, special moment when I had him all to myself.

I'd realised eventually that Marina, who I'd presumed as I grew up was my mother—I'd even shortened her name to "Ma"—was a glorified nursemaid, employed by Pa to take care of me because he was away such a lot. But of course, Marina was so much more than that to all of us girls. She was the one who had wiped our tears, berated us for sloppy table manners and steered us calmly through the difficult transition from childhood to womanhood.

She had always been there, and I could not have loved Ma any more if she had given birth to me.

During the first three years of my childhood, Marina and I had lived alone together in our magical castle on the shores of Lake Geneva as Pa Salt travelled the Seven Seas to conduct his business. And then, one by one, my sisters began to arrive.

Usually, Pa would bring me a present when he returned home. I'd hear the motor launch arriving, run across the sweeping lawns and through the trees to the jetty to greet him. Like any child, I'd want to see what he had hidden inside his magical pockets to delight me. On one particular occasion, however, after he'd presented me with an exquisitely carved wooden reindeer, which he assured me came from St Nicholas's workshop in the North Pole itself, a uniformed woman had stepped out from behind him, and in her arms was a bundle wrapped in a shawl. And the bundle was moving.

"This time, Maia, I've brought you back the most special gift. You have a new sister." He'd smiled at me as he lifted me into his arms. "Now you'll no longer be lonely when I have to go away."

After that, life had changed. The maternity nurse that Pa had brought with him disappeared after a few weeks and Marina took over the care of my baby sister. I couldn't understand how the red, squalling thing which often smelt and diverted attention from me could possibly be a gift. Until one morning, when Alcyone—named after the second star of The Seven Sisters—smiled at me from her high chair over breakfast.

"She knows who I am," I said in wonder to Marina, who was feeding her.

"Of course she does, Maia, dear. You're her big sister, the one she'll look up to. It'll be up to you to teach her lots of things that you know and she doesn't."

And as she grew, she became my shadow, following me everywhere, which pleased and irritated me in equal measure.

"Maia, wait me!" she'd demand loudly as she tottered along behind me.

Even though Ally—as I'd nicknamed her—had originally been an unwanted addition to my dreamlike existence at "Atlantis," I could not have asked for a sweeter, more loveable companion. She rarely, if ever, cried and there were none of the temper-tantrums associated with toddlers of her age. With her tumbling red-gold curls and her big blue eyes, Ally had a natural charm that drew people to her, including our father. On the occasions Pa Salt was home from one of his long trips abroad, I'd watch how his eyes lit up when he saw her, in a way I was sure they didn't for me. And whereas I was shy and reticent with strangers, Ally had an openness and a readiness to trust that endeared her to everyone.

She was also one of those children who seemed to excel at everything—particularly music, and any sport to do with water. I remember Pa teaching her to swim in our vast pool and, whereas I had struggled to stay afloat and hated being underwater, my little sister took to it like a mermaid. And while I couldn't find my sea legs even on *The Titan*, Pa's huge and beautiful ocean-going yacht, when we were at home Ally would beg him to take her out in the small Laser he kept moored on our private lakeside jetty. I'd crouch in the cramped stern of the boat while Pa and Ally took control as we sped across the glassy waters. Their joint passion for sailing bonded them in a way I felt I could never replicate.

Although Ally had studied music at the Conservatoire de

Musique de Genève and was a highly talented flautist who could have pursued a career with a professional orchestra, since leaving music school she had chosen the life of a full-time sailor. She now competed regularly in regattas, and had represented Switzerland on a number of occasions.

When Ally was almost three, Pa arrived home with our next sibling, who he named Asterope, after the third of the Seven Sisters.

"But we will call her Star," Pa had said, smiling at Marina, Ally and me as we studied the newest addition to the family lying in the bassinet.

By now I was attending lessons every morning with a private tutor, so my newest sister's arrival affected me less than Ally's had. Then, only six months later, another baby joined us, a twelve-week-old girl named Celaeno, whose name Ally immediately shortened to CeCe.

There was only three months' age difference between Star and CeCe, and from as far back as I can remember, the two of them forged a close bond. They were akin to twins, talking in their own private baby language, some of which the two of them still used to communicate to this day. They inhabited their own private world, to the exclusion of us other sisters. And even now in their twenties, nothing had changed. CeCe, the younger of the two, was always the boss, her stocky body and nut-brown skin in direct contrast to the pale, whippet-thin Star.

The following year, another baby arrived—Taygete, whom I nicknamed "Tiggy" because her short, dark hair sprouted out at strange angles on her tiny head and reminded me of the hedgehog in Beatrix Potter's famous story.

I was by now seven years old, and I'd bonded with Tiggy from the first moment I set eyes on her. She was the most delicate of us all, suffering one childhood illness after another, but even as an infant, she was stoic and undemanding. When yet another baby girl, named Electra, was brought home by Pa a few months later, an exhausted Marina would often ask me if I would mind sitting with Tiggy, who continually had a fever or croup. Eventually diagnosed as asthmatic, she rarely left the nursery to be wheeled outside in the pram, in case the cold air and heavy fog of a Geneva winter affected her chest.

Electra was the youngest of my siblings and her name suited her perfectly. By now, I was used to little babies and their demands, but my youngest sister was without doubt the most challenging of them all. Everything about her *was* electric; her innate ability to switch in an instant from dark to light and vice versa meant that our previously calm home rang daily with high-pitched screams. Her temper-tantrums resonated through my childhood consciousness and as she grew older, her fiery personality did not mellow.

Privately, Ally, Tiggy and I had our own nickname for her; she was known among the three of us as 'Tricky'. We all walked on eggshells around her, wishing to do nothing to set off a lightning change of mood. I can honestly say there were moments when I loathed her for the disruption she brought to "Atlantis."

And yet, when Electra knew one of us was in trouble, she was the first to offer help and support. Just as she was capable of huge selfishness, her generosity on other occasions was equally pronounced.

After Electra, the entire household was expecting the arrival of the Seventh Sister. After all, we'd been named after Pa Salt's favourite star cluster and we wouldn't be complete without her. We even knew her name—Merope—and wondered who she would be. But a year went past, and then another, and another, and no more babies arrived home with our father.

I remember vividly standing with him once in his observatory. I was fourteen years old and just on the brink of womanhood. We were waiting for an eclipse, which he'd told me was a seminal moment for humankind and usually brought change with it.

"Pa," I said, "will you ever bring home our seventh sister?"

At this, his strong, protective bulk had seemed to freeze for a few seconds. He'd looked suddenly as though he carried the weight of the world on his shoulders. Although he didn't turn around, for he was still concentrating on training the telescope on the coming eclipse, I knew instinctively that what I'd said had distressed him.

"No, Maia, I won't. Because I have never found her."

As the familiar thick hedge of spruce trees, which shielded our waterside home from prying eyes, came into view, I saw Marina standing on the jetty and the dreadful truth of losing Pa finally began to sink in.

And I realised that the man who had created the kingdom in which we had all been his princesses was no longer present to hold the enchantment in place.

About Lucinda Riley

Lucinda Riley was born in Ireland, and after an early career as an actress in film, theatre and television, wrote her first book aged twenty-four. Her books have been translated into thirty-seven languages and sold twenty million copies worldwide. She is a No.1 *Sunday Times* and *New York Times* bestseller.

Lucinda is currently writing The Seven Sisters series, which tells the story of adopted sisters and is based allegorically on the mythology of the famous star constellation. It has become a global phenomenon, with each book in the series being a No.1 bestseller across the world. The series is currently in development with a major Hollywood production company.

Discover the World Of Blue Box Press

Vist www.1001DarkNights.com for more information.

1001 Dark Nights

Collection One

Collection Two

Collection Three

Collection Four

Collection Five

Collection Six

Collection Seven

Bundles

Discovery Authors

Rising Storm

Liliana Hart's MacKenzie Family

Lexi Blake's Crossover Collection

Kristen Proby's Crossover Collection

On Behalf of Blue Box Press,

Liz Berry, M.J. Rose, and Jillian Stein would like to thank ~

Steve Berry
Doug Scofield
Benjamin Stein
Kim Guidroz
Social Butterfly PR
Asha Hossain
Chris Graham
Chelle Olson
Kasi Alexander
Jessica Johns
Dylan Stockton
Richard Blake
and Simon Lipskar

Made in the USA
Monee, IL
13 February 2021